Love
in the Time
of Cholera

Love in the Time of Cholera

GABRIEL GARCÍA MÁRQUEZ

Translated from the Spanish
by Edith Grossman

G.K.HALL &CO.
Boston, Massachusetts
1989

Copyright © 1988 by Gabriel García Márquez.

Originally published in Columbia as *El amor en los tiempos del cólera* by Editorial Oveja Negra Ltda., Bogotá.

A portion of this book originally appeared in
The New Yorker.

Published in Large Print by arrangement with
Alfred A. Knopf, Inc.

G.K. Hall Large Print Book Series.

Set in 16 pt Plantin.

Library of Congress Cataloging in Publication Data

García Márquez, Gabriel, 1928–
    Love in the time of cholera.

    (G.K. Hall large print book series)
    Translation of: El amor en los tiempos del cólera.
    I. Title.
[PQ8180.17.A73A813   1989b]   863   88-32863
ISBN 0-8161-4717-5 (lg. print)

For Mercedes, of course

The words I am about to express:
They now have their own crowned goddess.

LEANDRO DÍAZ

IT WAS INEVITABLE: the scent of bitter almonds always reminded him of the fate of unrequited love. Dr. Juvenal Urbino noticed it as soon as he entered the still darkened house where he had hurried on an urgent call to attend a case that for him had lost all urgency many years before. The Antillean refugee Jeremiah de Saint-Amour, disabled war veteran, photographer of children, and his most sympathetic opponent in chess, had escaped the torments of memory with the aromatic fumes of gold cyanide.

He found the corpse covered with a blanket on the campaign cot where he had always slept, and beside it was a stool with the developing tray he had used to vaporize the poison. On the floor, tied to a leg of the cot, lay the body of a black Great Dane with a snow-white chest, and next to him were the crutches. At one window the splendor of dawn was just beginning to illuminate the stifling, crowded room that served as both bedroom and laboratory, but there was enough light for him to recognize at once the authority of death. The other windows, as well as every other chink in the room, were muffled with rags or sealed with black cardboard, which increased the oppressive heaviness. A counter was crammed with jars and bottles without labels and two crumbling pewter trays under an ordinary light bulb covered with red paper. The third tray, the one for the fixative solution, was next to the body. There were old magazines and newspapers everywhere, piles of negatives on glass plates, broken furniture, but everything was kept free of dust by a diligent hand. Although the air coming through the window had purified the atmosphere, there still remained for the one who could identify it the dying embers of hapless love in the bitter almonds. Dr. Juvenal Urbino had often thought, with no premonitory intention, that this would not be a propitious place for dying in a state of grace. But in time he came to suppose that perhaps its disorder obeyed an obscure determination of Divine Providence.

A police inspector had come forward with a very young medical student who was completing his forensic training at the municipal dispensary, and it was they who had ventilated the room and covered the body while waiting for Dr. Urbino to arrive. They greeted him with a solemnity that on this occasion had more of condolence than veneration, for no one was unaware of the degree of his friendship with Jeremiah de Saint-Amour. The eminent teacher shook hands with each of them, as he always did with every one of his pupils before beginning the daily class in general clinical medicine, and then, as if it were a flower, he grasped the hem of the blanket with the tips of his index finger and his thumb, and slowly uncovered the body with sacramental circumspection. Jeremiah de Saint-Amour was completely naked, stiff and twisted, eyes open, body blue, looking fifty years older than he had the night before. He had luminous pupils, yellowish beard and hair, and an old scar sewn with baling knots across his stomach. The use of crutches had made his torso and arms as broad as a galley slave's, but his defenseless legs looked like an orphan's. Dr. Juvenal Urbino studied him for a moment, his heart aching as it rarely had in the long years of his futile struggle against death.

"Damn fool," he said. "The worst was over."

He covered him again with the blanket and regained his academic dignity. His eightieth birthday had been celebrated the year before with an official three-day jubilee, and in his thank-you speech he had once again resisted the temptation to retire. He had said: "I'll have plenty of time to rest when I die, but this eventuality is not yet part of my plans." Although he heard less and less with his right ear, and leaned on a silver-handled cane to conceal his faltering steps, he continued to wear a linen suit, with a gold watch chain across his vest, as smartly as he had in his younger years. His Pasteur beard, the color of mother-of-pearl, and his hair, the same color, carefully combed back and with a neat part in the middle, were faithful expressions of his character. He compensated as much as he could for an increasingly

3

disturbing erosion of memory by scribbling hurried notes on scraps of paper that ended in confusion in each of his pockets, as did the instruments, the bottles of medicine, and all the other things jumbled together in his crowded medical bag. He was not only the city's oldest and most illustrious physician, he was also its most fastidious man. Still, his too obvious display of learning and the disingenuous manner in which he used the power of his name had won him less affection than he deserved.

His instructions to the inspector and the intern were precise and rapid. There was no need for an autopsy; the odor in the house was sufficient proof that the cause of death had been the cyanide vapors activated in the tray by some photographic acid, and Jeremiah de Saint-Amour knew too much about those matters for it to have been an accident. When the inspector showed some hesitation, he cut him off with the kind of remark that was typical of his manner: "Don't forget that I am the one who signs the death certificate." The young doctor was disappointed: he had never had the opportunity to study the effects of gold cyanide on a cadaver. Dr. Juvenal Urbino had been surprised that he had not seen him at the Medical School, but he understood in an instant from the young man's easy blush and Andean accent that he was probably a recent arrival to the city. He said: "There is bound to be someone driven mad by love who will give you the chance one of these days." And only after he said it did he realize that among the countless suicides he could remember, this was the first with cyanide that had not been caused by the sufferings of love. Then something changed in the tone of his voice.

"And when you do find one, observe with care," he said to the intern: "they almost always have crystals in their heart."

Then he spoke to the inspector as he would have to a subordinate. He ordered him to circumvent all the legal procedures so that the burial could take place that same afternoon and with the greatest discretion. He said: "I will speak to the Mayor later." He knew that Jeremiah de Saint-Amour lived in primitive austerity and that he earned much more with his art than he needed, so that in one of the drawers in the house there was bound to be more than enough money for the funeral expenses.

"But if you do not find it, it does not matter," he said. "I will take care of everything."

He ordered him to tell the press that the photographer had died of natural causes, although he thought the news would in no way interest them. He said: "If it is necessary, I will speak to the Governor." The inspector, a serious and humble civil servant, knew that the Doctor's sense of civic duty exasperated even his closest friends, and he was surprised at the ease with which he skipped over legal formalities in order to expedite the burial. The only thing he was not willing to do was speak to the Archbishop so that Jeremiah de Saint-Amour could be buried in holy ground. The inspector,

5

astonished at his own impertinence, attempted to make excuses for him.

"I understood this man was a saint," he said.

"Something even rarer," said Dr. Urbino. "An atheistic saint. But those are matters for God to decide."

In the distance, on the other side of the colonial city, the bells of the Cathedral were ringing for High Mass. Dr. Urbino put on his half-moon glasses with the gold rims and consulted the watch on its chain, slim, elegant, with the cover that opened at a touch: he was about to miss Pentecost Mass.

In the parlor was a huge camera on wheels like the ones used in public parks, and the backdrop of a marine twilight, painted with homemade paints, and the walls papered with pictures of children at memorable moments: the first Communion, the bunny costume, the happy birthday. Year after year, during contemplative pauses on afternoons of chess, Dr. Urbino had seen the gradual covering over of the walls, and he had often thought with a shudder of sorrow that in the gallery of casual portraits lay the germ of the future city, governed and corrupted by those unknown children, where not even the ashes of his glory would remain.

On the desk, next to a jar that held several old sea dog's pipes, was the chessboard with an unfinished game. Despite his haste and his somber mood, Dr. Urbino could not resist the temptation to study it. He knew it was the previous night's game, for Jeremiah de Saint-Amour played at dusk every day of the week with at least three different opponents, but he always finished every game and then placed the board and chessmen in their box and stored the box in a desk drawer. The Doctor knew he played with the white pieces and that this time it was evident he was going to be defeated without mercy in four moves. "If there had been a crime, this would be a good clue," Urbino said to himself. "I know only one man capable of devising this masterful trap." If his life depended on it, he had to find out later why that indomitable soldier, accustomed to fighting to the last drop of blood, had left the final battle of his life unfinished.

At six that morning, as he was making his last rounds, the night watchman had seen the note nailed to the street door: *Come in without knocking and inform the police.* A short while later the inspector arrived with the intern, and the two of them had searched the house for some evidence that might contradict the unmistakable breath of bitter almonds. But in the brief minutes the Doctor needed to study the unfinished game, the inspector discovered an envelope among the papers on the desk, addressed to Dr. Juvenal Urbino and sealed with so much sealing wax that it had to be ripped to pieces to get the letter out. The Doctor opened the black curtain over the window to have more light, gave a quick glance at the eleven sheets covered on both sides by a diligent handwriting, and when he had read the first paragraph he knew that he would miss Pentecost Communion. He read with agitated breath, turning back on several pages to find the thread he had lost, and when he finished he seemed to return from very far away and very long ago. His despondency was obvious despite his effort to control it: his lips were as blue as the corpse and he could not stop the trembling of his fingers as he refolded the letter and placed it in his vest pocket. Then he remembered the inspector and the young doctor, and he smiled at them through the mists of grief.

"Nothing in particular," he said. "His final instructions."

It was a half-truth, but they thought it complete because he ordered them to lift a loose tile from the floor, where they found a worn account book that contained the combination to the strongbox. There was not as much money as they expected, but it was more than enough for the funeral expenses and to meet other minor obligations. Then Dr. Urbino realized that he could not get to the Cathedral before the Gospel reading.

"It's the third time I've missed Sunday Mass since I've had the use of my reason," he said. "But God understands."

So he chose to spend a few minutes more and attend to all the details, although he could hardly bear his intense longing to share the secrets of the letter with his wife. He promised to notify the numerous Caribbean refugees who lived in the city in case they wanted to pay their last respects to the man who had conducted himself as if he were the most respectable of them all, the most active and the most radical, even after it had become all too clear that he had been overwhelmed by the burden of disillusion. He would also inform his chess partners, who ranged from distinguished professional men to nameless laborers, as well as other, less intimate acquaintances who might perhaps wish to attend the funeral. Before he read the posthumous letter he had resolved to be first among them, but afterward he was not certain of anything. In any case, he was going to send a wreath of gardenias in the event that Jeremiah de Saint-Amour had repented at the last moment. The burial would be at five, which was the most suitable hour during the hottest months. If they needed him, from noon on he would be at the country house of Dr. Lácides Olivella, his beloved disciple, who was celebrating his silver anniversary in the profession with a formal luncheon that day.

Once the stormy years of his early struggles were over, Dr. Juvenal Urbino had followed a set routine and achieved a respectability and prestige that had no equal in the province. He arose at the crack of dawn, when he began to take his secret medicines: potassium bromide to raise his spirits, salicylates for the ache in his bones when it rained, ergosterol drops for vertigo, belladonna for sound sleep. He took something every hour, always in secret, because in his long life as a doctor and teacher he had always opposed prescribing palliatives for old age: it was easier for him to bear other people's pains than his own. In his pocket he always carried a little pad of camphor that he inhaled deeply when no one was watching to calm his fear of so many medicines mixed together.

He would spend an hour in his study preparing for the class in general clinical medicine that he taught at the Medical School every morning, Monday through Saturday, at eight o'clock, until the day before his death. He was also an avid reader of the latest books that his bookseller in Paris mailed to him, or the ones from Barcelona that his local bookseller ordered for him, although he did not follow Spanish literature as closely as French. In any case, he never read them in the morning, but only for an hour after his siesta and at night before he went to sleep. When he was finished in the study he did fifteen minutes of respiratory exercises in front of the open window in the bathroom, always breathing toward the side where the roosters were crowing, which was where the air was new. Then he bathed, arranged his beard and waxed his mustache in an atmosphere saturated with genuine cologne from Farina Gegenüber, and dressed in white linen, with a vest and a soft hat and cordovan boots. At eighty-one years of age he preserved the same easygoing manner and festive spirit that he had on his return from Paris soon after the great cholera epidemic, and except for the metallic color, his carefully combed hair with the center part was the same as it had been in his youth. He breakfasted *en famille* but followed his own personal regimen of an infusion of wormwood blossoms for his stomach and a head of garlic that he peeled and ate a clove at a time, chewing each one carefully with bread, to prevent heart failure. After class it was rare for him not to have an appointment related to his civic initiatives, or his Catholic service, or his artistic and social innovations.

He almost always ate lunch at home and had a ten-minute siesta on the terrace in the patio, hearing in his sleep the songs of the servant girls under the leaves of the mango trees, the cries of vendors on the street, the uproar of oil and motors from the bay whose exhaust fumes fluttered through the house on hot afternoons like an angel condemned to putrefaction. Then he read his new books for an hour, above all novels and works of history, and gave lessons in French and singing to the tame parrot who had been a local attraction for years. At four o'clock, after drinking a large glass of lemonade with ice, he left to call on his patients. In spite of his age he would not see patients in his office and continued to care for them in their homes as he always had, since the city was so domesticated that one could go anywhere in safety.

After he returned from Europe the first time, he used the family landau drawn by two golden chestnuts, but when this was no longer practical he changed it for a Victoria and a single horse, and he continued to use it, with a certain disdain for fashion, when carriages had already begun to disappear from the world and the only ones left in the city were for giving rides to tourists and carrying wreaths at funerals. Although he refused to retire, he was aware that he was called in only for

11

hopeless cases, but he considered this a form of specialization too. He could tell what was wrong with a patient just by looking at him, he grew more and more distrustful of patent medicines, and he viewed with alarm the vulgarization of surgery. He would say: "The scalpel is the greatest proof of the failure of medicine." He thought that, in a strict sense, all medication was poison and that seventy percent of common foods hastened death. "In any case," he would say in class, "the little medicine we know is known only by a few doctors." From youthful enthusiasm he had moved to a position that he himself defined as fatalistic humanism: "Each man is master of his own death, and all that we can do when the time comes is to help him die without fear of pain." But despite these extreme ideas, which were already part of local medical folklore, his former pupils continued to consult him even after they were established in the profession, for they recognized in him what was called in those days a clinical eye. In any event, he was always an expensive and exclusive doctor, and his patients were concentrated in the ancestral homes in the District of the Viceroys.

His daily schedule was so methodical that his wife knew where to send him a message if an emergency arose in the course of the afternoon. When he was a young man he would stop in the Parish Café before coming home, and this was where he perfected his chess game with his father-in-law's cronies and some Caribbean refugees. But

12

he had not returned to the Parish Café since the dawn of the new century, and he had attempted to organize national tournaments under the sponsorship of the Social Club. It was at this time that Jeremiah de Saint-Amour arrived, his knees already dead, not yet a photographer of children, yet in less than three months everyone who knew how to move a bishop across a chessboard knew who he was, because no one had been able to defeat him in a game. For Dr. Juvenal Urbino it was a miraculous meeting, at the very moment when chess had become an unconquerable passion for him and he no longer had many opponents who could satisfy it.

Thanks to him, Jeremiah de Saint-Amour could become what he was among us. Dr. Urbino made himself his unconditional protector, his guarantor in everything, without even taking the trouble to learn who he was or what he did or what inglorious wars he had come from in his crippled, broken state. He eventually lent him the money to set up his photography studio, and from the time he took his first picture of a child startled by the magnesium flash, Jeremiah de Saint-Amour paid back every last penny with religious regularity.

It was all for chess. At first they played after supper at seven o'clock, with a reasonable handicap for Jeremiah de Saint-Amour because of his notable superiority, but the handicap was reduced until at last they played as equals. Later, when Don Galileo Daconte opened the first outdoor cinema, Jeremiah de Saint-Amour was one of his

13

most dependable customers, and the games of chess were limited to the nights when a new film was not being shown. By then he and the Doctor had become such good friends that they would go to see the films together, but never with the Doctor's wife, in part because she did not have the patience to follow the complicated plot lines, and in part because it always seemed to her, through sheer intuition, that Jeremiah de Saint-Amour was not a good companion for anyone.

His Sundays were different. He would attend High Mass at the Cathedral and then return home to rest and read on the terrace in the patio. He seldom visited a patient on a holy day of obligation unless it was of extreme urgency, and for many years he had not accepted a social engagement that was not obligatory. On this Pentecost, in a rare coincidence, two extraordinary events had occurred: the death of a friend and the silver anniversary of an eminent pupil. Yet instead of going straight home as he had intended after certifying the death of Jeremiah de Saint-Amour, he allowed himself to be carried along by curiosity.

As soon as he was in his carriage, he again consulted the posthumous letter and told the coachman to take him to an obscure location in the old slave quarter. That decision was so foreign to his usual habits that the coachman wanted to make certain there was no mistake. No, no mistake: the address was clear and the man who had written it had more than enough reason to know it very well. Then Dr. Urbino returned to the first page of the letter and plunged once again into the flood of unsavory revelations that might have changed his life, even at his age, if he could have convinced himself that they were not the ravings of a dying man.

The sky had begun to threaten very early in the day and the weather was cloudy and cool, but there was no chance of rain before noon. In his effort to find a shorter route, the coachman braved the rough cobblestones of the colonial city and had to stop often to keep the horse from being frightened by the rowdiness of the religious societies and fraternities coming back from the Pentecost liturgy. The streets were full of paper garlands, music, flowers, and girls with colored parasols and muslin ruffles who watched the celebration from their balconies. In the Plaza of the Cathedral, where the statue of The Liberator was almost hidden among the African palm trees and the globes of the new streetlights, traffic was congested because Mass had ended, and not a seat was empty in the venerable and noisy Parish Café. Dr. Urbino's was the only horse-drawn carriage; it was distinguishable from the handful left in the city because the patent-leather roof was always kept polished, and it had fittings of bronze that would not be corroded by salt, and wheels and poles painted red with gilt trimming like gala nights at the Vienna Opera. Furthermore, while the most demanding families were satisfied if their drivers had a clean shirt, he still required his coachman to wear livery of faded velvet and a top hat like a circus ringmaster's, which, more than an anachronism, was thought to show a lack of compassion in the dog days of the Caribbean summer.

Despite his almost maniacal love for the city and a knowledge of it superior to anyone's, Dr. Juvenal Urbino had not often had reason as he did that Sunday to venture boldly into the tumult of the old slave quarter. The coachman had to make many turns and stop to ask directions several times in order to find the house. As they passed by the marshes, Dr. Urbino recognized their oppressive weight, their ominous silence, their suffocating gases, which on so many insomniac dawns had risen to his bedroom, blending with the fragrance of jasmine from the patio, and which he felt pass by him like a wind out of yesterday that had nothing to do with his life. But that pestilence so frequently idealized by nostalgia became an unbearable reality when the carriage began to lurch through the quagmire of the streets where buzzards fought over the slaughterhouse offal as it was swept along by the receding tide. Unlike the city of the Viceroys where the houses were made of masonry, here they were built of weathered boards and zinc roofs, and most of them rested on pilings to protect them from the flooding of the open sewers that had been inherited from the Spaniards. Everything looked wretched and desolate, but out of the sordid taverns came the thunder of riotous music, the godless drunken celebration of Pentecost by the poor. By the time they found the house, gangs of ragged children were chasing the

16

carriage and ridiculing the theatrical finery of the coachman, who had to drive them away with his whip. Dr. Urbino, prepared for a confidential visit, realized too late that there was no innocence more dangerous than the innocence of age.

The exterior of the unnumbered house was in no way distinguishable from its less fortunate neighbors, except for the window with lace curtains and an imposing front door taken from some old church. The coachman pounded the door knocker, and only when he had made certain that it was the right house did he help the Doctor out of the carriage. The door opened without a sound, and in the shadowy interior stood a mature woman dressed in black, with a red rose behind her ear. Despite her age, which was no less than forty, she was still a haughty mulatta with cruel golden eyes and hair tight to her skull like a helmet of steel wool. Dr. Urbino did not recognize her, although he had seen her several times in the gloom of the chess games in the photographer's studio, and he had once written her a prescription for tertian fever. He held out his hand and she took it between hers, less in greeting than to help him into the house. The parlor had the climate and invisible murmur of a forest glade and was crammed with furniture and exquisite objects, each in its natural place. Dr. Urbino recalled without bitterness an antiquarian's shop, No. 26 rue Montmartre in Paris, on an autumn Monday in the last century. The woman sat down across from him and spoke in accented Spanish.

"This is your house, Doctor," she said. "I did not expect you so soon."

Dr. Urbino felt betrayed. He stared at her openly, at her intense mourning, at the dignity of her grief, and then he understood that this was a useless visit because she knew more than he did about everything stated and explained in Jeremiah de Saint-Amour's posthumous letter. This was true. She had been with him until a very few hours before his death, as she had been with him for half his life, with a devotion and submissive tenderness that bore too close a resemblance to love, and without anyone knowing anything about it in this sleepy provincial capital where even state secrets were common knowledge. They had met in a convalescent home in Port-au-Prince, where she had been born and where he had spent his early years as a fugitive, and she had followed him here a year later for a brief visit, although both of them knew without agreeing to anything that she had come to stay forever. She cleaned and straightened the laboratory once a week, but not even the most evil-minded neighbors confused appearance with reality because they, like everyone else, supposed that Jeremiah de Saint-Amour's disability affected more than his capacity to walk. Dr. Urbino himself supposed as much for solid medical reasons, and never would have believed his friend had a woman if he himself had not revealed it in the letter. In any event, it was difficult for him to comprehend that two free adults without a past and living on the fringes of a closed society's prejudices had chosen the hazards of illicit love. She explained: "It was his wish." Moreover, a clandestine life shared with a man who was never completely hers, and in which they often knew the sudden explosion of happiness, did not seem to her a condition to be despised. On the contrary: life had shown her that perhaps it was exemplary.

On the previous night they had gone to the cinema, each one separately, and had sat apart as they had done at least twice a month since the Italian immigrant, Don Galileo Daconte, had installed his open-air theater in the ruins of a seventeenth-century convent. They saw *All Quiet on the Western Front,* a film based on a book that had been popular the year before and that Dr. Urbino had read, his heart devastated by the barbarism of war. They met afterward in the laboratory, she found him brooding and nostalgic, and thought it was because of the brutal scenes of wounded men dying in the mud. In an attempt to distract him, she invited him to play chess and he accepted to please her, but he played inattentively, with the white pieces, of course, until he discovered before she did that he was going to be defeated in four moves and surrendered without honor. Then the Doctor realized that she had been his opponent in the final game, and not General Jerónimo Argote, as he had supposed. He murmured in astonishment:

"It was masterful!"

She insisted that she deserved no praise, but rather that Jeremiah de Saint-Amour, already lost in the mists of death, had moved his pieces without love. When he stopped the game at about a quarter past eleven, for the music from the public dances had ended, he asked her to leave him. He wanted to write a letter to Dr. Juvenal Urbino, whom he considered the most honorable man he had ever known, and his soul's friend, as he liked to say, despite the fact that the only affinity between the two was their addiction to chess understood as a dialogue of reason and not as a science. And then she knew that Jeremiah de Saint-Amour had come to the end of his suffering and that he had only enough life left to write the letter. The Doctor could not believe it.

"So then you knew!" he exclaimed.

She not only knew, she agreed, but she had helped him to endure the suffering as lovingly as she had helped him to discover happiness. Because that was what his last eleven months had been: cruel suffering.

"Your duty was to report him," said the Doctor.

"I could not do that," she said, shocked. "I loved him too much."

Dr. Urbino, who thought he had heard everything, had never heard anything like that, and said with such simplicity. He looked straight at her and tried with all his senses to fix her in his memory as she was at that moment: she seemed like a river idol, undaunted in her black dress, with her serpent's eyes and the rose behind her ear. A long time ago, on a deserted beach in Haiti where the

20

two of them lay naked after love, Jeremiah de Saint-Amour had sighed; "I will never be old." She interpreted this as a heroic determination to struggle without quarter against the ravages of time, but he was more specific: he had made the irrevocable decision to take his own life when he was sixty years old.

He had turned sixty, in fact, on the twenty-third of January of that year, and then he had set the date as the night before Pentecost, the most important holiday in a city consecrated to the cult of the Holy Spirit. There was not a single detail of the previous night that she had not known about ahead of time, and they spoke of it often, suffering together the irreparable rush of days that neither of them could stop now. Jeremiah de Saint-Amour loved life with a senseless passion, he loved the sea and love, he loved his dog and her, and as the date approached he had gradually succumbed to despair as if his death had been not his own decision but an inexorable destiny.

"Last night, when I left him, he was no longer of this world," she said.

She had wanted to take the dog with her, but he looked at the animal dozing beside the crutches and caressed him with the tips of his fingers. He said: "I'm sorry, but Mister Woodrow Wilson is coming with me." He asked her to tie him to the leg of the cot while he wrote, and she used a false knot so that he could free himself. That had been her only act of disloyalty, and it was justified by her desire to remember the master in the wintry

21

eyes of his dog. But Dr. Urbino interrupted her to say that the dog had not freed himself. She said: "Then it was because he did not want to." And she was glad, because she preferred to evoke her dead lover as he had asked her to the night before, when he stopped writing the letter he had already begun and looked at her for the last time.

"Remember me with a rose," he said to her.

She had returned home a little after midnight. She lay down fully dressed on her bed, to smoke one cigarette after another and give him time to finish what she knew was a long and difficult letter, and a little before three o'clock, when the dogs began to howl, she put the water for coffee on the stove, dressed in full mourning, and cut the first rose of dawn in the patio. Dr. Urbino already realized how completely he would repudiate the memory of that irredeemable woman, and he thought he knew why: only a person without principles could be so complaisant toward grief.

And for the remainder of the visit she gave him even more justification. She would not go to the funeral, for that is what she had promised her lover, although Dr. Urbino thought he had read just the opposite in one of the paragraphs of the letter. She would not shed a tear, she would not waste the rest of her years simmering in the maggot broth of memory, she would not bury herself alive inside these four walls to sew her shroud, as native widows were expected to do. She intended to sell Jeremiah de Saint-Amour's house and all its contents, which, according to the letter, now belonged to her, and she would go on living as she always had, without complaining, in this death trap of the poor where she had been happy.

The words pursued Dr. Juvenal Urbino on the drive home: "this death trap of the poor." It was not a gratuitous description. For the city, his city, stood unchanging on the edge of time: the same burning dry city of his nocturnal terrors and the solitary pleasures of puberty, where flowers rusted and salt corroded, where nothing had happened for four centuries except a slow aging among withered laurels and putrefying swamps. In winter sudden devastating downpours flooded the latrines and turned the streets into sickening bogs. In summer an invisible dust as harsh as red-hot chalk was blown into even the best-protected corners of the imagination by mad winds that took the roofs off the houses and carried away children through the air. On Saturdays the poor mulattoes, along with all their domestic animals and kitchen utensils, tumultuously abandoned their hovels of cardboard and tin on the edges of the swamps and in jubilant assault took over the rocky beaches of the colonial district. Until a few years ago, some of the older ones still bore the royal slave brand that had been burned onto their chests with flaming irons. During the weekend they danced without mercy, drank themselves blind on home-brewed alcohol, made wild love among the icaco plants, and on Sunday at midnight they broke up their own party with bloody free-for-alls. During the rest of the week the same impetuous mob swarmed into the

23

plazas and alleys of the old neighborhoods with their stores of everything that could be bought and sold, and they infused the dead city with the frenzy of a human fair reeking of fried fish: a new life.

Independence from Spain and then the abolition of slavery precipitated the conditions of honorable decadence in which Dr. Juvenal Urbino had been born and raised. The great old families sank into their ruined palaces in silence. Along the rough cobbled streets that had served so well in surprise attacks and buccaneer landings, weeds hung from the balconies and opened cracks in the white-washed walls of even the best-kept mansions, and the only signs of life at two o'clock in the after-noon were languid piano exercises played in the dim light of siesta. Indoors, in the cool bedrooms saturated with incense, women protected them-selves from the sun as if it were a shameful infec-tion, and even at early Mass they hid their faces in their mantillas. Their love affairs were slow and difficult and were often disturbed by sinister omens, and life seemed interminable. At nightfall, at the oppressive moment of transition, a storm of carnivorous mosquitoes rose out of the swamps, and a tender breath of human shit, warm and sad, stirred the certainty of death in the depths of one's soul.

And so the very life of the colonial city, which the young Juvenal Urbino tended to idealize in his Parisian melancholy, was an illusion of memory. In the eighteenth century, the commerce of the

24

city had been the most prosperous in the Caribbean, owing in the main to the thankless privilege of its being the largest African slave market in the Americas. It was also the permanent residence of the Viceroys of the New Kingdom of Granada, who preferred to govern here on the shores of the world's ocean rather than in the distant freezing capital under a centuries-old drizzle that disturbed their sense of reality. Several times a year, fleets of galleons carrying the treasures of Potosí, Quito, and Veracruz gathered in the bay, and the city lived its years of glory. On Friday, June 8, 1708, at four o'clock in the afternoon, the galleon *San José,* set sail for Cádiz with a cargo of precious stones and metals valued at five hundred billion pesos in the currency of the day; it was sunk by an English squadron at the entrance to the port, and two long centuries later it had not yet been salvaged. That treasure lying in its bed of coral, and the corpse of the commander floating sideways on the bridge, were evoked by historians as an emblem of the city drowned in memories.

Across the bay, in the residential district of La Manga, Dr. Juvenal Urbino's house stood in another time. One-story, spacious and cool, it had a portico with Doric columns on the outside terrace, which commanded a view of the still, miasmic water and the debris from sunken ships in the bay. From the entrance door to the kitchen, the floor was covered with black and white checkerboard tiles, a fact often attributed to Dr. Urbino's ruling passion without taking into account that

25

this was a weakness common to the Catalonian craftsmen who built this district for the *nouveaux riches* at the beginning of the century. The large drawing room had the very high ceilings found throughout the rest of the house, and six full-length windows facing the street, and it was separated from the dining room by an enormous, elaborate glass door covered with branching vines and bunches of grapes and maidens seduced by the pipes of fauns in a bronze grove. The furnishings in the reception rooms, including the pendulum clock that stood like a living sentinel in the drawing room, were all original English pieces from the late nineteenth century, and the lamps that hung from the walls were all teardrop crystal, and there were Sèvres vases and bowls everywhere and little alabaster statues of pagan idylls. But that European coherence vanished in the rest of the house, where wicker armchairs were jumbled together with Viennese rockers and leather footstools made by local craftsmen. Splendid hammocks from San Jacinto, with multicolored fringe along the sides and the owner's name embroidered in Gothic letters with silk thread, hung in the bedrooms along with the beds. Next to the dining room, the space that had originally been designed for gala suppers was used as a small music room for intimate concerts when famous performers came to the city. In order to enhance the silence, the tiles had been covered with the Turkish rugs purchased at the World's Fair in Paris; a recent model of a victrola stood next to a stand that held records arranged with care, and in a corner, draped with a Manila shawl, was the piano that Dr. Urbino had not played for many years. Throughout the house one could detect the good sense and care of a woman whose feet were planted firmly on the ground.

But no other room displayed the meticulous solemnity of the library, the sanctuary of Dr. Urbino until old age carried him off. There, all around his father's walnut desk and the tufted leather easy chairs, he had lined the walls and even the windows with shelves behind glass doors, and had arranged in an almost demented order the three thousand volumes bound in identical calfskin with his initials in gold on the spines. Unlike the other rooms, which were at the mercy of noise and foul winds from the port, the library always enjoyed the tranquillity and fragrance of an abbey. Born and raised in the Caribbean superstition that one opened doors and windows to summon a coolness that in fact did not exist, Dr. Urbino and his wife at first felt their hearts oppressed by enclosure. But in the end they were convinced of the merits of the Roman strategy against heat, which consists of closing houses during the lethargy of August in order to keep out the burning air from the street, and then opening them up completely to the night breezes. And from that time on theirs was the coolest house under the furious La Manga sun, and it was a delight to take a siesta in the darkened bedrooms and to sit on the portico in the afternoon to watch the heavy, ash-gray freighters

27

from New Orleans pass by, and at dusk to see the wooden paddles of the riverboats with their shining lights, purifying the stagnant garbage heap of the bay with the wake of their music. It was also the best protected from December through March, when the northern winds tore away roofs and spent the night circling like hungry wolves looking for a crack where they could slip in. No one ever thought that a marriage rooted in such foundations could have any reason not to be happy.

In any case, Dr. Urbino was not when he returned home that morning before ten o'clock, shaken by the two visits that not only had obliged him to miss Pentecost Mass but also threatened to change him at an age when everything had seemed complete. He wanted a short siesta until it was time for Dr. Lácides Olivella's gala luncheon, but he found the servants in an uproar as they attempted to catch the parrot, who had flown to the highest branches of the mango tree when they took him from his cage to clip his wings. He was a deplumed, maniacal parrot who did not speak when asked to but only when it was least expected, but then he did so with a clarity and rationality that were uncommon among human beings. He had been tutored by Dr. Urbino himself, which afforded him privileges that no one else in the family ever had, not even the children when they were young.

He had lived in the house for over twenty years, and no one knew how many years he had been alive before then. Every afternoon after his siesta,

Dr. Urbino sat with him on the terrace in the patio, the coolest spot in the house, and he had summoned the most diligent reserves of his passion for pedagogy until the parrot learned to speak French like an academician. Then, just for love of the labor, he taught him the Latin accompaniment to the Mass and selected passages from the Gospel according to St. Matthew, and he tried without success to inculcate in him a working notion of the four arithmetic functions. On one of his last trips to Europe he brought back the first phonograph with a trumpet speaker, along with many of the latest popular records as well as those by his favorite classical composers. Day after day, over and over again for several months, he played the songs of Yvette Guilbert and Aristide Bruant, who had charmed France during the last century, until the parrot learned them by heart. He sang them in a woman's voice if they were hers, in a tenor's voice if they were his, and ended with impudent laughter that was a masterful imitation of the servant girls when they heard him singing in French. The fame of his accomplishments was so widespread that on occasion distinguished visitors who had traveled from the interior on the riverboats would ask permission to see him, and once some of the many English tourists, who in those days sailed the banana boats from New Orleans, would have bought him at any price. But the day of his greatest glory was when the President of the Republic, Don Marco Fidel Suárez, with his entourage of cabinet ministers, visited the house in order to confirm the truth of his reputation. They arrived at about three o'clock in the afternoon, suffocating in the top hats and frock coats they had worn during three days of official visits under the burning August sky, and they had to leave as curious as when they arrived, because for two desperate hours the parrot refused to say a single syllable, ignoring the pleas and threats and public humiliation of Dr. Urbino, who had insisted on that foolhardy invitation despite the sage warnings of his wife.

The fact that the parrot could maintain his privileges after that historic act of defiance was the ultimate proof of his sacred rights. No other animal was permitted in the house, with the exception of the land turtle who had reappeared in the kitchen after three or four years, when everyone thought he was lost forever. He, however, was not considered a living being but rather a mineral good luck charm whose location one could never be certain of. Dr. Urbino was reluctant to confess his hatred of animals, which he disguised with all kinds of scientific inventions and philosophical pretexts that convinced many, but not his wife. He said that people who loved them to excess were capable of the worst cruelties toward human beings. He said that dogs were not loyal but servile, that cats were opportunists and traitors, that peacocks were heralds of death, that macaws were simply decorative annoyances, that rabbits fomented greed, that monkeys carried the fever of lust, and that roosters were damned because they had been complicit in the three denials of Christ.

On the other hand, Fermina Daza, his wife, who at that time was seventy-two years old and had already lost the doe's gait of her younger days, was an irrational idolator of tropical flowers and domestic animals, and early in her marriage she had taken advantage of the novelty of love to keep many more of them in the house than good sense would allow. The first were three Dalmatians named after Roman emperors, who fought for the favors of a female who did honor to her name of Messalina, for it took her longer to give birth to nine pups than to conceive another ten. Then there were Abyssinian cats with the profiles of eagles and the manners of pharaohs, cross-eyed Siamese and palace Persians with orange eyes, who walked through the rooms like shadowy phantoms and shattered the night with the howling of their witches' sabbaths of love. For several years an Amazonian monkey, chained by his waist to the mango tree in the patio, elicited a certain compassion because he had the sorrowful face of Archbishop Obdulio y Rey, the same candid eyes, the same eloquent hands; that, however, was not the reason Fermina got rid of him, but because he had the bad habit of pleasuring himself in honor of the ladies.

There were all kinds of Guatemalan birds in cages along the passageways, and premonitory curlews, and swamp herons with long yellow legs, and a young stag who came in through the windows to eat the anthurium in the flowerpots. Shortly before the last civil war, when there was talk for the first time of a possible visit by the Pope, they had brought a bird of paradise from Guatemala, but it took longer to arrive than to return to its homeland when it was learned that the announcement of the pontifical visit had been a lie spread by the government to alarm the conspiratorial Liberals. Another time, on the smugglers' ships from Curaçao, they bought a wicker cage with six perfumed crows identical to the ones that Fermina Daza had kept as a girl in her father's house and that she still wanted to have as a married woman. But no one could bear the continual flapping of their wings that filled the house with the reek of funeral wreaths. They also brought in an anaconda, four meters long, whose insomniac hunter's sighs disturbed the darkness in the bedrooms although it accomplished what they had wanted, which was to frighten with its mortal breath the bats and salamanders and countless species of harmful insects that invaded the house during the rainy months. Dr. Juvenal Urbino, so occupied at that time with his professional obligations and so absorbed in his civic and cultural enterprises, was content to assume that in the midst of so many abominable creatures his wife was not only the most beautiful woman in the Caribbean but also the happiest. But one rainy afternoon, at the end of an exhausting day, he encountered a disaster in the house that brought him to his senses. Out of the drawing room, and for as far as the eye could see, a stream of dead animals floated in a marsh of blood. The servant girls had climbed on the chairs, not knowing what to do, and they had not yet recovered from the panic of the slaughter.

One of the German mastiffs, maddened by a sudden attack of rabies, had torn to pieces every animal of any kind that crossed its path, until the gardener from the house next door found the courage to face him and hack him to pieces with his machete. No one knew how many creatures he had bitten or contaminated with his green slaverings, and so Dr. Urbino ordered the survivors killed and their bodies burned in an isolated field, and he requested the services of Misericordia Hospital for a thorough disinfecting of the house. The only animal to escape, because nobody remembered him, was the giant lucky charm tortoise.

Fermina Daza admitted for the first time that her husband was right in a domestic matter, and for a long while afterward she was careful to say no more about animals. She consoled herself with color illustrations from Linnaeus's *Natural History,* which she framed and hung on the drawing room walls, and perhaps she would eventually have lost all hope of ever seeing an animal in the house again if it had not been for the thieves who, early one morning, forced a bathroom window and made off with the silver service that had been in the family for five generations. Dr. Urbino put double padlocks on the window frames, secured the doors on the inside with iron crossbars, placed his most valuable possessions in the strongbox, and belatedly acquired the wartime habit of sleeping with a revolver under his pillow. But he opposed the purchase of a fierce dog, vaccinated or unvaccinated, running loose or chained up, even if thieves were to steal everything he owned.

"Nothing that does not speak will come into this house," he said.

He said it to put an end to the specious arguments of his wife, who was once again determined to buy a dog, and he never imagined that his hasty generalization was to cost him his life. Fermina Daza, whose straightforward character had become more subtle with the years, seized on her husband's casual words and months after the robbery she returned to the ships from Curaçao and bought a royal Paramaribo parrot, who knew only the blasphemies of sailors but said them in a voice so human that he was well worth the extravagant price of twelve centavos.

He was a fine parrot, lighter than he seemed, with a yellow head and a black tongue, the only way to distinguish him from mangrove parrots who did not learn to speak even with turpentine suppositories. Dr. Urbino, a good loser, bowed to the ingenuity of his wife and was even surprised at how amused he was by the advances the parrot made when he was excited by the servant girls. On rainy afternoons, his tongue loosened by the pleasure of having his feathers drenched, he uttered phrases from another time, which he could

34

not have learned in the house and which led one to think that he was much older than he appeared. The Doctor's final doubts collapsed one night when the thieves tried to get in again through a skylight in the attic, and the parrot frightened them with a mastiff's barking that could not have been more realistic if it had been real, and with shouts of stop thief stop thief stop thief, two saving graces he had not learned in the house. It was then that Dr. Urbino took charge of him and ordered the construction of a perch under the mango tree with a container for water, another for ripe bananas, and a trapeze for acrobatics. From December through March, when the nights were cold and the north winds made living outdoors unbearable, he was taken inside to sleep in the bedrooms in a cage covered by a blanket, although Dr. Urbino suspected that his chronic swollen glands might be a threat to the healthy respiration of humans. For many years they clipped his wing feathers and let him wander wherever he chose to walk with his hulking old horseman's gait. But one day he began to do acrobatic tricks on the beams in the kitchen and fell into the pot of stew with a sailor's shout of every man for himself, and with such good luck that the cook managed to scoop him out with the ladle, scalded and deplumed but still alive. From then on he was kept in the cage even during the daytime, in defiance of the vulgar belief that caged parrots forget everything they have learned, and let out only in the four o'clock coolness for his classes with Dr. Urbino on the terrace in the patio. No one realized in time that his wings were too long, and they were about to clip them that morning when he escaped to the top of the mango tree.

And for three hours they had not been able to catch him. The servant girls, with the help of other maids in the neighborhood, had used all kinds of tricks to lure him down, but he insisted on staying where he was, laughing madly as he shouted long live the Liberal Party, long live the Liberal Party damn it, a reckless cry that had cost many a carefree drunk his life. Dr. Urbino could barely see him amid the leaves, and he tried to cajole him in Spanish and French and even in Latin, and the parrot responded in the same languages and with the same emphasis and timbre in his voice, but he did not move from his treetop. Convinced that no one was going to make him move voluntarily, Dr. Urbino had them send for the fire department, his most recent civic pastime.

Until just a short time before, in fact, fires had been put out by volunteers using brickmasons' ladders and buckets of water carried in from wherever it could be found, and methods so disorderly that they sometimes caused more damage than the fires. But for the past year, thanks to a fund organized by the Society for Public Improvement, of which Juvenal Urbino was honorary president, there was a corps of professional firemen and a water truck with a siren and a bell and two high-pressure hoses. They were so popular that classes were suspended when the church bells were heard

36

sounding the alarm, so that children could watch them fight the fire. At first that was all they did. But Dr. Urbino told the municipal authorities that in Hamburg he had seen firemen revive a boy found frozen in a basement after a three-day snowstorm. He had also seen them in a Neapolitan alley lowering a corpse in his coffin from a tenth-floor balcony because the stairway in the building had so many twists and turns that the family could not get him down to the street. That was how the local firemen learned to render other emergency services, such as forcing locks or killing poisonous snakes, and the Medical School offered them a special course in first aid for minor accidents. So it was in no way peculiar to ask them to please get a distinguished parrot, with all the qualities of a gentleman, out of a tree. Dr. Urbino said: "Tell them it's for me." And he went to his bedroom to dress for the gala luncheon. The truth was that at that moment, devastated by the letter from Jeremiah de Saint-Amour, he did not really care about the fate of the parrot.

Fermina Daza had put on a loose-fitting silk dress belted at the hip, a necklace of real pearls with six long, uneven loops, and high-heeled satin shoes that she wore only on very solemn occasions, for by now she was too old for such abuses. Her stylish attire did not seem appropriate for a venerable grandmother, but it suited her figure—long-boned and still slender and erect, her resilient hands without a single age spot, her steel-blue hair bobbed on a slant at her cheek. Her clear almond eyes and her inborn haughtiness were all that were left to her from her wedding portrait, but what she had been deprived of by age she more than made up for in character and diligence. She felt very well: the time of iron corsets, bound waists, and bustles that exaggerated buttocks was receding into the past. Liberated bodies, breathing freely, showed themselves for what they were. Even at the age of seventy-two.

Dr. Urbino found her sitting at her dressing table under the slow blades of the electric fan, putting on her bell-shaped hat decorated with felt violets. The bedroom was large and bright, with an English bed protected by mosquito netting embroidered in pink, and two windows open to the trees in the patio, where one could hear the clamor of cicadas, giddy with premonitions of rain. Ever since their return from their honeymoon, Fermina Daza had chosen her husband's clothes according to the weather and the occasion, and laid them out for him on a chair the night before so they would be ready for him when he came out of the bathroom. She could not remember when she had also begun to help him dress, and finally to dress him, and she was aware that at first she had done it for love, but for the past five years or so she had been obliged to do it regardless of the reason because he could not dress himself. They had just celebrated their golden wedding anniversary, and they were not capable of living for even an instant without the other, or without thinking about the other, and that capacity diminished as their age increased.

Neither could have said if their mutual dependence was based on love or convenience, but they had never asked the question with their hands on their hearts because both had always preferred not to know the answer. Little by little she had been discovering the uncertainty of her husband's step, his mood changes, the gaps in his memory, his recent habit of sobbing while he slept, but she did not identify these as the unequivocal signs of final decay but rather as a happy return to childhood. That was why she did not treat him like a difficult old man but as a senile baby, and that deception was providential for the two of them because it put them beyond the reach of pity.

Life would have been quite another matter for them both if they had learned in time that it was easier to avoid great matrimonial catastrophes than trivial everyday miseries. But if they had learned anything together, it was that wisdom comes to us when it can no longer do any good. For years Fermina Daza had endured her husband's jubilant dawns with a bitter heart. She clung to the last threads of sleep in order to avoid facing the fatality of another morning full of sinister premonitions, while he awoke with the innocence of a newborn: each new day was one more day he had won. She heard him awake with the roosters, and his first sign of life was a cough without rhyme or reason that seemed intended to awaken her too. She heard him grumble, just to annoy her, while he felt around for the slippers that were supposed to be next to the bed. She heard him make his way to the bathroom, groping in the dark. After an hour in his study, when she had fallen asleep again, he would come back to dress, still without turning on the light. Once, during a party game, he had been asked how he defined himself, and he had said: "I am a man who dresses in the dark." She heard him, knowing full well that not one of those noises was indispensable, and that he made them on purpose although he pretended not to, just as she was awake and pretended not to be. His motives were clear: he never needed her awake and lucid as much as he did during those fumbling moments.

There was no sleeper more elegant than she, with her curved body posed for a dance and her hand across her forehead, but there was also no one more ferocious when anyone disturbed the sensuality of her thinking she was still asleep when she no longer was. Dr. Urbino knew she was waiting for his slightest sound, that she even would be grateful for it, just so she could blame someone for waking her at five o'clock in the morning, so that on the few occasions when he had to feel around in the dark because he could not find his slippers in their customary place, she would suddenly say in a sleepy voice: "You left them in the bathroom last night." Then right after that, her voice fully awake with rage, she would curse: "The worst misfortune in this house is that nobody lets you sleep."

Then she would roll over in bed and turn on the light without the least mercy for herself, content with her first victory of the day. The truth was they both played a game, mythical and perverse, but for all that comforting: it was one of the many dangerous pleasures of domestic love. But one of those trivial games almost ended the first thirty years of their life together, because one day there was no soap in the bathroom.

It began with routine simplicity. Dr. Juvenal Urbino had returned to the bedroom, in the days when he still bathed without help, and begun to dress without turning on the light. As usual she was in her warm fetal state, her eyes closed, her breathing shallow, that arm from a sacred dance above her head. But she was only half asleep, as usual, and he knew it. After a prolonged sound of starched linen in the darkness, Dr. Urbino said to himself:

"I've been bathing for almost a week without any soap."

Then, fully awake, she remembered, and tossed and turned in fury with the world because in fact she had forgotten to replace the soap in the bathroom. She had noticed its absence three days earlier when she was already under the shower, and she had planned to replace it afterward, but then she forgot until the next day, and on the third day the same thing happened again. The truth was that a week had not gone by, as he said to make her feel more guilty, but three unpardonable days, and her anger at being found out in a mistake maddened her. As always, she defended herself by attacking.

41

"Well I've bathed every day," she shouted, beside herself with rage, "and there's always been soap."

Although he knew her battle tactics by heart, this time he could not abide them. On some professional pretext or other he went to live in the interns' quarters at Misericordia Hospital, returning home only to change his clothes before making his evening house calls. She headed for the kitchen when she heard him come in, pretending that she had something to do, and stayed there until she heard his carriage in the street. For the next three months, each time they tried to resolve the conflict they only inflamed their feelings even more. He was not ready to come back as long as she refused to admit there had been no soap in the bathroom, and she was not prepared to have him back until he recognized that he had consciously lied to torment her.

The incident, of course, gave them the opportunity to evoke many other trivial quarrels from many other dim and turbulent dawns. Resentments stirred up other resentments, reopened old scars, turned them into fresh wounds, and both were dismayed at the desolating proof that in so many years of conjugal battling they had done little more than nurture their rancor. At last he proposed that they both submit to an open confession, with the Archbishop himself if necessary, so that God could decide once and for all whether or not there had been soap in the soap dish in the bathroom. Then, despite all her self-control, she lost her temper with a historic cry:

"To hell with the Archbishop!"

The impropriety shook the very foundations of the city, gave rise to slanders that were not easy to disprove, and was preserved in popular tradition as if it were a line from an operetta: "To hell with the Archbishop!" Realizing she had gone too far, she anticipated her husband's predictable response and threatened to move back to her father's old house, which still belonged to her although it had been rented out for public offices, and live there by herself. And it was not an idle threat: she really did want to leave and did not care about the scandal, and her husband realized this in time. He did not have the courage to defy his own prejudices, and he capitulated. Not in the sense that he admitted there had been soap in the bathroom, but insofar as he continued to live in the same house with her, although they slept in separate rooms, and he did not say a word to her. They ate in silence, sparring with so much skill that they sent each other messages across the table through the children, and the children never realized that they were not speaking to each other.

Since the study had no bathroom, the arrangement solved the problem of noise in the morning, because he came in to bathe after preparing his class and made a sincere effort not to awaken his wife. They would often arrive at the bathroom at the same time, and then they took turns brushing their teeth before going to sleep. After four months had gone by, he lay down on their double bed one night to read until she came out of the bathroom, as he often did, and he fell asleep. She lay down beside him in a rather careless way so that he would wake up and leave. And in fact he did stir, but instead of getting up he turned out the light and settled himself on the pillow. She shook him by the shoulder to remind him that he was supposed to go to the study, but it felt so comfortable to be back in his great-grandparents' featherbed that he preferred to capitulate.

"Let me stay here," he said. "There was soap."

When they recalled this episode, now they had rounded the corner of old age, neither could believe the astonishing truth that this had been the most serious argument in fifty years of living together, and the only one that had made them both want to abandon their responsibilities and begin a new life. Even when they were old and placid they were careful about bringing it up, for the barely healed wounds could begin to bleed again as if they had been inflicted only yesterday.

He was the first man that Fermina Daza heard urinate. She heard him on their wedding night, while she lay prostrate with seasickness in the stateroom on the ship that was carrying them to France, and the sound of his stallion's stream seemed so potent, so replete with authority, that it increased her terror of the devastation to come. That memory often returned to her as the years weakened the stream, for she never could resign herself to his wetting the rim of the toilet bowl

44

each time he used it. Dr. Urbino tried to convince her, with arguments readily understandable to anyone who wished to understand them, that the mishap was not repeated every day through carelessness on his part, as she insisted, but because of organic reasons: as a young man his stream was so defined and so direct that when he was at school he won contests for marksmanship in filling bottles, but with the ravages of age it was not only decreasing, it was also becoming oblique and scattered, and had at last turned into a fantastic fountain, impossible to control despite his many efforts to direct it. He would say: "The toilet must have been invented by someone who knew nothing about men." He contributed to domestic peace with a quotidian act that was more humiliating than humble: he wiped the rim of the bowl with toilet paper each time he used it. She knew, but never said anything as long as the ammoniac fumes were not too strong in the bathroom, and then she proclaimed, as if she had uncovered a crime: "This stinks like a rabbit hutch." On the eve of old age this physical difficulty inspired Dr. Urbino with the ultimate solution: he urinated sitting down, as she did, which kept the bowl clean and him in a state of grace.

By this time he could do very little for himself, and the possibility of a fatal slip in the tub put him on his guard against the shower. The house was modern and did not have the pewter tub with lion's-paw feet common in the mansions of the old city. He had had it removed for hygienic reasons:

45

the bathtub was another piece of abominable junk invented by Europeans who bathed only on the last Friday of the month, and then in the same water made filthy by the very dirt they tried to remove from their bodies. So he had ordered an outsized washtub made of solid lignum vitae, in which Fermina Daza bathed her husband just as if he were a newborn child. Waters boiled with mallow leaves and orange skins were mixed into the bath that lasted over an hour, and the effect on him was so sedative that he sometimes fell asleep in the perfumed infusion. After bathing him, Fermina Daza helped him to dress: she sprinkled talcum powder between his legs, she smoothed cocoa butter on his rashes, she helped him put on his undershorts with as much love as if they had been a diaper, and continued dressing him, item by item, from his socks to the knot in his tie with the topaz pin. Their conjugal dawns grew calm because he had returned to the childhood his children had taken away from him. And she, in turn, at last accepted the domestic schedule because the years were passing for her too; she slept less and less, and by the time she was seventy she was awake before her husband.

On Pentecost Sunday, when he lifted the blanket to look at Jeremiah de Saint-Amour's body, Dr. Urbino experienced the revelation of something that had been denied him until then in his most lucid peregrinations as a physician and a believer. After so many years of familiarity with death, after battling it for so long, after so much turning it inside out and upside down, it was as if he had dared to look death in the face for the first time, and it had looked back at him. It was not the fear of death. No: that fear had been inside him for many years, it had lived with him, it had been another shadow cast over his own shadow ever since the night he awoke, shaken by a bad dream, and realized that death was not only a permanent probability, as he had always believed, but an immediate reality. What he had seen that day, however, was the physical presence of something that until that moment had been only an imagined certainty. He was very glad that the instrument used by Divine Providence for that overwhelming revelation had been Jeremiah de Saint-Amour, whom he had always considered a saint unaware of his own state of grace. But when the letter revealed his true identity, his sinister past, his inconceivable powers of deception, he felt that something definitive and irrevocable had occurred in his life.

Nevertheless Fermina Daza did not allow him to infect her with his somber mood. He tried, of course, while she helped him put his legs into his trousers and worked the long row of buttons on his shirt. But he failed because Fermina Daza was not easy to impress, least of all by the death of a man she did not care for. All she knew about him was that Jeremiah de Saint-Amour was a cripple on crutches whom she had never seen, that he had escaped the firing squad during one of many insurrections on one of many islands in the Antilles,

47

that he had become a photographer of children out of necessity and had become the most successful one in the province, and that he had won a game of chess from someone she remembered as Torremolinos but in reality was named Capablanca.

"But he was nothing more than a fugitive from Cayenne, condemned to life imprisonment for an atrocious crime," said Dr. Urbino. "Imagine, he had even eaten human flesh."

He handed her the letter whose secrets he wanted to carry with him to the grave, but she put the folded sheets in her dressing table without reading them and locked the drawer with a key. She was accustomed to her husband's unfathomable capacity for astonishment, his exaggerated opinions that became more incomprehensible as the years went by, his narrowness of mind that was out of tune with his public image. But this time he had outdone himself. She had supposed that her husband held Jeremiah de Saint-Amour in esteem not for what he had once been but for what he began to be after he arrived here with only his exile's rucksack, and she could not understand why he was so distressed by the disclosure of his true identity at this late date. She did not comprehend why he thought it an abomination that he had had a woman in secret, since that was an atavistic custom of a certain kind of man, himself included, yes even he in a moment of ingratitude, and besides, it seemed to her a heartbreaking proof of love that she had helped him carry out his decision to die. She said: "If you also decided to do that for reasons as serious as his, my duty would be to do what she did." Once again Dr. Urbino found himself face to face with the simple incomprehension that had exasperated him for a half a century.

"You don't understand anything," he said. "What infuriates me is not what he was or what he did, but the deception he practiced on all of us for so many years."

His eyes began to fill with easy tears, but she pretended not to see. "He did the right thing," she replied. "If he had told the truth, not you or that poor woman or anybody in this town would have loved him as much as they did."

She threaded his watch chain through the buttonhole in his vest. She put the finishing touches to the knot in his tie and pinned on his topaz tiepin. Then she dried his eyes and wiped his teary beard with the handkerchief sprinkled with florida water and put that in his breast pocket, its corners spread open like a magnolia. The eleven strokes of the pendulum clock sounded in the depths of the house.

"Hurry," she said, taking him by the arm. "We'll be late."

Aminta Dechamps, Dr. Lácides Olivella's wife, and her seven equally diligent daughters, had arranged every detail so that the silver anniversary luncheon would be the social event of the year. The family home, in the very center of the historic district, was the old mint, denatured by a Florentine architect who came through here like an ill wind blowing renovation and converted many

49

seventeenth-century relics into Venetian basilicas. It had six bedrooms and two large, well-ventilated dining and reception rooms, but that was not enough space for the guests from the city, not to mention the very select few from out of town. The patio was like an abbey cloister, with a stone fountain murmuring in the center and pots of heliotrope that perfumed the house at dusk, but the space among the arcades was inadequate for so many grand family names. So it was decided to hold the luncheon in their country house that was ten minutes away by automobile along the King's Highway and had over an acre of patio, and enormous Indian laurels, and local water lilies in a gently flowing river. The men from Don Sancho's Inn, under the supervision of Señora de Olivella, hung colored canvas awnings in the sunny areas and raised a platform under the laurels with tables for one hundred twenty-two guests, with a linen tablecloth on each of them and bouquets of the day's fresh roses for the table of honor. They also built a wooden dais for a woodwind band whose program was limited to contradances and national waltzes, and for a string quartet from the School of Fine Arts, which was Señora de Olivella's surprise for her husband's venerable teacher, who would preside over the luncheon. Although the date did not correspond exactly to the anniversary of his graduation, they chose Pentecost Sunday in order to magnify the significance of the celebration.

The preparations had begun three months earlier, for fear that something indispensable would be left undone for lack of time. They brought in live chickens from Ciénaga de Oro, famous all along the coast not only for their size and flavor but because in colonial times they had scratched for food in alluvial deposits and little nuggets of pure gold were found in their gizzards. Señora de Olivella herself, accompanied by some of her daughters and her domestic staff, boarded the luxury ocean liners and selected the best from everywhere to honor her husband's achievements. She had anticipated everything except that the celebration would take place on a Sunday in June in a year when the rains were late. She realized the danger that very morning when she went to High Mass and was horrified by the humidity and saw that the sky was heavy and low and that one could not see to the ocean's horizon. Despite these ominous signs, the Director of the Astronomical Observatory, whom she met at Mass, reminded her that in all the troubled history of the city, even during the cruelest winters, it had never rained on Pentecost. Still, when the clocks struck twelve and many of the guests were already having an aperitif outdoors, a single crash of thunder made the earth tremble, and a turbulent wind from the sea knocked over the tables and blew down the canopies, and the sky collapsed in a catastrophic downpour.

In the chaos of the storm Dr. Juvenal Urbino, along with the other late guests whom he had met on the road, had great difficulty reaching the house,

and like them he wanted to move from the carriage to the house by jumping from stone to stone
across the muddy patio, but at last he had to
accept the humiliation of being carried by Don
Sancho's men under a yellow canvas canopy. They
did the best they could to set up the separate
tables again inside the house—even in the bedrooms—and the guests made no effort to disguise
their surly, shipwrecked mood. It was as hot as a
ship's boiler room, for the windows had to be
closed to keep out the wind-driven rain. In the
patio each place at the tables had been marked
with a card bearing the name of the guest, one
side reserved for men and the other for women,
according to custom. But inside the house the
name cards were in confusion and people sat where
they could in an obligatory promiscuity that defied
our social superstitions on at least this one occasion. In the midst of the cataclysm Aminta de
Olivella seemed to be everywhere at once, her hair
soaking wet and her splendid dress spattered with
mud, but bearing up under the misfortune with
the invincible smile, learned from her husband,
that would give no quarter to adversity. With the
help of her daughters, who were cut from the
same cloth, she did everything possible to keep
the places at the table of honor in order, with Dr.
Juvenal Urbino in the center and Archbishop
Obdulio y Rey on his right. Fermina Daza sat
next to her husband, as she always did, for fear he
would fall asleep during the meal or spill soup on
his lapel. Across from him sat Dr. Lácides Olivella,

a well-preserved man of about fifty with an effeminate air, whose festive spirit seemed in no way related to his accurate diagnoses. The rest of the table was occupied by provincial and municipal officials and last year's beauty queen, whom the Governor escorted to the seat next to him. Although it was not customary for invitations to request special attire, least of all for a luncheon in the country, the women wore evening gowns and precious jewels and most of the men were dressed in dinner jackets with black ties, and some even wore frock coats. Only the most sophisticated, Dr. Urbino among them, wore their ordinary clothes. At each place was a menu printed in French, with golden vignettes.

Señora de Olivella, horror-struck by the devastating heat, went through the house pleading with the men to take off their jackets during the luncheon, but no one dared to be the first. The Archbishop commented to Dr. Urbino that in a sense this was a historic luncheon: there, together for the first time at the same table, their wounds healed and their anger dissipated, sat the two opposing sides in the civil wars that had bloodied the country ever since Independence. This thought accorded with the enthusiasm of the Liberals, especially the younger ones, who had succeeded in electing a president from their party after forty-five years of Conservative hegemony. Dr. Urbino did not agree: in his opinion a Liberal president was exactly the same as a Conservative president, but not as well dressed. But he did not want to contradict the Archbishop, although he would have liked to point out to him that guests were at that luncheon not because of what they thought but because of the merits of their lineage, which was something that had always stood over and above the hazards of politics and the horrors of war. From this point of view, in fact, not a single person was missing.

The downpour ended as suddenly as it had begun, and the sun began to shine in a cloudless sky, but the storm had been so violent that several trees were uprooted and the overflowing stream had turned the patio into a swamp. The greatest disaster had occurred in the kitchen. Wood fires had been built outdoors on bricks behind the house, and the cooks barely had time to rescue their pots from the rain. They lost precious time reorganizing the flooded kitchen and improvising new fires in the back gallery. But by one o'clock the crisis had been resolved and only the dessert was missing: the Sisters of St. Clare were in charge of that, and they had promised to send it before eleven. It was feared that the ditch along the King's Highway had flooded, as it did even in less severe winters, and in that case it would be at least two hours before the dessert arrived. As soon as the weather cleared they opened the windows, and the house was cooled by air that had been purified by the sulfurous storm. Then the band was told to play its program of waltzes on the terrace of the portico, and that only heightened the confusion because everyone had to shout to be heard over the banging of copper pots inside the house. Tired of waiting, smiling even on the verge of tears, Aminta de Olivella ordered luncheon to be served.

The group from the School of Fine Arts began their concert in the formal silence achieved for the opening bars of Mozart's "La Chasse." Despite the voices that grew louder and more confused and the intrusions of Don Sancho's black servants, who could barely squeeze past the tables with their steaming serving dishes, Dr. Urbino managed to keep a channel open to the music until the program was over. His powers of concentration had decreased so much with the passing years that he had to write down each chess move in order to remember what he had planned. Yet he could still engage in serious conversation and follow a concert at the same time, although he never reached the masterful extremes of a German orchestra conductor, a great friend of his during his time in Austria, who read the score of *Don Giovanni* while listening to *Tannhäuser*.

He thought that the second piece on the program, Schubert's "Death and the Maiden," was played with facile theatricality. While he strained to listen through the clatter of covered dishes, he stared at a blushing boy who nodded to him in greeting. He had seen him somewhere, no doubt about that, but he could not remember where. This often happened to him, above all with people's names, even those he knew well, or with a melody from other times, and it caused him such dreadful anguish that one night he would have preferred to die rather than endure it until dawn. He was on the verge of reaching that state now when a charitable flash illuminated his memory: the boy had been one of his students last year. He was surprised to see him there, in the kingdom of the elect, but Dr. Olivella reminded him that he was the son of the Minister of Health and was preparing a thesis in forensic medicine. Dr. Juvenal Urbino greeted him with a joyful wave of his hand and the young doctor stood up and responded with a bow. But not then, not ever, did he realize that this was the intern who had been with him that morning in the house of Jeremiah de Saint-Amour.

Comforted by yet another victory over old age, he surrendered to the diaphanous and fluid lyricism of the final piece on the program, which he could not identify. Later the young cellist, who had just returned from France, told him it was a quartet for strings by Gabriel Fauré, whom Dr. Urbino had not even heard of, although he was always very alert to the latest trends in Europe. Fermina Daza, who was keeping an eye on him as she always did, but most of all when she saw him becoming introspective in public, stopped eating and put her earthly hand on his. She said: "Don't think about it anymore." Dr. Urbino smiled at her from the far shore of ecstasy, and it was then that he began to think again about what she had feared. He remembered Jeremiah de Saint-Amour, on view at that hour in his coffin, in his bogus military uniform with his fake decorations, under the accusing eyes of the children in the portraits. He turned to the Archbishop to tell him about the suicide, but he had already heard the news. There had been a good deal of talk after High Mass, and he had even received a request from General Jerónimo Argote, on behalf of the Caribbean refugees, that he be buried in holy ground. He said: "The request itself, it seemed to me, showed a lack of respect." Then, in a more humane tone, he asked it anyone knew the reason for the suicide. Dr. Urbino answered: "Gerontophobia," the proper word although he thought he had just invented it. Dr. Olivella, attentive to the guests who were sitting closest to him, stopped listening to them for a moment to take part in his teacher's conversation. He said: "It is a pity to still find a suicide that is not for love." Dr. Urbino was not surprised to recognize his own thoughts in those of his favorite disciple.

"And worse yet," he said, "with gold cyanide."

When he said that, he once again felt compassion prevailing over the bitterness caused by the letter, for which he thanked not his wife but rather a miracle of the music. Then he spoke to the Archbishop of the lay saint he had known in their long twilights of chess, he spoke of the dedication of his art to the happiness of children, his rare erudition in all things of this world, his Spartan habits, and he himself was surprised by the purity of soul with which Jeremiah de Saint-Aniour had separated himself once and for all from his past. Then he spoke to the Mayor about the advantages of purchasing his files of photographic plates in order to preserve the images of a generation who might never again be happy outside their portraits and in whose hands lay the future of the city. The Archbishop was scandalized that a militant and educated Catholic would dare to think that a suicide was saintly, but he agreed with the plan to create an archive of the negatives. The Mayor wanted to know from whom they were to be purchased. Dr. Urbino's tongue burned with the live coal of the secret. "I will take care of it." And he felt redeemed by his own loyalty to the woman he had repudiated five hours earlier. Fermina Daza noticed it and in a low voice made him promise that he would attend the funeral. Relieved, he said that of course he would, that went without saying.

The speeches were brief and simple. The woodwind band began a popular tune that had not been announced on the program, and the guests strolled along the terraces, waiting for the men from Don Sancho's Inn to finish drying the patio in case anyone felt inclined to dance. The only guests who stayed in the drawing room were those at the table of honor, who were celebrating the fact that Dr. Urbino had drunk half a glass of brandy in one swallow in a final toast. No one recalled that he had already done the same thing with a glass of *grand cru* wine as accompaniment to a very special dish, but his heart had demanded it of him that afternoon, and his self-indulgence was well repaid: once again, after so many long years, he felt like singing. And he would have, no doubt, on the urging of the young cellist who offered to accompany him, if one of those new automobiles had not suddenly driven across the mudhole of the patio, splashing the musicians and rousing the ducks in the barnyards with the quacking of its horn. It stopped in front of the portico and Dr. Marco Aurelio Urbino Daza and his wife emerged, laughing for all they were worth and carrying a tray covered with lace cloths in each hand. Other trays just like them were on the jump seats and even on the floor next to the chauffeur. It was the belated dessert. When the applause and the shouted cordial jokes had ended, Dr. Urbino Daza explained in all seriousness that before the storm broke, the Sisters of St. Clare had asked him to please bring the dessert, but he had left the King's Highway because someone said that his parents' house was on fire. Dr. Juvenal Urbino became upset before his son could finish the story, but his wife reminded him in time that he himself had called for the firemen to rescue the parrot. Aminta de Olivella was radiant as she decided to serve the dessert on the terraces even though they had already had their coffee. But Dr. Juvenal Urbino and his wife left without tasting it, for there was barely enough time for him to have his sacred siesta before the funeral.

And he did have it, although his sleep was brief and restless because he discovered when he returned home that the firemen had caused almost as much damage as a fire. In their efforts to frighten the parrot they had stripped a tree with the pressure hoses, and a misdirected jet of water through the windows of the master bedroom had caused irreparable damage to the furniture and to the portraits of unknown forebears hanging on the walls. Thinking that there really was a fire, the neighbors had hurried over when they heard the bell on the fire truck, and if the disturbance was no worse, it was because the schools were closed on Sundays. When they realized they could not reach the parrot even with their extension ladders, the firemen began to chop at the branches with machetes, and only the opportune arrival of Dr. Urbino Daza prevented them from mutilating the tree all the way to the trunk. They left, saying they would return after five o'clock if they received permission to prune, and on their way out they muddied the interior terrace and the drawing room and ripped Fermina Daza's favorite Turkish rug. Needless disasters, all of them, because the general impression was that the parrot had taken advantage of the chaos to escape through neighboring patios. And in fact Dr. Urbino looked for him in the foliage, but there was no response in any language, not even to whistles and songs, so he gave him up for lost and went to sleep when it was almost three o'clock. But first he enjoyed the immediate pleasure of smelling a secret garden in his urine that had been purified by lukewarm asparagus.

He was awakened by sadness. Not the sadness he had felt that morning when he stood before the corpse of his friend, but the invisible cloud that would saturate his soul after his siesta and which he interpreted as divine notification that he was living his final afternoons. Until the age of fifty he had not been conscious of the size and weight and condition of his organs. Little by little, as he lay with his eyes closed after his daily siesta, he had begun to feel them, one by one, inside his body, feel the shape of his insomniac heart, his mysterious liver, his hermetic pancreas, and he had slowly discovered that even the oldest people were younger than he was and that he had become the only survivor of his generation's legendary group portraits. When he became aware of his first bouts of forgetfulness, he had recourse to a tactic he had heard about from one of his teachers at the Medical School: "The man who has no memory makes one out of paper." But this was a short-lived illusion, for he had reached the stage where he would forget what the written reminders in his pockets meant, search the entire house for the eyeglasses he was wearing, turn the key again after locking the doors, and lose the sense of what he was reading because he forgot the premise of the argument or the relationships among the characters. But what disturbed him most was his lack of confidence in his own power of reason: little by little, as in an ineluctable shipwreck, he felt himself losing his good judgment.

With no scientific basis except his own experience, Dr. Juvenal Urbino knew that most fatal diseases had their own specific odor, but that none was as specific as old age. He detected it in the cadavers slit open from head to toe on the dissecting table, he even recognized it in patients who hid their age with the greatest success, he smelled it in the perspiration on his own clothing and in the unguarded breathing of his sleeping wife. If he had not been what he was—in essence an old-style Christian—perhaps he would have agreed with Jeremiah de Saint-Amour that old age was an indecent state that had to be ended before it was too late. The only consolation, even for someone like him who had been a good man in bed, was sexual peace: the slow, merciful extinction of his venereal appetite. At eighty-one years of age he had enough lucidity to realize that he was attached to this world by a few slender threads that could break painlessly with a simple change of position while he slept, and if he did all he could to keep those threads intact, it was because of his terror of not finding God in the darkness of death.

Fermina Daza had been busy straightening the bedroom that had been destroyed by the firemen, and a little before four she sent for her husband's daily glass of lemonade with chipped ice and reminded him that he should dress for the funeral. That afternoon Dr. Urbino had two books by his hand: *Man, the Unknown* by Alexis Carrel and *The Story of San Michele* by Axel Munthe; the pages of the second book were still uncut, and he asked Digna Pardo, the cook, to bring him the marble paper cutter he had left in the bedroom. But when it was brought to him he was already reading *Man, the Unknown* at the place he had marked with an envelope: there were only a few pages left till the end. He read slowly, making his way through the meanderings of a slight headache that he attributed to the half glass of brandy at the final toast. When he paused in his reading he sipped the lemonade or took his time chewing on a piece of ice. He was wearing his socks, and his shirt without its starched collar; his elastic suspenders with the green stripes hung down from his waist. The mere idea of having to change for the funeral irritated him. Soon he stopped reading, placed one book on top of the other, and began to rock very slowly in the wicker rocking chair, contemplating with regret the banana plants in the mire of the patio, the stripped mango, the flying ants that came after the rain, the ephemeral splendor of another afternoon that would never return. He had forgotten that he ever owned a parrot from Paramaribo whom he loved as if he were a human being, when suddenly he heard him say: "Royal parrot." His voice sounded close by, almost next to him, and then he saw him in the lowest branch of the mango tree.

"You scoundrel!" he shouted.

The parrot answered in an identical voice:

"You're even more of a scoundrel, Doctor."

He continued to talk to him, keeping him in view while he put on his boots with great care so as not to frighten him and pulled his suspenders up over his arms and went down to the patio, which was still full of mud, testing the ground with his stick so that he would not trip on the three steps of the terrace. The parrot did not move, and perched so close to the ground that Dr. Urbino held out his walking stick for him so that he could sit on the silver handle, as was his custom, but the parrot sidestepped and jumped to the next branch, a little higher up but easier to reach since the house ladder had been leaning against it even before the arrival of the firemen. Dr. Urbino calculated the height and thought that if he climbed two rungs he would be able to catch him. He stepped onto the first, singing a disarming, friendly song to distract the attention of the churlish bird, who repeated the words without the music but sidled still farther out on the branch. He climbed to the second rung without difficulty, holding on to the ladder with both hands, and the parrot began to repeat the entire song without moving from the spot. He climbed to the third rung and then the fourth, for he had miscalculated the height of the branch, and then he grasped the ladder with his left hand and tried to seize the parrot with his right. Digna Pardo, the old servant, who was coming to remind him that he would be late for the funeral, saw the back of a man standing on the ladder, and she would not have believed that he was who he was if it had not been for the green stripes on the elastic suspenders.

"Santísimo Sacramento!" she shrieked. "You'll kill yourself!"

Dr. Urbino caught the parrot around the neck with a triumphant sigh: *ça y est*. But he released him immediately because the ladder slipped from under his feet and for an instant he was suspended in air and then he realized that he had died without Communion, without time to repent of anything or to say goodbye to anyone, at seven minutes after four on Pentecost Sunday.

Fermina Daza was in the kitchen tasting the soup for supper when she heard Digna Pardo's horrified shriek and the shouting of the servants and then of the entire neighborhood. She dropped the tasting spoon and tried her best to run despite the invincible weight of her age, screaming like a madwoman without knowing yet what had happened under the mango leaves, and her heart jumped inside her ribs when she saw her man lying on his back in the mud, dead to this life but still resisting death's final blow for one last minute so that she would have time to come to him. He recognized her despite the uproar, through his tears of unrepeatable sorrow at dying without her, and he looked at her for the last and final time with eyes more luminous, more grief-stricken, more grateful than she had ever seen them in half a century of a shared life, and he managed to say to her with his last breath:

"Only God knows how much I loved you."

It was a memorable death, and not without reason. Soon after he had completed his course of specialized studies in France, Dr. Juvenal Urbino became known in his country for the drastic new methods he used to ward off the last cholera epidemic suffered by the province. While he was still in Europe, the previous one had caused the death of a quarter of the urban population in less than three months; among the victims was his father, who was also a highly esteemed physician. With his immediate prestige and a sizable contribution from his own inheritance, he founded the Medical Society, the first and for many years the only one in the Caribbean provinces, of which he was lifetime president. He organized the construction of the first aqueduct, the first sewer system, and the covered public market that permitted filth to be cleaned out of Las Ánimas Bay. He was also president of the Academy of the Language and the Academy of History. For his service to the Church, the Latin Patriarch of Jerusalem made him a Knight of the Order of the Holy Sepulcher, and the French Government conferred upon him the rank of Commander in the Legion of Honor. He gave active encouragement to every religious and civic society in the city and had a special interest in the Patriotic Junta, composed of politically disinterested influential citizens who urged governments and local businesses to adopt progressive ideas that were too daring for the time. The most memorable of them was the testing of an aerostatic balloon that on its inaugural flight carried a letter to San Juan de la Ciénaga, long before anyone had thought of airmail as a rational possibility. The Center for the Arts, which was also his idea, established the School of Fine Arts in the same house where it is still located, and for many years he was a patron of the Poetic Festival in April.

Only he achieved what had seemed impossible for at least a century: the restoration of the Dramatic Theater, which had been used as a henhouse and a breeding farm for game cocks since colonial times. It was the culmination of a spectacular civic campaign that involved every sector of the city in a multitudinous mobilization that many thought worthy of a better cause. In any event, the new Dramatic Theater was inaugurated when it still lacked seats or lights, and the audience had to bring their own chairs and their own lighting for the intermissions. The same protocol held sway as at the great performances in Europe, and the ladies used the occasion to show off their long dresses and their fur coats in the dog days of the Caribbean summer, but it was also necessary to authorize the admission of servants to carry the chairs and lamps and all the things to eat that were deemed necessary to survive the interminable programs, one of which did not end until it was time for early Mass. The season opened with a French opera company whose novelty was a harp in the orchestra and whose unforgettable glory was the impeccable voice and dramatic talent of a Turkish soprano who sang barefoot and wore rings set with precious stones on her toes. After the first act the stage could barely be seen and the singers lost their voices because of the smoke from so many palm oil lamps, but the chroniclers of the city were very careful to delete these minor inconveniences and to magnify the memorable events. Without a doubt it was Dr. Urbino's most contagious initiative, for opera fever infected the most surprising elements in the city and gave rise to a whole generation of Isoldes and Otellos and Aïdas and Siegfrieds. But it never reached the extremes Dr. Urbino had hoped for, which was to see Italianizers and Wagnerians confronting each other with sticks and canes during the intermissions.

Dr. Juvenal Urbino never accepted the public positions that were offered to him with frequency and without conditions, and he was a pitiless critic of those physicians who used their professional prestige to attain political office. Although he was always considered a Liberal and was in the habit of voting for that party's candidates, it was more a question of tradition than conviction, and he was perhaps the last member of the great families who still knelt in the street when the Archbishop's carriage drove by. He defined himself as a natural pacifist, a partisan of definitive reconciliation between Liberals and Conservatives for the good of the nation. But his public conduct was so autonomous that no group claimed him for its own: the Liberals considered him a Gothic troglodyte, the Conservatives said he was almost a Mason, and the Masons repudiated him as a secret cleric in the service of the Holy See. His less savage critics thought he was just an aristocrat enraptured by the delights of the Poetic Festival while the nation bled to death in an endless civil war.

Only two of his actions did not seem to conform to this image. The first was his leaving the former palace of the Marquis de Casalduero, which had been the family mansion for over a century, and moving to a new house in a neighborhood of *nouveaux riches*. The other was his marriage to a beauty from the lower classes, without name or fortune, whom the ladies with long last names ridiculed in secret until they were forced to admit that she outshone them all in distinction and character. Dr. Urbino was always acutely aware of these and many other cracks in his public image, and no one was as conscious as he of being the last to bear a family name on its way to extinction. His children were two undistinguished ends of a line. After fifty years, his son, Marco Aurelio, a doctor like himself and like all the family's firstborn sons in every generation, had done nothing worthy of note—he had not even produced a child. Dr. Urbino's only daughter, Ofelia, was married to a solid bank employee from New Orleans, and had reached the climacteric with three daughters and no son. But although stemming the flow of his blood into the tide of history caused him pain, what worried Dr. Urbino most about dying was the solitary life Fermina Daza would lead without him.

In any event, the tragedy not only caused an uproar among his own household but spread to the common people as well. They thronged the streets in the hope of seeing something, even if it was only the brilliance of the legend. Three days of mourning were proclaimed, flags were flown at half mast in public buildings, and the bells in all the churches tolled without pause until the crypt in the family mausoleum was sealed. A group from the School of Fine Arts made a death mask that was to be used as the mold for a lifesize bust, but the project was canceled because no one thought the faithful rendering of his final terror was decent. A renowned artist who happened to be stopping here on his way to Europe painted, with pathos-laden realism, a gigantic canvas in which Dr. Urbino was depicted on the ladder at the fatal moment when he stretched out his hand to capture the parrot. The only element that contradicted the raw truth of the story was that in the painting he was wearing not the collarless shirt and the suspenders with green stripes, but rather a bowler hat and black frock coat copied from a rotogravure made during the years of the cholera epidemic. So that everyone would have the chance to see it, the painting was exhibited for a few months after the tragedy in the vast gallery of The Golden Wire, a shop that sold imported merchandise, and the entire city filed by. Then it was displayed on the walls of all the public and private institutions that felt obliged to pay tribute to the memory of their illustrious patron, and at last it was hung, after a second funeral, in the School of Fine Arts, where it was pulled down many years later by art students who burned it in the plaza of the University as a symbol of an aesthetic and a time they despised.

From her first moment as a widow, it was obvious that Fermina Daza was not as helpless as

70

her husband had feared. She was adamant in her determination not to allow the body to be used for any cause, and she remained so even after the honorific telegram from the president of the Republic ordering it to lie in state for public viewing in the Assembly Chamber of the Provincial Government. With the same serenity she opposed a vigil in the Cathedral, which the Archbishop himself had requested, and she agreed to the body's lying there only during the funeral Mass. Even after the mediation of her son, who was dumbfounded by so many different requests, Fermina Daza was firm in her rustic notion that the dead belong only to the family, and that the vigil would be kept at home, with mountain coffee and fritters and everyone free to weep for him in any way they chose. There would be no traditional nine-night wake: the doors were closed after the funeral and did not open again except for visits from intimate friends.

The house was under the rule of death. Every object of value had been locked away with care for safekeeping, and on the bare walls there were only the outlines of the pictures that had been taken down. Chairs from the house, and those lent by the neighbors, were lined up against the walls from the drawing room to the bedrooms, and the empty spaces seemed immense and the voices had a ghostly resonance because the large pieces of furniture had been moved to one side, except for the concert piano which stood in its corner under a white sheet. In the middle of the library, on his father's desk, what had once been Juvenal Urbino de la Calle was laid out with no coffin, with his final terror petrified on his face, and with the black cape and military sword of the Knights of the Holy Sepulcher. At his side, in complete mourning, tremulous, hardly moving, but very much in control of herself, Fermina Daza received condolences with no great display of feeling until eleven the following morning, when she bade farewell to her husband from the portico, waving goodbye with a handkerchief.

It had not been easy for her to regain her self-control after she heard Digna Pardo's shriek in the patio and found the old man of her life dying in the mud. Her first reaction was one of hope, because his eyes were open and shining with a radiant light she had never seen there before. She prayed to God to give him at least a moment so that he would not go without knowing how much she had loved him despite all their doubts, and she felt an irresistible longing to begin life with him over again so that they could say what they had left unsaid and do everything right that they had done badly in the past. But she had to give in to the intransigence of death. Her grief exploded into a blind rage against the world, even against herself, and that is what filled her with the control and the courage to face her solitude alone. From that time on she had no peace, but she was careful about any gesture that might seem to betray her grief. The only moment of pathos, although it was involuntary, occurred at eleven o'clock Sunday night when they brought in the episcopal coffin, still smelling of ship's wax, with its copper handles and tufted silk lining. Dr. Urbino Daza ordered it closed without delay since the air in the house was already rarefied with the heady fragrance of so many flowers in the sweltering heat, and he thought he had seen the first purplish shadows on his father's neck. An absentminded voice was heard in the silence: "At that age you're half decayed while you're still alive." Before they closed the coffin Fermina Daza took off her wedding ring and put it on her dead husband's finger, and then she covered his hand with hers, as she always did when she caught him digressing in public.

"We will see each other very soon," she said to him.

Florentino Ariza, unseen in the crowd of notable personages, felt a piercing pain in his side. Fermina Daza had not recognized him in the confusion of the first condolences, although no one would be more ready to serve or more useful during the night's urgent business. It was he who imposed order in the crowded kitchens so that there would be enough coffee. He found additional chairs when the neighbors' proved insufficient, and he ordered the extra wreaths to be put in the patio when there was no more room in the house. He made certain there was enough brandy for Dr. Lácides Olivella's guests, who had heard the bad news at the height of the silver anniversary celebration and had rushed in to continue the

73

party, sitting in a circle under the mango tree. He was the only one who knew how to react when the fugitive parrot appeared in the dining room at midnight with his head high and his wings spread, which caused a stupefied shudder to run through the house, for it seemed a sign of repentance. Florentino Ariza seized him by the neck before he had time to shout any of his witless stock phrases, and he carried him to the stable in a covered cage. He did everything this way, with so much discretion and such efficiency that it did not even occur to anyone that it might be an intrusion in other people's affairs; on the contrary, it seemed a priceless service when evil times had fallen on the house.

He was what he seemed: a useful and serious old man. His body was bony and erect, his skin dark and clean-shaven, his eyes avid behind round spectacles in silver frames, and he wore a romantic, old-fashioned mustache with waxed tips. He combed the last tufts of hair at his temples upward and plastered them with brilliantine to the middle of his shining skull as a solution to total baldness. His natural gallantry and languid manner were immediately charming, but they were also considered suspect virtues in a confirmed bachelor. He had spent a great deal of money, ingenuity, and willpower to disguise the seventy-six years he had completed in March, and he was convinced in the solitude of his soul that he had loved in silence for a much longer time than anyone else in this world ever had.

The night of Dr. Urbino's death, he was dressed just as he had been when he first heard the news, which was how he always dressed, even in the infernal heat of June: a dark suit with a vest, a silk bow tie and a celluloid collar, a felt hat, and a shiny black umbrella that he also used as a walking stick. But when it began to grow light he left the vigil for two hours and returned as fresh as the rising sun, carefully shaven and fragrant with lotions from his dressing table. He had changed into a black frock coat of the kind worn only for funerals and the offices of Holy Week, a wing collar with an artist's bow instead of a tie, and a bowler hat. He also carried his umbrella, not just out of habit but because he was certain that it would rain before noon, and he informed Dr. Urbino Daza of this in case the funeral could be held earlier. They tried to do so, in fact, because Florentino Ariza belonged to a shipping family and was himself President of the River Company of the Caribbean, which allowed one to suppose that he knew something about predicting the weather. But they could not alter the arrangements in time with the civil and military authorities, the public and private corporations, the military band, the School of Fine Arts orchestra, and the schools and religious fraternities, which were prepared for eleven o'clock, so the funeral that had been anticipated as a historic event turned into a rout because of a devastating downpour. Very few people splashed through the mud to the family mausoleum, protected by a colonial ceiba tree whose branches spread over the cemetery wall. On the previous afternoon, under those same branches but in the section on the other side of the wall reserved for suicides, the Caribbean refugees had buried Jeremiah de Saint-Amour with his dog beside him, as he had requested.

Florentino Ariza was one of the few who stayed until the funeral was over. He was soaked to the skin and returned home terrified that he would catch pneumonia after so many years of meticulous care and excessive precautions. He prepared hot lemonade with a shot of brandy, drank it in bed with two aspirin tablets, and, wrapped in a wool blanket, sweated by the bucketful until the proper equilibrium had been reestablished in his body. When he returned to the wake he felt his vitality completely restored. Fermina Daza had once again assumed command of the house, which was cleaned and ready to receive visitors, and on the altar in the library she had placed a portrait in pastels of her dead husband, with a black border around the frame. By eight o'clock there were as many people and as intense a heat as the night before, but after the rosary someone circulated the request that everyone leave early so that the widow could rest for the first time since Sunday afternoon.

Fermina Daza said goodbye to most of them at the altar, but she accompanied the last group of intimate friends to the street door so that she could lock it herself, as she had always done, as she was prepared to do with her final breath, when she saw Florentino Ariza, dressed in mourning and standing in the middle of the deserted drawing room. She was pleased, because for many years she had erased him from her life, and this was the first time she saw him clearly, purified by forgetfulness. But before she could thank him for the visit, he placed his hat over his heart, tremulous and dignified, and the abscess that had sustained his life finally burst.

"Fermina," he said, "I have waited for this opportunity for more than half a century, to repeat to you once again my vow of eternal fidelity and everlasting love."

Fermina Daza would have thought she was facing a madman if she had not had reason to believe that at that moment Florentino Ariza was inspired by the grace of the Holy Spirit. Her first impulse was to curse him for profaning the house when the body of her husband was still warm in the grave. But the dignity of her fury held her back. "Get out of here," she said. "And don't show your face again for the years of life that are left to you." She opened the street door, which she had begun to close, and concluded:

"And I hope there are very few of them."

When she heard his steps fade away in the deserted street she closed the door very slowly with the crossbar and the locks, and faced her destiny alone. Until that moment she had never been fully conscious of the weight and size of the drama that she had provoked when she was not yet eighteen, and that would pursue her until her death. She wept for the first time since the afternoon of the disaster, without witnesses, which was the only way she wept. She wept for the death of her husband, for her solitude and rage, and when she went into the empty bedroom she wept for herself because she had rarely slept alone in that bed since the loss of her virginity. Everything that belonged to her husband made her weep again: his tasseled slippers, his pajamas under the pillow, the space of his absence in the dressing table mirror, his own odor on her skin. A vague thought made her shudder: "The people one loves should take all their things with them when they die." She did not want anyone's help to get ready for bed, she did not want to eat anything before she went to sleep. Crushed by grief, she prayed to God to send her death that night while she slept, and with that hope she lay down, barefoot but fully dressed, and fell asleep on the spot. She slept without realizing it, but she knew in her sleep that she was still alive, and that she had half a bed to spare, that she was lying on her left side on the left-hand side of the bed as she always did, but that she missed the weight of the other body on the other side. Thinking as she slept, she thought that she would never again be able to sleep this way, and she began to sob in her sleep, and she slept, sobbing, without changing position on her side of the bed, until long after the roosters crowed and she was awakened by the despised sun of the morning without him. Only then did she realize that she had slept a long time without dying, sobbing in her sleep, and that while she slept, sobbing, she had thought more about Florentino Ariza than about her dead husband.

FLORENTINO ARIZA, ON the other hand, had not stopped thinking of her for a single moment since Fermina Daza had rejected him out of hand after a long and troubled love affair fifty-one years, nine months, and four days ago. He did not have to keep a running tally, drawing a line for each day on the walls of a cell, because not a day had passed that something did not happen to remind him of her. At the time of their separation he lived with his mother, Tránsito Ariza, in one half of a rented house on the Street of Windows, where she had kept a notions shop ever since she was a young woman, and where she also unraveled shirts and old rags to sell as bandages for the men wounded in the war. He was her only child, born of an occasional alliance with the well-known ship-owner Don Pius V Loayza, one of the three brothers who had founded the River Company of the Caribbean and thereby given new impetus to steam navigation along the Magdalena River.

Don Pius V Loayza died when his son was ten years old. Although he always took care of his expenses in secret, he never recognized him as his son before the law, nor did he leave him with his future secure, so that Florentino Ariza used only his mother's name even though his true parentage was always common knowledge. Florentino Ariza had to leave school after his father's death, and he went to work as an apprentice in the Postal Agency, where he was in charge of opening sacks, sorting the letters, and notifying the public that mail had arrived by flying the flag of its country of origin over the office door.

His good sense attracted the attention of the telegraph operator, the German émigré Lotario Thugut, who also played the organ for important ceremonies in the Cathedral and gave music lessons in the home. Lotario Thugut taught him the Morse code and the workings of the telegraph system, and after only a few lessons on the violin Florentino Ariza could play by ear like a professional. When he met Fermina Daza he was the most sought-after young man in his social circle, the one who knew how to dance the latest dances and recite sentimental poetry by heart, and who was always willing to play violin serenades to his friends' sweethearts. He was very thin, with Indian hair plastered down with scented pomade and eyeglasses for myopia, which added to his forlorn appearance. Aside from his defective vision, he suffered from chronic constipation, which forced him to take enemas throughout his life. He had one black suit, inherited from his dead father, but Tránsito Ariza took such good care of it that every Sunday it looked new. Despite his air of weakness, his reserve, and his somber clothes, the girls in his circle held secret lotteries to determine who would spend time with him, and he gambled on spending time with them until the day he met Fermina Daza and his innocence came to an end.

He had seen her for the first time one afternoon when Lotario Thugut told him to deliver a telegram to someone named Lorenzo Daza, with no known place of residence. He found him in one of the oldest houses on the Park of the Evangels; it was half in ruins, and its interior patio, with weeds in the flowerpots and a stone fountain with no water, resembled an abbey cloister. Florentino Ariza heard no human sound as he followed the barefoot maid under the arches of the passageway, where unopened moving cartons and bricklayer's tools lay among leftover lime and stacks of cement bags, for the house was undergoing drastic renovation. At the far end of the patio was a temporary office where a very fat man, whose curly sideburns grew into his mustache, sat behind a desk, taking his siesta. In fact his name was Lorenzo Daza, and he was not very well known in the city because he had arrived less than two years before and was not a man with many friends.

He received the telegram as if it were the continuation of an ominous dream. Florentino Ariza observed his livid eyes with a kind of official compassion, he observed his uncertain fingers trying to break the seal, the heartfelt fear that he had seen so many times in so many addressees who still could not think about telegrams without con-

necting them with death. After reading it he regained his composure. He sighed: "Good news."
And he handed Florentino Ariza the obligatory
five reales, letting him know with a relieved smile
that he would not have given them to him if the
news had been bad. Then he said goodbye with a
handshake, which was not the usual thing to do
with a telegraph messenger, and the maid accompanied him to the street door, more to keep an eye
on him than to lead the way. They retraced their
steps along the arcaded passageway, but this time
Florentino Ariza knew that there was someone else
in the house, because the brightness in the patio
was filled with the voice of a woman repeating a
reading lesson. As he passed the sewing room, he
saw through the window an older woman and a
young girl sitting very close together on two chairs
and following the reading in the book that the
woman held open on her lap. It seemed a strange
sight: the daughter teaching the mother to read.
His interpretation was incorrect only in part, because the woman was the aunt, not the mother of
the child, although she had raised her as if she
were her own. The lesson was not interrupted, but
the girl raised her eyes to see who was passing by
the window, and that casual glance was the beginning of a cataclysm of love that still had not ended
half a century later.

All that Florentino Ariza could learn about
Lorenzo Daza was that he had come from San
Juan de la Ciénaga with his only daughter and his
unmarried sister soon after the cholera epidemic,

and those who saw him disembark had no doubt that he had come to stay since he brought everything necessary for a well-furnished house. His wife had died when the girl was very young. His sister, named Escolástica, was forty years old, and she was fulfilling a vow to wear the habit of St. Francis when she went out on the street and the penitent's rope around her waist when she was at home. The girl was thirteen years old and had the same name as her dead mother: Fermina.

It was supposed that Lorenzo Daza was a man of means, because he lived well with no known employment and had paid hard cash for the Park of the Evangels house, whose restoration must have cost him at least twice the purchase price of two hundred gold pesos. His daughter was studying at the Academy of the Presentation of the Blessed Virgin, where for two centuries young ladies of society had learned the art and technique of being diligent and submissive wives. During the colonial period and the early years of the Republic, the school had accepted only those students with great family names. But the old families, ruined by Independence, had to submit to the realities of a new time, and the Academy opened its doors to all applicants who could pay the tuition, regardless of the color of their blood, on the essential condition that they were legitimate daughters of Catholic marriages. In any event, it was an expensive school, and the fact that Fermina Daza studied there was sufficient indication of her family's economic situation, if not of its social position. This news encouraged Florentino Ariza, since it indicated to him that the beautiful adolescent with the almond-shaped eyes was within reach of his dreams. But her father's strict regime soon provided an irremediable difficulty. Unlike the other students, who walked to school in groups or accompanied by an older servant, Fermina Daza always walked with her spinster aunt, and her behavior indicated that she was permitted no distraction.

It was in this innocent way that Florentino Ariza began his secret life as a solitary hunter. From seven o'clock in the morning, he sat on the most hidden bench in the little park, pretending to read a book of verse in the shade of the almond trees, until he saw the impossible maiden walk by in her blue-striped uniform, stockings that reached to her knees, masculine laced oxfords, and a single thick braid with a bow at the end, which hung down her back to her waist. She walked with natural haughtiness, her head high, her eyes unmoving, her step rapid, her nose pointing straight ahead, her bag of books held against her chest with crossed arms, her doe's gait making her seem immune to gravity. At her side, struggling to keep up with her, the aunt with the brown habit and rope of St. Francis did not allow him the slightest opportunity to approach. Florentino Ariza saw them pass back and forth four times a day and once on Sundays when they came out of High Mass, and just seeing the girl was enough for him. Little by little he idealized her, endowing her with improbable virtues and imaginary sentiments, and after two weeks he thought of nothing else but her. So he decided to send Fermina Daza a simple note written on both sides of the paper in his exquisite notary's hand. But he kept it in his pocket for several days, thinking about how to hand it to her, and while he thought he wrote several more pages before going to bed, so that the original letter was turning into a dictionary of compliments, inspired by books he had learned by heart because he read them so often during his vigils in the park.

Searching for a way to give her the letter, he tried to make the acquaintance of some of the other students at Presentation Academy, but they were too distant from his world. Besides, after much thought, it did not seem prudent to let anyone else know of his intentions. Still, he managed to find out that Fermina Daza had been invited to a Saturday dance a few days after their arrival in the city, and her father had not allowed her to go, with a conclusive: "Everything in due course." By the time the letter contained more than sixty pages written on both sides, Florentino Ariza could no longer endure the weight of his secret, and he unburdened himself to his mother, the only person with whom he allowed himself any confidences. Tránsito Ariza was moved to tears by her son's innocence in matters of love, and she tried to guide him with her own knowledge. She began by convincing him not to deliver the lyrical sheaf of papers, since it would only frighten the girl of his dreams, who she supposed was as green as he in matters of the heart. The first step, she said, was to make her aware of his interest so that his declaration would not take her so much by surprise and she would have time to think.

"But above all," she said, "the first person you have to win over is not the girl but her aunt."

Both pieces of advice were wise, no doubt, but they came too late. In reality, on the day when Fermina Daza let her mind wander for an instant from the reading lesson she was giving her aunt and raised her eyes to see who was walking along the passageway, Florentino Ariza had impressed her because of his air of vulnerability. That night, during supper, her father had mentioned the telegram, which was how she found out why Florentino Ariza had come to the house and what he did for a living. This information increased her interest, because for her, as for so many other people at that time, the invention of the telegraph had something magical about it. So that she recognized Florentino Ariza the first time she saw him reading under the trees in the little park, although it in no way disquieted her until her aunt told her he had been there for several weeks. Then, when they also saw him on Sundays as they came out of Mass, her aunt was convinced that all these meetings could not be casual. She said: "He is not going to all this trouble for me." For despite her austere conduct and penitential habit, Aunt Escolástica had an instinct for life and a vocation for complicity, which were her greatest virtues, and the mere idea that a man was interested in her niece awakened an irresistible emotion in her. Fermina Daza, however, was still safe from even simple curiosity about love, and the only feeling that Florentino Ariza inspired in her was a certain pity, because it seemed to her that he was sick. But her aunt told her that one had to live a long time to know a man's true nature, and she was convinced that the one who sat in the park to watch them walk by could only be sick with love.

Aunt Escolástica was a refuge of understanding and affection for the only child of a loveless marriage. She had raised her since the death of her mother, and in her relations with Lorenzo Daza she behaved more like an accomplice than an aunt. So that the appearance of Florentino Ariza was for them another of the many intimate diversions they invented to pass the time. Four times a day, when they walked through the little Park of the Evangels, both hurried to look with a rapid glance at the thin, timid, unimpressive sentinel who was almost always dressed in black despite the heat and who pretended to read under the trees. "There he is," said the one who saw him first, suppressing her laughter, before he raised his eyes and saw the two rigid, aloof women of his life as they crossed the park without looking at him.

"Poor thing," her aunt had said. "He does not dare approach you because I am with you, but one day he will if his intentions are serious, and then he will give you a letter."

Foreseeing all kinds of adversities, she taught her to communicate in sign language, an indispensable strategy in forbidden love. These unexpected, almost childish antics caused an unfamiliar curiosity in Fermina Daza, but for several months it did not occur to her that it could go any further. She never knew when the diversion became a preoccupation and her blood frothed with the need to see him, and one night she awoke in terror because she saw him looking at her from the darkness at the foot of the bed. Then she longed with all her soul for her aunt's predictions to come true, and in her prayers she begged God to give him the courage to hand her the letter just so she could know what it said.

But her prayers were not answered. On the contrary. This occurred at the time that Florentino Ariza made his confession to his mother, who dissuaded him from handing Fermina Daza his seventy pages of compliments, so that she continued to wait for the rest of the year. Her preoccupation turned into despair as the December vacation approached, and she asked herself over and over again how she would see him and let him see her during the three months when she would not be walking to school. Her doubts were still unresolved on Christmas Eve, when she was shaken by the presentiment that he was in the crowd at Midnight Mass, looking at her, and this uneasiness flooded her heart. She did not dare to turn her head, because she was sitting between her father and her aunt, and she had to control herself so that they would not notice her agitation. But in the crowd leaving the church she felt him so close, so clearly, that an irresistible power forced her to look over her shoulder as she walked along the central nave and then, a hand's breadth from her eyes, she saw those icy eyes, that livid face, those lips petrified by the terror of love. Dismayed by her own audacity, she seized Aunt Escolástica's arm so she would not fall, and her aunt felt the icy perspiration on her hand through the lace mitt, and she comforted her with an imperceptible sign of unconditional complicity. In the din of fireworks and native drums, of colored lights in the doorways and the clamor of the crowd yearning for peace, Florentino Ariza wandered like a sleepwalker until dawn, watching the fiesta through his tears, dazed by the hallucination that it was he and not God who had been born that night.

His delirium increased the following week, when he passed Fermina Daza's house in despair at the siesta hour and saw that she and her aunt were sitting under the almond trees at the doorway. It was an open-air repetition of the scene he had witnessed the first afternoon in the sewing room: the girl giving a reading lesson to her aunt. But Fermina Daza seemed different without the school uniform, for she wore a narrow tunic with many folds that fell from her shoulders in the Greek style, and on her head she wore a garland of fresh gardenias that made her look like a crowned goddess. Florentino Ariza sat in the park where he was sure he would be seen, and then he did not have recourse to his feigned reading but sat with the book open and his eyes fixed on the illusory maiden, who did not even respond with a charitable glance.

At first he thought that the lesson under the almond trees was a casual innovation due, perhaps, to the interminable repairs on the house, but in the days that followed he came to understand that Fermina Daza would be there, within view, every afternoon at the same time during the three months of vacation, and that certainty filled him with new hope. He did not have the impression that he was seen, he could not detect any sign of interest or rejection, but in her indifference there was a distinct radiance that encouraged him to persevere. Then, one afternoon toward the end of January, the aunt put her work on the chair and left her niece alone in the doorway under the shower of yellow leaves falling from the almond trees. Encouraged by the impetuous thought that this was an arranged opportunity, Florentino Ariza crossed the street and stopped in front of Fermina Daza, so close to her that he could detect the catches in her breathing and the floral scent that he would identify with her for the rest of his life. He spoke with his head high and with a determination that would be his again only half a century later, and for the same reason.

"All I ask is that you accept a letter from me," he said.

It was not the voice that Fermina Daza had expected from him: it was sharp and clear, with a control that had nothing to do with his languid manner. Without lifting her eyes from her embroidery, she replied: "I cannot accept it without my father's permission." Florentino Ariza shuddered at the warmth of that voice, whose hushed tones he was not to forget for the rest of his life. But he held himself steady and replied without hesitation: "Get it." Then he sweetened the command with a plea: "It is a matter of life and death." Fermina Daza did not look at him, she did not interrupt her embroidering, but her decision opened the door a crack, wide enough for the entire world to pass through.

"Come back every afternoon," she said to him, "and wait until I change my seat."

Florentino Ariza did not understand what she meant until the following Monday when, from the bench in the little park, he saw the same scene with one variation: when Aunt Escolástica went into the house, Fermina Daza stood up and then sat in the other chair. Florentino Ariza, with a white camellia in his lapel, crossed the street and stood in front of her. He said: "This is the greatest moment of my life." Fermina Daza did not raise her eyes to him, but she looked all around her and saw the deserted streets in the heat of the dry season and a swirl of dead leaves pulled along by the wind.

"Give it to me," she said.

Florentino Ariza had intended to give her the seventy sheets he could recite from memory after reading them so often, but then he decided on a sober and explicit half page in which he promised only what was essential: his perfect fidelity and his everlasting love. He took the letter out of his inside jacket pocket and held it before the eyes of the troubled embroiderer, who had still not dared to look at him. She saw the blue envelope trembling in a hand petrified with terror, and she raised the embroidery frame so he could put the letter on it, for she could not admit that she had noticed the trembling of his fingers. Then it happened: a bird shook himself among the leaves of the almond trees, and his droppings fell right on the embroidery. Fermina Daza moved the frame out of the way, hid it behind the chair so that he would not notice what had happened, and looked at him for the first time, her face aflame. Florentino Ariza was impassive as he held the letter in his hand and said: "It's good luck." She thanked him with her first smile and almost snatched the letter away from him, folded it, and hid it in her bodice. Then he offered her the camellia he wore in his lapel. She refused: "It is a flower of promises." Then, conscious that their time was almost over, she again took refuge in her composure.

"Now go," she said, "and don't come back until I tell you to."

After Florentino Ariza saw her for the first time, his mother knew before he told her because he lost his voice and his appetite and spent the entire night tossing and turning in his bed. But when he began to wait for the answer to his first letter, his anguish was complicated by diarrhea and green vomit, he became disoriented and suffered from sudden fainting spells, and his mother was terrified because his condition did not resemble the turmoil of love so much as the devastation of cholera. Florentino Ariza's godfather, an old homeopathic practitioner who had been Tránsito Ariza's confidant ever since her days as a secret mistress, was also alarmed at first by the patient's condition, because he had the weak pulse, the hoarse breathing, and the pale perspiration of a dying man. But his examination revealed that he had no fever, no pain anywhere, and that his only concrete feeling was an urgent desire to die. All that was needed was shrewd questioning, first of the patient and then of his mother, to conclude once again that the symptoms of love were the same as those of cholera. He prescribed infusions of linden blossoms to calm the nerves and suggested a change of air so he could find consolation in distance, but Florentino Ariza longed for just the opposite: to enjoy his martyrdom.

Tránsito Ariza was a freed quadroon whose instinct for happiness had been frustrated by poverty, and she took pleasure in her son's suffering as if it were her own. She made him drink the infusions when he became delirious, and she smothered him in wool blankets to keep away the chills, but at the same time she encouraged him to enjoy his prostration.

"Take advantage of it now, while you are young, and suffer all you can," she said to him, "because these things don't last your whole life."

In the Postal Agency, of course, they did not

agree. Florentino Ariza had become negligent, and he was so distracted that he confused the flags that announced the arrival of the mail, and one Wednesday he hoisted the Germany flag when the ship was from the Leyland Company and carried the mail from Liverpool, and on another day he flew the flag of the United States when the ship was from the Compagnie Générale Transatlantique and carried the mail from Saint-Nazaire. These confusions of love caused such chaos in the distribution of the mail and provoked so many protests from the public that if Florentino Ariza did not lose his job it was because Lotario Thugut kept him at the telegraph and took him to play the violin in the Cathedral choir. They had a friendship difficult to understand because of the difference in their ages, for they might have been grandfather and grandson, but they got along at work as well as they did in the taverns around the port, which were frequented by everyone out for the evening regardless of social class, from drunken beggars to young gentlemen in tuxedos who fled the gala parties at the Social Club to eat fried mullet and coconut rice. Lotario Thugut was in the habit of going there after the last shift at the telegraph office, and dawn often found him drinking Jamaican punch and playing the accordion with the crews of madmen from the Antillean schooners. He was corpulent and bull-necked, with a golden beard and a liberty cap that he wore when he went out at night, and all he needed was a string of bells to look like St. Nicholas. At least once a week he ended the evening with a little night bird, as he called them, one of the many who sold emergency love in a transient hotel for sailors. When he met Florentino Ariza, the first thing he did, with a certain magisterial delight, was to initiate him into the secrets of his paradise. He chose for him the little birds he thought best, he discussed their price and style with them and offered to pay in advance with his own money for their services. But Florentino Ariza did not accept: he was a virgin, and he had decided not to lose his virginity unless it was for love.

The hotel was a colonial palace that had seen better days, and its great marble salons and rooms were divided ito plasterboard cubicles with peep-holes, which were rented out as much for watching as for doing. There was talk of busybodies who had their eyes poked out with knitting needles, of a man who recognized his own wife as the woman he was spying on, of well-bred gentle-women who came disguised as tarts to forget who they were with the boatswains on shore leave, and of so many other misadventures of observers and observed that the mere idea of going into the next room terrified Florentino Ariza. And so Lotario Thugut could never persuade him that watching and letting himself be watched were the refinements of European princes.

As opposed to what his corpulence might suggest, Lotario Thugut had the rosebud genitals of a cherub, but this must have been a fortunate defect, because the most tarnished birds argued over who would have the chance to go to bed with him, and then they shrieked as if their throats were being cut, shaking the buttresses of the palace and making its ghosts tremble in fear. They said he used an ointment made of snake venom that inflamed women's loins, but he swore he had no resources other than those that God had given him. He would say with uproarious laughter: "It's pure love." Many years had to pass before Florentino Ariza would understand that perhaps he was right. He was convinced at last, at a more advanced stage of his sentimental education, when he met a man who lived like a king by exploiting three women at the same time. The three of them rendered their accounts at dawn, prostrate at his feet to beg forgiveness for their meager profits, and the only gratification they sought was that he go to bed with the one who brought him the most money. Florentino Ariza thought that terror alone could induce such indignities, but one of the three girls surprised him with the contradictory truth.

"These are things," she said, "you do only for love."

It was not so much for his talents as a fornicator as for his personal charm that Lotario Thugut had become one of the most esteemed clients of the hotel. Florentino Ariza, because he was so quiet and elusive, also earned the esteem of the owner, and during the most arduous period of his grief he would lock himself in the suffocating little rooms to read verses and tearful serialized love stories, and his reveries left nests of dark swallows on the balconies and the sound of kisses and the beating of wings in the stillness of siesta. At dusk, when it was cooler, it was impossible not to listen to the conversations of men who came to console themselves at the end of their day with hurried love. So that Florentino Ariza heard about many acts of disloyalty, and even some state secrets, which important clients and even local officials confided to their ephemeral lovers, not caring if they could be overheard in the adjoining rooms. This was also how he learned that four nautical leagues to the north of the Sotavento Archipelago, a Spanish galleon had been lying under water since the eighteenth century with its cargo of more than five hundred billion pesos in pure gold and precious stones. The story astounded him, but he did not think of it again until a few months later, when his love awakened in him an overwhelming desire to salvage the sunken treasure so that Fermina Daza could bathe in showers of gold.

Years later, when he tried to remember what the maiden idealized by the alchemy of poetry really was like, he could not distinguish her from the heartrending twilights of those times. Even when he observed her, unseen, during those days of longing when he waited for a reply to his first letter, he saw her transfigured in the afternoon shimmer of two o'clock in a shower of blossoms from the almond trees where it was always April regardless of the season of the year. The only reason he was interested in accompanying Lotario Thugut on his violin from the privileged vantage point in the choir was to see how her tunic fluttered in the breeze raised by the canticles. But his own delirium finally interfered with that pleasure, for the mystic music seemed so innocuous compared with the state of his soul that he attempted to make it more exciting with love waltzes, and Lotario Thugut found himself obliged to ask that he leave the choir. This was the time when he gave in to his desire to eat the gardenias that Tránsito Ariza grew in pots in the patio, so that he could know the taste of Fermina Daza. It was also the time when he happened to find in one of his mother's trunks a liter bottle of the cologne that the sailors from the Hamburg-American Line sold as contraband, and he could not resist the temptation to sample it in order to discover other tastes of his beloved. He continued to drink from the bottle until dawn, and he became drunk on Fermina Daza in abrasive swallows, first in the taverns around the port and then as he stared out to sea from the jetties where lovers without a roof over their heads made consoling love, until at last he succumbed to unconsciousness. Tránsito Ariza, who had waited for him until six o'clock in the morning with her heart in her mouth, searched for him in the most improbable hiding places, and a short while after noon she found him wallowing in a pool of fragrant vomit in a cove of the bay where drowning victims washed ashore.

She took advantage of the hiatus of his convalescence to reproach him for his passivity as he waited for the answer to his letter. She reminded him that the weak would never enter the kingdom of love, which is a harsh and ungenerous kingdom, and that women give themselves only to men of resolute spirit, who provide the security they need in order to face life. Florentino Ariza learned the lesson, perhaps too well. Tránsito Ariza could not hide a feeling of pride, more carnal than maternal, when she saw him leave the notions shop in his black suit and stiff felt hat, his lyrical bow tie and celluloid collar, and she asked him as a joke if he was going to a funeral. He answered, his ears flaming: "It's almost the same thing." She realized that he could hardly breathe with fear, but his determination was invincible. She gave him her final warnings and her blessing, and laughing for all she was worth, she promised him another bottle of cologne so they could celebrate his victory together.

He had given Fermina Daza the letter a month before, and since then he had often broken his promise not to return to the little park, but he had been very careful not to be seen. Nothing had changed. The reading lesson under the trees ended at about two o'clock, when the city was waking from its siesta, and Fermina Daza embroidered with her aunt until the day began to cool. Florentino Ariza did not wait for the aunt to go into the house, and he crossed the street with a martial stride that allowed him to overcome the weakness in his knees, but he spoke to her aunt, not to Fermina Daza.

"Please be so kind as to leave me alone for a

moment with the young lady," he said. "I have something important to tell her."

"What impertinence!" her aunt said to him. "There is nothing that has to do with her that I cannot hear."

"Then I will not say anything to her," he said, "but I warn you that you will be responsible for the consequences."

That was not the manner Escolástica Daza expected from the ideal sweetheart, but she stood up in alarm because for the first time she had the overwhelming impression that Florentino Ariza was speaking under the inspiration of the Holy Spirit. So she went into the house to change needles and left the two young people alone under the almond trees in the doorway.

In reality, Fermina Daza knew very little about this taciturn suitor who had appeared in her life like a winter swallow and whose name she would not even have known if it had not been for his signature on the letter. She had learned that he was the fatherless son of an unmarried woman who was hardworking and serious but forever marked by the fiery stigma of her single youthful mistake. She had learned that he was not a messenger, as she had supposed, but a well-qualified assistant with a promising future, and she thought that he had delivered the telegram to her father only as a pretext for seeing her. This idea moved her. She also knew that he was one of the musicians in the choir, and although she never dared raise her eyes to look at him during Mass, she had the revelation one Sunday that while the other instruments played for everyone, the violin played for her alone. He was not the kind of man she would have chosen. His foundling's eyeglasses, his clerical garb, his mysterious resources had awakened in her a curiosity that was difficult to resist, but she had never imagined that curiosity was one of the many masks of love.

She herself could not explain why she had accepted the letter. She did not reproach herself for doing so, but the ever-increasing pressure to respond complicated her life. Her father's every word, his casual glances, his most trivial gestures, seemed set with traps to uncover her secret. Her state of alarm was such that she avoided speaking at the table for fear some slip might betray her, and she became evasive even with her Aunt Escolástica, who nonetheless shared her repressed anxiety as if it were her own. She would lock herself in the bathroom at odd hours and for no reason other than to reread the letter, attempting to discover a secret code, a magic formula hidden in one of the three hundred fourteen letters of its fifty-eight words, in the hope they would tell her more than they said. But all she found was what she had understood on first reading, when she ran to lock herself in the bathroom, her heart in a frenzy, and tore open the envelope hoping for a long, feverish letter, and found only a perfumed note whose determination frightened her.

At first she had not even thought seriously that she was obliged to respond, but the letter was so explicit that there was no way to avoid it. Meanwhile, in the torment of her doubts, she was surprised to find herself thinking about Florentino Ariza with more frequency and interest than she cared to allow, and she even asked herself in great distress why he was not in the little park at the usual hour, forgetting that it was she who had asked him not to return while she was preparing her reply. And so she thought about him as she never could have imagined thinking about anyone, having premonitions that he would be where he was not, wanting him to be where he could not be, awaking with a start, with the physical sensation that he was looking at her in the darkness while she slept, so that on the afternoon when she heard his resolute steps on the yellow leaves in the little park it was difficult for her not to think this was yet another trick of her imagination. But when he demanded her answer with an authority that was so different from his languor, she managed to overcome her fear and tried to dodge the issue with the truth: she did not know how to answer him. But Florentino Ariza had not leapt across an abyss only to be shooed away with such excuses.

"If you accepted the letter," he said to her, "it shows a lack of courtesy not to answer it."

That was the end of the labyrinth. Fermina Daza regained her self-control, begged his pardon for the delay, and gave him her solemn word that he would have an answer before the end of the vacation. And he did. On the last Friday in February, three days before school reopened, Aunt

Escolástica went to the telegraph office to ask how much it cost to send a telegram to Piedras de Moler, a village that did not even appear on the list of places served by the telegraph, and she allowed Florentino Ariza to attend her as if she had never seen him before, but when she left she pretended to forget a breviary covered in lizard skin, leaving it on the counter, and in it there was an envelope made of linen paper with golden vignettes. Delirious with joy, Florentino Ariza spent the rest of the afternoon eating roses and reading the note letter by letter, over and over again, and the more he read the more roses he ate, and by midnight he had read it so many times and had eaten so many roses that his mother had to hold his head as if he were a calf and force him to swallow a dose of castor oil.

It was the year they fell into devastating love. Neither one could do anything except think about the other, dream about the other, and wait for letters with the same impatience they felt when they answered them. Never in that delirious spring, or in the following year, did they have the opportunity to speak to each other. Moreover, from the moment they saw each other for the first time until he reiterated his determination a half century later, they never had the opportunity to be alone or to talk of their love. But during the first three months not one day went by that they did not write to each other, and for a time they wrote twice a day, until Aunt Escolástica became frightened by the intensity of the blaze that she herself had helped to ignite.

After the first letter that she carried to the telegraph office with an ember of revenge against her own destiny, she had allowed an almost daily exchange of messages in what appeared to be casual encounters on the street, but she did not have the courage to permit a conversation, no matter how banal and fleeting it might be. Still, after three months she realized that her niece was not the victim of a girlish fancy, as it had seemed at first, and that her own life was threatened by the fire of love. The truth was that Escolástica Daza had no other means of support except her brother's charity, and she knew that his tyrannical nature would never forgive such a betrayal of his confidence. But when it was time for the final decision, she did not have the heart to cause her niece the same irreparable grief that she had been obliged to nurture ever since her youth, and she permitted her to use a strategy that allowed her the illusion of innocence. The method was simple: Fermina Daza would leave her letter in some hiding place along her daily route from the house to the Academy, and in that letter she would indicate to Florentino Ariza where she expected to find his answer. Florentino Ariza did the same. In this way, for the rest of the year, the conflicts in Aunt Escolástica's conscience were transferred to baptisteries in churches, holes in trees, and crannies in ruined colonial fortresses. Sometimes their letters were soaked by rain, soiled by mud, torn by adversity, and some were lost for a variety of other reasons, but they always found a way to be in touch with each other again.

Florentino Ariza wrote every night. Letter by letter, he had no mercy as he poisoned himself with the smoke from the palm oil lamps in the back room of the notions shop, and his letters became more discursive and more lunatic the more he tried to imitate his favorite poets from the Popular Library, which even at that time was approaching eighty volumes. His mother, who had urged him with so much fervor to enjoy his torment, became concerned for his health. "You are going to wear out your brains," she shouted at him from the bedroom when she heard the first roosters crow. "No woman is worth all that." She could not remember ever having known anyone in such a state of unbridled passion. But he paid no attention to her. Sometimes he went to the office without having slept, his hair in an uproar of love after leaving the letter in the prearranged hiding place so that Fermina Daza would find it on her way to school. She, on the other hand, under the watchful eye of her father and the vicious spying of the nuns, could barely manage to fill half a page from her notebook when she locked herself in the bathroom or pretended to take notes in class. But this was not only due to her limited time and the danger of being taken by surprise, it was also her nature that caused her letters to avoid emotional pitfalls and confine themselves to relating the events of her daily life in the utilitarian style of a ship's log. In reality they were distracted letters, intended to keep the coals alive without putting her hand in the fire, while Florentino Ariza burned himself alive in every line. Desperate to infect her with his own madness, he sent her miniaturist's verses inscribed with the point of a pin on camellia petals. It was he, not she, who had the audacity to enclose a lock of his hair in one letter, but he never received the response he longed for, which was an entire strand of Fermina Daza's braid. He did move her at last to take one step further, and from that time on she began to send him the veins of leaves dried in dictionaries, the wings of butterflies, the feathers of magic birds, and for his birthday she gave him a square centimeter of St. Peter Clavier's habit, which in those days was being sold in secret at a price far beyond the reach of a schoolgirl her age. One night, without any warning, Fermina Daza awoke with a start: a solo violin was serenading her, playing the same waltz over and over again. She shuddered when she realized that each note was an act of thanksgiving for the petals from her herbarium, for the moments stolen from arithemetic to write her letters, for her fear of examinations when she was thinking more about him than about the natural sciences, but she did not dare believe that Florentino Ariza was capable of such imprudence.

The next morning at breakfast Lorenzo Daza could not contain his curiosity—first because he did not know what playing a single piece meant in the language of serenades, and second because, despite the attention with which he had listened, he could not determine which house it had been intended for. Aunt Escolástica, with a sangfroid that took her niece's breath away, stated that she had seen through the bedroom curtains that the solitary violinist was standing on the other side of the park, and she said that in any event a single piece was notification of severed relations. In that day's letter Florentino Ariza confirmed that he had played the serenade, that he had composed the waltz, and that it bore the name he called Fermina Daza in his heart: "The Crowned Goddess." He did not play it in the park again, but on moonlit nights in places chosen so that she could listen without fear in her bedroom. One of his favored spots was the paupers' cemetery, exposed to the sun and the rain on an indigent hill, where turkey buzzards dozed and the music achieved a supernatural resonance. Later he learned to recognize the direction of the winds, and in this way he was certain that his melody carried as far as it had to.

In August of that year a new civil war, one of the many that had been devastating the country for over half a century, threatened to spread, and the government imposed martial law and a six o'clock curfew in the provinces along the Caribbean coast. Although some disturbances had already occurred, and the troops had committed all kinds of retaliatory abuses, Florentino Ariza was so befuddled that he was unaware of the state of the world, and a military patrol surprised him one dawn as he disturbed the chastity of the dead with his amorous provocations. By some miracle he escaped summary execution after he was accused of being a spy who sent messages in the key of G to the Liberal ships marauding in nearby waters.

"What the hell do you mean, a spy?" said Florentino Ariza. "I'm nothing but a poor lover."

For three nights he slept with irons around his ankles in the cells of the local garrison. But when he was released he felt defrauded by the brevity of his captivity, and even in the days of his old age, when so many other wars were confused in his memory, he still thought he was the only man in the city, and perhaps the country, who had dragged five-pound leg irons for the sake of love.

Their frenetic correspondence was almost two years old when Florentino Ariza, in a letter of only one paragraph, made a formal proposal of marriage to Fermina Daza. On several occasions during the preceding six months he had sent her a white camellia, but she would return it to him in her next letter so that he would have no doubt that she was disposed to continue writing to him, but without the seriousness of an engagement. The truth is that she had always taken the comings and goings of the camellia as a lovers' game, and it had never occurred to her to consider it as a crossroads in her destiny. But when the formal proposal arrived she felt herself wounded for the first time by the clawings of death. Panic-stricken, she told her Aunt Escolástica, who gave her advice with the courage and lucidity she had not had when she was twenty and was forced to decide her own fate.

"Tell him yes," she said. "Even if you are dying of fear, even if you are sorry later, because whatever you do, you will be sorry all the rest of your life if you say no."

Fermina Daza, however, was so confused that she asked for some time to think it over. First she asked for a month, then two, then three, and when the fourth month had ended and she had still not replied, she received a white camellia again, not alone in the envelope as on other occasions but with the peremptory notification that this was the last one: it was now or never. Then that same afternoon it was Florentino Ariza who saw the face of death when he received an envelope containing a strip of paper, torn from the margin of a school notebook, on which a one-line answer was written in pencil: *Very well, I will marry you if you promise not to make me eat eggplant.*

Florentino Ariza was not prepared for that answer, but his mother was. Since he had first spoken to her six months earlier about his intention to marry, Tránsito Ariza had begun negotiations for renting the entire house which, until that time, she had shared with two other families. A two-story structure dating from the seventeenth century, it was the building where the tobacco monopoly had been located under Spanish rule, and its ruined owners had been obliged to rent it out in bits and pieces because they did not have the money to maintain it. It had one section facing

110

the street, where the retail tobacco shop had been, another section at the rear of a paved patio, where the factory had been located, and a very large stable that the current tenants used in common for washing and drying their clothes. Tránsito Ariza occupied the first section, which was the most convenient and the best preserved, although it was also the smallest. The notions store was in the old tobacco shop, with a large door facing the street, and to one side was the former storeroom, with only a skylight for ventilation, where Tránsito Ariza slept. The stockroom took up half the space that was divided by a wooden partition. In it were a table and four chairs, used for both eating and writing, and it was there that Florentino Ariza hung his hammock when dawn did not find him writing. It was a good space for the two of them, but too small for a third person, least of all a young lady from the Academy of the Presentation of the Blessed Virgin whose father had restored a house in ruins until it was like new, while the families with seven titles went to bed with the fear that the roofs of their mansions would cave in on them while they slept. So Tránsito Ariza had arranged with the owner to let her also occupy the gallery in the patio, and in exchange she would keep the house in good condition for five years.

She had the resources to do so. In addition to the cash income from the notions store and the hemostatic rags, which sufficed for her modest life, she had multiplied her savings by lending them to a clientele made up of the embarrassed new poor, who accepted her excessive interest rates for the sake of her discretion. Ladies with the airs of queens descended from their carriages at the entrance to the notions shop, unencumbered by nursemaids or servants, and as they pretended to buy Holland laces and passementerie trimmings, they pawned, between sobs, the last glittering ornaments of their lost paradise. Tránsito Ariza rescued them from difficulties with so much consideration for their lineage that many of them left more grateful for the honor than for the favor they had received. In less than ten years she knew the jewels, so often redeemed and then tearfully pawned again, as if they had been her own, and at the time her son decided to marry, the profits, converted into gold, lay hidden in a clay jar under her bed. Then she did her accounts and discovered not only that she could undertake to keep the rented house standing for five years, but that with the same shrewdness and a little more luck she could perhaps buy it, before she died, for the twelve grandchildren she hoped to have. Florentino Ariza, for his part, had received provisional appointment as First Assistant at the telegraph office, and Lotario Thugut wanted him to head the office when he left to direct the School of Telegraphy and Magnetism, which he expected to do the following year.

So the practical side of the marriage was resolved. Still, Tránsito Ariza thought that two final conditions were prudent. The first was to find out who Lorenzo Daza really was, for though his accent left no doubt concerning his origins, no one had any certain information as to his identity and livelihood. The second was that the engagement be a long one so that the fiancés could come to know each other person to person, and that the strictest reserve be maintained until both felt very certain of their affections. She suggested they wait until the war was over. Florentino Ariza agreed to absolute secrecy, not only for his mother's reasons but because of the hermeticism of his own character. He also agreed to the delay, but its terms seemed unrealistic to him, since in over half a century of independent life the nation had not had a single day of civil peace.

"We'll grow old waiting," he said.

His godfather, the homeopathic practitioner, who happened to be taking part in the conversation, did not believe that the wars were an obstacle. He thought they were nothing more than the struggles of the poor, driven like oxen by the landowners, against barefoot soldiers who were driven in turn by the government.

"The war is in the mountains," he said. "For as long as I can remember, they have killed us in the cities with decrees, not with bullets."

In any case, the details of the engagement were settled in their letters during the weeks that followed. Fermina Daza, on the advice of her Aunt Escolástica, accepted both the two-year extension and the condition of absolute secrecy, and suggested that Florentino Ariza ask for her hand when she finished secondary school, during the Christ-

113

mas vacation. When the time came they would decide on how the engagement was to be formalized, depending on the degree of approval she obtained from her father. In the meantime, they continued to write to each other with the same ardor and frequency, but free of the turmoil they had felt before, and their letters tended toward a domestic tone that seemed appropriate to husband and wife. Nothing disturbed their dreams.

Florentino Ariza's life had changed. Requited love had given him a confidence and strength he had never known before, and he was so efficient in his work that Lotario Thugut had no trouble having him named his permanent assistant. By that time his plans for the School of Telegraphy and Magnetism had failed, and the German dedicated his free time to the only thing he really enjoyed: going to the port to play the accordion and drink beer with the sailors, finishing the evening at the transient hotel. It was a long time before Florentino Ariza realized that Lotario Thugut's influence in the palace of pleasure was due to the fact that he had become the owner of the establishment as well as impresario for the birds in the port. He had bought it gradually with his savings of many years, but the person who ran it for him was a lean, one-eyed little man with a polished head and a heart so kind that no one understood how he could be such a good manager. But he was. At least it seemed that way to Florentino Ariza when the manager told him, without his requesting it, that he had the permanent use of a room in the hotel, not only to resolve problems of the lower belly whenever he decided to do so, but so that he could have at his disposal a quiet place for his reading and his love letters. And as the long months passed until the formalizing of the engagement, he spent more time there than at the office or his house, and there were periods when Tránsito Ariza saw him only when he came home to change his clothes.

Reading had become his insatiable vice. Ever since she had taught him to read, his mother had bought him illustrated books by Nordic authors which were sold as stories for children but in reality were the cruelest and most perverse that one could read at any age. When he was five years old, Florentino Ariza would recite them from memory, both in his classes and at literary evenings at school, but his familiarity with them did not alleviate the terror they caused. On the contrary, it became acute. So that when he began to read poetry, by comparison it was like finding an oasis. Even during his adolescence he had devoured, in the order of their appearance, all the volumes of the Popular Library that Tránsito Ariza bought from the bargain booksellers at the Arcade of the Scribes, where one could find everything from Homer to the least meritorious of the local poets. But he made no distinctions: he read whatever came his way, as if it had been ordained by fate, and despite his many years of reading, he still could not judge what was good and what was not in all that he had read. The only thing clear to him was that he preferred verse to prose, and in verse he preferred love poems that he memorized without even intending to after the second reading, and the better rhymed and metered they were, and the more heartrending, the more easily he learned them.

They were the original source of his first letters to Fermina Daza, those half-baked endearments taken whole from the Spanish romantics, and his letters continued in that vein until real life obliged him to concern himself with matters more mundane than heartache. By that time he had moved on to tearful serialized novels and other, even more profane prose of the day. He had learned to cry with his mother as they read the pamphlets by local poets that were sold in plazas and arcades for two centavos each. But at the same time he was able to recite from memory the most exquisite Castilian poetry of the Golden Age. In general, he read everything that fell into his hands in the order in which it fell, so that long after those hard years of his first love, when he was no longer young, he would read from first page to last the twenty volumes of the Young People's Treasury, the complete catalogue of the Garnier Bros. Classics in translation, and the simplest works that Don Vicente Blasco Ibáñez published in the Prometeo collection.

In any event, his youthful adventures in the transient hotel were not limited to reading and composing feverish letters but also included his initiation into the secrets of loveless love. Life in

116

the house began after noon, when his friends the birds got up as bare as the day they were born, so that when Florentino Ariza arrived after work he found a palace populated by naked nymphs who shouted their commentaries on the secrets of the city, which they knew because of the faithlessness of the protagonists. Many displayed in their nudity traces of their past: scars of knife thrusts in the belly, starbursts of gunshot wounds, ridges of the razor cuts of love, Caesarean sections sewn up by butchers. Some of them had their young children with them during the day, those unfortunate fruits of youthful defiance or carelessness, and they took off their children's clothes as soon as they were brought in so they would not feel different in that paradise of nudity. Each one cooked her own food, and no one ate better than Florentino Ariza when they invited him for a meal, because he chose the best from each. It was a daily fiesta that lasted until dusk, when the naked women marched, singing, toward the bathrooms, asked to borrow soap, toothbrushes, scissors, cut each other's hair, dressed in borrowed clothes, painted themselves like lugubrious clowns, and went out to hunt the first prey of the night. Then life in the house became impersonal and dehumanized, and it was impossible to share in it without paying.

Since he had known Fermina Daza, there was no place where Florentino Ariza felt more at ease, because it was the only place where he felt that he was with her. Perhaps it was for similar reasons that an elegant older woman with beautiful silvery hair lived there but did not participate in the uninhibited life of the naked women, who professed sacramental respect for her. A premature sweetheart had taken her there when she was young, and after enjoying her for a time, abandoned her to her fate. Nevertheless, despite the stigma, she had made a good marriage. When she was quite old and alone, two sons and three daughters argued over who would have the pleasure of taking her to live with them, but she could not think of a better place to live than that hotel of her youthful debaucheries. Her permanent room was her only home, and this made for immediate communion with Florentino Ariza, who, she said, would become a wise man known throughout the world because he could enrich his soul with reading in a paradise of salaciousness. Florentino Ariza, for his part, developed so much affection for her that he helped her with her shopping and would spend the afternoons in conversation with her. He thought she was a woman wise in the ways of love, since she offered many insights into his affair without his having to reveal any secrets to her.

If he had not given in to the many temptations at hand before he experienced Fermina Daza's love, he certainly would not succumb now that she was his official betrothed. So Florentino Ariza lived with the girls and shared their pleasures and miseries, but it did not occur to him or them to go any further. An unforeseen event demonstrated the severity of his determination. One afternoon at six o'clock, when the girls were dressing to receive that evening's clients, the woman who cleaned the rooms on his floor in the hotel came into his cubicle. She was young, but haggard and old before her time, like a fully dressed penitent surrounded by glorious nakedness. He saw her every day without feeling himself observed: she walked through the rooms with her brooms, a bucket for the trash, and a special rag for picking up used condoms from the floor. She came into the room where Florentino Ariza lay reading, and as always she cleaned with great care so as not to disturb him. Then she passed close to the bed, and he felt a warm and tender hand low on his belly, he felt it searching, he felt it finding, he felt it unbuttoning his trousers while her breathing filled the room. He pretended to read until he could not bear it any longer and had to move his body out of the way.

She was dismayed, for the first thing they warned her about when they gave her the cleaning job was that she should not try to sleep with the clients. They did not have to tell her that, because she was one of those women who thought that prostitution did not mean going to bed for money but going to bed with a stranger. She had two children, each by a different father, not because they were casual adventures but because she could never love any man who came back after the third visit. Until that time she had been a woman without a sense of urgency, a woman whose nature prepared her to wait without despair, but life in that house proved stronger than her virtue. She came to work at six in the afternoon, and she spent the whole night going through the rooms, sweeping them out, picking up condoms, changing the sheets. It was difficult to imagine the number of things that men left after love. They left vomit and tears, which seemed understandable to her, but they also left many enigmas of intimacy: puddles of blood, patches of excrement, glass eyes, gold watches, false teeth, lockets with golden curls, love letters, business letters, condolence letters—all kinds of letters. Some came back for the items they had lost, but most were unclaimed, and Lotario Thugut kept them under lock and key and thought that sooner or later the palace that had seen better days, with its thousands of forgotten belongings, would become a museum of love.

The work was hard and the pay was low, but she did it well. What she could not endure were the sobs, the laments, the creaking of the bedsprings, which filled her blood with so much ardor and so much sorrow that by dawn she could not bear the desire to go to bed with the first beggar she met on the street, with any miserable drunk who would give her what she wanted with no pretensions and no questions. The appearance of a man like Florentino Ariza, young, clean, and without a woman, was for her a gift from heaven, because from the first moment she realized that he was just like her: someone in need of love. But he was unaware of her compelling desire. He had kept his virginity for Fermina Daza, and there was no force or argument in this world that could turn him from his purpose.

That was his life, four months before the date set for formalizing the engagement, when Lorenzo Daza showed up at the telegraph office one morning at seven o'clock and asked for him. Since he had not yet arrived, Lorenzo Daza waited on the bench until ten minutes after eight, slipping a heavy gold ring with its noble opal stone from one finger to another, and as soon as Florentino Ariza came in, he recognized him as the employee who had delivered the telegram, and he took him by the arm.

"Come with me, my boy," he said. "You and I have to talk for five minutes, man to man."

Florentino Ariza, as green as a corpse, let himself be led. He was not prepared for this meeting, because Fermina Daza had not found either the occasion or the means to warn him. The fact was that on the previous Saturday, Sister Franca de la Luz, Superior of the Academy of the Presentation of the Blessed Virgin, had come into the class on Ideas of Cosmogony with the stealth of a serpent, and spying on the students over their shoulders, she discovered that Fermina Daza was pretending to take notes in her notebook when in reality she was writing a love letter. According to the rules of the Academy, that error was reason for expulsion. Lorenzo Daza received an urgent summons to the rectory, where he discovered the leak through which his iron regime was trickling. Fermina Daza, with her innate fortitude, confessed to the error of the letter, but refused to reveal the identity of her secret sweetheart and refused again before the Tribunal of the Order which, therefore, confirmed the verdict of expulsion. Her father, however, searched her room, until then an inviolate sanctuary, and in the false bottom of her trunk he found the packets of three years' worth of letters hidden away with as much love as had inspired their writing. The signature was unequivocal, but Lorenzo Daza could not believe—not then, not ever—that his daughter knew nothing about her secret lover except that he worked as a telegraph operator and that he loved the violin.

Certain that such an intricate relationship was understandable only with the complicity of his sister, he did not grant her the grace of an excuse or the right of appeal, but shipped her on the schooner to San Juan de la Ciénaga. Fermina Daza never found relief from her last memory of her aunt on the afternoon when she said goodbye in the doorway, burning with fever inside her brown habit, bony and ashen, and then disappeared into the drizzle in the little park, carrying all that she owned in life: her spinster's sleeping mat and enough money for a month, wrapped in a handkerchief that she clutched in her fist. As soon as she had freed herself from her father's authority, Fermina Daza began a search for her in the Caribbean provinces, asking for information from everyone who might know her, and she could not find a trace of her until almost thirty years later when she received a letter that had taken a long time to pass through many hands, informing her that she had died in the Water of God leprosarium. Lorenzo Daza did not foresee the ferocity with which his daughter would react to the unjust punishment of her Aunt Escolástica, whom she had always identified with the mother she could barely remember. She locked herself in her room, refused to eat or drink, and when at last he persuaded her to open the door, first with threats and then with poorly dissimulated pleading, he found a wounded panther who would never be fifteen years old again.

He tried to seduce her with all kinds of flattery. He tried to make her understand that love at her age was an illusion, he tried to convince her to send back the letters and return to the Academy and beg forgiveness on her knees, and he gave his word of honor that he would be the first to help her find happiness with a worthy suitor. But it was like talking to a corpse. Defeated, he at last lost his temper at lunch on Monday, and while he choked back insults and blasphemies and was about to explode, she put the meat knife to her throat, without dramatics but with a steady hand and eyes so aghast that he did not dare to challenge her. That was when he took the risk of talking for five minutes, man to man, with the accursed upstart whom he did not remember ever having seen, and who had come into his life to his great sorrow. By force of habit he picked up his revolver before he went out, but he was careful to hide it under his shirt.

Florentino Ariza still had not recovered when

Lorenzo Daza held him by the arm and steered him across the Plaza of the Cathedral to the arcaded gallery of the Parish Café and invited him to sit on the terrace. There were no other customers at that hour: a black woman was scrubbing the tiles in the enormous salon with its chipped and dusty stained-glass windows, and the chairs were still upside down on the marble tables. Florentino Ariza had often seen Lorenzo Daza gambling and drinking cask wine there with the Asturians from the public market, while they shouted and argued about other longstanding wars that had nothing to do with our own. Conscious of the fatality of love, he had often wondered how the meeting would be that he was bound to have with Lorenzo Daza sooner or later, the meeting that no human power could forestall because it had been inscribed in both their destinies forever. He had supposed it would be an unequal dispute, not only because Fermina Daza had warned him in her letters of her father's stormy character, but because he himself had noted that his eyes seemed angry even when he was laughing at the gaming table. Everything about him was a testimony to crudeness: his ignoble belly, his emphatic speech, his lynx's sidewhiskers, his rough hands, the ring finger smothered by the opal setting. His only endearing trait, which Florentino Ariza recognized the first time he saw him walking, was that he had the same doe's gait as his daughter. However, when he showed him the chair so that he could sit down, he did not find Lorenzo Daza as harsh as he appeared to be, and his courage revived when he invited him to have a glass of anisette. Florentino Ariza had never had a drink at eight o'clock in the morning, but he accepted with gratitude because his need for one was urgent.

Lorenzo Daza, in fact, took no more than five minutes to say what he had to say, and he did so with a disarming sincerity that confounded Florentino Ariza. When his wife died he had set only one goal for himself: to turn his daughter into a great lady. The road was long and uncertain for a mule trader who did not know how to read or write and whose reputation as a horse thief was not so much proven as widespread in the province of San Juan de la Ciénaga. He lit a mule driver's cigar and lamented: "The only thing worse than bad health is a bad name." He said, however, that the real secret of his fortune was that none of his mules worked as hard and with so much determination as he did himself, even during the bitterest days of the wars when the villages awoke in ashes and the fields in ruins. Although his daughter was never aware of the premeditation in her destiny, she behaved as if she were an enthusiastic accomplice. She was intelligent and methodical, to the point where she taught her father to read as soon as she herself learned to, and at the age of twelve she had a mastery of reality that would have allowed her to run the house without the help of her Aunt Escolástica. He sighed: "She's a mule worth her weight in gold." When his daughter finished primary school with highest marks in every subject and honorable mention at graduation, he understood that San Juan de la Ciénaga was too narrow for his dreams. Then he liquidated lands and animals and moved with new impetus and seventy thousand gold pesos to this ruined city and its moth-eaten glories, where a beautiful woman with an old-fashioned upbringing still had the possibility of being reborn through a fortunate marriage. The sudden appearance of Florentino Ariza had been an unforeseen obstacle in his hard-fought plan. "So I have come to make a request of you," said Lorenzo Daza. He dipped the end of his cigar in the anisette, pulled on it and drew no smoke, then concluded in a sorrowful voice:

"Get out of our way."

Florentino Ariza had listened to him as he sipped his anisette, and was so absorbed in the disclosure of Fermina Daza's past that he did not even ask himself what he was going to say when it was his turn to speak. But when the moment arrived, he realized that anything he might say would compromise his destiny.

"Have you spoken to her?" he asked.

"That doesn't concern you," said Lorenzo Daza.

"I ask you the question," said Florentino Ariza, "because it seems to me that she is the one who has to decide."

"None of that," said Lorenzo Daza. "This is a matter for men and it will be decided by men."

His tone had become threatening, and a customer who had just sat down at a nearby table turned to look at them. Florentino Ariza spoke in

126

a most tenuous voice, but with the most imperious resolution of which he was capable:

"Be that as it may, I cannot answer without knowing what she thinks. It would be a betrayal."

Then Lorenzo Daza leaned back in his chair, his eyelids reddened and damp, and his left eye spun in its orbit and stayed twisted toward the outside. He, too, lowered his voice.

"Don't force me to shoot you," he said.

Florentino Ariza felt his intestines filling with cold froth. But his voice did not tremble because he felt himself illuminated by the Holy Spirit.

"Shoot me," he said, with his hand on his chest. "There is no greater glory than to die for love."

Lorenzo Daza had to look at him sideways, like a parrot, to see him with his twisted eye. He did not pronounce the four words so much as spit them out, one by one:

"Son of a bitch!"

That same week he took his daughter away on the journey that would make her forget. He gave her no explanation at all, but burst into her bedroom, his mustache stained with fury and his chewed cigar, and ordered her to pack. She asked him where they were going, and he answered: "To our death." Frightened by a response that seemed too close to the truth, she tried to face him with the courage of a few days before, but he took off his belt with its hammered copper buckle, twisted it around his fist, and hit the table with a blow that resounded through the house like a rifle shot.

Fermina Daza knew very well the extent and occasion of her own strength, and so she packed a bedroll with two straw mats and a hammock, and two large trunks with all her clothes, certain that this was a trip from which she would never return. Before she dressed, she locked herself in the bathroom and wrote a brief farewell letter to Florentino Ariza on a sheet torn from the pack of toilet paper. Then she cut off her entire braid at the nape of her neck with cuticle scissors, rolled it inside a velvet box embroidered with gold thread, and sent it along with the letter.

It was a demented trip. The first stage along the ridges of the Sierra Nevada, riding muleback in a caravan of Andean mule drivers, lasted eleven days, during which time they were stupefied by the naked sun or drenched by the horizontal October rains and almost always petrified by the numbing vapors rising from the precipices. On the third day a mule maddened by gadflies fell into a ravine with its rider, dragging along the entire line, and the screams of the man and his pack of seven animals tied to one another continued to rebound along the cliffs and gullies for several hours after the disaster, and continued to resound for years and years in the memory of Fermina Daza. All her baggage plunged over the side with the mules, but in the centuries-long instant of the fall until the scream of terror was extinguished at the bottom, she did not think of the poor dead mule driver or his mangled pack but of how unfortunate it was that the mule she was riding had not been tied to the others as well.

It was the first time she had ever ridden, but the terror and unspeakable privations of the trip would not have seemed so bitter to her if it had not been for the certainty that she would never see Florentino Ariza again or have the consolation of his letters. She had not said a word to her father since the beginning of the trip, and he was so confounded that he hardly spoke to her even when it was an absolute necessity to do so, or he sent the mule drivers to her with messages. When their luck was good they found some roadside inn that served rustic food which she refused to eat, and rented them canvas cots stained with rancid perspiration and urine. But more often they spent the night in Indian settlements, in open-air public dormitories built at the side of the road, with their rows of wooden poles and roofs of bitter palm where every passerby had the right to stay until dawn. Fermina Daza could not sleep through a single night as she sweated in fear and listened in the darkness to the coming and going of silent travelers who tied their animals to the poles and hung their hammocks where they could.

At nightfall, when the first travelers would arrive, the place was uncrowded and peaceful, but by dawn it had been transformed into a fairground, with a mass of hammocks hanging at different levels and Aruac Indians from the mountains sleeping on their haunches, with the raging of the tethered goats, and the uproar of the fighting cocks in their pharaonic crates, and the panting silence of the mountain dogs, who had been taught not to bark because of the dangers of war. Those privations were familiar to Lorenzo Daza, who had trafficked through the region for half his life and almost always met up with old friends at dawn. For his daughter it was perpetual agony. The stench of the loads of salted catfish added to the loss of appetite caused by her grief, and eventually destroyed her habit of eating, and if she did not go mad with despair it was because she always found relief in the memory of Florentino Ariza. She did not doubt that this was the land of forgetting.

Another constant terror was the war. Since the start of the journey there had been talk of the danger of running into scattered patrols, and the mule drivers had instructed them in the various ways of recognizing the two sides so that they could act accordingly. They often encountered squads of mounted soldiers under the command of an officer, who rounded up new recruits by roping them as if they were cattle on the hoof. Overwhelmed by so many horrors, Fermina Daza had forgotten about the one that seemed more legendary than imminent, until one night when a patrol of unknown affiliation captured two travelers from the caravan and hanged them from a campano tree half a league from the settlement. Lorenzo Daza did not even know them, but he had them taken down and he gave them a Christian burial in thanksgiving for not having met a similar fate. And he had reason: the assailants had awakened him with a rifle in his stomach, and a commander in rags, his face smeared with charcoal, had shone a light on him and asked him if he was Liberal or Conservative.

"Neither one or the other," said Lorenzo Daza. "I am a Spanish subject."

"What luck!" said the commander, and he left with his hand raised in a salute. "Long live the King!"

Two days later they descended to the luminous plain where the joyful town of Valledupar was located. There were cockfights in the patios, accordion music on the street corners, riders on thoroughbred horses, rockets and bells. A pyrotechnical castle was being assembled. Fermina Daza did not even notice the festivities. They stayed in the home of Uncle Lisímaco Sánchez, her mother's brother, who had come out to receive them on the King's Highway at the head of a noisy troop of young relatives riding the best-bred horses in the entire province, and they were led through the streets of the town to the accompaniment of exploding fireworks. The house was on the Grand Plaza, next to the colonial church that had been repaired several times, and it seemed more like the main house on a hacienda because of its large, somber rooms and its gallery that faced an orchard of fruit trees and smelled of hot sugarcane juice.

No sooner had they dismounted in the stables than the reception rooms were overflowing with numerous unknown relatives whose unbearable effusiveness was a scourge to Fermina Daza, for she

131

was incapable of ever loving anyone else in this world, she suffered from saddle burn, she was dying of fatigue and loose bowels, and all she longed for was a solitary and quiet place to cry. Her cousin Hildebranda Sánchez, two years older than she and with the same imperial haughtiness, was the only one who understood her condition as soon as she saw her, because she, too, was being consumed in the fiery coals of reckless love. When it grew dark she took her to the bedroom that she had prepared to share with her, and seeing the burning ulcers on her buttocks, she could not believe that she still lived. With the help of her mother, a very sweet woman who looked as much like her husband as if they were twins, she prepared a bath for her and cooled the burning with arnica compresses, while the thunder from the gunpowder castle shook the foundations of the house.

At midnight the visitors left, the public fiesta scattered into smoldering embers, and Cousin Hildebranda lent Fermina Daza a madapollam nightgown and helped her to lie down in a bed with smooth sheets and feather pillows, and without warning she was filled with the instantaneous panic of happiness. When at last they were alone in the bedroom, Cousin Hildebranda bolted the door with a crossbar and from under the straw matting of her bed took out a manila envelope sealed in wax with the emblem of the national telegraph. It was enough for Fermina Daza to see her cousin's expression of radiant malice for the pensive scent of white gardenias to grow again in her heart's memory, and then she tore the red sealing wax with her teeth and drenched the eleven forbidden telegrams in a shower of tears until dawn.

Then he knew. Before starting out on the journey, Lorenza Daza had made the mistake of telegraphing the news to his brother-in-law Lisímaco Sánchez, and he in turn had sent the news to his vast and intricate network of kinfolk in numerous towns and villages throughout the province. So that Florentino Ariza not only learned the complete itinerary but also established an extensive brotherhood of telegraph operators who would follow the trail of Fermina Daza to the last settlement in Cabo de la Vela. This allowed him to maintain intensive communications with her from the time of her arrival in Valledupar, where she stayed three months, until the end of her journey in Riohacha, a year and a half later, when Lorenzo Daza took it for granted that his daughter had at last forgotten and he decided to return home. Perhaps he was not even aware of how much he had relaxed his vigilance, distracted as he was by the flattering words of the in-laws who after so many years had put aside their tribal prejudices and welcomed him with open arms as one of their own. The visit was a belated reconciliation, although that had not been its purpose. As a matter of fact, the family of Fermina Sánchez had been opposed in every way to her marrying an immigrant with no background who was a braggart and a boor and who was always traveling, trading his unbroken mules in a business that seemed too simple to be honest. Lorenzo Daza played for high stakes, because his sweetheart was the darling of a typical family of the region: an intricate tribe of wild women and softhearted men who were obsessed to the point of dementia with their sense of honor. Fermina Sánchez, however, settled on her desire with the blind determination of love when it is opposed, and she married him despite her family, with so much speed and so much secrecy that it seemed as if she had done so not for love but to cover over with a sacramental cloak some premature mistake.

Twenty-five years later, Lorenzo Daza did not realize that this intransigence in his daughter's love affair was a vicious repetition of his own past, and he complained of his misfortune to the same in-laws who had opposed him, as they had complained in their day to their own kin. Still, the time he spent in lamentation was time his daughter gained for her love affair. So that while he went about castrating calves and taming mules on the prosperous lands of his in-laws, she was free to spend time with a troop of female cousins under the command of Hildebranda Sánchez, the most beautiful and obliging of them all, whose hopeless passion for a married man, a father who was twenty years older than she, had to be satisfied with furtive glances.

After their prolonged stay in Valledupar they continued their journey through the foothills of the mountains, crossing flowering meadows and dreamlike mesas, and in all the villages they were received as they had been in the first, with music and fireworks and new conspiratorial cousins and punctual messages in the telegraph offices. Fermina Daza soon realized that the afternoon of their arrival in Valledupar had not been unusual, but rather that in this fertile province every day of the week was lived as if it were a holiday. The visitors slept wherever they happened to be at nightfall, and they ate wherever they happened to be hungry, for these were houses with open doors, where there was always a hammock hanging and a three-meat stew simmering on the stove in case guests arrived before the telegram announcing their arrival, as was almost always the case. Hildebranda Sánchez accompanied her cousin for the remainder of the trip, guiding her with joyful spirit through the tangled complexities of her blood to the very source of her origins. Fermina Daza learned about herself, she felt free for the first time, she felt herself befriended and protected, her lungs full of the air of liberty, which restored her tranquillity and her will to live. In her final years she would still recall the trip that, with the perverse lucidity of nostalgia, became more and more recent in her memory.

One night she came back from her daily walk stunned by the revelation that one could be happy not only without love, but despite it. The revelation alarmed her, because one of her cousins had surprised her parents in conversation with Lorenzo

Daza, who had suggested the idea of arranging the marriage of his daughter to the only heir to the fabulous fortune of Cleofás Moscote. Fermina Daza knew who he was. She had seen him in the plazas, pirouetting his perfect horses with trappings so rich they seemed ornaments used for the Mass, and he was elegant and clever and had a dreamer's eyelashes that could make the stones sigh, but she compared him to her memory of poor emaciated Florentino Ariza sitting under the almond trees in the little park, with the book of verses on his lap, and she did not find even the shadow of a doubt in her heart.

In those days Hildebranda Sánchez was delirious with hope after visiting a fortune-teller whose clairvoyance had astonished her. Dismayed by her father's intentions, Fermina Daza also went to consult with her. The cards said there was no obstacle in her future to a long and happy marriage, and that prediction gave her back her courage because she could not conceive of such a fortunate destiny with any man other than the one she loved. Exalted by that certainty, she assumed command of her fate. That was how the telegraphic correspondence with Florentino Ariza stopped being a concerto of intentions and illusory promises and became methodical and practical and more intense than ever. They set dates, established means, pledged their lives to their mutual determination to marry without consulting anyone, wherever and however they could, as soon as they were together again. Fermina Daza considered this commitment so binding that the night her father gave her permission to attend her first adult dance in the town of Fonseca, she did not think it was decent to accept without the consent of her fiancé. Florentino Ariza was in the transient hotel that night, playing cards with Lotario Thugut, when he was told he had an urgent telegram on the line.

It was the telegraph operator from Fonseca, who had keyed in through seven intermediate stations so that Fermina Daza could ask permission to attend the dance. When she obtained it, however, she was not satisfied with the simple affirmative answer but asked for proof that in fact it was Florentino Ariza operating the telegraph key at the other end of the line. More astonished than flattered, he composed an identifying phrase: *Tell her that I swear by the crowned goddess*. Fermina Daza recognized the password and stayed at her first adult dance until seven in the morning, when she had to change in a rush in order not to be late for Mass. By then she had more letters and telegrams in the bottom of her trunk than her father had taken away from her, and she had learned to behave with the air of a married woman. Lorenzo Daza interpreted these changes in her manner as proof that distance and time had cured her of her juvenile fantasies, but he never spoke to her about his plans for the arranged marriage. Their relations had become fluid within the formal reserve that she had imposed since the expulsion of Aunt Escolástica, and this allowed them such a comfortable modus vivendi that no one would have doubted that it was based on affection.

It was at this time that Florentino Ariza decided to tell her in his letters of his determination to salvage the treasure of the sunken galleon for her. It was true, and it had come to him in a flash of inspiration one sunlit afternoon when the sea seemed paved with aluminum because of the numbers of fish brought to the surface by mullein. All the birds of the air were in an uproar because of the kill, and the fishermen had to drive them away with their oars so they would not have to fight with them for the fruits of that prohibited miracle. The use of the mullein plant to put the fish to sleep had been prohibited by law since colonial times, but it continued to be a common practice among the fishermen of the Caribbean until it was replaced by dynamite. One of Florentino Ariza's pastimes during Fermina Daza's journey was to watch from the jetties as the fishermen loaded their canoes with enormous nets filled with sleeping fish. At the same time, a gang of boys who swam like sharks asked curious bystanders to toss coins into the water so they could dive to the bottom for them. They were the same boys who swam out to meet the ocean liners for that purpose, and whose skill in the art of diving had been the subject of so many tourist accounts written in the United States and Europe. Florentino Ariza had always known about them, even before he knew about love, but it had never occurred to him that perhaps they might be able to bring up the fortune from the galleon. It occurred to him that afternoon, and from the following Sunday until Fermina Daza's return almost a year later, he had an additional motive for delirium.

After talking to him for only ten minutes, Euclides, one of the boy swimmers, became as excited as he was at the idea of an underwater exploration. Florentino Ariza did not reveal the whole truth of the enterprise, but he informed himself thoroughly regarding his abilities as a diver and navigator. He asked him if he could descend without air to a depth of twenty meters, and Euclides told him yes. He asked him if he was prepared to sail a fisherman's canoe by himself in the open sea in the middle of a storm with no instruments other than his instinct, and Euclides told him yes. He asked him if he could find a specific spot sixteen nautical miles to the northwest of the largest island in the Sotavento Archipelago, and Euclides told him yes. He asked him if he was capable of navigating by the stars at night, and Euclides told him yes. He asked him if he was prepared to do so for the same wages the fishermen paid him for helping them to fish, and Euclides told him yes, but with an additional five reales on Sundays. He asked him if he knew how to defend himself against sharks, and Euclides told him yes, for he had magic tricks to frighten them away. He asked him if he was able to keep a secret even if they put him in the torture chambers of the Inquisition, and Euclides told him yes, in fact he did not say no to anything, and he knew how to say yes with so much conviction that there was no way to doubt him. Then the boy reckoned expenses: renting the canoe, renting the canoe paddle, renting fishing equipment so that no one would suspect the truth behind their incursions. It was also necessary to take along food, a demijohn of fresh water, an oil lamp, a pack of tallow candles, and a hunter's horn to call for help in case of emergency.

Euclides was about twelve years old, and he was fast and clever and an incessant talker, with an eel's body that could slither through a bull's-eye. The weather had tanned his skin to such a degree that it was impossible to imagine his original color, and this made his big yellow eyes seem more radiant. Florentino Ariza decided on the spot that he was the perfect companion for an adventure of such magnitude, and they embarked without further delay the following Sunday.

They sailed out of the fishermen's port at dawn, well provisioned and better disposed, Euclides almost naked, with only the loincloth that he always wore, and Florentino Ariza with his frock coat, his tenebrous hat, his patent-leather boots, the poet's bow at his neck, and a book to pass the time during the crossing to the islands. From the very first Sunday he realized that Euclides was as good a navigator as he was a diver, and that he had astonishing knowledge of the character of the sea and the debris in the bay. He could recount in the most unexpected detail the history of each rusting hulk of a boat, he knew the age of each buoy, the

140

origin of every piece of rubbish, the number of links in the chain with which the Spaniards closed off the entrance of the bay. Fearing that he might also know the real purpose of his expedition, Florentino Ariza asked him sly questions and in this way realized that Euclides did not have the slightest suspicion about the sunken galleon.

Ever since he had first heard the story of the treasure in the transient hotel, Florentino Ariza had learned all he could about the habits of galleons. He learned that the *San José* was not the only ship in the coral depths. It was, in fact, the flagship of the Terra Firma fleet, and had arrived here after May 1708, having sailed from the legendary fair of Portobello in Panama where it had taken on part of its fortune: three hundred trunks of silver from Peru and Veracruz, and one hundred ten trunks of pearls gathered and counted on the island of Contadora. During the long month it had remained here, the days and nights had been devoted to popular fiestas, and the rest of the treasure intended to save the Kingdom of Spain from poverty had been taken aboard: one hundred sixteen trunks of emeralds from Muzo and Somondoco and thirty million gold coins.

The Terra Firma fleet was composed of no less than twelve supply ships of varying sizes, and it set sail from this port traveling in a convoy with a French squadron that was heavily armed but still incapable of protecting the expedition from the accurate cannon shot of the English squadron under Commander Charles Wager, who waited for it in the Sotavento Archipelago, at the entrance to the bay. So the *San José* was not the only sunken vessel, although there was no reliable documented record of how many had succumbed and how many had managed to escape the English fire. What was certain was that the flagship had been among the first to sink, along with the entire crew and the commander standing straight on the quarterdeck, and that she alone carried most of the cargo.

Florentino Ariza had learned the route of the galleons from the navigation charts of the period, and he thought he had determined the site of the shipwreck. They left the bay between the two fortresses of Boca Chica, and after four hours of sailing they entered the interior still waters of the archipelago in whose coral depths they could pick up sleeping lobsters with their hands. The air was so soft and the sea so calm and clear that Florentino Ariza felt as if he were his own reflection in the water. At the far end of the backwater, two hours from the largest island, was the site of the shipwreck.

Suffocating in his formal clothes under the infernal sun, Florentino Ariza indicated to Euclides that he should try to dive to a depth of twenty meters and bring back anything he might find at the bottom. The water was so clear that he saw him moving below like a tarnished shark among the blue ones that crossed his path without touching him. Then he saw him disappear into a thicket of coral, and just when he thought that he could

142

not possibly have any more air in his lungs, he heard his voice at his back. Euclides was standing on the bottom, with his arms raised and the water up to his waist. And so they continued exploring deeper sites, always moving toward the north, sailing over the indifferent manta rays, the timid squid, the rosebushes in the shadows, until Euclides concluded that they were wasting their time.

"If you don't tell me what you want me to find, I don't know how I am going to find it," he said.

But he did not tell him. Then Euclides proposed to him that he take off his clothes and dive with him, even if it was only to see that other sky below the world, the coral depths. But Florentino Ariza always said that God had made the sea to look at through the window, and he had never learned to swim. A short while later, the afternoon grew cloudy and the air turned cold and damp, and it grew dark with so little warning that they had to navigate by the lighthouse to find the port. Before they entered the bay, the enormous white ocean liner from France passed very close to them, all its lights blazing as it trailed a wake of tender stew and boiled cauliflower.

They wasted three Sundays in this way, and they would have continued to waste them all if Florentino Ariza had not decided to share his secret with Euclides, who then modified the entire search plan, and they sailed along the old channel of the galleons, more than twenty nautical leagues to the east of the spot Florentino Ariza had decided on. Less than two months had gone by when, one rainy afternoon out at sea, Euclides spent considerable time down on the bottom and the canoe drifted so much that he had to swim almost half an hour to reach it because Florentino Ariza could not row it closer to him. When at last he climbed on board, he took two pieces of woman's jewelry out of his mouth and displayed them as if they were the prize for his perseverance.

What he recounted then was so fascinating that Florentino Ariza promised himself that he would learn to swim and dive as far under water as possible just so he could see it with his own eyes. He said that in that spot, only eighteen meters down, there were so many old sailing ships lying among the coral reefs that it was impossible to even calculate the number, and they were spread over so extensive an area that you could not see to the end of them. He said that the most surprising thing was that none of the old wrecks afloat in the bay was in such good condition as the sunken vessels. He said that there were several caravelles with their sails still intact, and that the sunken ships were visible even on the bottom, for it seemed as if they had sunk along with their own space and time, so that they were still illumined by the same eleven o'clock sun that was shining on Saturday, June 9, when they went down. Choking on the driving force of his imagination, he said that the easiest one to distinguish was the galleon *San José*, for its name could be seen on the poop in gold letters, but it was also the ship most damaged by

144

English artillery. He said he had seen an octopus inside, more than three centuries old, whose tentacles emerged through the openings in the cannon and who had grown to such a size in the dining room that one would have to destroy the ship to free him. He said he had seen the body of the commander, dressed for battle and floating sideways inside the aquarium of the forecastle, and that if he had not dived down to the hold with all its treasure, it was because he did not have enough air in his lungs. There were the proofs: an emerald earring and a medal of the Virgin, the chain corroded by salt.

That was when Florentino Ariza first mentioned the treasure to Fermina Daza in a letter he sent to Fonseca a short while before her return. The history of the sunken galleon was familiar to her because she had heard it many times from Lorenzo Daza, who had lost both time and money trying to convince a company of German divers to join with him in salvaging the sunken treasure. He would have persevered in the enterprise if several members of the Academy of History had not convinced him that the legend of the shipwrecked galleon had been invented by some brigand of a viceroy to hide his theft of the treasures of the Crown. In any case, Fermina Daza knew that the galleon lay beyond the reach of any human being, at a depth of two hundred meters, not the twenty claimed by Florentino Ariza. But she was so accustomed to his poetic excesses that she celebrated the adventure of the galleon as one of his most successful.

Still, when she continued to receive other letters with still more fantastic details, written with as much seriousness as his promises of love, she had to confess to Hildebranda Sánchez her fear that her bedazzled sweetheart must have lost his mind.

During this time Euclides had surfaced with so many proofs of his tale that it was no longer a question of playing with earrings and rings scattered amid the coral but of financing a major enterprise to salvage the fifty ships with their cargo of Babylonian treasure. Then what had to happen sooner or later happened: Florentino Ariza asked his mother for help in bringing his adventure to a successful conclusion. All she had to do was bite the metal settings and look at the gems made of glass against the light to realize that someone was taking advantage of her son's innocence. Euclides went down on his knees and swore to Florentino Ariza that he had done nothing wrong, but he was not seen the following Sunday in the fishermen's port, or anywhere else ever again.

The only thing Florentino Ariza salvaged from that disaster was the loving shelter of the lighthouse. He had gone there in Euclides' canoe one night when a storm at sea took them by surprise, and from that time on he would go there in the afternoons to talk to the lighthouse keeper about the innumerable marvels on land and water that the keeper had knowledge of. It was the beginning of a friendship that survived the many changes in the world. Florentino Ariza learned to feed the fire, first with loads of wood and then with large earthen jars of oil, before electrical energy came to us. He learned to direct the light and augment it with mirrors, and on several occasions, when the lighthouse keeper could not do so, he stayed to keep watch over the night at sea from the tower. He learned to know the ships by their voices, by the size of their lights on the horizon, and to sense that something of them came back to him in the flashing beacon of the lighthouse.

During the day, above all on Sundays, there was another kind of pleasure. In the District of the Viceroys, where the wealthy people of the old city lived, the women's beaches were separated from those of the men by a plaster wall: one lay to the right and the other to the left of the lighthouse. And so the lighthouse keeper installed a spyglass through which one could contemplate the women's beach by paying a centavo. Without knowing they were being observed, the young society ladies displayed themselves to the best of their ability in ruffled bathing suits and slippers and hats that hid their bodies almost as much as their street clothes did and were less attractive besides. Their mothers, sitting out in the sun in wicker rocking chairs, wearing the same dresses, the same feathered hats, and holding the same organdy parasols as they had at High Mass, watched over them from the shore, for fear the men from the neighboring beaches would seduce their daughters under the water. The reality was that one could not see anything more, or anything more exciting, through the spyglass than one could see on the street, but there were many clients who came every Sunday to wrangle over the telescope for the pure delight of tasting the insipid forbidden fruits of the walled area that was denied them.

Florentino Ariza was one of them, more from boredom than for pleasure, but it was not because of that additional attraction that he became a good friend of the lighthouse keeper. The real reason was that after Fermina Daza rejected him, when he contracted the fever of many disparate loves in his effort to replace her, it was in the lighthouse and nowhere else that he lived his happiest hours and found the best consolation for his misfortunes. It was the place he loved most, so much so that for years he tried to convince his mother, and later his Uncle Leo XII, to help him buy it. For in those days the lighthouses in the Caribbean were private property, and their owners charged ships according to their size for the right to enter the port. Florentino Ariza thought that it was the only honorable way to make a profit out of poetry, but neither his mother nor his uncle agreed with him, and by the time he had the resources to do it on his own, the lighthouses had become the property of the state.

None of these dreams was in vain, however. The tale of the galleon and the novelty of the lighthouse helped to alleviate the absence of Fermina Daza, and then, when he least expected it, he received the news of her return. And in fact, after a prolonged stay in Riohacha, Lorenzo Daza had decided to come home. It was not the most benign season on the ocean, due to the December trade winds, and the historic schooner, the only one that would risk the crossing, might find itself blown by a contrary wind back to the port where it had started. And that is what happened. Fermina Daza spent an agonized night vomiting bile, strapped to her bunk in a cabin that resembled a tavern latrine not only because of its oppressive narrowness but also because of the pestilential stench and the heat. The motion was so strong that she had the impression several times that the straps on the bed would fly apart; on the deck she heard fragments of shouted lamentations that sounded like a shipwreck, and her father's tigerish snoring in the next bunk added yet another ingredient to her terror. For the first time in almost three years she spent an entire night awake without thinking for even one moment of Florentino Ariza, while he, on the other hand, lay sleepless in his hammock in the back room, counting the eternal minutes one by one until her return. At dawn the wind suddenly died down and the sea grew calm, and Fermina Daza realized that she had slept despite her devastating seasickness, because the noise of the anchor chains awakened her. Then she loosened the straps and went to the porthole, hoping to see Florentino Ariza in the tumult of the port, but all she saw were the customs sheds among the palm trees gilded by the first rays of the sun and the rotting boards of the dock in Riohacha, where the schooner had set sail the night before.

The rest of the day was like a hallucination: she

was in the same house where she had been until yesterday, receiving the same visitors who had said goodbye to her, talking about the same things, bewildered by the impression that she was reliving a piece of life she had already lived. It was such a faithful repetition that Fermina Daza trembled at the thought that the schooner trip would be a repetition, too, for the mere memory of it terrified her. However, the only other possible means of returning home was two weeks on muleback over the mountains in circumstances even more dangerous than the first time, since a new civil war that had begun in the Andean state of Cauca was spreading throughout the Caribbean provinces. And so at eight o'clock that night she was once again accompanied to the port by the same troop of noisy relatives shedding the same tears of farewell and with the same jumble of last-minute gifts and packages that did not fit in the cabins. When it was time to sail, the men in the family saluted the schooner with a volley of shots fired into the air, and Lorenzo Daza responded from the deck with five shots from his revolver. Fermina Daza's fears dissipated because the wind was favorable all night, and there was a scent of flowers at sea that helped her to sleep soundly without the safety straps. She dreamed that she was seeing Florentino Ariza again, and that he took off the face that she had always seen on him because in fact it was a mask, but his real face was identical to the false one. She got up very early, intrigued by the enigma of the dream, and she found her father drinking mountain coffee with brandy in the captain's bar, his eye twisted by alcohol, but he did not show the slightest hint of uncertainty regarding their return.

They were coming into port. The schooner slipped in silence through the labyrinth of sailing ships anchored in the cove of the public market whose stench could be smelled several leagues out to sea, and the dawn was saturated by a steady drizzle that soon broke into a full-fledged downpour. Standing watch on the balcony of the telegraph office, Florentino Ariza recognized the schooner, its sails disheartened by the rain, as it crossed Las Ánimas Bay and anchored at the market pier. The morning before, he had waited until eleven o'clock, when he learned through a casual telegram of the contrary winds that had delayed the schooner, and on this day he had returned to his vigil at four o'clock in the morning. He continued to wait, not taking his eyes off the launch that carried ashore the few passengers who had decided to disembark despite the storm. Halfway across, the launch ran aground, and most of them had to abandon ship and splash through the mud to the pier. At eight o'clock, after they had waited in vain for the rain to stop, a black stevedore in water up to his waist received Fermina Daza at the rail of the schooner and carried her ashore in his arms, but she was so drenched that Florentino Ariza did not recognize her.

She herself was not aware of how much she had matured during the trip until she walked into her closed house and at once undertook the heroic task of making it livable again with the help of Gala Placidia, the black servant who came back from her old slave quarters as soon as she was told of their return. Fermina Daza was no longer the only child, both spoiled and tyrannized by her father, but the lady and mistress of an empire of dust and cobwebs that could be saved only by the strength of invincible love. She was not intimidated because she felt herself inspired by an exalted courage that would have enabled her to move the world. The very night of their return, while they were having hot chocolate and crullers at the large kitchen table, her father delegated to her the authority to run the house, and he did so with as much formality as if it were a sacred rite.

"I turn over to you the keys to your life," he said.

She, with all of her seventeen years behind her, accepted with a firm hand, conscious that every inch of liberty she won was for the sake of love. The next day, after a night of bad dreams, she suffered her first sense of displeasure at being home when she opened the balcony window and saw again the sad drizzle in the little park, the statue of the decapitated hero, the marble bench where Florentino Ariza used to sit with his book of verses. She no longer thought of him as the impossible sweetheart but as the certain husband to whom she belonged heart and soul. She felt the heavy weight of the time they had lost while she was away, she felt how hard it was to be alive and how much love she was going to need to love her man as God demanded. She was surprised that he was not in the little park, as he had been so many times despite the rain, and that she had received no sign of any kind from him, not even a premonition, and she was shaken by the sudden idea that he had died. But she put aside the evil thought at once, for in the recent frenzy of telegrams regarding her imminent return they had forgotten to agree on a way to continue communicating once she was home.

The truth is that Florentino Ariza was sure she had not returned, until the telegraph operator in Riohacha confirmed that they had embarked on Friday aboard the very same schooner that did not arrive the day before because of contrary winds, so that during the weekend he watched for any sign of life in her house, and at dusk on Monday he saw through the windows a light that moved through the house and was extinguished, a little after nine, in the bedroom with the balcony. He did not sleep, victim to the same fearful nausea that had disturbed his first nights of love. Tránsito Ariza arose with the first roosters, alarmed that her son had gone out to the patio at midnight and had not yet come back inside, and she did not find him in the house. He had gone to wander along the jetties, reciting love poetry into the wind and crying with joy until daybreak. At eight o'clock he was sitting under the arches of the Parish Café, delirious with fatigue, trying to think of how to send his welcome to Fermina Daza, when he felt himself shaken by a seismic tremor that tore his heart.

It was she, crossing the Plaza of the Cathedral, accompanied by Gala Placidia who was carrying the baskets for their marketing, and for the first time she was not wearing her school uniform. She was taller than when she had left, more polished and intense, her beauty purified by the restraint of maturity. Her braid had grown in, but instead of letting it hang down her back she wore it twisted over her left shoulder, and that simple change had erased all girlish traces from her. Florentino Ariza sat bedazzled until the child of his vision had crossed the plaza, looking to neither the left nor the right. But then the same irresistible power that had paralyzed him obliged him to hurry after her when she turned the corner of the Cathedral and was lost in the deafening noise of the market's rough cobblestones.

He followed her without letting himself be seen, watching the ordinary gestures, the grace, the premature maturity of the being he loved most in the world and whom he was seeing for the first time in her natural state. He was amazed by the fluidity with which she made her way through the crowd. While Gala Placidia bumped into people and became entangled in her baskets and had to run to keep up with her, she navigated the disorder of the street in her own time and space, not colliding with anyone, like a bat in the darkness. She had often been to the market with her Aunt Escolástica, but they made only minor purchases, since her

154

father himself took charge of provisioning the household, not only with furniture and food but even with women's clothing. So this first excursion was for her a fascinating adventure idealized in her girlhood dreams.

She paid no attention to the urgings of the snake charmers who offered her a syrup for eternal love, or to the pleas of the beggars lying in doorways with their running sores, or to the false Indian who tried to sell her a trained alligator. She made a long and detailed tour with no planned itinerary, stopping with no other motive than her unhurried delight in the spirit of things. She entered every doorway where there was something for sale, and everywhere she found something that increased her desire to live. She relished the aroma of vetiver in the cloth in the great chests, she wrapped herself in embossed silks, she laughed at her own laughter when she saw herself in the full-length mirror in The Golden Wire disguised as a woman from Madrid, with a comb in her hair and a fan painted with flowers. In the store that sold imported foods she lifted the lid of a barrel of pickled herring that reminded her of nights in the northeast when she was a very little girl in San Juan de la Ciénaga. She sampled an Alicante sausage that tasted of licorice, and she bought two for Saturday's breakfast, as well as some slices of cod and a jar of red currants in aguardiente. In the spice shop she crushed leaves of sage and oregano in the palms of her hands for the pure pleasure of smelling them, and bought a handful of cloves,

155

another of star anise, and one each of ginger root and juniper, and she walked away with tears of laughter in her eyes because the smell of the cayenne pepper made her sneeze so much. In the French cosmetics shop, as she was buying Reuter soaps and balsam water, they put a touch of the latest perfume from Paris behind her ear and gave her a breath tablet to use after smoking.

She played at buying, it is true, but what she really needed she bought without hesitation, with an authority that allowed no one to think that she was doing so for the first time, for she was conscious that she was buying not only for herself but for him as well: twelve yards of linen for their table, percale for the marriage sheets that by dawn would be damp with moisture from both their bodies, the most exquisite of everything for both of them to enjoy in the house of love. She asked for discounts and she got them, she argued with grace and dignity until she obtained the best, and she paid with pieces of gold that the shopkeepers tested for the sheer pleasure of hearing them sing against the marble counters.

Florentino Ariza spied on her in astonishment, he pursued her breathlessly, he tripped several times over the baskets of the maid who responded to his excuses with a smile, and she passed so close to him that he could smell her scent, and if she did not see him then it was not because she could not but because of the haughty manner in which she walked. To him she seemed so beautiful, so seductive, so different from ordinary people, that he could not understand why no one was as disturbed as he by the clicking of her heels on the paving stones, why no one else's heart was wild with the breeze stirred by the sighs of her veils, why everyone did not go mad with the movements of her braid, the flight of her hands, the gold of her laughter. He had not missed a single one of her gestures, not one of the indications of her character, but he did not dare approach her for fear of destroying the spell. Nevertheless, when she entered the riotous noise of the Arcade of the Scribes, he realized that he might lose the moment he had craved for so many years.

Fermina Daza shared with her schoolmates the singular idea that the Arcade of the Scribes was a place of perdition that was forbidden, of course, to decent young ladies. It was an arcaded gallery across from a little plaza where carriages and freight carts drawn by donkeys were for hire, where popular commerce became noisier and more dense. The name dated from colonial times, when the taciturn scribes in their vests and false cuffs first began to sit there, waiting for a poor man's fee to write all kinds of documents: memoranda of complaints or petition, legal testimony, cards of congratulation or condolence, love letters appropriate to any stage in an affair. They, of course, were not the ones who had given that thundering market its bad reputation but more recent peddlers who made illegal sales of all kinds of questionable merchandise smuggled in on European ships, from obscene postcards and aphrodisiac ointments to the famous

Catalonian condoms with iguana crests that fluttered when circumstances required or with flowers
at the tip that would open their petals at the will
of the user. Fermina Daza, somewhat unskilled in
the customs of the street, went through the Arcade
without noticing where she was going as she
searched for a shady refuge from the fierce eleven
o'clock sun.

She sank into the hot clamor of the shoeshine
boys and the bird sellers, the hawkers of cheap
books and the witch doctors and the sellers of
sweets who shouted over the din of the crowd:
pineapple sweets for your sweetie, coconut candy
is dandy, brown-sugar loaf for your sugar. But,
indifferent to the uproar, she was captivated on
the spot by a paper seller who was demonstrating
magic inks, red inks with an ambience of blood,
inks of sad aspect for messages of condolence,
phosphorescent inks for reading in the dark, invisible inks that revealed themselves in the light. She
wanted all of them so she could amuse Florentino
Ariza and astound him with her wit, but after
several trials she decided on a bottle of gold ink.
Then she went to the candy sellers sitting behind
their big round jars and she bought six of each
kind, pointing at the glass because she could not
make herself heard over all the shouting: six angel
hair, six tinned milk, six sesame seed bars, six
cassava pastries, six chocolate bars, six blanc-
manges, six tidbits of the queen, six of this and six
of that, six of everything, and she tossed them into
the maid's baskets with an irresistible grace and a

158

complete detachment from the stormclouds of flies on the syrup, from the continual hullabaloo and the vapor of rancid sweat that reverberated in the deadly heat. She was awakened from the spell by a good-natured black woman with a colored cloth around her head who was round and handsome and offered her a triangle of pineapple speared on the tip of a butcher's knife. She took it, she put it whole into her mouth, she tasted it, and was chewing it as her eyes wandered over the crowd, when a sudden shock rooted her on the spot. Behind her, so close to her ear that only she could hear it in the tumult, she heard his voice:

"This is not the place for a crowned goddess."

She turned her head and saw, a hand's breadth from her eyes, those other glacial eyes, that livid face, those lips petrified with fear, just as she had seen them in the crowd at Midnight Mass the first time he was so close to her, but now, instead of the commotion of love, she felt the abyss of disenchantment. In an instant the magnitude of her own mistake was revealed to her, and she asked herself, appalled, how she could have nurtured such a chimera in her heart for so long and with so much ferocity. She just managed to think: My God, poor man! Florentino Ariza smiled, tried to say something, tried to follow her, but she erased him from her life with a wave of her hand.

"No, please," she said to him. "Forget it."

That afternoon, while her father was taking his siesta, she sent Gala Placidia with a two-line letter: "Today, when I saw you, I realized that what is

159

between us is nothing more than an illusion." The maid also returned his telegrams, his verses, his dry camellias, and asked him to send back her letters and gifts, Aunt Escolástica's missal, the veins of leaves from her herbariums, the square centimeter of the habit of St. Peter Clavier, the saints' medals, the braid of her fifteenth year tied with the silk ribbon of her school uniform. In the days that followed, on the verge of madness, he wrote her countless desperate letters and besieged the maid to take them to her, but she obeyed her unequivocal instructions not to accept anything but the returned gifts. She insisted with so much zeal that Florentino Ariza sent them all back except the braid, which he would return only to Fermina Daza in person so they could talk, if just for a moment. But she refused. Fearing a decision fatal to her son, Tránsito Ariza swallowed her pride and asked Fermina Daza to grant her the favor of five minutes of her time, and Fermina Daza received her for a moment in the doorway of her house, not asking her to sit down, not asking her to come in, and without the slightest trace of weakening. Two days later, after an argument with his mother, Florentino Ariza took down from the wall of his room the stained-glass case where he displayed the braid as if it were a holy relic, and Tránsito Ariza herself returned it in the velvet box embroidered with gold thread. Florentino Ariza never had another opportunity to see or talk to Fermina Daza alone in the many chance encounters of their very long lives until fifty-one years and nine months and four days later, when he repeated his vow of eternal fidelity and everlasting love on her first night as a widow.

AT THE AGE of twenty-eight, Dr. Juvenal Urbino had been the most desirable of bachelors. He had returned from a long stay in Paris, where he had completed advanced studies in medicine and surgery, and from the time he set foot on solid ground he gave overwhelming indications that he had not wasted a minute of his time. He returned more fastidious than when he left, more in control of his nature, and none of his contemporaries seemed as rigorous and as learned as he in his science, and none could dance better to the music of the day or improvise as well on the piano. Seduced by his personal charms and by the certainty of his family fortune, the girls in his circle held secret lotteries to determine who would spend time with him, and he gambled, too, on being with them, but he managed to keep himself in a state of grace, intact and tempting, until he succumbed without resistance to the plebeian charms of Fermina Daza.

He liked to say that this love was the result of a clinical error. He himself could not believe that it had happened, least of all at that time in his life when all his reserves of passion were concentrated on the destiny of his city which, he said with great frequency and no second thoughts, had no equal in the world. In Paris, strolling arm in arm with a casual sweetheart through a late autumn, it seemed impossible to imagine a purer happiness than those golden afternoons, with the woody odor of chestnuts on the braziers, the languid accordions, the insatiable lovers kissing on the open terraces, and still he had told himself with his hand on his heart that he was not prepared to exchange all that for a single instant of his Caribbean in April. He was still too young to know that the heart's memory eliminates the bad and magnifies the good, and that thanks to this artifice we manage to endure the burden of the past. But when he stood at the railing of the ship and saw the white promontory of the colonial district again, the motionless buzzards on the roofs, the washing of the poor hung out to dry on the balconies, only then did he understand to what extent he had been an easy victim to the charitable deceptions of nostalgia.

The ship made its way across the bay through a floating blanket of drowned animals, and most of the passengers took refuge in their cabins to escape the stench. The young doctor walked down the gangplank dressed in perfect alpaca, wearing a vest and dustcoat, with the beard of a young Pasteur and his hair divided by a neat, pale part, and with enough self-control to hide the lump in his throat caused not by terror but by sadness. On the nearly deserted dock guarded by barefoot soldiers without uniforms, his sisters and mother were

163

waiting for him, along with his closest friends, whom he found insipid and without expectations despite their sophisticated airs; they spoke about the crisis of the civil war as if it were remote and foreign, but they all had an evasive tremor in their voices and an uncertainty in their eyes that belied their words. His mother moved him most of all. She was still young, a woman who had made a mark on life with her elegance and social drive, but who was now slowly withering in the aroma of camphor that rose from her widow's crepe. She must have seen herself in her son's confusion, and she asked in immediate self-defense why his skin was as pale as wax.

"It's life over there, Mother," he said. "You turn green in Paris."

A short while later, suffocating with the heat as he sat next to her in the closed carriage, he could no longer endure the unmerciful reality that came pouring in through the window. The ocean looked like ashes, the old palaces of the marquises were about to succumb to a proliferation of beggars, and it was impossible to discern the ardent scent of jasmine behind the vapors of death from the open sewers. Everything seemed smaller to him than when he left, poorer and sadder, and there were so many hungry rats in the rubbish heaps of the streets that the carriage horses stumbled in fright. On the long trip from the port to his house, located in the heart of the District of the Viceroys, he found nothing that seemed worthy of his nostalgia. Defeated, he turned his head away so that

164

his mother would not see, and he began to cry in silence.

The former palace of the Marquis de Casalduero, historic residence of the Urbino de la Calle family, had not escaped the surrounding wreckage. Dr. Juvenal Urbino discovered this with a broken heart when he entered the house through the gloomy portico and saw the dusty fountain in the interior garden and the wild brambles in flower beds where iguanas wandered, and he realized that many marble flagstones were missing and others were broken on the huge stairway with its copper railings that led to the principal rooms. His father, a physician who was more self-sacrificing than eminent, had died in the epidemic of Asian cholera that had devastated the population six years earlier, and with him had died the spirit of the house. Doña Blanca, his mother, smothered by mourning that was considered eternal, had substituted evening novenas for her dead husband's celebrated lyrical soirées and chamber concerts. His two sisters, despite their natural inclinations and festive vocation, were fodder for the covenant.

Dr. Juvenal Urbino did not sleep at all on the night of his return; he was frightened by the darkness and the silence, and he said three rosaries to the Holy Spirit and all the prayers he could remember to ward off calamities and shipwrecks and all manner of night terrors, while a curlew that had come in through a half-closed door sang every hour on the hour in his bedroom. He was tormented by the hallucinating screams of the madwomen in the Divine Shepherdess Asylum next door, the harsh dripping from the water jar into the washbasin which resonated throughout the house, the long-legged steps of the curlew wandering in his bedroom, his congenital fear of the dark, and the invisible presence of his dead father in the vast, sleeping mansion. When the curlew sang five o'clock along with the local roosters, Dr. Juvenal Urbino commended himself body and soul to Divine Providence because he did not have the heart to live another day in his rubble-strewn homeland. But in time the affection of his family, the Sundays in the country, and the covetous attentions of the unmarried women of his class mitigated the bitterness of his first impression. Little by little he grew accustomed to the sultry heat of October, to the excessive odors, to the hasty judgments of his friends, to the We'll see tomorrow, Doctor, don't worry, and at last he gave in to the spell of habit. It did not take him long to invent an easy justification for his surrender. This was his world, he said to himself, the sad, oppressive world that God had provided for him, and he was responsible to it.

The first thing he did was to take possession of his father's office. He kept in place the hard, somber English furniture made of wood that sighed in the icy cold of dawn, but he consigned to the attic the treatises on viceregal science and romantic medicine and filled the bookshelves behind their glass doors with the writings of the new French school. He took down the faded pictures, except for the one of the physician arguing with Death for the nude body of a female patient, and the Hippocratic Oath printed in Gothic letters, and he hung in their place, next to his father's only diploma, the many diverse ones he himself had received with highest honors from various schools in Europe.

He tried to impose the latest ideas at Misericordia Hospital, but this was not as easy as it had seemed in his youthful enthusiasm, for the antiquated house of health was stubborn in its attachment to atavistic superstitions, such as standing beds in pots of water to prevent disease from climbing up the legs, or requiring evening wear and chamois gloves in the operating room because it was taken for granted that elegance was an essential condition for asepsis. They could not tolerate the young newcomer's tasting a patient's urine to determine the presence of sugar, quoting Charcot and Trousseau as if they were his roommates, issuing severe warnings in class against the mortal risks of vaccines while maintaining a suspicious faith in the recent invention of suppositories. He was in conflict with everything: his renovating spirit, his maniacal sense of civic duty, his slow humor in a land of immortal pranksters—everything, in fact, that constituted his most estimable virtues provoked the resentment of his older colleagues and the sly jokes of the younger ones.

His obsession was the dangerous lack of sanitation in the city. He appealed to the highest authorities to fill in the Spanish sewers that were an immense breeding ground for rats, and to build in their place a closed sewage system whose contents would not empty into the cove at the market, as had always been the case, but into some distant drainage area instead. The well-equipped colonial houses had latrines with septic tanks, but two thirds of the population lived in shanties at the edge of the swamps and relieved themselves in the open air. The excrement dried in the sun, turned to dust, and was inhaled by everyone along with the joys of Christmas in the cool, gentle breezes of December. Dr. Juvenal Urbino attempted to force the City Council to impose an obligatory training course so that the poor could learn how to build their own latrines. He fought in vain to stop them from tossing garbage into the mangrove thickets that over the centuries had become swamps of putrefaction, and to have them collect it instead at least twice a week and incinerate it in some uninhabited area.

He was aware of the mortal threat of the drinking water. The mere idea of building an aqueduct seemed fantastic, since those who might have supported it had underground cisterns at their disposal, where water rained down over the years was collected under a thick layer of scum. Among the most valued household articles of the time were carved wooden water collectors whose stone filters dripped day and night into large earthen water jars. To prevent anyone from drinking from the aluminum cup used to dip out the water, its edges were as jagged as the crown of a mock king. The water was crystalline and cool in the dark clay, and it tasted of the forest. But Dr. Juvenal Urbino was not taken in by these appearances of purity, for he knew that despite all precautions, the bottom of each earthen jar was a sanctuary for waterworms. He had spent the slow hours of his childhood watching them with an almost mystical astonishment, convinced along with so many other people at the time that waterworms were *animes*, supernatural creatures who, from the sediment in still water, courted young maidens and could inflict furious vengeance because of love. As a boy he had seen the havoc they had wreaked in the house of Lázara Conde, a schoolteacher who dared to rebuff the *animes*, and he had seen the watery trail of glass in the street and the mountain of stones they had thrown at her windows for three days and three nights. And so it was a long while before he learned that waterworms were in reality the larvae of mosquitoes, but once he learned it he never forgot it, because from that moment on he realized that they and many other evil *animes* could pass through our simple stone filters intact.

For a long time the water in the cisterns had been honored as the cause of the scrotal hernia that so many men in the city endured not only without embarrassment but with a certain patriotic insolence. When Juvenal Urbino was in elementary school, he could not avoid a spasm of horror at the sight of men with ruptures sitting in their doorways on hot afternoons, fanning their enormous testicle as if it were a child sleeping between their legs. It was said that the hernia whistled like a lugubrious bird on stormy nights and twisted in unbearable pain when a buzzard feather was burned nearby, but no one complained about those discomforts because a large, well-carried rupture was, more than anything else, a display of masculine honor. When Dr. Juvenal Urbino returned from Europe he was already well aware of the scientific fallacy in these beliefs, but they were so rooted in local superstition that many people opposed the mineral enrichment of the water in the cisterns for fear of destroying its ability to cause an honorable rupture.

Impure water was not all that alarmed Dr. Juvenal Urbino. He was just as concerned with the lack of hygiene at the public market, a vast extension of cleared land along Las Ánimas Bay where the sailing ships from the Antilles would dock. An illustrious traveler of the period described the market as one of the most varied in the world. It was rich, in fact, and profuse and noisy, but also, perhaps, the most alarming of markets. Set on its own garbage heap, at the mercy of capricious tides, it was the spot where the bay belched filth from the sewers back onto land. The offal from the adjoining slaughterhouse was also thrown away there—severed heads, rotting viscera, animal refuse that floated, in sunshine and starshine, in a swamp of blood. The buzzards fought for it with the rats and the dogs in a perpetual scramble among the deer and succulent capons from Sotavento hanging from the eaves of the market stalls, and the spring vegetables from Arjona displayed on straw mats spread over the ground. Dr. Urbino wanted to make the place sanitary, he wanted a slaughterhouse built somewhere else and a covered market constructed with stained-glass turrets, like the one he had seen in the old *boquerías* in Barcelona, where the provisions looked so splendid and clean that it seemed a shame to eat them. But even the most complaisant of his notable friends pitied his illusory passion. That is how they were: they spent their lives proclaiming their proud origins, the historic merits of the city, the value of its relics, its heroism, its beauty, but they were blind to the decay of the years. Dr. Juvenal Urbino, on the other hand, loved it enough to see it with the eyes of truth.

"How noble this city must be," he would say, "for we have spent four hundred years trying to finish it off and we still have not succeeded."

They almost had, however. The epidemic of *cholera morbus*, whose first victims were struck down in the standing water of the market, had, in eleven weeks, been responsible for the greatest death toll in our history. Until that time the eminent dead were interred under the flagstones in the churches, in the exclusive vicinity of archbishops and capitulars, while the less wealthy were buried in the patios of convents. The poor were sent to the colonial cemetery, located on a windy hill that was separated from the city by a dry canal whose mortar bridge bore the legend carved there by order of some clairvoyant mayor: *Lasciate ogni speranza voi ch'entrate.* After the first two weeks of the cholera epidemic, the cemetery was overflowing and there was no room left in the churches despite the fact that they had dispatched the decayed remains of many nameless civic heroes to the communal ossuary. The air in the Cathedral grew thin with the vapors from badly sealed crypts, and its doors did not open again until three years later, at the time that Fermina Daza saw Florentino Ariza at close quarters as she left Midnight Mass. By the third week the cloister of the Convent of St. Clare was full all the way to its poplar-lined walks, and it was necessary to use the Community's orchard, which was twice as large, as a cemetery. There graves were dug deep enough to bury the dead on three levels, without delay and without coffins, but this had to be stopped because the brimming ground turned into a sponge that oozed sickening, infected blood at every step. Then arrangements were made to continue burying in The Hand of God, a cattle ranch less than a league from the city, which was later consecrated as the Universal Cemetery.

From the time the cholera proclamation was issued, the local garrison shot a cannon from the fortress every quarter hour, day and night, in accordance with the local superstition that gunpowder purified the atmosphere. The cholera was much more devastating to the black population, which was larger and poorer, but in reality it had no regard for color or background. It ended as suddenly as it had begun, and the extent of its

172

ravages was never known, not because this was impossible to establish but because one of our most widespread virtues was a certain reticence concerning personal misfortune.

Dr. Marco Aurelio Urbino, the father of Juvenal, was a civic hero during that dreadful time, as well as its most distinguished victim. By official decree he personally designed and directed public health measures, but on his own initiative he intervened to such an extent in every social question that during the most critical moments of the plague no higher authority seemed to exist. Years later, reviewing the chronicle of those days, Dr. Juvenal Urbino confirmed that his father's methodology had been more charitable than scientific and, in many ways, contrary to reason, so that in large measure it had fostered the voraciousness of the plague. He confirmed this with the compassion of sons whom life has turned, little by little, into the fathers of their fathers, and for the first time he regretted not having stood with his father in the solitude of his errors. But he did not dispute his merits: his diligence and his self-sacrifice and above all his personal courage deserved the many honors rendered him when the city recovered from the disaster, and it was with justice that his name was found among those of so many other heroes of less honorable wars.

He did not live to see his own glory. When he recognized in himself the irreversible symptoms that he had seen and pitied in others, he did not even attempt a useless struggle but withdrew from the world so as not to infect anyone else. Locked in a utility room at Misericordia Hospital, deaf to the calls of his colleagues and the pleas of his family, removed from the horror of the plague victims dying on the floor in the packed corridors, he wrote a letter of feverish love to his wife and children, a letter of gratitude for his existence in which he revealed how much and with how much fervor he had loved life. It was a farewell of twenty heartrending pages in which the progress of the disease could be observed in the deteriorating script, and it was not necessary to know the writer to realize that he had signed his name with his last breath. In accordance with his instructions, his ashen body was mingled with others in the communal cemetery and was not seen by anyone who loved him.

Three days later, in Paris, Dr. Juvenal Urbino received a telegram during supper with friends, and he toasted the memory of his father with champagne. He said: "He was a good man." Later he would reproach himself for his lack of maturity: he had avoided reality in order not to cry. But three weeks later he received a copy of the posthumous letter, and then he surrendered to the truth. All at once the image of the man he had known before he knew any other was revealed to him in all its profundity, the man who had raised him and taught him and had slept and fornicated with his mother for thirty-two years and yet who, before that letter, had never revealed himself body and soul because of timidity, pure and simple.

174

Until then Dr. Juvenal Urbino and his family had conceived of death as a misfortune that befell others, other people's fathers and mothers, other people's brothers and sisters and husbands and wives, but not theirs. They were people whose lives were slow, who did not see themselves growing old, or falling sick, or dying, but who disappeared little by little in their own time, turning into memories, mists from other days, until they were absorbed into oblivion. His father's posthumous letter, more than the telegram with the bad news, hurled him headlong against the certainty of death. And yet one of his oldest memories, when he was nine years old perhaps, perhaps when he was eleven, was in a way an early sign of death in the person of his father. One rainy afternoon the two of them were in the office his father kept in the house; he was drawing larks and sunflowers with colored chalk on the tiled floor, and his father was reading by the light shining through the window, his vest unbuttoned and elastic armbands on his shirt sleeves. Suddenly he stopped reading to scratch his back with a long-handled back scratcher that had a little silver hand on the end. Since he could not reach the spot that itched, he asked his son to scratch him with his nails, and as the boy did so he had the strange sensation of not feeling his own body. At last his father looked at him over his shoulder with a sad smile.

"If I died now," he said, "you would hardly remember me when you are my age."

He said it for no apparent reason, and the angel

of death hovered for a moment in the cool shadows of the office and flew out again through the window, leaving a trail of feathers fluttering in his wake, but the boy did not see them. More than twenty years had gone by since then, and Juvenal Urbino would very soon be as old as his father was that afternoon. He knew he was identical to him, and to that awareness had now been added the awful consciousness that he was also as mortal.

Cholera became an obsession for him. He did not know much more about it than he had learned in a routine manner in some marginal course, when he had found it difficult to believe that only thirty years before, it had been responsible for more than one hundred forty thousand deaths in France, including Paris. But after the death of his father he learned all there was to know about the different forms of cholera, almost as a penance to appease his memory, and he studied with the most outstanding epidemiologist of his time and the creator of the *cordons sanitaires*, Professor Adrien Proust, father of the great novelist. So that when he returned to his country and smelled the stench of the market while he was still out at sea and saw the rats in the sewers and the children rolling naked in the puddles on the streets, he not only understood how the tragedy had occurred but was certain that it would be repeated at any moment.

The moment was not long in coming. In less than a year his students at Misericordia Hospital asked for his help in treating a charity patient with a strange blue coloration all over his body. Dr.

Juvenal Urbino had only to see him from the doorway to recognize the enemy. But they were in luck: the patient had arrived three days earlier on a schooner from Curaçao and had come to the hospital clinic by himself, and it did not seem probable that he had infected anyone else. In any event, Dr. Juvenal Urbino alerted his colleagues and had the authorities warn the neighboring ports so that they could locate and quarantine the contaminated schooner, and he had to restrain the military commander of the city who wanted to declare martial law and initiate the therapeutic strategy of firing the cannon every quarter hour.

"Save that powder for when the Liberals come," he said with good humor. "We are no longer in the Middle Ages."

The patient died in four days, choked by a grainy white vomit, but in the following weeks no other case was discovered despite constant vigilance. A short while later, *The Commercial Daily* published the news that two children had died of cholera in different locations in the city. It was learned that one of them had had common dysentery, but the other, a girl of five, appeared to have been, in fact, a victim of cholera. Her parents and three brothers were separated and placed under individual quarantine, and the entire neighborhood was subjected to strict medical supervision. One of the children contracted cholera but recovered very soon, and the entire family returned home when the danger was over. Eleven more cases were reported in the next three months, and in the fifth there was an alarming outbreak, but by the end of the year it was believed that the danger of an epidemic had been averted. No one doubted that the sanitary rigor of Dr. Juvenal Urbino, more than the efficacy of his pronouncements, had made the miracle possible. From that time on, and well into this century, cholera was endemic not only in the city but along most of the Caribbean coast and the valley of the Magdalena, but it never again flared into an epidemic. The crisis meant that Dr. Juvenal Urbino's warnings were heard with greater seriousness by public officials. They established an obligatory Chair of Cholera and Yellow Fever in the Medical School, and realized the urgency of closing up the sewers and building a market far from the garbage dump. By that time, however, Dr. Urbino was not concerned with proclaiming victory, nor was he moved to persevere in his social mission, for at that moment one of his wings was broken, he was distracted and in disarray and ready to forget everything else in life, because he had been struck by the lightning of his love for Fermina Daza.

It was, in fact, the result of a clinical error. A physician who was a friend of his thought he detected the warning symptoms of cholera in an eighteen-year-old patient, and he asked Dr. Juvenal Urbino to see her. He called that very afternoon, alarmed at the possibility that the plague had entered the sanctuary of the old city, for all the cases until that time had occurred in the poor neighborhoods, and almost all of those among the black population. He encountered other, less unpleasant, surprises. From the outside, the house, shaded by the almond trees in the Park of the Evangels, appeared to be in ruins, as did the others in the colonial district, but inside there was a harmony of beauty and an astonishing light that seemed to come from another age. The entrance opened directly into a square Sevillian patio that was white with a recent coat of lime and had flowering orange trees and the same tiles on the floor as on the walls. There was an invisible sound of running water, and pots with carnations on the cornices, and cages of strange birds in the arcades. The strangest of all were three crows in a very large cage, who filled the patio with an ambiguous perfume every time they flapped their wings. Several dogs, chained elsewhere in the house, began to bark, maddened by the scent of a stranger, but a woman's shout stopped them dead, and numerous cats leapt all around the patio and hid among the flowers, frightened by the authority in the voice. Then there was such a diaphanous silence that despite the disorder of the birds and the syllables of water on stone, one could hear the desolate breath of the sea.

Shaken by the conviction that God was present, Dr. Juvenal Urbino thought that such a house was immune to the plague. He followed Gala Placidia along the arcaded corridor, passed by the window of the sewing room where Florentino Ariza had seen Fermina Daza for the first time, when the patio was still a shambles, climbed the new marble

179

stairs to the second floor, and waited to be announced before going into the patient's bedroom. But Gala Placidia came out again with a message.

"The señorita says you cannot come in now because her papa is not at home."

And so he returned at five in the afternoon, in accordance with the maid's instructions, and Lorenzo Daza himself opened the street door and led him to his daughter's bedroom. There he remained, sitting in a dark corner with his arms folded, and making futile efforts to control his ragged breathing during the examination. It was not easy to know who was more constrained, the doctor with his chaste touch or the patient in the silk chemise with her virgin's modesty, but neither one looked the other in the eye; instead, he asked questions in an impersonal voice and she responded in a tremulous voice, both of them very conscious of the man sitting in the shadows. At last Dr. Juvenal Urbino asked the patient to sit up, and with exquisite care he opened her nightdress down to the waist; her pure high breasts with the childish nipples shone for an instant in the darkness of the bedroom, like a flash of gunpowder, before she hurried to cover them with crossed arms. Imperturbable, the physician opened her arms without looking at her and examined her by direct auscultation, his ear against her skin, first the chest and then the back.

Dr. Juvenal Urbino used to say that he experienced no emotion when he met the woman with whom he would live until the day of his death. He remembered the sky-blue chemise edged in lace, the feverish eyes, the long hair hanging loose over her shoulders, but he was so concerned with the outbreak of cholera in the colonial district that he took no notice of her flowering adolescence: he had eyes only for the slightest hint that she might be a victim of the plague. She was more explicit: the young doctor she had heard so much about in connection with the cholera epidemic seemed a pedant incapable of loving anyone but himself. The diagnosis was an intestinal infection of alimentary origin, which was cured by three days of treatment at home. Relieved by this proof that his daughter had not contracted cholera, Lorenzo Daza accompanied Dr. Juvenal Urbino to the door of his carriage, paid him a gold peso for the visit, a fee that seemed excessive even for a physician to the rich, and he said goodbye with immoderate expressions of gratitude. He was overwhelmed by the splendor of the Doctor's family names, and he not only did not hide it but would have done anything to see him again, under less formal circumstances.

The case should have been considered closed. But on Tuesday of the following week, without being called and with no prior announcement, Dr. Juvenal Urbino returned to the house at the inconvenient hour of three in the afternoon. Fermina Daza was in the sewing room, having a lesson in oil painting with two of her friends, when he appeared at the window in his spotless white frock coat and his white top hat and signaled to her to come over to him. She put her palette down on a chair and tiptoed to the window, her ruffled skirt raised to keep it from dragging on the floor. She wore a diadem with a jewel that hung on her forehead, and the luminous stone was the same aloof color as her eyes, and everything in her breathed an aura of coolness. The Doctor was struck by the fact that she was dressed for painting at home as if she were going to a party. He took her pulse through the open window, he had her stick out her tongue, he examined her throat with an aluminum tongue depressor, he looked inside her lower eyelids, and each time he nodded in approval. He was less inhibited than on the previous visit, but she was more so, because she could not understand the reason for the unexpected examination if he himself had said that he would not come back unless they called him because of some change. And even more important: she did not ever want to see him again. When he finished his examination, the Doctor put the tongue depressor back into his bag, crowded with instruments and bottles of medicine, and closed it with a resounding snap.

"You are like a new-sprung rose," he said.

"Thank you."

"Thank God," he said, and he misquoted St. Thomas: "Remember that everything that is good, whatever its origin, comes from the Holy Spirit. Do you like music?"

"What is the point of that question?" she asked in turn.

"Music is important for one's health," he said.

He really thought it was, and she was going to know very soon, and for the rest of her life, that the topic of music was almost a magic formula that he used to propose friendship, but at that moment she interpreted it as a joke. Besides, her two friends, who had pretended to paint while she and Dr. Juvenal Urbino were talking at the window, tittered and hid their faces behind their palettes, and this made Fermina Daza lose her self-control. Blind with fury, she slammed the window shut. The Doctor stared at the sheer lace curtains in bewilderment, he tried to find the street door but lost his way, and in his confusion he knocked into the cage with the perfumed crows. They broke into sordid shrieking, flapped their wings in fright, and saturated the Doctor's clothing with a feminine fragrance. The thundering voice of Lorenzo Daza rooted him to the spot:

"Doctor—wait for me there."

He had seen everything from the upper floor and, swollen and livid, he came down the stairs buttoning his shirt, his side-whiskers still in an uproar after a restless siesta. The Doctor tried to overcome his embarrassment.

"I told your daughter that she is like a rose."

"True enough," said Lorenzo Daza, "but one with too many thorns."

He walked past Dr. Urbino without greeting him. He pushed open the sewing room window and shouted a rough command to his daughter:

"Come here and beg the Doctor's pardon."

The Doctor tried to intervene and stop him, but Lorenzo Daza paid no attention to him. He insisted: "Hurry up." She looked at her friends with a secret plea for understanding, and she said to her father that she had nothing to beg pardon for, she had only closed the window to keep out the sun. Dr. Urbino, with good humor, tried to confirm her words, but Lorenzo Daza insisted that he be obeyed. Then Fermina Daza, pale with rage, turned toward the window, and extending her right foot as she raised her skirt with her fingertips, she made a theatrical curtsy to the Doctor.

"I give you my most heartfelt apologies, sir," she said.

Dr. Juvenal Urbino imitated her with good humor, making a cavalier's flourish with his top hat, but he did not win the compassionate smile he had hoped for. Then Lorenzo Daza invited him to have a cup of coffee in his office to set things right, and he accepted with pleasure so that there would be no doubt whatsoever that he did not harbor a shred of resentment in his heart.

The truth was that Dr. Juvenal Urbino did not drink coffee, except for a cup first thing in the morning. He did not drink alcohol either, except for a glass of wine with meals on solemn occasions, but he not only drank down the coffee that Lorenzo Daza offered him, he also accepted a glass of anisette. Then he accepted another coffee with another anisette, and then another and another, even though he still had to make a few more calls. At first he listened with attention to the excuses that Lorenzo Daza continued to offer in the name of his daughter, whom he defined as an intelligent and serious girl, worthy of a prince whether he came from here or anywhere else, whose only defect, so he said, was her mulish character. But after the second anisette, the Doctor thought he heard Fermina Daza's voice at the other end of the patio, and his imagination went after her, followed her through the night that had just descended in the house as she lit the lights in the corridor, fumigated the bedrooms with the insecticide bomb, uncovered the pot of soup on the stove, which she was going to share that night with her father, the two of them alone at the table, she not raising her eyes, not tasting the soup, not breaking the rancorous spell, until he was forced to give in and ask her to forgive his severity that afternoon.

Dr. Urbino knew enough about women to realize that Fermina Daza would not pass by the office until he left, but he stayed nevertheless because he felt that wounded pride would give him no peace after the humiliations of the afternoon. Lorenzo Daza, who by now was almost drunk, did not seem to notice his lack of attention, for he was satisfied with his own indomitable eloquence. He talked at full gallop, chewing the flower of his unlit cigar, coughing in shouts, trying to clear his throat, attempting with great difficulty to find a comfortable position in the swivel chair, whose springs wailed like an animal in heat. He had drunk three glasses of anisette to each one drunk by his guest, and he paused only when he realized that they could no longer see each other, and he stood up to light the lamp. Dr. Juvenal Urbino looked at him in the new light, he saw that one eye was twisted like a fish's and that his words did not correspond to the movement of his lips, and he thought these were hallucinations brought on by his abuse of alcohol. Then he stood up, with the fascinating sensation that he was inside a body that belonged not to him but to someone who was still in the chair where he had been sitting, and he had to make a great effort not to lose his mind.

It was after seven o'clock when he left the office, preceded by Lorenzo Daza. There was a full moon. The patio, idealized by anisette, floated at the bottom of an aquarium, and the cages covered with cloths looked like ghosts sleeping under the hot scent of new orange blossoms. The sewing room window was open, there was a lighted lamp on the worktable, and the unfinished paintings were on their easels as if they were on exhibit. "Where art thou that thou art not here," said Dr. Urbino as he passed by, but Fermina Daza did not hear him, she could not hear him, because she was crying with rage in her bedroom, lying face down on the bed and waiting for her father so that she could make him pay for the afternoon's humiliation. The Doctor did not renounce his hope of saying goodbye to her, but Lorenzo Daza did not suggest it. He yearned for the innocence of her pulse, her cat's tongue, her tender tonsils, but he was disheartened by the idea that she never wanted to see him again and would never permit him to try to see her. When Lorenzo Daza walked into the entryway, the crows, awake under their sheets, emitted a funereal shriek. "They will peck out your eyes," the Doctor said aloud, thinking of her, and Lorenzo Daza turned around to ask him what he had said.

"It was not me," he said. "It was the anisette."

Lorenzo Daza accompanied him to his carriage, trying to force him to accept a gold peso for the second visit, but he would not take it. He gave the correct instructions to the driver for taking him to the houses of the two patients he still had to see, and he climbed into the carriage without help. But he began to feel sick as they bounced along the cobbled streets, so that he ordered the driver to take a different route. He looked at himself for a moment in the carriage mirror and saw that his image, too, was still thinking about Fermina Daza. He shrugged his shoulders. Then he belched, lowered his head to his chest, and fell asleep, and in his dream he began to hear funeral bells. First he heard those of the Cathedral and then he heard those of all the other churches, one after another, even the cracked pots of St. Julian the Hospitaler.

"Shit," he murmured in his sleep, "the dead have died."

His mother and sisters were having *café con leche* and crullers for supper at the formal table in the large dining room when they saw him appear in the door, his face haggard and his entire being dishonored by the whorish perfume of the crows. The largest bell of the adjacent Cathedral resounded in the immense empty space of the house. His mother asked him in alarm where in the world he had been, for they had looked everywhere for him so that he could attend General Ignacio María, the last grandson of the Marquis de Jaraíz de la Vera, who had been struck down that afternoon by a cerebral hemorrhage: it was for him that the bells were tolling. Dr. Juvenal Urbino listened to his mother without hearing her as he clutched the doorframe, and then he gave a half turn, trying to reach his bedroom, but he fell flat on his face in an explosion of star anise vomit.

"Mother of God," shouted his mother. "Something very strange must have happened for you to show up in your own house in this state."

The strangest thing, however, had not yet occurred. Taking advantage of the visit of the famous pianist Romeo Lussich, who played a cycle of Mozart sonatas as soon as the city had recovered from mourning the death of General Ignacio María, Dr. Juvenal Urbino had the piano from the Music School placed in a mule-drawn wagon and brought a history-making serenade to Fermina Daza. She was awakened by the first measures, and she did not have to look out the grating on the balcony to know who was the sponsor of that uncommon tribute. The only thing she regretted was not having the courage of other harassed maidens, who emptied their chamber pots on the heads of unwanted suitors. Lorenzo Daza, on the other hand, dressed without delay as the serenade was playing, and when it was over he had Dr. Juvenal Urbino and the pianist, still wearing their formal concert clothes, come in to the visitors' parlor, where he thanked them for the serenade with a glass of good brandy.

Fermina Daza soon realized that her father was trying to soften her heart. The day after the serenade, he said to her in a casual manner: "Imagine how your mother would feel if she knew you were being courted by an Urbino de la Calle." Her dry response was: "She would turn over in her grave." The friends who painted with her told her that Lorenzo Daza had been invited to lunch at the Social Club by Dr. Juvenal Urbino, who had received a severe reprimand for breaking club rules. It was only then that she learned that her father had applied for membership in the Social Club on several occasions, and that each time he had been rejected with such a large number of black balls that another attempt was not possible. But Lorenzo Daza had an infinite capacity for assimilating humiliations, and he continued his ingenious strategies for arranging casual encounters with Juvenal Urbino, not realizing that it was Juvenal Urbino who went out of his way to let himself be encountered. At times they spend hours chatting in the office, while the house seemed suspended at the edge of time because Fermina Daza would not permit anything to run its normal course until he left. The Parish Café was a good intermediate haven. It was there that Lorenzo Daza gave Juvenal

Urbino his first lessons in chess, and he was such a diligent pupil that chess became an incurable addiction that tormented him until the day of his death.

One night, a short while after the serenade by solo piano, Lorenzo Daza discovered a letter, its envelope sealed with wax, in the entryway to his house. It was addressed to his daughter and the monogram "J.U.C." was imprinted on the seal. He slipped it under the door as he passed Fermina's bedroom, and she never understood how it had come there, since it was inconceivable to her that her father had changed so much that he would bring her a letter from a suitor. She left it on the night table, for the truth was she did not know what to do with it, and there it stayed, unopened, for several days, until one rainy afternoon when Fermina Daza dreamed that Juvenal Urbino had returned to the house to give her the tongue depressor he had used to examine her throat. In the dream, the tongue depressor was made not of aluminum but of a delicious metal that she had tasted with pleasure in other dreams, so that she broke it in two unequal pieces and gave him the smaller one.

When she awoke she opened the letter. It was brief and proper, and all that Juvenal Urbino asked was permission to request her father's permission to visit her. She was impressed by its simplicity and seriousness, and the rage she had cultivated with so much love for so many days faded away on the spot. She kept the letter in the bottom of

190

her trunk, but she remembered that she had also kept Florentino Ariza's perfumed letters there, and she took it out of the chest to find another place for it, shaken by a rush of shame. Then it seemed that the most decent thing to do was to pretend she had not received it, and she burned it in the lamp, watching how the drops of wax exploded into blue bubbles above the flame. She sighed: "Poor man." And then she realized that it was the second time she had said those words in little more than a year, and for a moment she thought about Florentino Ariza, and even she was surprised at how removed he was from her life: poor man.

Three more letters arrived with the last rains in October, the first of them accompanied by a little box of violet pastilles from Flavigny Abbey. Two had been delivered at the door by Dr. Juvenal Urbino's coachman, and the Doctor had greeted Gala Placidia from the carriage window, first so that there would be no doubt that the letters were his, and second so that no one could tell him they had not been received. Moreover, both of them were sealed with his monogram in wax and written in the cryptic scrawl that Fermina Daza already recognized as a physician's handwriting. Both of them said in substance what had been said in the first, and were conceived in the same submissive spirit, but underneath their propriety one could begin to detect an impatience that was never evident in the parsimonious letters of Florentino Ariza. Fermina Daza read them as soon as they were delivered, two weeks apart, and without knowing why, she changed her mind as she was about to throw them into the fire. But she never thought of answering them.

The third letter in October had been slipped under the street door, and was in every way different from the previous ones. The handwriting was so childish that there was no doubt it had been scrawled with the left hand, but Fermina Daza did not realize that until the text itself proved to be a poison pen letter. Whoever had written it took for granted that Fermina Daza had bewitched Dr. Juvenal Urbino with her love potions, and from that supposition sinister conclusions had been drawn. It ended with a threat: if Fermina Daza did not renounce her efforts to move up in the world by means of the most desirable man in the city, she would be exposed to public disgrace.

She felt herself the victim of a grave injustice, but her reaction was not vindictive. On the contrary: she would have liked to discover who the author of the anonymous letter was in order to convince him of his error with all the pertinent explanations, for she felt certain that never, for any reason, would she respond to the wooing of Juvenal Urbino. In the days that followed she received two more unsigned letters, as perfidious as the first, but none of the three seemed to be written by the same person. Either she was the victim of a plot, or the false version of her secret love affair had gone further than anyone could imagine. She was disturbed by the idea that it was all the result of a simple indiscretion on the part of Juvenal Urbino. It occurred to her that perhaps he was different from his worthy appearance, that perhaps he talked too much when he was making house calls and boasted of imaginary conquests, as did so many other men of his class. She thought about writing him a letter to reproach him for the insult to her honor, but then she decided against the idea because that might be just what he wanted. She tried to learn more from the friends who painted with her in the sewing room, but they had heard only benign comments concerning the serenade by solo piano. She felt furious, impotent, humiliated. In contrast to her initial feeling that she wanted to meet with her invisible enemy in order to convince him of his errors, now she only wanted to cut him to ribbons with the pruning shears. She spent sleepless nights analyzing details and phrases in the anonymous letters in the hope of finding some shred of comfort. It was a vain hope: Fermina Daza was, by nature, alien to the inner world of the Urbino de la Calle family, and she had weapons for defending herself from their good actions but not from their evil ones.

This conviction became even more bitter after the fear caused by the black doll that was sent to her without any letter, but whose origin seemed easy to imagine: only Dr. Juvenal Urbino could have sent it. It had been bought in Martinique, according to the original tag, and it was dressed in an exquisite gown, its hair rippled with gold threads, and it closed its eyes when it was laid down. It seemed so charming to Fermina Daza that she overcame her scruples and laid it on her pillow during the day and grew accustomed to sleeping with it at night. After a time, however, she discovered when she awoke from an exhausting dream that the doll was growing: the original exquisite dress she had arrived in was up above her thighs, and her shoes had burst from the pressure of her feet. Fermina Daza had heard of African spells, but none as frightening as this. On the other hand, she could not imagine that a man like Juvenal Urbino would be capable of such an atrocity. She was right: the doll had been brought not by his coachman but by an itinerant shrimp-monger whom no one knew. Trying to solve the enigma, Fermina Daza thought for a moment of Florentino Ariza, whose depressed condition caused her dismay, but life convinced her of her error. The mystery was never clarified, and just thinking about it made her shudder with fear long after she was married and had children and thought of herself as destiny's darling: the happiest woman in the world.

Dr. Urbino's last resort was the mediation of Sister Franca de la Luz, Superior of the Academy of the Presentation of the Blessed Virgin, who could not deny the request of a family that had supported her Community since its establishment in the Americas. She appeared one morning at nine o'clock in the company of a novice, and for half an hour the two of them had to amuse themselves with the birdcages while Fermina Daza finished her bath. She was a masculine German with a metallic accent and an imperious gaze that had no relationship to her puerile passions. Fermina Daza hated her and everything that had to do with her more than anything in this world, and the mere memory of her false piety made scorpions crawl in her belly. Just the sight of her from the bathroom door was enough to revive the torture of school, the unbearable boredom of daily Mass, the terror of examinations, the servile diligence of the novices, all of that life distorted by the prism of spiritual poverty. Sister Franca de la Luz, on the other hand, greeted her with a joy that seemed sincere. She was surprised at how much she had grown and matured, and she praised the good judgment with which she managed the house, the good taste evident in the patio, the brazier filled with orange blossoms. She ordered the novice to wait for her without getting too close to the crows, who in a careless moment might peck out her eyes, and she looked for a private spot where she could sit down and talk alone with Fermina, who invited her into the drawing room.

It was a brief and bitter visit. Sister Franca de la Luz, wasting no time on formalities, offered honorable reinstatement to Fermina Daza. The reason for her expulsion would be erased not only from the records but also from the memory of the Community, and this would allow her to finish her studies and receive her baccalaureate degree. Fermina Daza was perplexed and wanted to know why.

"It is the request of someone who deserves everything he desires and whose only wish is to make you happy," said the nun. "Do you know who that is?"

Then she understood. She asked herself with what authority a woman who had made her life miserable because of an innocent letter served as the emissary of love, but she did not dare to speak of it. Instead she said yes, she knew that man, and by the same token she also knew that he had no right to interfere in her life.

"All he asks is that you allow him to speak with you for five minutes," said the nun. "I am certain your father will agree."

Fermina Daza's anger grew more intense at the idea that her father was an accessory to the visit.

"We saw each other twice when I was sick," she said. "Now there is no reason for us to see each other again."

"For any woman with a shred of sense, that man is a gift from Divine Providence," said the nun.

She continued to speak of his virtues, of his devotion, of his dedication to serving those in pain. As she spoke she pulled from her sleeve a gold rosary with Christ carved in marble, and dangled it in front of Fermina Daza's eyes. It was a family heirloom, more than a hundred years old, carved by a goldsmith from Siena and blessed by Clement IV.

"It is yours," she said.

Fermina Daza felt the blood pounding through her veins, and then she dared.

"I do not understand how you can lend yourself to this," she said, "if you think that love is a sin."

Sister Franca de la Luz pretended not to notice the remark, but her eyelids flamed. She continued to dangle the rosary in front of Fermina Daza's eyes.

"It would be better for you to come to an understanding with me," she said, "because after me comes His Grace the Archbishop, and it is a different story with him."

"Let him come," said Fermina Daza.

Sister Franca de la Luz tucked the gold rosary into her sleeve. Then from the other she took a well-used handkerchief squeezed into a ball and held it tight in her fist, looking at Fermina Daza from a great distance and with a smile of commiseration.

"My poor child," she sighed, "you are still thinking about that man."

Fermina Daza chewed on the impertinence as she looked at the nun without blinking, looked her straight in the eye without speaking, chewing in silence, until she saw with infinite satisfaction that those masculine eyes had filled with tears. Sister Franca de la Luz dried them with the ball of the handkerchief and stood up.

"Your father is right when he says that you are a mule," she said.

The Archbishop did not come. So the siege might have ended that day if Hildebranda Sánchez had not arrived to spend Christmas with her cousin, and life changed for both of them. They met her on the schooner from Riohacha at five o'clock in the morning, surrounded by a crowd of passengers half dead from seasickness, but she walked off the boat radiant, very much a woman, and excited after the bad night at sea. She arrived with crates of live turkeys and all the fruits of her fertile lands so that no one would lack for food during her visit. Lisímaco Sánchez, her father, sent a message asking if they needed musicians for their holiday parties, because he had the best at his disposal, and he promised to send a load of fireworks later on. He also announced that he could not come for his daughter before March, so there was plenty of time for them to enjoy life.

The two cousins began at once. From the first afternoon they bathed together, naked, the two of them making their reciprocal ablutions with water from the cistern. They soaped each other, they removed each other's nits, they compared their buttocks, their quiet breasts, each looking at herself in the other's mirror to judge with what cruelty time had treated them since the last occasion when they had seen each other undressed. Hildebranda was large and solid, with golden skin, but all the hair on her body was like a mulatta's, as short and curly as steel wool. Fermina Daza, on the other hand, had a pale nakedness, with long lines, serene skin, and straight hair. Gala Placidia had two identical beds placed in the bedroom, but at times they lay together in one and talked in the dark until dawn. They smoked long, thin highwaymen's cigars that Hildebranda had hidden in the lining of her trunk, and afterward they had to burn Armenian paper to purify the rank smell they left behind in the bedroom. Fermina Daza had smoked for the first time in Valledupar, and had continued in Fonseca and Riohacha, where as many as ten cousins would lock themselves in a room to talk about men and to smoke. She learned to smoke backward, with the lit end in her mouth, the way men smoked at night during the wars so that the glow of their cigarettes would not betray them. But she had never smoked alone. With Hildebranda in her house, she smoked every night before going to sleep, and it was then that she acquired the habit although she always hid it, even from her husband and her children, not only because it was thought improper for a woman to smoke in public but because she associated the pleasure with secrecy.

Hildebranda's trip had also been imposed by her parents in an effort to put distance between her and her impossible love, although they wanted her to think that it was to help Fermina decide on a good match. Hildebranda had accepted, hoping to mock forgetfulness as her cousin had done before her, and she had arranged with the telegraph operator in Fonseca to send her messages with the greatest prudence. And that is why her disillusion was so bitter when she learned that Fermina Daza had rejected Florentino Ariza. Moreover, Hildebranda had a universal conception of love, and she

199

believed that whatever happened to one love affected all other loves throughout the world. Still, she did not renounce her plan. With an audacity that caused a crisis of dismay in Fermina Daza, she went to the telegraph office alone, intending to win the favor of Florentino Ariza.

She would not have recognized him, for there was nothing about him that corresponded to the image she had formed from Fermina Daza. At first glance it seemed impossible that her cousin could have been on the verge of madness because of that almost invisible clerk with his air of a whipped dog, whose clothing, worthy of a rabbi in disgrace, and whose solemn manner could not perturb anyone's heart. But she soon repented of her first impression, for Florentino Ariza placed himself at her unconditional service without knowing who she was: he never found out. No one could have understood her as he did, so that he did not ask for identification or even for her address. His solution was very simple: she would pass by the telegraph office on Wednesday afternoons so that he could place her lover's answers in her hand, and nothing more. And yet when he read the written message that Hildebranda brought him, he asked if she would accept a suggestion, and she agreed. Florentino Ariza first made some corrections between the lines, erased them, rewrote them, had no more room, and at last tore up the page and wrote a completely new message that she thought very touching. When she left the telegraph office, Hildebranda was on the verge of tears.

"He is ugly and sad," she said to Fermina Daza, "but he is all love."

What most struck Hildebranda was her cousin's solitude. She seemed, she told her, an old maid of twenty. Accustomed to large scattered families in houses where no one was certain how many people were living or eating at any given time, Hildebranda could not imagine a girl her age reduced to the cloister of a private life. That was true: from the time she awoke at six in the morning until she turned out the light in the bedroom, Fermina Daza devoted herself to killing time. Life was imposed on her from outside. First, at the final rooster crow, the milkman woke her with his rapping on the door knocker. Then came the knock of the fishwife with her box of red snappers dying on a bed of algae, the sumptuous fruit sellers with vegetables from María la Baja and fruit from San Jacinto. And then, for the rest of the day, everyone knocked at the door: beggars, girls with lottery tickets, the Sisters of Charity, the knife grinder with the gossip, the man who bought bottles, the man who bought old gold, the man who bought newspapers, the fake gypsies who offered to read one's destiny in cards, in the lines of one's palm, in coffee grounds, in the water in washbasins. Gala Placidia spent the week opening and closing the street door to say no, another day, or shouting from the balcony in a foul humor to stop bothering us, damn it, we already bought everything we need. She had replaced Aunt Escolástica with so much fervor and so much grace that Fermina confused them to the point of loving her. She had the obsessions of a slave. Whenever she had free time she would go to the workroom to iron the linens; she kept them perfect, she kept them in cupboards with lavender, and she ironed and folded not only what she had just washed but also what might have lost its brightness through disuse. With the same care she continued to maintain the wardrobe of Fermina Sánchez, Fermina's mother, who had died fourteen years before. But Fermina Daza was the one who made the decisions. She ordered what they would eat, what they would buy, what had to be done in every circumstance, and in that way she determined the life in a house where in reality nothing had to be determined. When she finished washing the cages and feeding the birds, and making certain that the flowers wanted for nothing, she was at a loss. Often, after she was expelled from school, she would fall asleep at siesta and not wake up until the next day. The painting classes were only a more amusing way to kill time.

Her relationship with her father had lacked affection since the expulsion of Aunt Escolástica, although they had found the way to live together without bothering each other. When she awoke, he had already gone to his business. He rarely missed the ritual of lunch, although he almost never ate, for the aperitifs and Galician appetizers at the Parish Café satisfied him. He did not eat supper either: they left his meal on the table, everything on one plate covered by another, although they knew that he would not eat it until the next day when it was reheated for his breakfast. Once a week he gave his daughter money for expenses, which he calculated with care and she administered with rigor, but he listened with pleasure to any request she might make for unforeseen expenses. He never questioned a penny she spent, he never asked her for any explanations, but she behaved as if she had to make an accounting before the Tribunal of the Holy Office. He had never spoken to her about the nature or condition of his business, and he had never taken her to his offices in the port, which were in a location forbidden to decent young ladies even if accompanied by their fathers. Lorenzo Daza did not come home before ten o'clock at night, which was the curfew hour during the less critical periods of the wars. Until that time he would stay at the Parish Café, playing one game or another, for he was an expert in all salon games and a good teacher as well. He always came home sober, not disturbing his daughter, despite the fact that he had his first anisette when he awoke and continued chewing the end of his unlit cigar and drinking at regular intervals throughout the day. One night, however, Fermina heard him come in. She heard his cossack's step on the stair, his heavy breathing in the second-floor hallway, his pounding with the flat of his hand on her bedroom door. She opened it, and for the first time she was frightened by his twisted eye and the slurring of his words.

"We are ruined," he said. "Total ruin, so now you know."

That was all he said, and he never said it again, and nothing happened to indicate whether he had told the truth, but after that night Fermina Daza knew that she was alone in the world. She lived in a social limbo. Her former schoolmates were in a heaven that was closed to her, above all after the dishonor of her expulsion, and she was not a neighbor to her neighbors, because they had known her without a past, in the uniform of the Academy of the Presentation of the Blessed Virgin. Her father's world was one of traders and stevedores, of war refugees in the public shelter of the Parish Café, of solitary men. In the last year the painting classes had alleviated her seclusion somewhat, for the teacher preferred group classes and would bring the other pupils to the sewing room. But they were girls of varying and undefined social circumstances, and for Fermina Daza they were no more than borrowed friends whose affection ended with each class. Hildebranda wanted to open the house, air it, bring in her father's musicians and fireworks and castles of gunpowder, and have a Carnival dance whose gale winds would clear out her cousin's moth-eaten spirit, but she soon realized that her proposals were to no avail, and for a very simple reason: there was no one to invite.

In any case, it was she who thrust Fermina Daza into life. In the afternoon, after the painting classes, she allowed herself to be taken out to see the city. Fermina Daza showed her the route she had taken every day with Aunt Escolástica, the bench in the little park where Florentino Ariza pretended to read while he waited for her, the narrow streets along which he followed her, the hiding places for their letters, the sinister palace where the prison of the Holy Office had been located, later restored and converted into the Academy of the Presentation of the Blessed Virgin, which she hated with all her soul. They climbed the hill of the paupers' cemetery, where Florentino Ariza played the violin according to the direction of the winds so that she could listen to him in bed, and from there they viewed the entire historic city, the broken roofs and the decaying walls, the rubble of fortresses among the brambles, the trail of islands in the bay, the hovels of the poor around the swamps, the immense Caribbean.

On Christmas Eve they went to Midnight Mass in the Cathedral. Fermina sat where she used to hear Florentino Ariza's confidential music with greatest clarity, and she showed her cousin the exact spot where, on a night like this, she had seen his frightened eyes up close for the first time. They ventured alone as far as the Arcade of the Scribes, they bought sweets, they were amused in the shop that sold fancy paper, and Fermina Daza showed her cousin the place where she suddenly discovered that her love was nothing more than an illusion. She herself had not realized that every step she took from her house to school, every spot in the city, every moment of her recent past, did not seem to exist except by the grace of Florentino Ariza. Hildebranda pointed this out to her, but she did not admit it because she never would have admitted that Florentino Ariza, for better or for worse, was the only thing that had ever happened to her in her life.

It was during this time that a Belgian photographer came to the city and set up his studio at the end of the Arcade of the Scribes, and all those with the money to pay took advantage of the opportunity to have their pictures taken. Fermina and Hildebranda were among the first. They emptied Fermina Sánchez's clothes closet, they shared the finest dresses, the parasols, the party shoes, the hats, and they dressed as midcentury ladies. Gala Placidia helped them lace up the corsets, she showed them how to move inside the wire frames of the hoop skirts, how to wear the gloves, how to button the high-heeled boots. Hildebranda preferred a broad-brimmed hat with ostrich feathers that hung down over her shoulder. Fermina wore a more recent model decorated with painted plaster fruit and crinoline flowers. At last they giggled when they looked in the mirror and saw the resemblance to the daguerreotypes of their grandmothers, and they went off happy, laughing for all they were worth, to have the photograph of their lives taken. Gala Placidia watched from the balcony as they crossed the park with their parasols open, tottering on their high heels and pushing against the hoop skirts with their bodies as if they were children's walkers, and she gave them her blessing so that God would help them in their portraits.

There was a mob in front of the Belgian's studio because photographs were being taken of Beny Centeno, who had won the boxing championship in Panama. He wore his boxing trunks and his boxing gloves and his crown, and it was not easy to photograph him because he had to hold a fighting stance for a whole minute and breathe as little as possible, but as soon as he put up his guard, his fans burst into cheers and he could not resist the temptation to please them by showing off his skill. When it was the cousins' turn, the sky had clouded over and rain seemed imminent, but they allowed their faces to be powdered with starch and they leaned against an alabaster column with such ease that they remained motionless for more time than seemed reasonable. It was an immortal portrait. When Hildebranda died on her ranch at Flores de María, when she was almost one hundred years old, they found her copy locked in the bedroom closet, hidden among the folds of the perfumed sheets along with the fossil of a thought in a letter that had faded with time. For many years Fermina Daza kept hers on the first page of a family album, then it disappeared without anyone's knowing how, or when, and came into the possession of Florentino Ariza, through a series of unbelievable coincidences, when they were both over sixty years old.

When Fermina and Hildebranda came out of

the Belgian's studio, there were so many people in the plaza across from the Arcade of the Scribes that even the balconies were crowded. They had forgotten that their faces were white with starch and that their lips were painted with a chocolate-colored salve and that their clothes were not appropriate to the time of day or the age. The street greeted them with catcalls and mockery. They were cornered, trying to escape public derision, when the landau drawn by the golden chestnuts opened a path through the crowd. The catcalls ceased and the hostile groups dispersed. Hildebranda was never to forget her first sight of the man who appeared on the footboard: his satin top hat, his brocaded vest, his knowing gestures, the sweetness in his eyes, the authority of his presence.

Although she had never seen him before, she recognized him immediately. The previous month, Fermina Daza had spoken about him, in an offhand way and with no sign of interest, one afternoon when she did not want to pass by the house of the Marquis de Casalduero because the landau with the golden horses was stopped in front of the door. She told her who the owner was and attempted to explain the reasons for her antipathy, although she did not say a word about his courting her. Hildebranda thought no more about him. But when she identified him as a vision out of legend, standing in the carriage door with one foot on the ground and the other on the footboard, she could not understand her cousin's motives.

"Please get in," said Dr. Juvenal Urbino. "I will take you wherever you want to go."

Fermina Daza began a gesture of refusal, but Hildebranda had already accepted. Dr. Juvenal Urbino jumped down, and with his fingertips, almost without touching her, he helped her into the carriage. Fermina had no alternative but to climb in after her, her face blazing with embarrassment.

The house was only three blocks away. The cousins did not realize that Dr. Urbino had given instructions to the coachman, but he must have done so, because it took the carriage almost half an hour to reach its destination. The girls were on the principal seat and he sat opposite them, facing the back of the carriage. Fermina turned her head toward the window and was lost in the void. Hildebranda, on the other hand, was delighted, and Dr. Urbino was even more delighted by her delight. As soon as the carriage began to move, she sensed the warm odor of the leather seats, the intimacy of the padded interior, and she said that it seemed a nice place to spend the rest of one's life. Very soon they began to laugh, to exchange jokes as if they were old friends, and they began to match wits in a simple word game that consisted of placing a nonsense syllable after every other syllable. They pretended that Fermina did not understand them, although they knew she not only understood but was listening as well, which is why they did it. After much laughter, Hildebranda confessed that she could no longer endure the torture of her boots.

"Nothing could be simpler," said Dr. Urbino. "Let us see who finishes first."

He began to unlace his own boots, and Hildebranda accepted the challenge. It was not easy for her to do because the stays in the corset did not allow her to bend, but Dr. Urbino dallied until she took her boots out from under her skirt with a triumphant laugh, as if she had just fished them out of a pond. Then both of them looked at Fermina and saw her magnificent golden oriole's profile sharper than ever against the blaze of the setting sun. She was furious for three reasons: because of the undeserved situation in which she found herself, because of Hildebranda's libertine behavior, and because she was certain that the carriage was driving in circles in order to postpone their arrival. But Hildebranda had lost all restraint.

"Now I realize," she said, "that what bothered me was not my shoes but this wire cage."

Dr. Urbino understood that she was referring to her hoop skirt, and he seized the opportunity as it flew by. "Nothing could be simpler," he said. "Take it off." With the rapid movements of a prestidigitator, he removed his handkerchief from his pocket and covered his eyes with it.

"I won't look," he said.

The blindfold emphasized the purity of his lips surrounded by his round black beard and his mustache with the waxed tips, and she felt herself shaken by a sudden surge of panic. She looked at

210

Fermina, and now she saw that she was not furious but terrified that she might be capable of taking off her skirt. Hildebranda became serious and asked her in sign language: "What shall we do?" Fermina answered in the same code that if they did not go straight home she would throw herself out of the moving carriage.

"I am waiting," said the Doctor.

"You can look now," said Hildebranda.

When Dr. Juvenal Urbino removed the blindfold he found her changed, and he understood that the game had ended, and had not ended well. At a sign from him, the coachman turned the carriage around and drove into the Park of the Evangels, just as the lamplighter was making his rounds. All the churches were ringing the Angelus. Hildebranda hurried out of the carriage, somewhat disturbed at the idea that she had offended her cousin, and she said goodbye to the Doctor with a perfunctory handshake. Fermina did the same, but when she tried to withdraw her hand in its satin glove, Dr. Urbino squeezed her ring finger.

"I am waiting for your answer," he said.

Then Fermina pulled harder and her empty glove was left dangling in the Doctor's hand, but she did not wait to retrieve it. She went to bed without eating. Hildebranda, as if nothing had happened, came into the bedroom after her supper with Gala Placidia in the kitchen, and with her inborn wit, commented on the events of the afternoon. She did not attempt to hide her enthusiasm for Dr. Urbino, for his elegance and charm, and Fermina refused to comment, but was brimming with anger. At one point Hildebranda confessed that when Dr. Juvenal Urbino covered his eyes and she saw the splendor of his perfect teeth between his rosy lips, she had felt an irresistible desire to devour him with kisses. Fermina Daza turned to the wall and with no wish to offend, but smiling and with all her heart, put an end to the conversation:

"What a whore you are!" she said.

Her sleep was restless; she saw Dr. Juvenal Urbino everywhere, she saw him laughing, singing, emitting sulfurous sparks from between his teeth with his eyes blindfolded, mocking her with a word game that had no fixed rules, driving up to the paupers' cemetery in a different carriage. She awoke long before dawn and lay exhausted and wakeful, with her eyes closed, thinking of the countless years she still had to live. Later, while Hildebranda was bathing, she wrote a letter as quickly as possible, folded it as quickly as possible, put it in an envelope as quickly as possible, and before Hildebranda came out of the bathroom she had Gala Placidia deliver it to Dr. Juvenal Urbino. It was one of her typical letters, not a syllable too many or too few, in which she told the Doctor yes, he could speak to her father.

When Florentino Ariza learned that Fermina Daza was going to marry a physician with family and fortune, educated in Europe and with an extraordinary reputation for a man of his years, there was no power on earth that could raise him from his prostration. Tránsito Ariza did all she could and more, using all the stratagems of a sweetheart to console him when she realized that he had lost his speech and his appetite and was spending nights on end in constant weeping, and by the end of the week he was eating again. Then she spoke to Don Leo XII Loayza, the only one of the three brothers who was still alive, and without telling him the reason, she pleaded with him to give his nephew any job at all in the navigation company, as long as it was in a port lost in the jungle of the Magdalena, where there was no mail and no telegraph and no one who would tell him anything about this damnable city. His uncle did not give him the job out of deference to his brother's widow, for she could not bear the very existence of her husband's illegitimate son, but he did find him employment as a telegraph operator in Villa de Leyva, a dreamy city more than twenty days' journey away and almost three thousand meters above the level of the Street of Windows.

Florentino Ariza was never very conscious of that curative journey. He would remember it always, as he remembered everything that happened during that period, through the rarefied lenses of his misfortune. When he received the telegram informing him of his appointment, it did not even occur to him to consider it, but Lotario Thugut convinced him with Germanic arguments that a brilliant career awaited him in public administration. He told him: "The telegraph is the profession of the future." He gave him a pair of gloves lined with rabbit fur, a hat worthy of the steppes, and an overcoat with a plush collar, tried and proven in the icy winters of Bavaria. Uncle Leo XII gave him two serge suits and a pair of waterproof boots that had belonged to his older brother, and he also gave him cabin passage on the next boat. Tránsito Ariza altered the clothing and made it smaller for her son, who was less corpulent than his father and much shorter than the German, and she bought him woolen socks and long underwear so that he would have everything he needed to resist the rigors of the mountain wastelands. Florentino Ariza, hardened by so much suffering, attended to the preparations for his journey as if he were a dead man attending to the preparations for his own funeral. The same iron hermeticism with which he had revealed to no one but his mother the secret of his repressed passion meant that he did not tell anyone he was going away and did not say goodbye to anyone, but on the eve of his departure he committed, with full awareness, a final mad act of the heart that might well have cost him his life. At midnight he put on his Sunday suit and went to stand alone under Fermina Daza's balcony to play the love waltz he had composed for her, which was known only to the two of them and which for three years had been the emblem of their frustrated complicity. He played, murmuring the words, his violin bathed in tears, with an inspiration so intense that with the first measures the dogs on the street and then the dogs all over the city began to howl, but then, little by little, they were quieted by the spell of the music, and the waltz ended in supernatural silence. The balcony did not open, and no one appeared on the street, not even the night watchman, who almost always came running with his oil lamp in an effort to profit in some small way from serenades. The act was an exorcism of relief for Florentino Ariza, for when he put the violin back into its case and walked down the dead streets without looking back, he no longer felt that he was leaving the next morning but that he had gone away many years before with the irrevocable determination never to return.

The boat, one of three identical vessels belonging to the River Company of the Caribbean, had been renamed in honor of the founder: *Pius V Loayza*. It was a floating two-story wooden house on a wide, level iron hull, and its maximum draft of five feet allowed it to negotiate the variable depths of the river. The older boats had been built in Cincinnati in midcentury on the legendary model of the vessels that traveled the Ohio and the Mississippi, with a wheel on each side powered by a wood-fed boiler. Like them, the boats of the River Company of the Caribbean had a lower deck almost level with the water, with the steam engines and the galleys and the sleeping quarters like henhouses where the crew hung their hammocks criss-crossed at different heights. On the upper deck were the bridge, the cabins of the Captain and his officers, and a recreation and dining room, where notable passengers were invited at least once to have dinner and play cards. On the middle deck were six first-class cabins on either side of a passage that served as a common dining room, and in the prow was a sitting room open to the river, with carved wood railings and iron columns, where most of the passengers hung their hammocks at night. Unlike the older boats, these did not have paddle wheels at the sides; instead, there was an enormous wheel with horizontal paddles at the stern, just underneath the suffocating toilets on the passenger deck. Florentino Ariza had not taken the trouble to explore the boat when he came aboard on a Sunday in July at seven o'clock in the morning, as those traveling for the first time did almost by instinct. He became aware of his new milieu only at dusk, as they were sailing past the hamlet of Calamar, when he went to the stern to urinate and saw, through the opening in the toilet, the gigantic paddle wheel turning under his feet with a volcanic display of foam and steam.

He had never traveled before. He had with him a tin trunk with his clothes for the mountain wastelands, the illustrated novels that he bought in pamphlet form every month and that he himself sewed into cardboard covers, and the books of love poetry that he recited from memory and that were about to crumble into dust with so much reading. He had left behind his violin, for he identified it too closely with his misfortune, but his mother had obliged him to take his *petate*, a very popular and practical bedroll, with its pillow, sheet, small pewter chamber pot, and mosquito netting, all of this wrapped in straw matting tied with two hemp ropes for hanging a hammock in an emergency. Florentino Ariza had not wanted to take it, for he thought it would be useless in a cabin that provided bed and bedclothes, but from the very first night he had reason once again to be grateful for his mother's good sense. At the last moment, a passenger dressed in evening clothes boarded the boat; he had arrived early that morning on a ship from Europe and was accompanied by the Provincial Governor himself. He wanted to continue his journey without delay, along with his wife and daughter and liveried servant and seven trunks with gold fittings, which were almost too bulky for the stairway. To accommodate the unexpected travelers, the Captain, a giant from Curaçao, called on the passengers' indigenous sense of patriotism. In a jumble of Spanish and Curaçao patois, he explained to Florentino Ariza that the man in evening dress was the new plenipotentiary from England, on his way to the capital of the Republic; he reminded him of how that kingdom had provided us with decisive resources in our struggle for independence from Spanish rule, and that as a consequence no sacrifice was too great if it would allow a family of such distinction to feel more at home in our country than in their own. Florentino Ariza, of course, gave up his cabin.

At first he did not regret it, for the river was high at that time of year and the boat navigated without any difficulty for the first two nights.

After dinner, at five o'clock, the crew distributed folding canvas cots to the passengers, and each person opened his bed wherever he could find room, arranged it with the bedclothes from his *petate*, and set the mosquito netting over that. Those with hammocks hung them in the salon, and those who had nothing slept on the tables in the dining room, wrapped in the tablecloths that were not changed more than twice during the trip. Florentino Ariza was awake most of the night, thinking that he heard the voice of Fermina Daza in the fresh river breeze, ministering to his solitude with her memory, hearing her sing in the respiration of the boat as it moved like a great animal through the darkness, until the first rosy streaks appeared on the horizon and the new day suddenly broke over deserted pastureland and misty swamps. Then his journey seemed yet another proof of his mother's wisdom, and he felt that he had the fortitude to endure forgetting.

After three days of favorable water, however, it became more difficult to navigate between inopportune sandbanks and deceptive rapids. The river turned muddy and grew narrower and narrower in a tangled jungle of colossal trees where there was only an occasional straw hut next to the piles of wood for the ship's boilers. The screeching of the parrots and the chattering of the invisible monkeys seemed to intensify the midday heat. At night it was necessary to anchor the boat in order to sleep, and then the simple fact of being alive became unendurable. To the heat and the mosquitoes was

218

added the reek of strips of salted meat hung to dry on the railings. Most of the passengers, above all the Europeans, abandoned the pestilential stench of their cabins and spent the night walking the decks, brushing away all sorts of predatory creatures with the same towel they used to dry their incessant perspiration, and at dawn they were exhausted and swollen with bites.

Moreover, another episode of the intermittent civil war between Liberals and Conservatives had broken out that year, and the Captain had taken very strict precautions to maintain internal order and protect the safety of the passengers. Trying to avoid misunderstandings and provocations, he prohibited the favorite pastime during river voyages in those days, which was to shoot the alligators sunning themselves on the broad sandy banks. Later on, when some of the passengers divided into two opposing camps during an argument, he confiscated everyone's weapons and gave his word of honor that they would be returned at the end of the journey. He was inflexible even with the British minister who, on the morning following their departure, appeared in a hunting outfit, with a precision carbine and a double-barreled rifle for killing tigers. The restrictions became even more drastic above the port of Tenerife, where they passed a boat flying the yellow plague flag. The Captain could not obtain any further information regarding that alarming sign because the other vessel did not respond to his signals. But that same day they encountered another boat, with a cargo of cattle for Jamaica, and were informed that the vessel with the plague flag was carrying two people sick with cholera, and that the epidemic was wreaking havoc along the portion of the river they still had to travel. Then the passengers were prohibited from leaving the boat, not only in the ports but even in the uninhabited places where they stopped to take on wood. So that until they reached the final port, a trip of six days, the passengers acquired the habits of prisoners, including the pernicious contemplation of a packet of pornographic Dutch postcards that circulated from hand to hand without anyone's knowing where it came from, although no veteran of the river was unaware that this was only a tiny sampling of the Captain's legendary collection. But, in the end, even that distraction with no expectation only increased the tedium.

Florentino Ariza endured the hardships of the journey with the mineral patience that had brought sorrow to his mother and exasperation to his friends. He spoke to no one. The days were easy for him as he sat at the rail, watching the motionless alligators sunning themselves on sandy banks, their mouths open to catch butterflies, watching the flocks of startled herons that rose without warning from the marshes, the manatees that nursed their young at large maternal teats and startled the passengers with their woman's cries. On a single day he saw three bloated, green, human corpses float past, with buzzards sitting on them. First the bodies of two men went by, one of them without a head, and then a very young girl, whose medusan locks undulated in the boat's wake. He never knew, because no one ever knew, if they were victims of the cholera or the war, but the nauseating stench contaminated his memory of Fermina Daza.

That was always the case: any event, good or bad, had some relationship to her. At night, when the boat was anchored and most of the passengers walked the decks in despair, he perused the illustrated novels he knew almost by heart under the carbide lamp in the dining room, which was the only one kept burning until dawn, and the dramas he had read so often regained their original magic when he replaced the imaginary protagonists with people he knew in real life, reserving for himself and Fermina Daza the roles of star-crossed lovers. On other nights he wrote anguished letters and then scattered their fragments over the water that flowed toward her without pause. And so the most difficult hours passed for him, at times in the person of a timid prince or a paladin of love, at other times in his own scalded hide of a lover in the middle of forgetting, until the first breezes began to blow and he went to doze in the lounge chairs by the railing.

One night when he stopped his reading earlier than usual and was walking, distracted, toward the toilets, a door opened as he passed through the dining room, and a hand like the talon of a hawk seized him by the shirt sleeve and pulled him into a cabin. In the darkness he could barely see the

221

naked woman, her ageless body soaked in hot perspiration, her breathing heavy, who pushed him onto the bunk face up, unbuckled his belt, unbuttoned his trousers, impaled herself on him as if she were riding horseback, and stripped him, without glory, of his virginity. Both of them fell, in an agony of desire, into the void of a bottomless pit that smelled of a salt marsh full of prawns. Then she lay for a moment on top of him, gasping for breath, and she ceased to exist in the darkness.

"Now go and forget all about it," she said. "This never happened."

The assault had been so rapid and so triumphant that it could only be understood not as a sudden madness caused by boredom but as the fruit of a plan elaborated over time and down to its smallest detail. This gratifying certainty increased Florentino Ariza's eagerness, for at the height of pleasure he had experienced a revelation that he could not believe, that he even refused to admit, which was that his illusory love for Fermina Daza could be replaced by an earthly passion. And so it was that he felt compelled to discover the identity of the mistress of violation in whose panther's instincts he might find the cure for his misfortune. But he was not successful. On the contrary, the more he delved into the search the further he felt from the truth.

The assault had taken place in the last cabin, but this communicated with the one next to it by a door, so that the two rooms had been converted into family sleeping quarters with four bunks. The occupants were two young women, another who was rather mature but very attractive, and an infant a few months old. They had boarded in Barranco de Loba, the port where cargo and passengers from Mompox were picked up ever since that city had been excluded from the itineraries of the steamboats because of the river's caprices, and Florentino Ariza had noticed them only because they carried the sleeping child in a large birdcage.

They dressed as if they were traveling on a fashionable ocean liner, with bustles under their silk skirts and lace gorgets and broad-brimmed hats trimmed with crinoline flowers, and the two younger women changed their entire outfits several times a day, so that they seemed to carry with them their own springlike ambience while the other passengers were suffocating in the heat. All three were skilled in the use of parasols and feathered fans, but their intentions were as indecipherable as those of other women from Mompox. Florentino Ariza could not even determine their relationship to one another, although he had no doubt they came from the same family. At first he thought that the older one might be the mother of the other two, but then he realized she was not old enough for that, and that she also wore partial mourning that the others did not share. He could not imagine that one of them would have dared to do what she did while the others were sleeping in the nearby bunks, and the only reasonable supposition was that she had taken advantage of a fortuitous, or perhaps prearranged, moment when she was alone in the cabin. He observed that at times two of them stayed out for a breath of cool air until very late, while the third remained behind, caring for the infant, but one night when it was very hot all three of them left the cabin, carrying the baby, who was asleep in the wicker cage covered with gauze.

Despite the tangle of clues, Florentino Ariza soon rejected the possibility that the oldest had been the perpetrator of the assault, and with as much dispatch he also absolved the youngest, who was the most beautiful and the boldest of the three. He did so without valid reasons, but only because his avid observations of the three women had persuaded him to accept as truth the profound hope that his sudden lover was in fact the mother of the caged infant. That supposition was so seductive that he began to think about her with more intensity than he thought about Fermina Daza, ignoring the evidence that this recent mother lived only for her child. She was no more than twenty-five, she was slender and golden, she had Portuguese eyelids that made her seem even more aloof, and any man would have been satisfied with only the crumbs of the tenderness that she lavished on her son. From breakfast until bedtime she was busy with him in the salon, while the other two played Chinese checkers, and when at last she managed to put him to sleep she would hang the wicker cage from the ceiling on the cooler side of the railing. She did not ignore him, however, even when he was asleep, but would rock the cage, singing love songs under her breath while her thoughts flew high above the miseries of the journey. Florentino Ariza clung to the illusion that sooner or later she would betray herself, if only with a gesture. He even observed the changes in her breathing, watching the reliquary that hung on her batiste blouse as he looked at her without dissimulation over the book he pretended to read, and he committed the calculated impertinence of changing his seat in the dining room so that he would face her. But he could not find the slightest hint that she was in fact the repository of the other half of his secret. The only thing of hers he had, and that only because her younger companion called to her, was her first name: Rosalba.

On the eighth day, the boat navigated with great difficulty through a turbulent strait squeezed between marble cliffs, and after lunch it anchored in Puerto Nare. This was the disembarkation point for those passengers who would continue their journey into Antioquia, one of the provinces most affected by the new civil war. The port consisted of half a dozen palm huts and a store made of wood, with a zinc roof, and it was protected by several squads of barefoot and ill-armed soldiers because there had been rumors of a plan by the insurrectionists to plunder the boats. Behind the houses, reaching to the sky, rose a promontory of uncultivated highland with a wrought-iron cornice at the edge of the precipice. No one on board slept well that night, but the attack did not materialize, and in the morning the port was transformed into a Sunday fair, with Indians selling Tagua amulets and love potions amid packs of animals ready to begin the six-day ascent to the orchid jungles of the central mountain range.

Florentino Ariza passed the time watching black men unload the boat onto their backs, he watched them carry off crates of china, and pianos for the spinsters of Envigado, and he did not realize until it was too late that Rosalba and her party were among the passengers who had stayed on shore. He saw them when they were already sitting side-saddle, with their Amazons' boots and their parasols in equatorial colors, and then he took the step he had not dared to take during the preceding days: he waved goodbye to Rosalba, and the three women responded in kind, with a familiarity that cut him to the quick because his boldness came too late. He saw them round the corner of the store, followed by the mules carrying their trunks, their hatboxes, and the baby's cage, and soon afterward he saw them ascend along the edge of the precipice like a line of ants and disappear from his life. Then he felt alone in the world, and the memory of Fermina Daza, lying in ambush in recent days, dealt him a mortal blow.

He knew that she was to have an elaborate wedding, and then the being who loved her most, who would love her forever, would not even have the right to die for her. Jealousy, which until that time had been drowned in weeping, took possession of his soul. He prayed to God that the lightning of divine justice would strike Fermina Daza as she was about to give her vow of love and obedience to a man who wanted her for his wife only as a social adornment, and he went into rapture at the vision of the bride, his bride or no one's, lying face up on the flagstones of the Cathedral, her orange blossoms laden with the dew of death, and the foaming torrent of her veil covering the funerary marbles of the fourteen bishops who were buried in front of the main altar. Once his revenge was consummated, however, he repented of his own wickedness, and then he saw Fermina Daza rising from the ground, her spirit intact, distant but alive, because it was not possible for him to imagine the world without her. He did not sleep again, and if at times he sat down to pick at food, it was in the hope that Fermina Daza would be at the table or, conversely, to deny her the homage of fasting for her sake. At times his solace was the certainty that during the intoxication of her wedding celebration, even during the feverish nights of her honeymoon, Fermina Daza would suffer one moment, one at least but one in any event, when the phantom of the sweetheart she had scorned, humiliated, and insulted would appear in her thoughts, and all her happiness would be destroyed.

The night before they reached the port of Caracolí, which was the end of the journey, the Captain gave the traditional farewell party, with a woodwind orchestra composed of crew members, and fireworks from the bridge. The minister from Great Britain had survived the odyssey with exemplary stoicism, shooting with his camera the animals they would not allow him to kill with his rifles, and not a night went by that he was not seen in evening dress in the dining room. But he came to the final party wearing the tartans of the MacTavish clan, and he played the bagpipe for everyone's entertainment and taught those who were interested how to dance his national dances, and before daybreak he almost had to be carried to his cabin. Florentino Ariza, prostrate with grief, had gone to the farthest corner of the deck where the noise of the revelry could not reach him, and he put on Lotario Thugut's overcoat in an effort to overcome the shivering in his bones. He had awakened at five that morning, as the condemned man awakens at dawn on the day of his execution, and for that entire day he had done nothing but imagine, minute by minute, each of the events at Fermina Daza's wedding. Later, when he returned home, he realized that he had made a mistake in the time and that everything had been different from what he had imagined, and he even had the good sense to laugh at his fantasy.

But in any case, it was a Saturday of passion, which culminated in a new crisis of fever when he thought the moment had come for the newlyweds to flee in secret through a false door to give themselves over to the delights of their first night. Someone saw him shivering with fever and informed the Captain, who, fearing a case of cholera, left the party with the ship's doctor, and the doctor took the precaution of sending Florentino to the quarantine cabin with a dose of bromides. The next day, however, when they sighted the cliffs of Caracolí, his fever had disappeared and his spirits were elated, because in the marasmus of the sedatives he had resolved once and for all that he did not give a damn about the brilliant future of the telegraph and that he would take this very same boat back to his old Street of Windows.

It was not difficult to persuade them to give him return passage in exchange for the cabin he had surrendered to the representative of Queen Victoria. The Captain also attempted to dissuade him, arguing that the telegraph was the science of the future. So much so, he said, that they were already devising a system for installing it on boats. But he resisted all arguments, and in the end the Captain took him home, not because he owed him the price of the cabin but because he knew of his excellent connections to the River Company of the Caribbean.

The trip downriver took less than six days, and Florentino Ariza felt that he was home again from the moment they entered Mercedes Lagoon at dawn and he saw the trail of lights on the fishing canoes undulating in the wake of the boat. It was still dark when they docked in Niño Perdido Cove, nine leagues from the bay and the last port for riverboats until the old Spanish channel was dredged and put back into service. The passengers would have to wait until six o'clock in the morning to board the fleet of sloops for hire that would carry them to their final destination. But Florentino

Ariza was so eager that he sailed much earlier on the mail sloop, whose crew acknowledged him as one of their own. Before he left the boat he succumbed to the temptation of a symbolic act: he threw his *petate* into the water, and followed it with his eyes as it floated past the beacon lights of the invisible fishermen, left the lagoon, and disappeared in the ocean. He was sure he would not need it again for all the rest of his days. Never again, because never again would he abandon the city of Fermina Daza.

The bay was calm at daybreak. Above the floating mist Florentino Ariza saw the dome of the Cathedral, gilded by the first light of dawn, he saw the dovecotes on the flat roofs, and orienting himself by them, he located the balcony of the palace of the Marquis de Casalduero, where he supposed that the lady of his misfortune was still dozing, her head on the shoulder of her satiated husband. That idea broke his heart, but he did nothing to suppress it; on the contrary, he took pleasure in his pain. The sun was beginning to grow hot as the mail sloop made its way through the labyrinth of sailing ships that lay at anchor where the countless odors from the public market and the decaying matter on the bottom of the bay blended into one pestilential stench. The schooner from Riohacha had just arrived, and gangs of stevedores in water up to their waists lifted the passengers over the side and carried them to shore. Florentino Ariza was the first to jump on land from the mail sloop, and from that time on he no longer detected the fetid reek of the bay in the city, but was aware only of the personal fragrance of Fermina Daza. Everything smelled of her.

He did not return to the telegraph office. His only interest seemed to be the serialized love novels and the volumes of the Popular Library that his mother continued to buy for him and that he continued to read again and again, lying in his hammock, until he learned them by heart. He did not even ask for his violin. He reestablished relations with his closest friends, and sometimes they played billiards or conversed in the outdoor cafés under the arches around the Plaza of the Cathedral, but he did not go back to the Saturday night dances: he could not conceive of them without her.

On the morning of his return from his inconclusive journey, he learned that Fermina Daza was spending her honeymoon in Europe, and his agitated heart took it for granted that she would live there, if not forever then for many years to come. This certainty filled him with his first hope of forgetting. He thought of Rosalba, whose memory burned brighter as the other's dimmed. It was during this time that he grew the mustache with the waxed tips that he would keep for the rest of his life and that changed his entire being, and the idea of substituting one love for another carried him along surprising paths. Little by little the fragrance of Fermina Daza became less frequent and less intense, and at last it remained only in white gardenias.

One night during the war, when he was drifting, not knowing what direction his life should take, the celebrated Widow Nazaret took refuge in his house because hers had been destroyed by cannon fire during the siege by the rebel general Ricardo Gaitán Obeso. It was Tránsito Ariza who took control of the situation and sent the widow to her son's bedroom on the pretext that there was no space in hers, but actually in the hope that another love would cure him of the one that did not allow him to live. Florentino Ariza had not made love since he lost his virginity to Rosalba in the cabin on the boat, and in this emergency it seemed natural to him that the widow should sleep in the bed and he in the hammock. But she had already made the decision for him. She sat on the edge of the bed where Florentino Ariza was lying, not knowing what to do, and she began to speak to him of her inconsolable grief for the husband who had died three years earlier, and in the meantime she removed her widow's weeds and tossed them in the air until she was not even wearing her wedding ring. She took off the taffeta blouse with the beaded embroidery and threw it across the room onto the easy chair in the corner, she tossed her bodice over her shoulder to the other side of the bed, with one pull she removed her long ruffled skirt, her satin garter belt and funereal stockings, and she threw everything on the floor until the room was carpeted with the last remnants of her mourning. She did it with so much joy, and with such well-measured pauses, that each of her

232

gestures seemed to be saluted by the cannon of the attacking troops, which shook the city down to its foundations. Florentino Ariza tried to help her unfasten her stays, but she anticipated him with a deft maneuver, for in five years of matrimonial devotion she learned to depend on herself in all phases of love, even the preliminary stages, with no help from anyone. Then she removed her lace panties, sliding them down her legs with the rapid movements of a swimmer, and at last she was naked.

She was twenty-eight years old and had given birth three times, but her naked body preserved intact the giddy excitement of an unmarried woman. Florentino Ariza was never to understand how a few articles of penitential clothing could have hidden the drives of that wild mare who, choking on her own feverish desire, undressed him as she had never been able to undress her husband, who would have thought her perverse, and tried, with the confusion and innocence of five years of conjugal fidelity, to satisfy in a single assault the iron abstinence of her mourning. Before that night, and from the hour of grace when her mother gave birth to her, she had never even been in the same bed with any man other than her dead husband.

She did not permit herself the vulgarity of remorse. On the contrary. Kept awake by the gunfire whizzing over the roofs, she continued to evoke her husband's excellent qualities until daybreak, not reproaching him for any disloyalty other than his having died without her, which was mitigated by her conviction that he had never belonged to her as much as he did now that he was in the coffin nailed shut with a dozen three-inch nails and two meters under the ground.

"I am happy," she said, "because only now do I know for certain where he is when he is not at home."

That night she stopped wearing mourning once and for all, without passing through the useless intermediate stage of blouses with little gray flowers, and her life was filled with love songs and provocative dresses decorated with macaws and spotted butterflies, and she began to share her body with anyone who cared to ask for it. When the troops of General Gaitán Obeso were defeated after a sixty-three-day siege, she rebuilt the house that had been damaged by cannon fire, adding a beautiful sea terrace that overlooked the breakwater where the surf would vent its fury during the stormy season. That was her love nest, as she called it without irony, where she would receive only men she liked, when she liked, how she liked, and without charging one red cent, because in her opinion it was the men who were doing her the favor. In a very few cases she would accept a gift, as long as it was not made of gold, and she managed everything with so much skill that no one could have presented conclusive evidence of improper conduct. On only one occasion did she hover on the edge of public scandal, when the rumor circulated that Archbishop Dante de Luna had not died by accident after eating a plate of poisonous mushrooms but had eaten them intentionally because she threatened to expose him if he persisted in his sacrilegious solicitations. As she used to say between peals of laughter, she was the only free woman in the province.

The Widow Nazaret never missed her occasional appointments with Florentino Ariza, not even during her busiest times, and it was always without pretensions of loving or being loved, although always in the hope of finding something that resembled love, but without the problems of love. Sometimes he went to her house, and then they liked to sit on the sea terrace, drenched by salt spray, watching the dawn of the whole world on the horizon. With all his perseverance, he tried to teach her the tricks he had seen others perform through the peepholes in the transient hotel, along with the theoretical formulations preached by Lotario Thugut on his nights of debauchery. He persuaded her to let themselves be observed while they made love, to replace the conventional missionary position with the bicycle on the sea, or the chicken on the grill, or the drawn-and-quartered angel, and they almost broke their necks when the cords snapped as they were trying to devise something new in a hammock. The lessons were to no avail. The truth is that she was a fearless apprentice but lacked all talent for guided fornication. She never understood the charm of serenity in bed, never had a moment of invention, and her orgasms were inopportune and epidermic: an

235

uninspired lay. For a long time Florentino Ariza lived with the deception that he was the only one, and she humored him in that belief until she had the bad luck to talk in her sleep. Little by little, listening to her sleep, he pieced together the navigation chart of her dreams and sailed among the countless islands of her secret life. In this way he learned that she did not want to marry him, but did feel joined to his life because of her immense gratitude to him for having corrupted her. She often said to him:

"I adore you because you made me a whore."

Said in another way, she was right. Florentino Ariza had stripped her of the virginity of a conventional marriage, more pernicious than congenital virginity or the abstinence of widowhood. He had taught her that nothing one does in bed is immoral if it helps to perpetuate love. And something else that from that time on would be her reason for living: he convinced her that one comes into the world with a predetermined allotment of lays, and whoever does not use them for whatever reason, one's own or someone else's, willingly or unwillingly, loses them forever. It was to her credit that she took him at his word. Still, because he thought he knew her better than anyone else, Florentino Ariza could not understand why a woman of such puerile resources should be so popular—a woman, moreover, who never stopped talking in bed about the grief she felt for her dead husband. The only explanation he could think of, one that could not be denied, was that the Widow

Nazaret had enough tenderness to make up for what she lacked in the marital arts. They began to see each other with less frequency as she widened her horizons and he exploited his, trying to find solace in other hearts for his pain, and at last, with no sorrow, they forgot each other.

That was Florentino Ariza's first bedroom love. But instead of their forming a permanent union, of the kind his mother dreamed about, both used it to embark on a profligate way of life. Florentino Ariza developed methods that seemed incredible in someone like him, taciturn and thin and dressed like an old man from another time. He had two advantages working in his favor, however. One was an unerring eye that promptly spotted the woman, even in a crowd, who was waiting for him, though even then he courted her with caution, for he felt that nothing was more embarrassing or more demeaning than a refusal. The other was that women promptly identified him as a solitary man in need of love, a street beggar as humble as a whipped dog, who made them yield without conditions, without asking him for anything, without hoping for anything from him except the tranquillity of knowing they had done him a favor. These were his only weapons, and with them he joined in historic battles of absolute secrecy, which he recorded with the rigor of a notary in a coded book, recognizable among many others by the title that said everything: *Women*. His first notation was the Widow Nazaret. Fifty years later, when Fermina Daza was freed from her sacramental sentence, he had some twenty-five notebooks, with six hundred twenty-two entries of long-term liaisons, apart from the countless fleeting adventures that did not even deserve a charitable note.

After six months of furious lovemaking with the Widow Nazaret, Florentino Ariza himself was convinced that he had survived the torment of Fermina Daza. He not only believed it, he also discussed it several times with Tránsito Ariza during the two years of Fermina Daza's wedding trip, and he continued to believe it with a feeling of boundless freedom until one fateful Sunday when, with no warning and no presentiments, he saw her leaving High Mass on her husband's arm, besieged by the curiosity and flattery of her new world. The same ladies from fine families who at first had scorned and ridiculed her for being an upstart without a name went out of their way to make her feel like one of them, and she intoxicated them with her charm. She had assumed the condition of woman of the world to such perfection that Florentino Ariza needed a moment of reflection to recognize her. She was another person: the composure of an older woman, the high boots, the hat with the veil and colored plume from some Oriental bird—everything about her was distinctive and confident, as if it had been hers from birth. He found her more beautiful and youthful than ever, but more lost to him than she had ever been, although he did not understand why until he saw the curve of her belly under the silk tunic: she was in her sixth month of pregnancy. But what impressed him most was that she and her husband made an admirable couple, and both of them negotiated the world with so much fluidity that they seemed to float above the pitfalls of reality. Florentino Ariza did not feel either jealousy or rage—only great contempt for himself. He felt poor, ugly, inferior, and unworthy not only of her but of any other woman on the face of the earth.

So she had returned. She came back without any reason to repent of the sudden change she had made in her life. On the contrary, she had fewer and fewer such reasons, above all after surviving the difficulties of the early years, which was especially admirable in her case, for she had come to her wedding night still trailing clouds of innocence. She had begun to lose them during her journey through Cousin Hildebranda's province. In Valledupar she realized at last why the roosters chase the hens, she witnessed the brutal ceremony of the burros, she watched the birth of calves, and she listened to her cousins talking with great naturalness about which couples in the family still made love and which ones had stopped, and when, and why, even though they continued to live together. That was when she was initiated into solitary love, with the strange sensation of discovering something that her instincts had always known, first in bed, holding her breath so she would not give herself away in the bedroom she shared with half a dozen cousins, and then, with eagerness and unconcern, sprawling on the bathroom floor, her

239

hair loose, smoking her first mule drivers' cigarette. She always did it with certain pangs of conscience, which she could overcome only after she was married, and always in absolute secrecy, although her cousins boasted to each other not only about the number of orgasms they had in one day but even about their form and size. But despite those bewitching first rites, she was still burdened by the belief that the loss of virginity was a bloody sacrifice.

So that her wedding, one of the most spectacular of the final years of the last century, was for her the prelude to horror. The anguish of the honeymoon affected her much more than the social uproar caused by her marriage to the most incomparably elegant young man of the day. When the banns were announced at High Mass in the Cathedral, Fermina Daza received anonymous letters again, some of them containing death threats, but she took scant notice of them because all the fear of which she was capable was centered on her imminent violation. Although that was not her intention, it was the correct way to respond to anonymous letters from a class accustomed by the affronts of history to bow before faits accomplis. So that little by little they swallowed their opposition as it became clear that the marriage was irrevocable. She noticed the gradual changes in the attention paid her by livid women, degraded by arthritis and resentment, who one day were convinced of the uselessness of their intrigues and appeared unannounced in the little Park of the

Evangels as if it were their own home, bearing recipes and engagement gifts. Tránsito Ariza knew that world, although this was the only time it caused her suffering in her own person, and she knew that her clients always reappeared on the eve of great parties to ask her please to dig down into her jars and lend thcm their pawned jewels for only twenty-four hours in exchange for the payment of additional interest. It had been a long while since this had occurred to the extent it did now, the jars emptied so that the ladies with long last names could emerge from their shadowy sanctuaries and, radiant in their own borrowed jewels, appear at a wedding more splendid than any that would be seen for the rest of the century and whose ultimate glory was the sponsorship of Dr. Rafael Núñez, three times President of the Republic, philosopher, poet, and author of the words to the national anthem, as anyone could learn, from that time on, in some of the more recent dictionaries. Fermina Daza came to the main altar of the Cathedral on the arm of her father, whose formal dress lent him, for the day, an ambiguous air of respectability. She was married forever after at the main altar of the Cathedral, with a Mass at which three bishops officiated, at eleven o'clock in the morning on the day of the Holy Trinity, and without a single charitable thought for Florentino Ariza, who at that hour was delirious with fever, dying because of her, lying without shelter on a boat that was not to carry him to forgetting. During the ceremony, and later at the reception, she wore a smile that seemed painted on with white lead, a soulless grimace that some interpreted as a mocking smile of victory, but in reality was her poor attempt at disguising the terror of a virgin bride.

It was fortunate that unforeseen circumstances, combined with her husband's understanding, re-solved the first three nights without pain. It was providential. The ship of the Compagnie Générale Transatlantique, its itinerary upset by bad weather in the Caribbean, announced only three days in advance that its departure had been moved ahead by twenty-four hours, so that it would not sail for La Rochelle on the day following the wedding, as had been planned for the past six months, but on that same night. No one believed that the change was not another of the many elegant surprises the wedding had to offer, for the reception ended after midnight on board the brightly lit ocean liner, with a Viennese orchestra that was premiering the most recent waltzes by Johann Strauss on this voyage. So that various members of the wedding party, soggy with champagne, had to be dragged ashore by their long-suffering wives when they began to ask the stewards if there were any free cabins so they could continue the celebration all the way to Paris. The last to leave saw Lorenzo Daza outside the port taverns, sitting on the ground in the middle of the street, his tuxedo in ruins. He was crying with tremendous loud wails, the way Arabs cry for their dead, sitting in a trickle of fouled water that might well have been a pool of tears.

Not on the first night on rough seas, or on the following nights of smooth sailing, or ever in her very long married life did the barbarous acts occur that Fermina Daza had feared. Despite the size of the ship and the luxuries of their stateroom, the first night was a horrible repetition of the schooner trip from Riohacha, and her husband, a diligent physician, did not sleep at all so he could comfort her, which was all that an overly distinguished physician knew how to do for seasickness. But the storm abated on the third day, after the port of Guayra, and by that time they had spent so much time together and had talked so much that they felt like old friends. On the fourth night, when both resumed their ordinary habits, Dr. Juvenal Urbino was surprised that his young wife did not pray before going to sleep. She was frank with him: the duplicity of the nuns had provoked in her a certain resistance to rituals, but her faith was intact, and she had learned to maintain it in silence. She said: "I prefer direct communication with God." He understood her reasoning, and from then on they each practiced the same religion in their own way. They had had a brief engagement, but a rather informal one for that time: Dr. Urbino had visited her in her house, without a chaperone, every day at sunset. She would not have permitted him to touch even her fingertips before the episcopal blessing, but he had not attempted to. It was on the first calm night, when they were in bed but still dressed, that he began his first caresses with so much care that his suggestion that she put on her nightdress seemed natural to her. She went into the bathroom to change, but first she turned out the lights in the stateroom, and when she came out in her chemise she covered the cracks around the door with articles of clothing so she could return to bed in absolute darkness. As she did so, she said with good humor:

"What do you expect, Doctor? This is the first time I have slept with a stranger."

Dr. Urbino felt her slide in next to him like a startled little animal, trying to keep as far away as possible in a bunk where it was difficult for two people to be together without touching. He took her hand, cold and twitching with terror, he entwined his fingers with hers, and almost in a whisper he began to recount his recollections of other ocean voyages. She was tense again because when she came back to bed she realized that he had taken off all his clothes while she was in the bathroom, which revived her terror of what was to come. But what was to come took several hours, for Dr. Urbino continued talking very slowly as he won her body's confidence millimeter by millimeter. He spoke to her of Paris, of love in Paris, of the lovers in Paris who kissed on the street, on the omnibus, on the flowering terraces of the cafés opened to the burning winds and languid accordions of summer, who made love standing up on the quays of the Seine without anyone disturbing them.

As he spoke in the darkness he caressed the curve of her neck with his fingertips, he caressed the fine silky hair on her arms, her evasive belly, and when he felt that her tension had given way he made his first attempt to raise her nightgown, but she stopped him with an impulse typical of her character. She said: "I know how to do it myself." She took it off, in fact, and then she was so still that Dr. Urbino might have thought she was no longer there if it had not been for the glint of her body in the darkness.

After a while he took her hand again, and this time it was warm and relaxed but still moist with a tender dew. They were silent and unmoving for a while longer, he looking for the opportunity to take the next step and she waiting for it without knowing where it would come from, while the darkness expanded as their breathing grew more and more intense. Without warning he let go of her hand and made his leap into the void: he wet the tip of his forefinger with his tongue and grazed her nipple when it was caught off guard, and she felt a mortal explosion as if he had touched a raw nerve. She was glad of the darkness so he could not see the searing blush that shook her all the way to the base of her skull. "Don't worry," he said with great calm. "Don't forget that I've met them already." He felt her smile, and her voice was sweet and new in the darkness.

"I remember it very well," she said, "and I'm still angry."

Then he knew that they had rounded the cape

of good hope, and he took her large, soft hand again and covered it with forlorn little kisses, first the hard metacarpus, the long, discerning fingers, the diaphanous nails, and then the hieroglyphics of her destiny on her perspiring palm. She never knew how her hand came to his chest and felt something it could not decipher. He said: "It is a scapular." She caressed the hairs on his chest one by one and then seized all the hair in her fist to pull it out by the roots. "Harder," he said. She tried, until she knew she was not hurting him, and then it was her hand that sought his, lost in the darkness. But he did not allow their fingers to intertwine; instead he grasped her by the wrist and moved her hand along his body with an invisible but well-directed strength until she felt the ardent breath of a naked animal without bodily form, but eager and erect. Contrary to what he had imagined, even contrary to what she herself had imagined, she did not withdraw her hand or let it lie inert where he placed it, but instead she commended herself body and soul to the Blessed Virgin, clenched her teeth for fear she would laugh out loud at her own madness, and began to identify her rearing adversary by touch, discovering its size, the strength of its shaft, the extension of its wings, amazed by its determination but pitying its solitude, making it her own with a detailed curiosity that someone less experienced than her husband might have confused with caresses. He summoned all his reserves of strength to overcome the vertigo of her implacable scrutiny, until she released it with childish unconcern as if she were tossing it into the trash.

"I have never been able to understand how that thing works," she said.

Then, with authoritative methodology, he explained it to her in all seriousness while he moved her hand to the places he mentioned and she allowed it to be moved with the obedience of an exemplary pupil. At a propitious moment he suggested that all of this was easier in the light. He was going to turn it on, but she held his arm, saying: "I see better with my hands." In reality she wanted to turn on the light as well, but she wanted to be the one to do it, without anyone's ordering her to, and she had her way. Then he saw her in the sudden brightness, huddled in the fetal position beneath the sheet. But he watched as she grasped the animal under study without hesitation, turned it this way and that, observed it with an interest that was beginning to seem more than scientific, and said when she was finished: "How ugly it is, even uglier than a woman's thing." He agreed, and pointed out other disadvantages more serious than ugliness. He said: "It is like a firstborn son: you spend your life working for him, sacrificing everything for him, and at the moment of truth he does just as he pleases." She continued to examine it, asking what this was for and what that was for, and when she felt satisfied with her information she hefted it in both hands to confirm that it did not weigh enough to bother with, and let it drop with a gesture of disdain.

247

"Besides, I think it has too many things on it," she said.

He was astounded. The original thesis of his dissertation had been just that: the advantage of simplifying the human organism. It seemed anti-quated to him, with many useless or duplicated functions that had been essential in other stages of the human race but were not in ours. Yes: it could be more simple and by the same token less vulner-able. He concluded: "It is something that only God can do, of course, but in any event it would be good to have it established in theoretical terms." She laughed with amusement and so much natu-ralness that he took advantage of the opportunity to embrace her and kiss her for the first time on the mouth. She responded, and he continued giv-ing her very soft kisses on her cheeks, her nose, her eyelids, while he slipped his hand under the sheet and caressed her flat, straight pubic hair: the pubic hair of a Japanese. She did not move his hand away, but she kept hers on the alert in the event that he took one step further.

"Let's not go on with the medical lesson," she said.

"No," he said. "This is going to be a lesson in love."

Then he pulled down the sheet and she not only did not object but kicked it away from the bunk with a rapid movement of her feet because she could no longer bear the heat. Her body was undulant and elastic, much more serious than it appeared when dressed, with its own scent of a forest animal, which distinguished her from all the other women in the world. Defenseless in the light, she felt a rush of blood surge up to her face, and the only way she could think of to hide it was to throw her arms around her husband's neck and give him a hard, thorough kiss that lasted until they were both gasping for breath.

He was aware that he did not love her. He had married her because he liked her haughtiness, her seriousness, her strength, and also because of some vanity on his part, but as she kissed him for the first time he was sure there would be no obstacle to their inventing true love. They did not speak of it that first night, when they spoke of everything until dawn, nor would they ever speak of it. But in the long run, neither of them had made a mistake.

At dawn, when they fell asleep, she was still a virgin, but she would not be one much longer. The following night, in fact, after he taught her how to dance Viennese waltzes under the starry Caribbean sky, he went to the bathroom after she did, and when he returned to the stateroom he found her waiting for him naked in the bed. Then it was she who took the initiative, and gave herself without fear, without regret, with the joy of an adventure on the high seas, and with no traces of bloody ceremony except for the rose of honor on the sheet. They both made love well, almost as if by miracle, and they continued to make love well, night and day and better each time for the rest of

249

the voyage, and when they reached La Rochelle they got along as if they were old lovers.

They stayed in Europe, with Paris as their base, and made short trips to neighboring countries. During that time they made love every day, more than once on winter Sundays when they frolicked in bed until it was time for lunch. He was a man of strong impulses, and well disciplined besides, and she was not one to let anyone take advantage of her, so they had to be content with sharing power in bed. After three months of feverish lovemaking he concluded that one of them was sterile, and they both submitted to rigorous examinations at the Hôpital de la Salpêtrière, where he had been an intern. It was an arduous but fruitless effort. However, when they least expected it, and with no scientific intervention, the miracle occurred. When they returned home, Fermina was in the sixth month of her pregnancy and thought herself the happiest woman on earth. The child they had both longed for was born without incident under the sign of Aquarius and baptized in honor of the grandfather who had died of cholera.

It was impossible to know if it was Europe or love that changed them, for both occurred at the same time. They were, in essence, not only between themselves but with everyone else, just as Florentino Ariza perceived them when he saw them leaving Mass two weeks after their return on that Sunday of his misfortune. They came back with a new conception of life, bringing with them the latest trends in the world and ready to lead, he with the most recent developments in literature, music, and above all in his science. He had a subscription to *Le Figaro,* so he would not lose touch with reality, and another to the *Revue des Deux Mondes,* so that he would not lose touch with poetry. He had also arranged with his bookseller in Paris to receive works by the most widely read authors, among them Anatole France and Pierre Loti, and by those he liked best, including Rémy de Gourmont and Paul Bourget, but under no circumstances anything by Émile Zola, whom he found intolerable despite his valiant intervention in the Dreyfus affair. The same bookseller agreed to mail him the most attractive scores from the Ricordi catalogue, chamber music above all, so that he could maintain the well-deserved title earned by his father as the greatest friend of concerts in the city.

Fermina Daza, always resistant to the demands of fashion, brought back six trunks of clothing from different periods, for the great labels did not convince her. She had been in the Tuileries in the middle of winter for the launching of the collection by Worth, the indisputable tyrant of *haute couture,* and the only thing she got was a case of bronchitis that kept her in bed for five days. Laferrière seemed less pretentious and voracious to her, but her wise decision was to buy her fill of what she liked best in the secondhand shops, although her husband swore in dismay that it was corpses' clothing. In the same way she brought back quantities of Italian shoes without brand names, which she preferred to the renowned and famous shoes by Ferry, and she brought back a parasol from Dupuy, as red as the fires of hell, which gave our alarmed social chroniclers much to write about. She bought only one hat from Madame Reboux, but on the other hand she filled a trunk with sprigs of artificial cherries, stalks of all the felt flowers she could find, branches of ostrich plumes, crests of peacocks, tailfeathers of Asiatic roosters, entire pheasants, hummingbirds, and a countless variety of exotic birds preserved in midflight, midcall, midagony: everything that had been used in the past twenty years to change the appearance of hats. She brought back a collection of fans from countries all over the world, each one appropriate to a different occasion. She brought back a disturbing fragrance chosen from many at the perfume shop in the Bazar de la Charité, before the spring winds leveled everything with ashes, but she used it only once because she did not recognize herself in the new scent. She also brought back a cosmetic case that was the latest thing in seductiveness, and she took it to parties at a time when the simple act of checking one's makeup in public was considered indecent.

They also brought back three indelible memories: the unprecedented opening of *The Tales of Hoffmann* in Paris, the terrifying blaze that destroyed almost all the gondolas off St. Mark's Square in Venice, which they witnessed with grieving hearts from the window of their hotel, and their fleeting glimpse of Oscar Wilde during the first snowfall in January. But amid these and so many other memories, Dr. Juvenal Urbino had one that he always regretted not sharing with his wife, for it came from his days as a bachelor student in Paris. It was the memory of Victor Hugo, who enjoyed an impassioned fame here that had nothing to do with his books, because someone said that he had said, although no one actually heard him say it, that our Constitution was meant for a nation not of men but of angels. From that time on, special homage was paid to him, and most of our many compatriots who traveled to France went out of their way to see him. A half-dozen students, among them Juvenal Urbino, stood guard for a time outside his residence on Avenue Eylau, and at the cafés where it was said he came without fail and never came, and at last they sent a written request for a private audience in the name of the angels of the Constitution of Rionegro. They never received a reply. One day, when Juvenal Urbino happened to be passing the Luxembourg Gardens, he saw him come out of the Senate with a young woman on his arm. He seemed very old, he walked with difficulty, his beard and hair were less brilliant than in his pictures, and he wore an overcoat that seemed to belong to a larger man. He did not want to ruin the memory with an impertinent greeting: he was satisfied with the almost unreal vision that he would keep for the rest of his life. When he returned to Paris as a married man, in a position to see him under more formal circumstances, Victor Hugo had already died.

As a consolation, Juvenal Urbino and Fermina Daza brought back the shared memory of a snowy afternoon when they were intrigued by a crowd that defied the storm outside a small bookshop on the Boulevard des Capucines because Oscar Wilde was inside. When he came out at last, elegant indeed but perhaps too conscious of being so, the group surrounded him, asking that he sign their books. Dr. Urbino had stopped just to watch him, but his impulsive wife wanted to cross the boulevard so that he could sign the only thing she thought appropriate, given the fact that she did not have a book: her beautiful gazelle-skin glove, long, smooth, soft, the same color as her newlywed's skin. She was sure that a man as refined as he would appreciate the gesture. But her husband objected with firmness, and when she tried to go despite his arguments, he did not feel he could survive the embarrassment.

"If you cross that street," he said to her, "when you get back here you will find me dead."

It was something natural in her. Before she had been married a year, she moved through the world with the same assurance that had been hers as a little girl in the wilds of San Juan de la Ciénaga, as if she had been born with it, and she had a facility for dealing with strangers that left her husband dumbfounded, and a mysterious talent for making herself understood in Spanish with anyone, anywhere. "You have to know languages when you go to sell something," she said with mocking laughter. "But when you go to buy, everyone does what he must to understand you." It was difficult to imagine anyone who could have assimilated the daily life of Paris with so much speed and so much joy, and who learned to love her memory of it despite the eternal rain. Nevertheless, when she returned home overwhelmed by so many experiences, tired of traveling, drowsy with her pregnancy, the first thing she was asked in the port was what she thought of the marvels of Europe, and she summed up many months of bliss with four words of Caribbean slang:

"It's not so much."

THE DAY THAT Florentino Ariza saw Fermina Daza in the atrium of the Cathedral, in the sixth month of her pregnancy and in full command of her new condition as a woman of the world, he made a fierce decision to win fame and fortune in order to deserve her. He did not even stop to think about the obstacle of her being married, because at the same time he decided, as if it depended on himself alone, that Dr. Juvenal Urbino had to die. He did not know when or how, but he considered it an ineluctable event that he was resolved to wait for without impatience or violence, even till the end of time.

He began at the beginning. He presented himself unannounced in the office of Uncle Leo XII, President of the Board of Directors and General Manager of the River Company of the Caribbean, and expressed his willingness to yield to his plans. His uncle was angry with him because of the manner in which he had thrown away the good position of telegraph operator in Villa de Leyva, but he allowed himself to be swayed by his conviction that human beings are not born once and for all on the day their mothers give birth to them, but that life obliges them over and over again to give birth to themselves. Besides, his brother's widow had died the year before, still smarting from rancor but without any heirs. And so he gave the job to his errant nephew.

It was a decision typical of Don Leo XII Loayza. Inside the shell of a soulless merchant was hidden a genial lunatic, as willing to bring forth a spring of lemonade in the Guajira Desert as to flood a solemn funeral with weeping at his heartbreaking rendition of "In Questa Tomba Oscura." His head was covered with curls, he had the lips of a faun, and all he needed was a lyre and a laurel wreath to be the image of the incendiary Nero of Christian mythology. When he was not occupied with the administration of his decrepit vessels, still afloat out of sheer distraction on the part of fate, or with the problems of river navigation, which grew more and more critical every day, he devoted his free time to the enrichment of his lyric repertoire. He liked nothing better than to sing at funerals. He had the voice of a galley slave, untrained but capable of impressive registers. Someone had told him that Enrico Caruso could shatter a vase with the power of his voice, and he had spent years trying to imitate him, even with the windowpanes. His friends brought him the most delicate vases they had come across in their travels through the world, and they organized special parties so that he might at last achieve the culmination of his dream. He never succeeded. Still, in the depth of his thundering there was a glimmer of tenderness that broke the hearts of his listeners as if they were the crystal vases of the great Caruso, and it was this that made him so revered at funerals. Except at one, when he thought it a good idea to sing "When I Wake Up in Glory," a beautiful and moving funeral song from Louisiana, and he was told to be quiet by the priest, who could not understand that Protestant intrusion in his church.

And so, between operatic encores and Neapolitan serenades, his creative talent and his invincible entrepreneurial spirit made him the hero of river navigation during the time of its greatest splendor. He had come from nothing, like his dead brothers, and all of them went as far as they wished despite the stigma of being illegitimate children and, even worse, illegitimate children who had never been recognized. They were the cream of what in those days was called the "shop-counter aristocracy," whose sanctuary was the Commercial Club. And yet, even when he had the resources to live like the Roman emperor he resembled, Uncle Leo XII lived in the old city because it was convenient to his business, in such an austere manner and in such a plain house that he could never shake off an unmerited reputation for miserliness. His only luxury was even simpler: a house by the sea, two leagues from his offices, furnished only with six handmade stools, a stand for earthenware jars, and a hammock on the terrace where he could lie down to think on Sundays. No one described him better than he did when someone accused him of being rich.

"No, not rich," he said. "I am a poor man with money, which is not the same thing."

His strange nature, which someone once praised in a speech as lucid dementia, allowed him to see in an instant what no one else ever saw in Florentino Ariza. From the day he came to his office to ask for work, with his doleful appearance and his twenty-six useless years behind him, he had tested him with the severity of a barracks training that could have broken the hardest man. But he did not intimidate him. What Uncle Leo XII never suspected was that his nephew's courage did not come from the need to survive or from a brute indifference inherited from his father, but from a driving need for love, which no obstacle in this world or the next would ever break.

The worst years were the early ones, when he was appointed clerk to the Board of Directors, which seemed a position made to order for him. Lotario Thugut, Uncle Leo XII's old music teacher, was the one who advised him to give his nephew a writing job because he was a voracious wholesale consumer of literature, although he preferred the worst to the best. Uncle Leo XII disregarded what he said concerning his nephew's bad taste in reading, for Lotario Thugut would also say of him that he had been his worst voice student, and still he could make even tombstones cry. In any case, the German was correct in regard to what he had thought about least, which was that

Florentino Ariza wrote everything with so much passion that even official documents seemed to be about love. His bills of lading were rhymed no matter how he tried to avoid it, and routine business letters had a lyrical spirit that diminished their authority. His uncle himself came to his office one day with a packet of correspondence that he had not dared put his name to, and he gave him his last chance to save his soul.

"If you cannot write a business letter you will pick up the trash on the dock," he said.

Florentino Ariza accepted the challenge. He made a supreme effort to learn the mundane simplicity of mercantile prose, imitating models from notarial files with the same diligence he had once used for popular poets. This was the period when he spent his free time in the Arcade of the Scribes, helping unlettered lovers to write their scented love notes, in order to unburden his heart of all the words of love that he could not use in customs reports. But at the end of six months, no matter how hard he twisted, he could not wring the neck of his diehard swan. So that when Uncle Leo XII reproached him a second time, he admitted defeat, but with a certain haughtiness.

"Love is the only thing that interests me," he said.

"The trouble," his uncle said to him, "is that without river navigation there is no love."

He kept his threat to have him pick up trash on the dock, but he gave him his word that he would promote him, step by step, up the ladder of faithful service until he found his place. And he did. No work could defeat him, no matter how hard or humiliating it was, no salary, no matter how miserable, could demoralize him, and he never lost his essential fearlessness when faced with the insolence of his superiors. But he was not an innocent, either: everyone who crossed his path suffered the consequences of the overwhelming determination, capable of anything, that lay behind his helpless appearance. Just as Uncle Leo XII had foreseen, and according to his desire that his nephew not be ignorant of any secret in the business, Florentino Ariza moved through every post during thirty years of dedication and tenacity in the face of every trial. He fulfilled all his duties with admirable skill, studying every thread in that mysterious warp that had so much to do with the offices of poetry, but he never won the honor he most desired, which was to write one, just one, acceptable business letter. Without intending to, without even knowing it, he demonstrated with his life that his father had been right when he repeated until his dying day that there was no one with more common sense, no stonecutter more obstinate, no manager more lucid or dangerous, than a poet. That, at least, is what he was told by Uncle Leo XII, who talked to him about his father during moments of sentimental leisure and created an image that resembled a dreamer more than it did a businessman.

He told him that Pius V Loayza used the offices for matters more pleasant than work, and that he always arranged to leave the house on Sundays, with the excuse that he had to meet or dispatch a boat. What is more, he had an old boiler installed in the warehouse patio, with a steam whistle that someone would sound with navigation signals in the event his wife became suspicious. According to his calculations, Uncle Leo XII was certain that Florentino Ariza had been conceived on a desk in some unlocked office on a hot Sunday afternoon, while from her house his father's wife heard the farewells of a boat that never sailed. By the time she learned the truth it was too late to accuse him of infamy because her husband was already dead. She survived him by many years, destroyed by the bitterness of not having a child and asking God in her prayers for the eternal damnation of his bastard son.

The image of his father disturbed Florentino Ariza. His mother had spoken of him as a great man with no commercial vocation, who had at last gone into the river business because his older brother had been a very close collaborator of the German commodore Johann B. Elbers, the father of river navigation. They were the illegitimate sons of the same mother, a cook by trade, who had them by different men, and all bore her surname and the name of a pope chosen at random from the calendar of saints' days, except for Uncle Leo XII, named after the Pope in office when he was born. The man called Florentino was their maternal grandfather, so that the name had come down to the son of Tránsito Ariza after skipping over an entire generation of pontiffs.

Florentino always kept the notebook in which his father wrote love poems, some of them inspired by Tránsito Ariza, its pages decorated with drawings of broken hearts. Two things surprised him. One was the character of his father's handwriting, identical to his own although he had chosen his because it was the one he liked best of the many he saw in a manual. The other was finding a sentence that he thought he had composed but that his father had written in the notebook long before he was born: *The only regret I will have in dying is if it is not for love.*

He had also seen the only two pictures of his father. One had been taken in Santa Fe, when he was very young, the same age as Florentino Ariza when he saw the photograph for the first time, and in it he was wearing an overcoat that made him look as if he were stuffed inside a bear, and he was leaning against a pedestal that supported the decapitated gaiters of a statue. The little boy beside him was Uncle Leo XII, wearing a ship captain's hat. In the other photograph, his father was with a group of soldiers in God knows which of so many wars, and he held the longest rifle, and his mustache had a gunpowder smell that wafted out of the picture. He was a Liberal and a Mason, just like his brothers, and yet he wanted his son to go to the seminary. Florentino Ariza did not see the resemblance that people observed, but according to his Uncle Leo XII, Pius V was also reprimanded for the lyricism of his documents. In any case, he did not resemble him in the pictures, or in his memories of him, or in the image transfigured by love that his mother painted, or in the one unpainted by his Uncle Leo XII with his cruel wit. Nevertheless, Florentino Ariza discovered the resemblance many years later, as he was combing his hair in front of the mirror, and only then did he understand that a man knows when he is growing old because he begins to look like his father.

He had no memory of him on the Street of Windows. He thought he knew that at one time his father slept there, very early in his love affair with Tránsito Ariza, but that he did not visit her again after the birth of Florentino. For many years the baptismal certificate was our only valid means of identification, and Florentino Ariza's, recorded in the parish church of St. Tiburtius, said only that he was the natural son of an unwed natural daughter called Tránsito Ariza. The name of his father did not appear on it, although Pius V took care of his son's needs in secret until the day he died. This social condition closed the doors of the seminary to Florentino Ariza, but he also escaped military service during the bloodiest period of our wars because he was the only son of an unmarried woman.

Every Friday after school he sat across from the offices of the River Company of the Caribbean, looking at pictures of animals in a book that was falling apart because he had looked at it so often. His father would walk into the building without looking at him, wearing the frock coats that Tránsito Ariza later had to alter for him, and with a face identical to that of St. John the Evangelist on the altars. When he came out, many hours later, he would make certain that no one saw him, not even his coachman, and he would give him money for the week's expenses. They did not speak, not only because his father made no effort to, but because he was terrified of him. One day, after he waited much longer than usual, his father gave him the coins and said:

"Take them and do not come back again."

It was the last time he saw him. But in time he was to learn that Uncle Leo XII, who was some ten years younger, continued to bring money to Tránsito Ariza, and was the one who took care of her after Pius V died of an untreated colic without leaving anything in writing and without the time to make any provisions for his only child: a child of the streets.

The drama of Florentino Ariza while he was a clerk for the River Company of the Caribbean was that he could not avoid lyricism because he was always thinking about Fermina Daza, and he had never learned to write without thinking about her. Later, when he was moved to other posts, he had so much love left over inside that he did not know what to do with it, and he offered it to unlettered lovers free of charge, writing their love missives for them in the Arcade of the Scribes. That is where he went after work. He would take off his frock coat with his circumspect gestures and hang it over the back of the chair, he would put on the cuffs so he would not dirty his shirt sleeves, he would unbutton his vest so he could think better, and sometimes until very late at night he would encourage the hopeless with letters of mad adoration. From time to time he would be approached by a poor woman who had a problem with one of her children, a war veteran who persisted in demanding payment of his pension, someone who had been robbed and wanted to file a complaint with the government, but no matter how he tried, he could not satisfy them, because the only convincing document he could write was a love letter. He did not even ask his new clients any questions, because all he had to do was look at the whites of their eyes to know what their problem was, and he would write page after page of uncontrolled love, following the infallible formula of writing as he thought about Fermina Daza and nothing but Fermina Daza. After the first month he had to establish a system of appointments made in advance so that he would not be swamped by yearning lovers.

His most pleasant memory of that time was of a very timid young girl, almost a child, who trembled as she asked him to write an answer to an irresistible letter that she had just received, and that Florentino Ariza recognized as one he had written on the previous afternoon. He answered it in a different style, one that was in tune with the emotions and the age of the girl, and in a hand that also seemed to be hers, for he knew how to create a handwriting for every occasion, according to the character of each person. He wrote, imagining to himself what Fermina Daza would have said to him if she had loved him as much as that helpless child loved her suitor. Two days later, of course, he had to write the boy's reply with the same hand, style, and kind of love that he had attributed to him in the first letter, and so it was that he became involved in a feverish correspondence with himself. Before a month had passed, each came to him separately to thank him for what he himself had proposed in the boy's letter and accepted with devotion in the girl's response: they were going to marry.

Only when they had their first child did they realize, after a casual conversation, that their letters had been written by the same scribe, and for the first time they went together to the Arcade to ask him to be the child's godfather. Florentino Ariza was so enraptured by the practical evidence of his dreams that he used time he did not have to write a *Lovers' Companion* that was more poetic and extensive than the one sold in doorways for twenty centavos and that half the city knew by heart. He categorized all the imaginable situations in which he and Fermina Daza might find themselves, and for all of them he wrote as many models and alternatives as he could think of. When he finished, he had some thousand letters in three volumes as complete as the Covarrubias Dictionary, but no printer in the city would take the risk of publishing them, and they ended up in an attic along with other papers from the past, for Tránsito Ariza flatly refused to dig out the earthenware jars and squander the savings of a lifetime on a mad publishing venture. Years later, when Florentino Ariza had the resources to publish the book himself, it was difficult for him to accept the reality that love letters had gone out of fashion.

As he was starting out in the River Company of the Caribbean and writing letters free of charge in the Arcade of the Scribes, the friends of Florentino Ariza's youth were certain that they were slowly losing him beyond recall. And they were right. When he returned from his voyage along the river, he still saw some of them in the hope of dimming the memory of Fermina Daza, he played billiards with them, he went to their dances, he allowed himself to be raffled off among the girls, he allowed himself to do everything he thought would help him to become the man he had once been. Later, when Uncle Leo XII took him on as an employee, he played dominoes with his officemates in the Commercial Club, and they began to accept him as one of their own when he spoke to them of nothing but the navigation company, which he did not call by its complete name but by its initials: the R.C.C. He even changed the way he ate. As indifferent and irregular as he had been until then regarding food, that was how habitual and austere he became until the end of his days: a large cup of black coffee for breakfast, a slice of poached fish with white rice for lunch, a cup of *café con leche* and a piece of cheese before going to bed. He drank black coffee at any hour, anywhere, under any circumstances, as many as thirty little cups a day: a brew like crude oil which he preferred to prepare himself and which he always kept near at hand in a thermos. He was another person, despite his firm decision and anguished efforts to continue to be the same man he had been before his mortal encounter with love.

The truth is that he was never the same again. Winning back Fermina Daza was the sole purpose of his life, and he was so certain of achieving it sooner or later that he convinced Tránsito Ariza to continue with the restoration of the house so that it would be ready to receive her whenever the miracle took place. In contrast to her reaction to the proposed publication of the *Lovers' Companion*, Tránsito Ariza went much further: she bought the house at once and undertook a complete renovation. They made a reception room where the bedroom had been, on the upper floor they built two spacious, bright bedrooms, one for the married couple and another for the children they were going to have, and in the space where the old tobacco factory had been they put in an extensive garden with all kinds of roses, which Florentino Ariza himself tended during his free time at dawn. The only thing they left intact, as a kind of testimony of gratitude to the past, was the notions shop. The back room where Florentino Ariza had slept they left it as it had always been, with the hammock hanging and the writing table covered with untidy piles of books, but he moved to the room planned as the conjugal bedroom on the upper floor. This was the largest and airiest in the house, and it had an interior terrace where it was pleasant to sit at night because of the sea breeze and the scent of the rosebushes, but it was also the room that best reflected Florentino Ariza's Trappist severity. The plain whitewashed walls were rough and unadorned, and the only furniture was a prison cot, a night table with a candle in a bottle, an old wardrobe, and a washstand with its basin and bowl.

The work took almost three years, and it coincided with a brief civic revival owing to the boom in river navigation and trade, the same factors that had maintained the city's greatness during colonial times and for more than two centuries had made her the gateway to America. But that was also the period when Tránsito Ariza manifested the first symptoms of her incurable disease. Her regular clients were older, paler, and more faded each time they came to the notions shop, and she did not recognize them after dealing with them for half a lifetime, or she confused the affairs of one with those of another, which was a very grave matter in a business like hers, in which no papers were signed to protect her honor or theirs, and one's word of honor was given and accepted as sufficient guarantee. At first it seemed she was growing deaf, but it soon became evident that her memory was trickling away. And so she liquidated her pawn business, the treasure in the jars paid for completing and furnishing the house, and still left over were many of the most valuable old jewels in the city, whose owners did not have funds to redeem them.

During this period Florentino Ariza had to attend to too many responsibilities at the same time, but his spirits never flagged as he sought to expand his work as a furtive hunter. After his erratic experience with the Widow Nazaret, which opened the door to street love, he continued to hunt the abandoned little birds of the night for several years, still hoping to find a cure for the pain of Fermina Daza. But by then he could no longer tell if his habit of fornicating without hope was a mental necessity or a simple vice of his body. His visits to the transient hotel became less frequent, not only because his interests lay elsewhere but because he did not like them to see him there under circumstances that were different from the chaste domesticity of the past. Nevertheless, in three emergency situations he had recourse to the simple strategy of an era before his time: he disguised his friends, who were afraid of being recognized, as men, and they walked into the hotel together as if they were two gentlemen out on the town. Yet on two of these occasions someone realized that he and his presumptive male companion did not go to the bar but to a room, and the already tarnished reputation of Florentino Ariza received the coup de grace. At last he stopped going there, except for the very few times he did so not to catch up on what he had missed but for just the opposite reason: to find a refuge where he could recuperate from his excesses.

And it was just as well. No sooner did he leave his office at five in the afternoon than he began to hunt like a chicken hawk. At first he was content with what the night provided. He picked up serving girls in the parks, black women in the market, sophisticated young ladies from the interior on the beaches, gringas on the boats from New Orleans. He took them to the jetties where half the city also went after nightfall, he took them wherever he could, and sometimes even where he could not, and not infrequently he had to hurry into a dark entryway and do what he could, however he could do it, behind the gate.

The lighthouse was always a blessed refuge in a storm, which he evoked with nostalgia in the dawn of his old age when he had everything settled, because it was a good place to be happy, above all at night, and he thought that something of his loves from that time flashed out to the sailors with every turn of the light. So that he continued to go there more than to any other spot, while his friend the lighthouse keeper was delighted to receive him with a simpleminded expression on his face that was the best guarantee of discretion for the frightened little birds. There was a house at the foot of the tower, close to the thunder of the waves breaking against the cliffs, where love was more intense because it seemed like a shipwreck. But Florentino Ariza preferred the light tower itself, late at night, because one could see the entire city and the trail of lights on the fishing boats at sea, and even in the distant swamps.

It was in those days that he devised his rather simplistic theories concerning the relationship between a woman's appearance and her aptitude for love. He distrusted the sensual type, the ones who looked as if they could eat an alligator raw and tended to be the most passive in bed. The type he preferred was just the opposite: those skinny little tadpoles that no one bothered to turn around and look at in the street, who seemed to disappear when they took off their clothes, who made you feel sorry for them when their bones cracked at the first impact, and yet who could leave the man who bragged the most about his virility ready for the trashcan. He had made notes of these premature observations, intending to write a practical supplement to the *Lovers' Companion,* but the project met the same fate as the previous one after Ausencia Santander sent him tumbling with her old dog's wisdom, stood him on his head, tossed him up and threw him down, made him as good as new, shattered all his virtuous theories, and taught him the only thing he had to learn about love: that nobody teaches life anything.

Ausencia Santander had had a conventional marriage for twenty years, which left her with three children who had married and had children in turn, so that she boasted of being the grandmother with the best bed in the city. It was never clear if she had abandoned her husband, or if he had abandoned her, or if they had abandoned each

273

other at the same time, but he went to live with his regular mistress, and then she felt free, in the middle of the day and at the front door, to receive Rosendo de la Rosa, a riverboat captain whom she had often received in the middle of the night at the back door. Without giving the matter a second thought, he brought Florentino Ariza to meet her.

He brought him for lunch. He also brought a demijohn of homemade aguardiente and ingredients of the highest quality for an epic *sancocho*, the kind that was possible only with chickens from the patio, meat with tender bones, rubbish-heap pork, and greens and vegetables from the towns along the river. Nevertheless, from the very first, Florentino Ariza was not as enthusiastic about the excellence of the cuisine or the exuberance of the lady of the house as he was about the beauty of the house itself. He liked her because of her house, bright and cool, with four large windows facing the sea and beyond that a complete view of the old city. He liked the quantity and the splendor of the things that gave the living room a confused and at the same time rigorous appearance, with all kinds of handcrafted objects that Captain Rosendo de la Rosa brought back from each trip until there was no room left for another piece. On the sea terrace, sitting on his private ring, was a cockatoo from Malaya, with unbelievable white plumage and a pensive tranquillity that gave one much to think about: it was the most beautiful animal that Florentino Ariza had ever seen.

Captain Rosendo de la Rosa was enthusiastic

about his guest's enthusiasm, and he told him in detail the history of each object. As he spoke he sipped aguardiente without pause. He seemed to be made of reinforced concrete: he was enormous, with hair all over his body except on his head, a mustache like a housepainter's brush, a voice like a capstan, which would have been his alone, and an exquisite courtesy. But not even his body could resist the way he drank. Before they sat down to the table he had finished half of the demijohn, and he fell forward onto the tray of glasses and bottles with a slow sound of demolition. Ausencia Santander had to ask Florentino Ariza to help her drag the inert body of the beached whale to bed and undress him as he slept. Then, in a flash of inspiration that they attributed to a conjunction of their stars, the two of them undressed in the next room without agreeing to, without even suggesting it or proposing it to each other, and for more than seven years they continued undressing wherever they could while the Captain was on a trip. There was no danger of his surprising them, because he had the good sailor's habit of advising the port of his arrival by sounding the ship's horn, even at dawn, first with three long howls for his wife and nine children, and then with two short, melancholy ones for his mistress.

Ausencia Santander was almost fifty years old and looked it, but she had such a personal instinct for love that no homegrown or scientific theories could interfere with it. Florentino Ariza knew from the ship's itineraries when he could visit her, and he always went unannounced, whenever he wanted to, at any hour of the day or night, and never once was she not waiting for him. She would open the door as her mother had raised her until she was seven years old: stark naked, with an organdy ribbon in her hair. She would not let him take another step until she had undressed him, because she thought it was bad luck to have a clothed man in the house. This was the cause of constant discord with Captain Rosendo de la Rosa, because he had the superstitious belief that smoking naked brought bad luck, and at times he preferred to put off love rather than put out his inevitable Cuban cigar. On the other hand, Florentino Ariza was very taken with the charms of nudity, and she removed his clothes with sure delight as soon as she closed the door, not even giving him time to greet her, or to take off his hat or his glasses, kissing him and letting him kiss her with sharp-toothed kisses, unfastening his clothes from bottom to top, first the buttons of his fly, one by one after each kiss, then his belt buckle, and at the last his vest and shirt, until he was like a live fish that had been slit open from head to tail. Then she sat him in the living room and took off his boots, pulled on his trouser cuffs so that she could take off his pants while she removed his long underwear, and at last she undid the garters around his calves and took off his socks. Then Florentino Ariza stopped kissing her and letting her kiss him so that he could do the only thing he was responsible for in that precise ceremony: he took his watch and chain out of the buttonhole in his vest and took off his glasses and put them in his boots so he would be sure not to forget them. He always took that precaution, always without fail, whenever he undressed in someone else's house.

As soon as he had done that, she attacked him without giving him time for anything else, there on the same sofa where she had just undressed him, and only on rare occasions in the bed. She mounted him and took control of all of him for all of her, absorbed in herself, her eyes closed, gauging the situation in her absolute inner darkness, advancing here, retreating there, correcting her invisible route, trying another, more intense path, another means of proceeding without drowning in the slimy marsh that flowed from her womb, droning like a horsefly as she asked herself questions and answered in her native jargon; where was that something in the shadows that only she knew about and that she longed for just for herself, until she succumbed without waiting for anybody, she fell alone into her abyss with a jubilant explosion of total victory that made the world tremble. Florentino Ariza was left exhausted, incomplete, floating in a puddle of their perspiration, but with the impression of being no more than an instrument of pleasure. He would say: "You treat me as if I were just anybody." She would roar with the laughter of a free female and say: "Not at all: as if you were nobody." He was left with the impression that she took away everything with mean-spirited greed, and his pride would rebel and he would leave the house determined never to return. But then he would wake for no reason in the middle of the night, and the memory of the self-absorbed love of Ausencia Santander was revealed to him for what it was: a pitfall of happiness that he despised and desired at the same time, but from which it was impossible to escape.

One Sunday, two years after they met, the first thing she did when he arrived was to take off his glasses instead of undressing him, so that she could kiss him with greater ease, and this was how Florentino Ariza learned that she had begun to love him. Despite the fact that from the first day he had felt very comfortable in the house that he now loved as if it were his own, he had never stayed longer than two hours, and he had never slept there, and he had eaten there only once because she had given him a formal invitation. He went there, in fact, only for what he had come for, always bringing his only gift, a single rose, and then he would disappear until the next unforesee-able time. But on the Sunday when she took off his glasses to kiss him, in part because of that and in part because they fell asleep after gentle lovemaking, they spent the afternoon naked in the Captain's enormous bed. When he awoke from his nap, Florentino Ariza still remembered the shriek-ing of the cockatoo, whose strident calls belied his beauty. But the silence was diaphanous in the four o'clock heat, and through the bedroom window one could see the outline of the old city with the afternoon sun at its back, its golden domes, its sea in flames all the way to Jamaica. Ausencia Santander stretched out an adventurous hand, seeking the sleeping beast, but Florentino Ariza moved it away. He said: "Not now. I feel something strange, as if someone were watching us." She aroused the cockatoo again with her joyous laughter. She said: "Not even Jonah's wife would swallow that story." Neither did she, of course, but she admitted it was a good one, and the two of them loved each other for a long time in silence without making love again. At five o'clock, with the sun still high, she jumped out of bed, naked as always and with the organdy ribbon in her hair, and went to find something to drink in the kitchen. But she had not taken a single step out of the bedroom when she screamed in horror.

She could not believe it. The only objects left in the house were the lamps attached to the walls. All the rest, the signed furniture, the Indian rugs, the statues and the hand-woven tapestries, the countless trinkets made of precious stones and metals, everything that had made hers one of the most pleasant and best decorated houses in the city, everything, even the sacred cockatoo, everything had vanished. It had been carried out through the sea terrace without disturbing their love. All that was left were empty rooms with the four open windows, and a message painted on the rear wall: *This is what you get for fucking around*. Captain Rosendo de la Rosa could never understand why Ausencia Santander did not report the robbery, or try to get in touch with the dealers in stolen

279

goods, or permit her misfortune to be mentioned again.

Florentino Ariza continued to visit her in the looted house, whose furnishings were reduced to three leather stools that the thieves forgot in the kitchen, and the contents of the bedroom where the two of them had been. But he did not visit her as often as before, not because of the desolation in the house, as she supposed and as she said to him, but because of the novelty of a mule-drawn trolley at the turn of the new century, which proved to be a prodigious and original nest of free-flying little birds. He rode it four times a day, twice to go to the office, twice to return home, and sometimes when his reading was real, and most of the time when it was pretense, he would take the first steps, at least, toward a future tryst. Later, when Uncle Leo XII put at his disposal a carriage drawn by two little gray mules with golden trappings, just like the one that belonged to President Rafael Núñez, he would long for those times on the trolley as the most fruitful of all his adventures in falconry. He was right: there is no worse enemy of secret love than a carriage waiting at the door. In fact, he almost always left it hidden at his house and made his hawkish rounds on foot so that he would not leave wheel marks in the dust. That is why he evoked with such great nostalgia the old trolley with its emaciated mules covered with sores, in which a sideways glance was all one needed to know where love was. However, in the midst of so many tender memories, he could not elude his recollection of a helpless little bird whose name he never knew and with whom he spent no more than half a frenetic night, but that had been enough to ruin the innocent rowdiness of Carnival for him for the rest of his life.

She had attracted his attention on the trolley for the fearlessness with which she traveled through the riotous public celebration. She could not have been more than twenty years old, and she did not seem to share the spirit of Carnival, unless she was disguised as an invalid: her hair was very light, long, and straight, hanging loose over her shoulders, and she wore a tunic of plain, unadorned linen. She was completely removed from the confusion of music in the streets, the handfuls of rice powder, the showers of aniline thrown at the passengers on the trolley, whose mules were whitened with cornstarch and wore flowered hats during those three days of madness. Taking advantage of the confusion, Florentino Ariza invited her to have an ice with him, because he did not think he could ask for anything more. She looked at him without surprise. She said: "I am happy to accept, but I warn you that I am crazy." He laughed at her witticism, and took her to see the parade of floats from the balcony of the ice cream shop. Then he put on a rented cape, and the two of them joined the dancing in the Plaza of the Customhouse, and enjoyed themselves like newborn sweethearts, for her indifference went to the opposite extreme in the uproar of the night: she danced like a professional, she was imaginative and daring in her revelry, and she had devastating charm.

"You don't know the trouble you've gotten into with me," she shouted, laughing in the fever of Carnival. "I'm a crazy woman from the insane asylum."

For Florentino Ariza, that night was a return to the innocent unruliness of adolescence, when he had not yet been wounded by love. But he knew, more from hearsay than from personal experience, that such easy happiness could not last very long. And so before the night began to degenerate, as it always did after prizes were distributed for the best costumes, he suggested to the girl that they go to the lighthouse to watch the sunrise. She accepted with pleasure, but she wanted to wait until after they had given out the prizes.

Florentino Ariza was certain that the delay saved his life. In fact, the girl had indicated to him that they should leave for the lighthouse, when she was seized by two guards and a nurse from Divine Shepherdess Asylum. They had been looking for her since her escape at three o'clock that afternoon—they and the entire police force. She had decapitated a guard and seriously wounded two others with a machete that she had snatched away from the gardener because she wanted to go dancing at Carnival. It had not occurred to anyone that she might be dancing in the streets; they thought she would be hiding in one of the many houses where they had searched even the cisterns.

It was not easy to take her away. She defended

herself with a pair of gardening shears that she had hidden in her bodice, and six men were needed to put her in the straitjacket while the crowd jammed into the Plaza of the Customhouse applauded and whistled with glee in the belief that the bloody capture was one of many Carnival farces. Florentino Ariza was heartbroken, and beginning on Ash Wednesday he would walk down Divine Shepherdess Street with a box of English chocolates for her. He would stand and look at the inmates, who shouted all kinds of profanities and compliments at him through the windows, and he would show them the box of chocolates in case luck would have it that she, too, might look out at him through the iron bars. But he never saw her. Months later, as he was getting off the mule-drawn trolley, a little girl walking with her father asked him for a piece of chocolate from the box he was carrying in his hand. Her father reprimanded her and begged Florentino Ariza's pardon. But he gave the whole box to the child, thinking that the action would redeem him from all bitterness, and he soothed the father with a pat on the back.

"They were for a love that has gone all to hell," he said.

As a kind of compensation from fate, it was also in the mule-drawn trolley that Florentino Ariza met Leona Cassiani, who was the true woman in his life although neither of them ever knew it and they never made love. He had sensed her before he saw her as he was going home on the trolley at five o'clock; it was a tangible look that touched him as if it were a finger. He raised his eyes and saw her, at the far end of the trolley, but standing out with great clarity from the other passengers. She did not look away. On the contrary: she continued to look at him with such boldness that he could not help thinking what he thought: black, young, pretty, but a whore beyond the shadow of a doubt. He rejected her from his life, because he could not conceive of anything more contemptible than paying for love: he had never done it.

Florentino Ariza got off at the Plaza of the Carriages, which was the end of the line, hurried through the labyrinth of commerce because his mother was expecting him at six, and when he emerged on the other side of the crowd, he heard the tapping heels of a loose woman on the paving stones and turned around so that he would be certain of what he already knew: it was she, dressed like the slave girls in engravings, with a skirt of veils that was raised with the gesture of a dancer when she stepped over the puddles in the streets, a low-cut top that left her shoulders bare, a handful of colored necklaces, and a white turban. He knew them from the transient hotel. It often happened that at six in the afternoon they were still eating breakfast, and then all they could do was to use sex as if it were a bandit's knife and put it to the throat of the first man they passed on the street: your prick or your life. As a final test, Florentino Ariza changed direction and went down the deserted Oil Lamp Alley, and she followed, coming closer and closer to him. Then he stopped, turned around, blocked her way on the sidewalk, and leaned on his umbrella with both hands. She stood facing him.

"You made a mistake, good-looking," he said. "I don't do that."

"Of course you do," she said. "One can see it in your face."

Florentino Ariza remembered a phrase from his childhood, something that the family doctor, his godfather, had said regarding his chronic constipation: "The world is divided into those who can shit and those who cannot." On the basis of this dogma the Doctor had elaborated an entire theory of character, which he considered more accurate than astrology. But with what he had learned over the years, Florentino Ariza stated it another way: "The world is divided into those who screw and those who do not." He distrusted those who did not: when they strayed from the straight and narrow, it was something so unusual for them that they bragged about love as if they had just invented it. Those who did it often, on the other hand, lived for that alone. They felt so good that their lips were sealed as if they were tombs, because they knew that their lives depended on their discretion. They never spoke of their exploits, they confided in no one, they feigned indifference to the point where they earned the reputation of being impotent, or frigid, or above all timid fairies, as in the case of Florentino Ariza. But they took pleasure in the error because the error protected them. They formed a secret society, whose members recognized each other all over the world without need of a common language, which is why Florentino Ariza was not surprised by the girl's reply: she was one of them, and therefore she knew that he knew that she knew.

It was the great mistake of his life, as his conscience was to remind him every hour of every day until the final day of his life. What she wanted from him was not love, least of all love that was paid for, but a job, any kind of job, at any salary, in the River Company of the Caribbean. Florentino Ariza felt so ashamed of his own conduct that he took her to the head of Personnel, who gave her the lowest-level job in the General Section, which she performed with seriousness, modesty, and dedication for three years.

Ever since its founding, the R.C.C. had had its offices across from the river dock, and it had nothing in common with the port for ocean liners on the opposite side of the bay, or with the market pier on Las Ánimas Bay. The building was of wood, with a sloping tin roof, a single long balcony with columns at the front, and windows, covered with wire mesh, on all four sides through which one had complete views of the boats at the dock as if they were paintings hanging on the wall. When the German founders built it, they painted the tin roof red and the wooden walls a brilliant white, so that the building itself bore some resemblance to a riverboat. Later it was painted all blue, and at the time that Florentino Ariza began to work for the company it was a dusty shed of no definite color, and on the rusting roof there were patches of new tin plates over the original ones. Behind the building, in a gravel patio surrounded by chicken wire, stood two large warehouses of more recent construction, and at the back there was a closed sewer pipe, dirty and foul-smelling, where the refuse of a half a century of river navigation lay rotting: the debris of historic boats, from the early one with a single smokestack, christened by Simón Bolívar, to some so recent that they had electric fans in the cabins. Most of them had been dismantled for materials to be used in building other boats, but many were in such good condition that it seemed possible to give them a coat of paint and launch them without frightening away the iguanas or disturbing the foliage of the large yellow flowers that made them even more nostalgic.

The Administrative Section was on the upper floor of the building, in small but comfortable and well-appointed offices similar to the cabins on the boats, for they had been built not by civil architects but by naval engineers. At the end of the corridor, like any employee, Uncle Leo XII dispatched his business in an office similar to all the others, the one exception being that every morning he found a glass vase filled with sweet-smelling flowers on his desk. On the ground floor was the Passenger Section, with a waiting room that had rustic benches and a counter for selling tickets and handling baggage. Last of all was the confusing General Section, its name alone suggesting the vagueness of its functions, where problems that had not been solved elsewhere in the company went to die an ignominious death. There sat Leona Cassiani, lost behind a student's desk surrounded by corn stacked for shipping and unresolved papers, on the day that Uncle Leo XII himself went to see what the devil he could think of to make the General Section good for something. After three hours of questions, theoretical assumptions, and concrete evidence, with all the employees in the middle of the room, he returned to his office tormented by the certainty that instead of a solution to so many problems, he had found just the opposite: new and different problems with no solution.

The next day, when Florentino Ariza came into his office, he found a memorandum from Leona Cassiani, with the request that he study it and then show it to his uncle if he thought it appropriate. She was the only one who had not said a word during the inspection the previous afternoon. She had remained silent in full awareness of the worth of her position as a charity employee, but in the memorandum she noted that she had said nothing not because of negligence but out of respect for the hierarchies in the section. It had an alarming simplicity. Uncle Leo XII had proposed a thorough reorganization, but Leona Cassiani did not agree, for the simple reason that in reality the General Section did not exist: it was the dumping ground for annoying but minor problems that the other sections wanted to get rid of. As a consequence, the solution was to eliminate the General Section and return the problems to the sections where they had originated, to be solved there.

Uncle Leo XII did not have the slightest idea who Leona Cassiani was, and he could not remember having seen anyone who could be Leona Cassiani at the meeting on the previous afternoon, but when he read the memorandum he called her to his office and talked with her behind closed doors for two hours. They spoke about everything, in accordance with the method he used to learn about people. The memorandum showed simple common sense, and her suggestion, in fact, would produce the desired result. But Uncle Leo XII was not interested in that: he was interested in her. What most attracted his attention was that her only education after elementary school had been in the School of Millinery. Moreover, she was learning English at home, using an accelerated method with no teacher, and for the past three months she had been taking evening classes in typing, a new kind of work with a wonderful future, as they used to say about the telegraph and before that the steam engine.

When she left the meeting, Uncle Leo XII had already begun to call her what he would always call her: my namesake Leona. He had decided to eliminate with the stroke of a pen the troublesome section and distribute the problems so that they could be solved by the people who had created them, in accordance with Leona Cassiani's suggestion, and he had created a new position for her, which had no title or specific duties but in effect was his Personal Assistant. That afternoon, after the inglorious burial of the General Section, Uncle Leo XII asked Florentino Ariza where he had found Leona Cassiani, and he answered with the truth.

"Well, then, go back to the trolley and bring me every girl like her that you find," his uncle said. "With two or three more, we'll salvage your galleon."

Florentino Ariza took this as one of Uncle Leo XII's typical jokes, but the next day he found himself without the carriage that had been assigned to him six months earlier, and that was taken back now so that he could continue to look for hidden talent on the trolleys. Leona Cassiani, for her part, soon overcame her initial scruples, and she revealed what she had kept hidden with so much astuteness during her first three years. In three more years she had taken control of everything, and in the next four she stood on the threshold of the General Secretaryship, but she refused to cross it because it was only one step below Florentino Ariza. Until then she had taken orders from him, and she wanted to continue to do so, although the fact of the matter was that Florentino himself did not realize that he took orders from her. Indeed, he had done nothing more on the Board of Directors than follow her suggestions, which helped him to move up despite the traps set by his secret enemies.

Leona Cassiani had a diabolical talent for handling secrets, and she always knew how to be where she had to be at the right time. She was dynamic and quiet, with a wise sweetness. But when it was indispensable she would, with sorrow in her heart, give free rein to a character of solid iron. However, she never did that for herself. Her only objective was to clear the ladder at any cost, with blood if necessary, so that Florentino Ariza could move up to the position he had proposed for himself without calculating his own strength very well. She would have done this in any event, of course, because she had an indomitable will to power, but the truth was that she did it consciously, out of simple gratitude. Her determination was so great that Florentino Ariza himself lost his way in her schemes, and on one unfortunate occasion he attempted to block her, thinking that she was trying to do the same to him. Leona Cassiani put him in his place.

"Make no mistake," she said to him. "I will withdraw from all this whenever you wish, but think it over carefully."

Florentino Ariza, who in fact had never thought about it, thought about it then, as well as he could, and he surrendered his weapons. The truth is that in the midst of that sordid internecine battle in a company in perpetual crisis, in the midst of his disasters as a tireless falconer and the more and more uncertain dream of Fermina Daza, the impassive Florentino Ariza had not had a moment of inner peace as he confronted the fascinating spectacle of that fierce black woman smeared with shit and love in the fever of battle. Many times he regretted in secret that she had not been in fact what he thought she was on the afternoon he met her, so that he could wipe his ass with his principles and make love to her even if it cost nuggets of shining gold. For Leona Cassiani was still the woman she had been that afternoon on the trolley, with the same clothes, worthy of an impetuous runaway slave, her mad turbans, her earrings and bracelets made of bone, her necklaces, her rings with fake stones on every finger: a lioness in the streets. The years had changed her appearance very little, and that little became her very well. She moved in splendid maturity, her feminine charms were even more exciting, and her ardent African body was becoming more compact. Florentino Ariza had made no propositions to her in ten years, a hard penance for his original error, and she had helped him in everything except that.

One night when he had worked late, something he did often after his mother's death, Florentino Ariza was about to leave when he saw a light burning in Leona Cassiani's office. He opened the door without knocking, and there she was: alone at her desk, absorbed, serious, with the new eyeglasses that gave her an academic air. Florentino Ariza realized with joyful fear that the two of them were alone in the building, the piers were deserted, the city asleep, the night eternal over the dark sea, and the horn mournful on the ship that would not dock for another hour. Florentino Ariza leaned both hands on his umbrella, just as he had done in Oil Lamp Alley when he barred her way, only now he did it to hide the trembling in his knees.

"Tell me something, lionlady of my soul," he said. "When are we ever going to stop this?"

She took off her glasses without surprise, with absolute self-control, and dazzled him with her solar laugh. It was the first time she used the familiar form of address with him.

"Ay, Florentino Ariza," she said, "I've been sitting here for ten years waiting for you to ask me that."

It was too late: the opportunity had been there with her in the mule-drawn trolley, it had always been with her there on the chair where she was sitting, but now it was gone forever. The truth was that after all the dirty tricks she had done for him, after so much sordidness endured for him, she had moved on in life and was far beyond his twenty-year advantage in age: she had grown too old for him. She loved him so much that instead of deceiving him she preferred to continue loving him, although she had to let him know in a brutal manner.

"No," she said to him. "I would feel as if I were going to bed with the son I never had."

Florentino Ariza was left with the nagging suspicion that this was not her last word. He believed that when a woman says no, she is waiting to be urged before making her final decision, but with her he could not risk making the same mistake twice. He withdrew without protest, and even with a certain grace, which was not easy for him. From that night on, any cloud there might have been between them was dissipated without bitterness, and Florentino Ariza understood at last that it is possible to be a woman's friend and not go to bed with her.

Leona Cassiani was the only human being to whom Florentino Ariza was tempted to reveal the secret of Fermina Daza. The few people who had known were beginning to forget for reasons over which they had no control. Three of them were, beyond the shadow of any doubt, in the grave: his mother, whose memory had been erased long before she died; Gala Placidia, who had died of old age in the service of one who had been like a daughter to her; and the unforgettable Escolástica Daza, the woman who had brought him the first love letter he had ever received in his life, hidden in her prayerbook, and who could not still be alive after so many years. Lorenzo Daza (no one knew if he was alive or dead) might have revealed the secret to Sister Franca de la Luz when he was trying to stop Fermina Daza's expulsion, but it was unlikely that it had gone any further. That left the eleven telegraph operators in Hildebranda Sánchez's province who had handled telegrams with their complete names and exact addresses, and Hildebranda Sánchez herself, and her court of indomitable cousins.

What Florentino Ariza did not know was that Dr. Juvenal Urbino should have been included on the list. Hildebranda Sánchez had revealed the secret to him during one of her many visits in the early years. But she did so in such a casual way and at such an inopportune moment that it did not go in one of Dr. Urbino's ears and out the other, as she thought; it did not go in at all. Hildebranda had mentioned Florentino Ariza as one of the secret poets who, in her opinion, might win the Poetic Festival. Dr. Urbino could not remember who he was, and she told him—she did not need to, but there was no hint of malice in it—that he was Fermina Daza's only sweetheart before she married. She told him, convinced that it had been something so innocent and ephemeral that in fact it was rather touching. Dr. Urbino replied without looking at her: "I did not know that fellow was a poet." And then he wiped him from his memory, because among other things, his profession had accustomed him to the ethical management of forgetfulness.

Florentino Ariza observed that, with the exception of his mother, the keepers of the secret belonged to Fermina Daza's world. In his, he was alone with the crushing weight of a burden that he had often needed to share, but until then there had been no one worthy of so much trust. Leona Cassiani was the only one, and all he needed was the opportunity and the means. This was what he was thinking on the hot summer afternoon when Dr. Juvenal Urbino climbed the steep stairs of the R.C.C., paused on each step in order to survive the three o'clock heat, appeared in Florentino Ariza's office, panting and soaked with perspiration down to his trousers, and gasped with his last breath: "I believe a cyclone is coming." Florentino Ariza had seen him there many times, asking for Uncle Leo XII, but never until now had it seemed so clear to him that this uninvited guest had something to do with his life.

This was during the time that Dr. Juvenal Urbino had overcome the pitfalls of his profession, and was going from door to door, almost like a beggar with his hat in his hand, asking for contributions to his artistic enterprises. Uncle Leo XII had always been one of his most faithful and generous contributors, but just at that moment he had begun his daily ten-minute siesta, sitting in the swivel chair at his desk. Florentino Ariza asked Dr. Juvenal Urbino to please wait in his office, which was next to Uncle Leo XII's and, in a certain sense, served as his waiting room.

They had seen each other on various occasions, but they had never before been face to face as they were now, and once again Florentino Ariza experienced the nausea of feeling himself inferior. The ten minutes were an eternity, during which he stood up three times in the hope that his uncle had awakened early, and he drank an entire thermos of black coffee. Dr. Urbino refused to drink even a single cup. He said: "Coffee is poison." And he continued to chat about one thing and another and did not even care if anyone was listening to him. Florentino Ariza could not bear his natural distinction, the fluidity and precision of his words, his faint scent of camphor, his personal charm, the easy and elegant manner in which he made his most frivolous sentences seem essential only because he had said them. Then, without warning, the Doctor changed the subject.

"Do you like music?"

He was taken by surprise. In reality, Florentino Ariza attended every concert and opera performed in the city, but he did not feel capable of engaging in a critical or well-informed discussion. He had a weakness for popular music, above all sentimental waltzes, whose similarity to the ones he had composed as an adolescent, or to his secret verses, could not be denied. He had only to hear them once, and then for nights on end there was no power in heaven or earth that could shake the melody out of his head. But that would not be a serious answer to a serious question put to him by a specialist.

"I like Gardel," he said.

Dr. Urbino understood. "I see," he said. "He is popular." And he slipped into a recounting of his many new projects which, as always, had to be realized without official backing. He called to his attention the disheartening inferiority of the performances that could be heard here now, compared with the splendid ones of the previous century. That was true: he had spent a year selling subscriptions to bring the Cortot-Casals-Thibaud trio to the Dramatic Theater, and there was no one in the government who even knew who they were, while this very month there were no seats left for the Ramón Caralt company that performed detective dramas, for the Operetta and Zarzuela Company of Don Manolo de la Presa, for the Santanelas, ineffable mimics, illusionists, and artistes, who could change their clothes on stage in the wink of an eye, for Danyse D'Altaine, advertised as a former dancer with the Folies-Bergère, and even for the abominable Ursus, a Basque madman who took on a fighting bull all by himself. There was no reason to complain, however, if the Europeans themselves were once again setting the bad example of a barbaric war when we had begun to live in peace after nine civil wars in half a century, which, if the truth were told, were all one war: always the same war. What most attracted Florentino Ariza's attention in that intriguing speech was the possibility of reviving the Poetic Festival, the most renowned and long-lasting of the enterprises that Dr. Juvenal Urbino had conceived in the past. He had to bite his tongue to keep from telling him that he had been an assiduous participant in the annual competition that had eventually interested famous poets, not only in the rest of the country but in other nations of the Caribbean as well.

No sooner had the conversation begun than the hot, steamy air suddenly cooled and a storm of crosswinds shook doors and windows with great blasts, while the office groaned down to its foundations like a sailing ship set adrift. Dr. Juvenal Urbino did not seem to notice. He made some casual reference to the lunatic cyclones of June and then, out of the blue, he began to speak of his wife. He considered her not only his most enthusiastic collaborator, but the very soul of his endeavors. He said: "Without her I would be nothing." Florentino Ariza listened to him, impassive, nodding his agreement with a slight motion of his head, not daring to say anything for fear his voice would betray him. Two or three sentences more, however, were enough for him to understand that Dr. Juvenal Urbino, in the midst of so many absorbing commitments, still had more than enough time to adore his wife almost as much as he did, and that truth stunned him. But he could not respond as he would have liked, because then his heart played one of those whorish tricks that only hearts can play: it revealed to him that he and this man, whom he had always considered his personal enemy, were victims of the same fate and shared the hazards of a common passion; they were two animals yoked together. For the first time in the interminable twenty-seven years that he had been waiting, Florentino Ariza could not endure the pangs of grief at the thought that this admirable man would have to die in order for him to be happy.

The cyclone passed by at last, but in fifteen minutes its gusting northwest winds had devastated the neighborhoods by the swamps and caused severe damage in half the city. Dr. Juvenal Urbino, gratified once again by the generosity of Uncle Leo XII, did not wait for the weather to clear, and without thinking he accepted the umbrella that Florentino Ariza lent him for walking to his carriage. But he did not mind. On the contrary: he was happy thinking about what Fermina Daza would think when she learned who the owner of the umbrella was. He was still troubled by the unsettling interview when Leona Cassiani came into his office, and this seemed to him a unique opportunity to stop beating about the bush and to reveal his secret, as if he were squeezing a boil that would not leave him in peace: it was now or never. He began by asking her what she thought of Dr. Juvenal Urbino. She answered almost without thinking: "He is a man who does many things, too many perhaps, but I believe that no one knows what he thinks." Then she reflected, shredding the eraser on a pencil with her long, sharp, black woman's teeth, and at last she shrugged her shoulders to put an end to a matter that did not concern her.

"That may be the reason he does so many things," she said, "so that he will not have to think."

Florentino Ariza tried to keep her with him.

"What hurts me is that he has to die," he said.

"Everybody has to die," she said.

"Yes," he said, "but he more than anyone else."

She understood none of it: she shrugged her shoulders again without speaking and left. Then Florentino Ariza knew that some night, sometime in the future, in a joyous bed with Fermina Daza, he was going to tell her that he had not revealed the secret of his love, not even to the one person who had earned the right to know it. No: he would never reveal it, not even to Leona Cassiani, not because he did not want to open the chest where he had kept it so carefully hidden for half his life, but because he realized only then that he had lost the key.

That, however, was not the most staggering event of the afternoon. He still had the nostalgic memory of his youth, his vivid recollection of the Poetic Festival, whose thunder sounded throughout the Antilles every April 15. He was always one of the protagonists, but always, as in almost everything he did, a secret protagonist. He had participated several times since the inaugural competition, and he had never received even honorable mention. But that did not matter to him, for he did compete not out of ambition for the prize but because the contest held an additional attraction for him: in the first session Fermina Daza had opened the sealed envelopes and announced the names of the winners, and then it was established that she would continue to do so in the years that followed.

Hidden in the darkness of an orchestra seat, a fresh camellia in the buttonhole of his lapel throbbing with the strength of his desire, Florentino Ariza saw Fermina Daza open the three sealed envelopes on the stage of the old National Theater on the night of the first Festival. He asked himself what was going to happen in her heart when she discovered that he was the winner of the Golden Orchid. He was certain she would recognize his handwriting, and that then she would evoke the afternoons of embroidery under the almond trees in the little park, the scent of faded gardenias in his letters, the private Waltz of the Crowned Goddess at windblown daybreak. It did not happen. Even worse, the Golden Orchid, the most sought-after prize among the nation's poets, was awarded to a Chinese immigrant. The public scandal provoked by that unheard-of decision threw doubts on the seriousness of the competition. But the decision was correct, and the unanimity of the judges had its justification in the excellence of the sonnet.

No one believed that the author was the Chinese who received the prize. At the end of the last century, fleeing the scourge of yellow fever that devastated Panama during the construction of the railroad between the two oceans, he had arrived along with many others who stayed here until they died, living in Chinese, reproducing in Chinese, and looking so much alike that no one could tell one from the other. At first there were no more than ten, some of them with their wives and children and edible dogs, but in a few years four narrow streets in the slums along the port were overflowing with other, unexpected Chinese, who came into the country without leaving a trace in the customs records. Some of the young ones turned into venerable patriarchs with so much haste that no one could explain how they had time to grow old. In the popular view they were divided into two kinds: bad Chinese and good Chinese. The bad ones were those in the lugubrious restaurants along the waterfront, where one was as likely to eat like a king as to die a sudden death at the table, sitting before a plate of rat meat with sunflowers, and which were thought to be nothing more than fronts for white slavery and many other kinds of traffic. The good ones were the Chinese in the laundries, heirs of a sacred knowledge, who returned one's shirts cleaner than new, with collars and cuffs like recently ironed Communion wafers. The man who defeated seventy-two well-prepared rivals in the Poetic Festival was one of these good Chinese.

When a bewildered Fermina Daza read out the name, no one understood it, not only because it was an unusual name but because no one knew for certain what Chinese were called. But it was not necessary to think about it very much, because the victorious Chinese walked from the back of the theater with that celestial smile Chinese wear when they come home early. He had been so sure of victory that he had put on a yellow silk robe, appropriate to the rites of spring, in order to accept the prize. He received the eighteen-carat Golden Orchid and kissed it with joy in the midst of the thundering jeers of the incredulous. He did not react. He waited in the middle of the stage, as imperturbable as the apostle of a Divine Providence less dramatic than ours, and as soon as it was quiet he read the winning poem. No one understood him. But when the new round of jeers and whistles was over, an impassive Fermina Daza read it again, in her hoarse, suggestive voice, and amazement reigned after the first line. It was a perfect sonnet in the purest Parnassian tradition, and through it there wafted a breath of inspiration that revealed the involvement of a master hand. The only possible explanation was that one of the great poets had devised the joke in order to ridicule the Poetic Festival, and that the Chinese had been a party to it and was determined to keep the secret until the day he died. The *Commercial Daily*, our traditional newspaper, tried to save our civic honor with an erudite and rather confused essay concerning the antiquity and cultural influence of the Chinese in the Caribbean, and the right they had earned to participate in Poetic Festivals. The author of the essay did not doubt that the writer of the sonnet was in fact who he said he was, and he defended him in a straightforward manner, beginning with the title itself: "All Chinese Are Poets." The instigators of the plot, if there was one, rotted in their graves along with the secret. For his part, the Chinese who had won died without confession at an Oriental age and was buried with the Golden Orchid in his coffin, but also with the bitterness of never having achieved the only thing he wanted in his life, which was recognition as a poet. On his death, the press recalled the forgotten incident of the Poetic Festival and reprinted the sonnet with a Modernist vignette of fleshy maidens and gold cornucopias, and the guardian angels of poetry took advantage of the opportunity to clarify matters: the sonnet seemed so bad to the younger generation that no one could doubt any longer that it had, in fact, been composed by the dead Chinese.

Florentino Ariza always associated that scandalous event with the memory of an opulent stranger who sat beside him. He had noticed her at the beginning of the ceremony, but then he had forgotten her in the frightful suspense of anticipation. She attracted his attention because of her mother-of-pearl whiteness, her happy plump woman's scent, her immense soprano's bosom crowned by an artificial magnolia. She wore a very close-fitting black velvet dress, as black as her eager warm eyes, and her hair, caught at the nape of her neck with a gypsy comb, was blacker still. She wore pendant earrings, a matching necklace, and identical rings, shaped like sparkling roses, on several fingers. A beauty mark had been drawn with pencil on her right cheek. In the din of the final applause, she looked at Florentino Ariza with sincere grief.

"Believe me, my heart goes out to you," she said to him.

Florentino Ariza was amazed, not because of the condolences, which he in fact deserved, but because of his overwhelming astonishment that anyone knew his secret. She explained: "I knew because of how the flower trembled in your lapel as they opened the envelopes." She showed him the velvet magnolia in her hand, and she opened her heart to him.

"That is why I took off mine," she said.

She was on the verge of tears because of his

305

defeat, but Florentino Ariza raised her spirits with his instincts of a nocturnal hunter.

"Let us go someplace where we can cry together," he said.

He accompanied her to her house. At the door, since it was almost midnight and there was no one on the street, he persuaded her to invite him in for a brandy while they looked at the scrapbooks and photograph albums, containing over ten years of public events, which she had told him she owned. It was an old trick even then, but this time it was guileless, because she was the one who had talked about her albums as they walked from the National Theater. They went in. The first thing Florentino Ariza observed in the living room was that the door to the only bedroom was open, and that the bed was huge and luxurious with a brocaded quilt and a headboard with brass foliage. That disturbed him. She must have realized it, for she crossed the living room and closed the bedroom door. Then she invited him to sit down on a flowered cretonne sofa where a sleeping cat was lying, and she placed her collection of albums on the coffee table. Florentino Ariza began to leaf through them in an unhurried way, thinking more about his next step than about what he was seeing, and then he looked up and saw that her eyes were full of tears. He advised her to cry to her heart's content, and to feel no shame, for there was no greater relief than weeping, but he suggested that she loosen her bodice first. He hurried to help her, because her bodice was tightly fastened in the back with a long closure of crossed laces. He did not have to unlace them all, for the bodice burst open from sheer internal pressure, and her astronomical bosom was able to breathe freely.

Florentino Ariza, who had never lost the timidity of a novice even in comfortable circumstances, risked a superficial caress on her neck with the tips of his fingers, and she writhed and moaned like a spoiled child and did not stop crying. Then he kissed her on the same spot, just as softly, and he could not kiss her a second time because she turned toward him with all her monumental body, eager and warm, and they rolled in an embrace on the floor. The cat on the sofa awoke with a screech and jumped on top of them. They groped like desperate virgins and found each other any way they could, wallowing in the torn albums, fully dressed, soaked with sweat, and more concerned with avoiding the furious claws of the cat than with the disastrous love they were making. But beginning the following night, their scratches still bleeding, they continued to make love for several years.

When he realized that he had begun to love her, she was in the fullness of her years, and he was approaching his thirtieth birthday. Her name was Sara Noriega, and she had enjoyed fifteen minutes of fame in her youth when she won a competition with a collection of poems about love among the poor, a book that was never published. She was a teacher of deportment and civics in the public schools, and she lived on her salary in a rented flat

307

in the motley Sweethearts' Mews in the old Gethsemane District. She had had several occasional lovers, but none with intentions of matrimony, because it was difficult for a man of her time and place to marry a woman he had taken to bed. Nor did she cherish that dream again after her first formal fiancé, whom she loved with the almost demented passion of which one is capable at the age of eighteen, broke the engagement one week before the date they had set for the wedding, and left her to wander the limbo of abandoned brides. Or of used goods, as they used to say in those days. And yet that first experience, although cruel and short-lived, did not leave her bitter; rather, she had the overwhelming conviction that with or without marriage, or God, or the law, life was not worth living without a man in her bed. What Florentino Ariza liked best about her was that in order to reach the heights of glory, she had to suck on an infant's pacifier while they made love. Eventually they had a string of them, in every size, shape, and color they could find in the market, and Sara Noriega hung them on the headboard so she could reach them without looking in her moments of extreme urgency.

Although she was as free as he was, and perhaps would not have been opposed to making their relationship public, from the very first Florentino Ariza considered it a clandestine adventure. He would slip in by the back door, almost always very late at night, and sneak away on tiptoe just before dawn. He knew as well as she that in a crowded and subdivided building like hers the neighbors had to know more than they pretended. But although it was a mere formality, that was how Florentino Ariza was, how he would be with all women for the rest of his life. He never made a slip, with her or with any other woman; he never betrayed their confidence. He did not exaggerate: on only one occasion did he leave a compromising trace or written evidence, and this might have cost him his life. In truth, he always behaved as if he were the eternal husband of Fermina Daza, an unfaithful husband but a tenacious one, who fought endlessly to free himself from his servitude without causing her the displeasure of a betrayal.

Such secretiveness could not flourish without misapprehensions. Tránsito Ariza died in the conviction that the son she had conceived in love and raised for love was immune to any kind of love because of his first youthful misfortune. But many less benevolent people who were very close to him, who were familiar with his mysterious character and his fondness for mystic ceremonies and strange lotions, shared the suspicion that he was immune not to love but only to women. Florentino Ariza knew it and never did anything to disprove it. It did not worry Sara Noriega either. Like the countless other women who loved him, and even those who gave and received pleasure without loving him, she accepted him for what he really was: a man passing through.

He eventually showed up at her house at any hour, above all on Sunday mornings, the most peaceful time. She would leave whatever she was doing, no matter what it was, and devote her entire body to trying to make him happy in the enormous mythic bed that was always ready for him, and in which she never permitted the invocation of liturgical formalisms. Florentino Ariza did not understand how a single woman without a past could be so wise in the ways of men, or how she could move her sweet porpoise body with as much lightness and tenderness as if she were moving under water. She would defend herself, saying that love, no matter what else it might be, was a natural talent. She would say: "You are either born knowing how, or you never know." Florentino Ariza writhed with retrogressive jealousy, thinking that perhaps she had more of a past than she pretended, but he had to swallow everything she said because he told her, as he told them all, that she had been his only lover. Among many other things that he did not like, he had to resign himself to having the furious cat in bed with them, although Sara Noriega had his claws removed so he would not tear them apart while they made love.

However, almost as much as rolling in bed until they were exhausted, she liked to devote the aftermath of love to the cult of poetry. She had an astonishing memory for the sentimental verses of her own time, which were sold in the street in pamphlet form for two centavos as soon as they were written, and she also pinned on the walls the poems she liked most, so that she could read them aloud whenever she wished. She had written versions of the deportment and civics texts in hendecasyllabic couplets, like those used for spelling, but she could not obtain official approval for them. Her declamatory passion was such that at times she continued to shout her recitation as they made love, and Florentino Ariza had to force a pacifier into her mouth, as one did with children to make them stop crying.

In the plenitude of their relationship, Florentino Ariza had asked himself which of the two was love: the turbulent bed or the peaceful Sunday afternoons, and Sara Noriega calmed him with the simple argument that love was everything they did naked. She said: "Spiritual love from the waist up and physical love from the waist down." Sara Noriega thought this definition would be good for a poem about divided love, which they wrote together and which she submitted to the Fifth Poetic Festival, convinced that no participant had ever presented such an original poem. But she lost again.

She was in a rage as Florentino Ariza accompanied her to her house. For some reason she could not explain, she was convinced that Fermina Daza had plotted against her so that her poem would not win first prize. Florentino Ariza paid no attention to her. He had been in a somber mood ever since the awarding of the prizes, for he had not seen Fermina Daza in a long time, and that night he had the impression that she had undergone a profound change: for the first time one could tell just by looking at her that she was a mother. This came as no surprise to him, for he knew that her son was already in school. However, her maternal age had never seemed so apparent to him as it did that night, as much for the size of her waist and the slight shortness of breath when she walked as for the break in her voice when she read the list of prizewinners.

In an attempt to document his memories, he leafed through the albums of the Poetic Festivals while Sara Noriega prepared something to eat. He saw magazine photographs in color, yellowing postcards of the sort sold in arcades for souvenirs, and it was a kind of ghostly review of the fallacy of his own life. Until that time he had maintained the fiction that it was the world that was changing, and its customs and styles: everything but her. But that night he saw for the first time in a conscious way how Fermina Daza's life was passing, and how his was passing, while he did nothing more than wait. He had never spoken about her to anyone, because he knew he was incapable of saying her name without everyone's noticing the pallor of his lips. But that night, as he looked through the albums as he had done on so many other evenings of Sunday tedium, Sara Noriega made one of those casual observations that freeze the blood.

"She's a whore," she said.

She said it as she walked past him and saw a print of Fermina Daza disguised as a black panther at a masquerade ball, and she did not have to

312

mention anyone by name for Florentino Ariza to know whom she was talking about. Fearing a revelation that would shake his very life, he hurried to a cautious defense. He objected that he knew Fermina Daza only from a distance, that they had never gone further than formal greetings, that he had no information about her private life, but was certain she was an admirable woman who had come out of nowhere and risen to the top by virtue of her own merits.

"By virtue of marrying a man she does not love for money," interrupted Sara Noriega. "That's the lowest kind of whore." His mother had told Florentino Ariza the same thing, with less crudeness but with the same moral rigidity, when she tried to console him for his misfortunes. Shaken to the very core, he could find no appropriate response to Sara Noriega's harshness, and he attempted to change the subject. But Sara Noriega would not allow that to happen until she had given vent to her feelings. In a flash of inspiration that she could not have explained, she was convinced that Fermina Daza had been the one behind the conspiracy to cheat her of the prize. There was no reason to think so: they did not know each other, they had never met, and Fermina Daza had nothing to do with the decision of the judges even though she was privy to their secrets. Sara Noriega said in a categorical manner: "We women intuit these things." And that ended the discussion.

From that moment on, Florentino Ariza began to see her with different eyes. The years were passing for her too. Her abundant sexuality was withering without glory, her lovemaking was slowed by her sobbing, and her eyelids were beginning to darken with old bitterness. She was yesterday's flower. Besides, in her fury at the defeat, she had lost count of her brandies. It was not her night: while they were eating their reheated coconut rice, she tried to establish how much each of them had contributed to the losing poem, in order to determine how many petals of the Golden Orchid would have gone to each one. This was not the first time they had amused themselves with Byzantine competitions, but he took advantage of the opportunity to speak through his own newly opened wound, and they became entangled in a mean-spirited argument that stirred up in both of them the rancor of almost five years of divided love.

At ten minutes before twelve, Sara Noriega climbed up on a chair to wind the pendulum clock, and she reset it on the hour, perhaps trying to tell him without saying so that it was time to leave. Then Florentino Ariza felt an urgent need to put a definitive end to that loveless relationship, and he looked for the opportunity to be the one to take the initiative: as he would always do. Praying that Sara Noriega would let him into her bed so that he could tell her no, that everything was over, he asked her to sit next to him when she finished winding the clock. But she preferred to keep her distance in the visitor's easy chair. Then Florentino Ariza extended his index finger, wet with brandy, so that she could suck it, as she had liked to do in the past during their preambles to love. She refused.

"Not now," she said. "I'm expecting someone.

Ever since his rejection by Fermina Daza, Florentino Ariza had learned to always keep the final decision for himself. In less bitter circumstances he would have persisted in his pursuit of Sara Noriega, certain of ending the evening rolling in bed with her, for he was convinced that once a woman goes to bed with a man, she will continue to go to bed with him whenever he desires, as long as he knows how to move her to passion each time. He had endured everything because of that conviction, he had overlooked everything, even the dirtiest dealings in love, so that he would not have to grant to any woman born of woman the opportunity to make the final decision. But that night he felt so humiliated that he gulped down the brandy in a single swallow, doing all he could to display anger, and left without saying goodbye. They never saw each other again.

The relationship with Sara Noriega was one of Florentino Ariza's longest and most stable affairs, although it was not his only one during those five years. When he realized that he felt happy with her, above all in bed, but that she would never replace Fermina Daza, he had another outbreak of his nights as a solitary hunter, and he arranged matters so that he could portion out his time and strength as far as they would go. Sara Noriega, however, achieved the miracle of curing him for a time. At least now he could live without seeing Fermina Daza, instead of interrupting whatever he was doing at any hour of the day to search for her along the uncertain pathways of his presentiments, on the most unlikely streets, in unreal places where she could not possibly be, wandering without reason, with a longing in his breast that gave him no rest until he saw her, even for an instant. The break with Sara Noriega, however, revived his dormant grief, and once again he felt as he did on those afternoons of endless reading in the little park, but this time it was exacerbated by his urgent need for Dr. Juvenal Urbino to die.

He had known for a long time that he was predestined to make a widow happy, and that she would make him happy, and that did not worry him. On the contrary: he was prepared. After having known so many of them during his incursions as a solitary hunter, Florentino Ariza had come to realize that the world was full of happy widows. He had seen them go mad with grief at the sight of their husband's corpse, pleading to be buried alive in the same coffin so they would not have to face the future without him, but as they grew reconciled to the reality of their new condition he had seen them rise up from the ashes with renewed vitality. They began by living like parasites of gloom in their big empty houses, they became the confidantes of their servants, lovers of their pillows, with nothing to do after so many years of sterile captivity. They wasted their overabundant hours doing what they had not had time for before, sewing the buttons on the dead man's clothes, ironing and reironing the shirts with stiff collar and cuffs so that they would always in in perfect condition. They continued to put his soap in the bathroom, his monogrammed pillowcase on the bed; his place was always set at the table, in case he returned from the dead without warning, as he tended to do in life. But in those solitary Masses they began to be aware that once again they were mistresses of their fate, after having renounced not only their family name but their own identity in exchange for a security that was no more than another of a bride's many illusions. They alone knew how tiresome was the man they loved to distraction, who perhaps loved them but whom they had to continue nurturing until his last breath as if he were a child, suckling him, changing his soiled diapers, distracting him with a mother's tricks to ease his terror at going out each morning to face reality. And nevertheless, when they watched him leave the house, this man they themselves had urged to conquer the world, then they were the ones left with the terror that he would never return. That was their life. Love, if it existed, was something separate: another life.

In the restorative idleness of solitude, on the other hand, the widows discovered that the honorable way to live was at the body's bidding, eating only when one was hungry, loving without lies, sleeping without having to feign sleep in order to escape the indecency of official love, possessed at last of the right to an entire bed to themselves, where no one fought them for half of the sheet, half of the air they breathed, half of their night, until their bodies were satisfied with dreaming their own dreams, and they woke alone. In the dawns of his furtive hunting, Florentino Ariza would see them coming out of five o'clock Mass, shrouded in black and with the raven of destiny on their shoulder. As soon as they spotted him in the light of dawn, they would cross the street to walk on the other side with their small, hesitant steps, the steps of a little bird, for just walking near a man might stain their honor. And yet he was convinced that a disconsolate widow, more than any other woman, might carry within her the seed of happiness.

So many widows in his life, since the Widow Nazaret, had made it possible for him to discern how happy they were after the death of their husbands. What had been only a dream until then was changed, thanks to them, into a possibility that he could seize with both hands. He saw no reason why Fermina Daza should not be a widow like them, prepared by life to accept him just as he was, without fantasies of guilt because of her dead husband, resolved to discover with him the other happiness of being happy twice, with one love for everyday use which would become, more and more, a miracle of being alive, and the other love that belonged to her alone, the love immunized by death against all contagion.

Perhaps he would not have been as enthusiastic if he had even suspected how far Fermina Daza was from those illusory calculations, at a time when she was just beginning to perceive the horizon of a world in which everything was foreseen except adversity. In those days, being rich had many advantages, and many disadvantages as well, of course, but half the world longed for it as the most probable way to live forever. Fermina Daza had rejected Florentino Ariza in a lightning flash of maturity which she paid for immediately with a crisis of pity, but she never doubted that her decision had been correct. At the time she could not explain what hidden impulses of her reason had allowed her that clairvoyance, but many years later, on the eve of old age, she uncovered them suddenly and without knowing how during a casual conversation about Florentino Ariza. Everyone knew that he was heir apparent to the River Company of the Caribbean during its greatest period; they were all sure they had seen him many times, and had even had dealings with him, but no one could remember what he was like. It was then that Fermina Daza experienced the revelation of the unconscious motives that had kept her from loving him. She said: "It is as if he were not a person but only a shadow." That is what he was: the shadow of someone whom no one had ever known. But while she resisted the siege of Dr. Juvenal Urbino, who was just the opposite, she felt herself tormented by the phantom of guilt: the only emotion she could not bear. When she felt it coming on, a kind of panic overtook her which she could control only if she found someone to soothe her conscience. Ever since she was a little girl, when a plate broke in the kitchen, when someone fell, when she herself caught her finger in the door, she would turn in dismay to the nearest adult and make her accusation: "It was your fault." Although in reality she was not concerned with who was responsible or with convincing herself of her own innocence: she was satisfied at having established it.

The specter was so notorious that Dr. Urbino realized how much it threatened the harmony of his home, and as soon as he detected it he hastened to tell his wife: "Don't worry, my love, it was my fault." For he feared nothing so much as his wife's sudden categorical decisions, and he was convinced that they always originated in a feeling of guilt. The confusion caused by her rejection of Florentino Ariza, however, had not been resolved with comforting words. For several months Fermina Daza continued to open up the balcony in the morning, and she always missed the solitary phantom watching her from the deserted little park; she saw the tree that had been his, the most obscure bench where he would sit to read as he thought about her, suffered for her, and she would have to close the window again, sighing: "Poor man." When it was already too late to make up for the past, she even suffered the disillusionment of knowing that he was not as tenacious as she had supposed, and from time to time she would still feel a belated longing for a letter that never arrived. But when she had to face the decision of marrying Juvenal Urbino, she succumbed, in a major crisis, when she realized that she had no valid reasons for preferring him after she had rejected Florentino Ariza without valid reasons. In fact, she loved him as little as she had loved the other one, but knew much less about him, and his letters did not have the fervor of the other one's, nor had he given her so many moving proofs of his determination. The truth is that Juvenal Urbino's suit had never been undertaken in the name of love, and it was curious, to say the least, that a militant Catholic like him would offer her only worldly goods: security, order, happiness, contiguous numbers that, once they were added together, might resemble love, almost be love. But they were not love, and these doubts increased her confusion, because she was also not convinced that love was really what she most needed to live.

In any case, the principal factor operating against Dr. Juvenal Urbino was his more than suspect resemblance to the ideal man that Lorenzo Daza had so wanted for his daughter. It was impossible not to see him as the creature of a paternal plot, even if in reality he was not, but Fermina Daza became convinced that he was from the time she saw him come to her house for a second, unsolicited medical call. In the end, her conversations with Cousin Hildebranda only confused her. Because of Cousin Hildebranda's own situation as a victim, she tended to identify with Florentino Ariza, forgetting that perhaps Lorenzo Daza had arranged her visit so that she could use her influence in favor of Dr. Urbino. God alone knows what it cost Fermina Daza not to accompany her cousin when she went to meet Florentino Ariza in the telegraph office. She would have liked to see him again to present him with her doubts, to speak with him alone, to learn to know him well so that she could be certain that her impulsive decision would not precipitate her into another, more serious one: capitulation in her personal war against her father. But that is what she did at a crucial moment in her life, giving no importance whatsoever to the handsomeness of her suitor, or his legendary wealth, or his youthful glory, or any of his numerous virtues; rather, she was stunned by the fear of an opportunity slipping away, and by the imminence of her twenty-first birthday, which was her private time limit for surrendering to fate. That one moment was enough for her to make the decision that was foreseen in the laws of God and man: until death do you part. Then all her doubts vanished, and she could accomplish without remorse what reason indicated as the most decent thing to do: with no tears, she wiped away the memory of Florentino Ariza, she erased him completely, and in the space that he had occupied in her memory she allowed a field of poppies to bloom. All that she permitted herself was one final sigh that was deeper than usual: "Poor man!"

The most fearful doubts began, however, when she returned from her honeymoon. As soon as they opened the trunks, unpacked the furniture, and emptied the eleven chests she had brought in

322

order to take possession as lady and mistress of the former palace of the Marquis de Casalduero, she realized with mortal vertigo that she was a prisoner in the wrong house and, even worse, with a man who was not. It took her six years to leave, the worst years of her life, when she was in despair because of the bitterness of Doña Blanca, her mother-in-law, and the mental lethargy of her sisters-in-law, who did not go to rot in a convent cell only because they already carried one inside themselves.

Dr. Urbino, resigned to paying homage to his lineage, turned a deaf ear to her pleas, confident that the wisdom of God and his wife's infinite capacity to adapt would resolve the situation. He was pained by the deterioration of his mother, whose joy in living had, at one time, sparked the desire to live in even the most skeptical. It was true: that beautiful, intelligent woman, with a human sensibility not at all common in her milieu, had been the soul and body of her social paradise for almost forty years. Widowhood had so embittered her that she did not seem the same person; it had made her flabby and sour and the enemy of the world. The only possible explanation for her decline was the rancor she felt because her husband had knowingly sacrificed himself for a black rabble, as she used to say, when the only fitting sacrifice would have been to survive for her sake. In any case, Fermina Daza's happy marriage lasted as long as the honeymoon, and the only person who could help her to prevent its final wreckage was paralyzed by terror in the presence of his mother's power. It was he, and not her imbecilic sisters-in-law and her half-mad mother-in-law, whom Fermina Daza blamed for the death trap that held her. She suspected too late that behind his professional authority and worldly charm, the man she had married was a hopeless weakling: a poor devil made bold by the social weight of his family names.

She took refuge in her newborn son. She had felt him leave her body with a sensation of relief at freeing herself from something that did not belong to her, and she had been horrified at herself when she confirmed that she did not feel the slightest affection for that calf from her womb the midwife showed her in the raw, smeared with grease and blood and with the umbilical cord rolled around his neck. But in her loneliness in the palace she learned to know him, they learned to know each other, and she discovered with great delight that one does not love one's children just because they are one's children but because of the friendship formed while raising them. She came to despise anything and anyone who was not him in the house of her misfortune. She was depressed by the solitude, the cemetery garden, the squandering of time in the enormous, windowless rooms. During the endless nights she felt herself losing her mind, as the madwomen screamed in the asylum next door. She was ashamed of their custom of setting the banquet table every day with embroidered tablecloths, silver service, and funereal candelabra so that five phantoms could dine on *café con leche* and crullers. She detested the rosary at dusk, the affected table etiquette, the constant criticism of the way she held her silverware, the way she walked in mystical strides like a woman of the streets, the way she dressed as if she were in the circus, and even the rustic way she treated her husband and nursed her child without covering her breast with her mantilla. When she issued her first invitations to five o'clock tea, with little imperial cakes and candied flowers, in accordance with recent English fashion, Doña Blanca objected to serving remedies for sweating out a fever in her house instead of chocolate with aged cheese and rounded loaves of cassava bread. Not even dreams escaped her notice. One morning when Fermina Daza said she had dreamed about a naked stranger who walked through the salons of the palace scattering fistfuls of ashes, Doña Blanca cut her off:

"A decent woman cannot have that kind of dream."

Along with the feeling of always being in someone else's house came two even greater misfortunes. One was the almost daily diet of eggplant in all its forms, which Doña Blanca refused to vary out of respect for her dead husband, and which Fermina Daza refused to eat. She had despised eggplants ever since she was a little girl, even before she had tasted them, because it always seemed to her that they were the color of poison. Only now she had to admit that in this case something had changed for the better in her life, because at the age of five she had said the same thing at the table, and her father had forced her to eat the entire casserole intended for six people. She thought she was going to die, first because she vomited pulverized eggplant and then because of the cupful of castor oil she had to take as a cure for the punishment. Both things were confused in her memory as a single purgative, as much for the taste as for her terror of the poison, and at the abominable lunches in the palace of the Marquis de Casalduero she had to look away so as not to repay their kindness with the icy nausea of castor oil.

The other misfortune was the harp. One day, very conscious of what she meant, Doña Blanca had said: "I do not believe in decent women who do not know how to play the piano." It was an order that even her son tried to dispute, for the best years of his childhood had been spent in the galley slavery of piano lessons, although as an adult he would be grateful for them. He could not imagine his wife, with her character, subjected to the same punishment at the age of twenty-five. But the only concession he could wring from his mother, with the puerile argument that it was the instrument of the angels, was to substitute the harp for the piano. And so it was that they brought a magnificent harp from Vienna that seemed to be gold and sounded as if it were, and that was one of the most valued heirlooms in the Museum of the City until it and all it contained were consumed in flames. Fermina Daza submitted to this deluxe prison sentence in an attempt to avoid catastrophe with one final sacrifice. She began to study with a teacher of teachers, whom they brought for that purpose from the city of Mompox, and who died unexpectedly two weeks later, and she continued for several years with the best musician at the seminary, whose gravedigger's breath distorted her arpeggios.

She herself was surprised at her obedience. For although she did not admit it in her innermost thoughts, or in the silent arguments she had with her husband during the hours they had once devoted to love, she had been caught up more quickly than she had believed in the tangle of conventions and prejudices of her new world. At first she had a ritual phrase that affirmed her freedom of thought: "To hell with a fan when the wind is blowing." But later, jealous of her carefully won privileges, fearful of embarrassment and scorn, she demonstrated her willingness to endure even humiliation in the hope that God would at last take pity on Doña Blanca, who never tired of begging Him in her prayers to send her death.

Dr. Urbino justified his own weakness with grave arguments, not even asking himself if they were in conflict with the Church. He would not admit that the difficulties with his wife had their origin in the rarefied air of the house, but blamed them on the very nature of matrimony: an absurd invention that could exist only by the infinite grace of God. It was against all scientific reason for two people who hardly knew each other, with no ties at all between them, with different characters, different upbringings, and even different genders, to suddenly find themselves committed to living together, to sleeping in the same bed, to sharing two destinies that perhaps were fated to go in opposite directions. He would say: "The problem with marriage is that it ends every night after making love, and it must be rebuilt every morning before breakfast." And worst of all was theirs, arising out of two opposing classes, in a city that still dreamed of the return of the Viceroys. The only possible bond was something as improbable and fickle as love, if there was any, and in their case there was none when they married, and when they were on the verge of inventing it, fate had done nothing more than confront them with reality.

That was the condition of their lives during the period of the harp. They had left behind the delicious coincidences of her coming in while he was taking a bath, when, despite the arguments and the poisonous eggplant, and despite his demented sisters and the mother who bore them, he still had enough love to ask her to soap him. She began to do it with the crumbs of love that still remained from Europe, and both allowed themselves to be betrayed by memories, softening without wanting to, desiring each other without saying so, and at last they would die of love on the floor, spattered with fragrant suds, as they heard the maids talking about them in the laundry room: "If they don't have more children it's because they don't fuck." From time to time, when they came home from a wild fiesta, the nostalgia crouching behind the door would knock them down with one blow of its paw, and then there would be a marvelous explosion in which everything was the way it used to be and for five minutes they were once again the uninhibited lovers of their honeymoon.

But except for those rare occasions, one of them was always more tired than the other when it was time to go to bed. She would dawdle in the bathroom, rolling her cigarettes in perfumed paper, smoking alone, relapsing into her consolatory love as she did when she was young and free in her own house, mistress of her own body. She always had a headache, or it was too hot, always, or she pretended to be asleep, or she had her period again, her period, always her period. So much so that Dr. Urbino had dared to say in class, only for the relief of unburdening himself without confession, that after ten years of marriage women had their periods as often as three times a week.

Misfortune piled on misfortune, and in the worst of those years Fermina Daza had to face what was bound to come sooner or later: the truth of her father's fabulous and always mysterious dealings. The Governor of the Province made an appointment with Juvenal Urbino in his office to bring him up to date on the excesses of his father-in-law, which he summed up in a single sentence: "There is no law, human or divine, that this man has not ignored." Some of his most serious schemes had been carried out in the shadow of his son-in-law's prestige, and it would have been difficult to believe that he and his wife knew nothing about them. Realizing that the only reputation to protect was his own, because it was the only one still standing, Dr. Juvenal Urbino intervened with all the weight of his prestige, and he succeeded in covering up the scandal with his word of honor. So that Lorenzo Daza left the country on the first boat, never to return. He went back to his native country as if it were one of those little trips one takes from time to time to ward off nostalgia, and at the bottom of that appearance there was some truth: for a long time he had boarded ships from his country just to drink a glass of water from the cisterns filled with the rains of the village where he was born. He left without having his arm twisted, protesting his innocence, and still trying to convince his son-in-law that he had been the victim of a political conspiracy. He left crying for his girl, as he had called Fermina Daza since her marriage, crying for his grandson, for the land in which he had become rich and free and where, on the basis of his shady dealings, he had won the power to turn his daughter into an exquisite lady. He left old and sick, but still he lived much longer than any of his victims might have desired. Fermina Daza could not repress a sigh of relief when she received news of his death, and in order to avoid questions she did not wear mourning, but for several months she wept with mute fury without knowing why when she locked herself in the bathroom to smoke, and it was because she was crying for him.

The most absurd element in their situation was that they never seemed so happy in public as during those years of misery. For this was the time of their greatest victories over the subterranean hostility of a milieu that resisted accepting them as they were: different and modern, and for that reason transgressors against the traditional order. That, however, had been the easy part for Fermina Daza. Life in the world, which had caused her so much uncertainty before she was familiar with it, was nothing more than a system of atavistic contracts, banal ceremonies, preordained words, with which people entertained each other in society in order not to commit murder. The dominant sign in that paradise of provincial frivolity was fear of the unknown. She had defined it in a simpler way: "The problem in public life is learning to overcome terror; the problem in married life is learning to overcome boredom." She had made this sudden discovery with the clarity of a revelation when, trailing her endless bridal train behind her, she had entered the vast salon of the Social Club, where the air was thin with the mingled scent of so many flowers, the brilliance of the waltzes, the tumult of perspiring men and tremulous women who looked at her not knowing how they were going to exorcise the dazzling menace that had come to them from the outside world. She had just turned twenty-one and had done little more than leave her house to go to school, but with one look around her she understood that her adversaries were not convulsed with hatred but

331

paralyzed by fear. Instead of frightening them even more, as she was already doing, she had the compassion to help them learn to know her. They were no different from what she wanted them to be, just as in the case of cities, which did not seem better or worse to her, but only as she made them in her heart. Despite the perpetual rain, the sordid merchants, and the Homeric vulgarity of its carriage drivers, she would always remember Paris as the most beautiful city in the world, not because of what it was or was not in reality, but because it was linked to the memory of her happiest years. Dr. Urbino, for his part, commanded respect with the same weapons that were used against him, except that his were wielded with more intelligence and with calculated solemnity. Nothing happened without them: civic exhibitions, the Poetic Festival, artistic events, charity raffles, patriotic ceremonies, the first journey in a balloon. They were there for everything, and almost always from its inception and at the forefront. During those unfortunate years no one could have imagined anyone happier than they or a marriage more harmonious than theirs.

The house left by her father gave Fermina Daza a refuge from the asphyxiation of the family palace. As soon as she could escape from public view, she would go in secret to the Park of the Evangels, and there she would visit with new friends and some old ones from school or the painting classes: an innocent substitute for infidelity. She spent tranquil hours as a single mother, surrounded by what remained of her girlhood memories. She replaced the perfumed crows, found cats on the street and placed them in the care of Gala Placidia, who by this time was old and somewhat slowed by rheumatism but still willing to bring the house back to life. She opened the sewing room where Florentino Ariza saw her for the first time, where Dr. Juvenal Urbino had her stick out her tongue so that he could try to read her heart, and she turned it into a sanctuary of the past. One winter afternoon she went to close the balcony because a heavy storm was threatening, and she saw Florentino Ariza on his bench under the almond trees in the little park, with his father's suit altered to fit him and his book open on his lap, but this time she did not see him as she had seen him by accident on various occasions, but at the age at which he remained in her memory. She was afraid that the vision was an omen of death, and she was grief-stricken. She dared to tell herself that perhaps she would have been happier with him, alone with him in that house she had restored for him with as much love as he had felt when he restored his house for her, and that simple hypothesis dismayed her because it permitted her to realize the extreme of unhappiness she had reached. Then she summoned her last strength and obliged her husband to talk to her without evasion, to confront her, to argue with her, to cry with her in rage at the loss of paradise, until they heard the last rooster crow, and the light filtered in through the lace curtains of the palace, and the sun rose, and her husband, puffy with so much talk, exhausted with lack of sleep, his heart fortified with so much weeping, laced his shoes, tightened his belt, fastened everything that remained to him of his manhood, and told her yes, my love, they were going to look for the love they had lost in Europe: starting tomorrow and forever after. It was such a firm decision that he arranged with the Treasury Bank, his general administrator, for the immediate liquidation of the vast family fortune, which was dispersed, and had been from the very beginning, in all kinds of businesses, investments, and long-term, sacred bonds, and which only he knew was not as excessive as legend would have it: just large enough so one did not need to think about it. What there was of it was converted into stamped gold, to be invested little by little in his foreign bank accounts until he and his wife would own nothing in this harsh country, not even a plot of ground to die on.

And yet Florentino Ariza actually existed, contrary to what she had decided to believe. He was on the pier where the French ocean liner was docked when she arrived with her husband and child in the landau drawn by the golden horses, and he saw them emerge as he had so often seen them at public ceremonies: perfect. They were leaving with their son, raised in such a way that one could already see what he would be like as an adult: and so he was. Juvenal Urbino greeted Florentino Ariza with a joyous wave of his hat: "We're off to conquer Flanders." Fermina Daza nodded, and Florentino Ariza took off his hat and made a slight bow, and she looked at him without the slightest compassion for the premature ravages of baldness. There he was, just as she saw him: the shadow of someone she had never met.

These were not the best times for Florentino Ariza either. In addition to his work, which grew more and more intense, and the tedium of his furtive hunting, and the dead calm of the years, there was also the final crisis of Tránsito Ariza, whose mind had been left almost without memories, almost a blank, to the point where she would turn to him at times, see him reading in the armchair he always sat in, and ask him in surprise: "And whose son are you?" He would always reply with the truth, but she would interrupt him again without delay:

"And tell me something, my boy," she would ask. "Who am I?"

She had grown so fat that she could not move, and she spent the day in the notions shop, where there was no longer anything to sell, primping and dressing in finery from the time she awoke with the first roosters until the following dawn, for she slept very little. She would put garlands of flowers on her head, paint her lips, powder her face and arms, and at last she would ask whoever was with her, "Who am I now?" The neighbors knew that she always expected the same reply: "You are Little Roachie Martínez." This identity, stolen from a character in a children's story, was the only one that satisfied her. She continued to rock and to fan herself with long pink feathers, until she began all over again: the crown of paper flowers, violet on her eyelids, red on her lips, dead white on her face. And again the question to whoever was nearby: "Who am I now?" When she became the laughingstock of the neighborhood, Florentino Ariza had the counter and the storage drawers of the old notions shop dismantled in one night, and the street door sealed, and the space arranged just as he had heard her describe Roachie Martínez's bedroom, and she never asked again who she was.

At the suggestion of Uncle Leo XII, he found an older woman to take care of her, but the poor thing was always more asleep than awake, and at times she gave the impression that she, too, forgot who she was. So that Florentino Ariza would stay home from the time he left the office until he managed to put his mother to sleep. He no longer played dominoes at the Commercial Club, and for a long time he did not visit the few women friends he had continued to see, for something very profound had changed in his heart after his dreadful meeting with Olimpia Zuleta.

It was as if he had been struck by lightning. Florentino Ariza had just taken Uncle Leo XII home during one of those October storms that would leave us reeling, when he saw from his carriage a slight, very agile girl in a dress covered with organza ruffles that looked like a bridal gown. He saw her running in alarm from one side of the street to the other, because the wind had snatched away her parasol and was blowing it out to sea. He rescued her in his carriage and went out of his way to take her to her house, an old converted hermitage that faced the open sea and whose patio, visible from the street, was full of pigeon coops. On the way, she told him that she had been married less than a year to a man who sold trinkets in the market, whom Florentino Ariza had often seen on his company's boats unloading cartons of all kinds of salable merchandise and with a multitude of pigeons in a wicker cage of the sort mothers used on riverboats for carrying infants. Olimpia Zuleta seemed to belong to the wasp family, not only because of her high buttocks and meager bosom, but because of everything about her: her hair like copper wire, her freckles, her round, animated eyes that were farther apart than normal, and her melodious voice that she used only for saying intelligent and amusing things. Florentino Ariza thought she was more witty than attractive, and he forgot her as soon as he left her at her house, where she lived with her husband, his father, and other members of his family.

A few days later he saw her husband at the port, loading merchandise instead of unloading it, and when the ship weighed anchor Florentino heard, with great clarity, the voice of the devil in his ear. That afternoon, after taking Uncle Leo XII home, he passed by Olimpia Zuleta's house as if by accident, and he saw her over the fence, feeding the noisy pigeons. He called to her from his carriage: "How much for a pigeon?" She recognized him and answered in a merry voice: "They

337

are not for sale." He asked: "Then what must I do to get one?" Still feeding the pigeons, she replied: "You drive her back to the coop when you find her lost in a storm." So that Florentino Ariza arrived home that night with a thank-you gift from Olimpia Zuleta: a carrier pigeon with a metal ring around its leg.

The next afternoon, just at dinnertime, the beautiful pigeon fancier saw the gift carrier pigeon in the dovecote and thought it had escaped. But when she picked it up to examine it, she realized that there was a slip of paper inside the ring: a declaration of love. It was the first time that Florentino Ariza had left a written trace, and it would not be the last, although on this occasion he had been prudent enough not to sign his name. He was going into his house the following afternoon, a Wednesday, when a street boy handed him the same pigeon in a cage, with a memorized message that the pigeon lady hereby sends you this, and says to tell you to please keep the cage locked because if not it will fly away again and this is the last time she will send it back. He had no idea how to interpret this: either the pigeon had lost the note en route, or the pigeonkeeper had decided to play innocent, or she had returned the pigeon so that he could send it back to her again. If that was true, however, the natural thing would have been for her to return the pigeon with a reply.

On Saturday morning, after much thought, Florentino Ariza sent back the pigeon with another unsigned letter. This time he did not have to wait until the next day. In the afternoon the same boy brought it back in another cage, with a message that said she hereby sends back the pigeon that flew away again, and that the day before yesterday she returned it out of courtesy and this time she returns it out of pity, but that now it is really true that she will not return it again if it flies away another time. Tránsito Ariza played with the pigeon until very late, she took it out of the cage, she rocked it in her arms, she tried to lull it to sleep with children's songs, and then suddenly Florentino Ariza realized that in the ring around its leg was a little piece of paper with one line written on it: *I do not accept anonymous letters*. Florentino Ariza read it, his heart wild with joy as if this were the culmination of his first adventure, and he did not sleep a wink that night as he tossed and turned with impatience. Very early the next day, before he left for the office, he once again set the pigeon free, carrying a love note that bore his clear signature, and he also put in the ring the freshest, reddest, and most fragrant rose from his garden.

It was not that easy. After three months of pursuit, the beautiful pigeon fancier was still sending the same answer: *I am not one of those women*. But she never refused to accept his messages or broke any of the dates that Florentino Ariza arranged so that they would seem to be casual encounters. He was a different person: the lover who never showed his face, the man most avid for love as well as most niggardly with it, the man who gave nothing and wanted everything, the man who did not allow anyone to leave a trace of her passing in his heart, the hunter lying in ambush—this man went out on the street in the midst of ecstatic signed letters, gallant gifts, imprudent vigils at the pigeonkeeper's house, even on two occasions when her husband was not on a trip or at the market. It was the only time, since his youngest days, when he felt himself run through by the lance of love.

Six months after their first meeting, they found themselves at last in a cabin on a riverboat that was being painted at the docks. It was a marvelous afternoon. Olimpia Zuleta had the joyous love of a startled pigeon fancier, and she preferred to remain naked for several hours in a slow-moving repose that was, for her, as loving as love itself. The cabin was dismantled, half painted, and they would take the odor of turpentine away with them in the memory of a happy afternoon. In a sudden inspiration, Florentino Ariza opened a can of red paint that was within reach of the bunk, wet his index finger, and painted the pubis of the beautiful pigeon fancier with an arrow of blood pointing south, and on her belly the words: *This pussy is mine*. That same night, Olimpia Zuleta undressed in front of her husband, having forgotten what was scrawled there, and he did not say a word, his breathing did not even change, nothing, but he went to the bathroom for his razor while she was putting on her nightgown, and in a single slash he cut her throat.

Florentino did not find out until many days later, when the fugitive husband was captured and told the newspapers the reasons for the crime and how he had committed it. For many years he thought with terror about the signed letters, he kept track of the prison term of the murderer, who knew him because of his dealings with the boat company, but it was not so much fear of a knife at his throat or a public scandal as the misfortune of Fermina Daza's learning about his infidelity. One day during his years of waiting, the woman who took care of Tránsito Ariza had to stay at the market longer than expected because of an unseasonable downpour, and when she returned to the house she found her sitting in the rocking chair, painted and bedecked as always, and with eyes so animated and a smile so mischievous that her caretaker did not realize she was dead until two hours later. Shortly before her death she had distributed to the neighborhood children the fortune in gold and jewels hidden in the jars buried under her bed, saying they could eat them like candy, and some of the most valuable were impossible to recover. Florentino Ariza buried her in the former Hand of God ranch, which was still known as the Cholera Cemetery, and he planted a rosebush on her grave.

After his first few visits to the cemetery, Florentino Ariza discovered that Olimpia Zuleta was buried very close by, without a tombstone but with her name and the date scrawled in the fresh cement of the crypt, and he thought in horror that this was one of her husband's sanguinary jokes. When the roses bloomed he would place a flower on her grave if there was no one in sight, and later he planted a cutting taken from his mother's rosebush. Both bloomed in such profusion that Florentino Ariza had to bring shears and other garden tools to keep them under control. But the task was beyond him: after a few years the two rosebushes had spread like weeds among the graves, and from then on, the unadorned cemetery of the plague was called the Cemetery of Roses, until some mayor who was less realistic than popular wisdom cleared out the roses one night and hung a republican sign from the arch of the entrance gate: Universal Cemetery.

The death of his mother left Florentino Ariza condemned once again to his maniacal pursuits: the office, his meetings in strict rotation with his regular mistresses, the domino games at the Commercial Club, the same books of love, the Sunday visits to the cemetery. It was the rust of routine, which he had despised and feared so much, but which had protected him from an awareness of his age. However, one Sunday in December, when the rosebushes on the tombs had already defeated the garden shears, he saw the swallows on the recently installed electric wires and he suddenly realized how much time had gone by since the death of his mother, and how much since the murder of Olimpia Zuleta, and how very much since that other distant December afternoon when Fermina Daza sent him a letter saying yes, she would love him always. Until then he had behaved as if time would not pass for him but only for others. Just the week before, he happened to meet on the street one of the many couples who had married because of the letters he had written, and he did not recognize their oldest child, who was his godson. He smoothed over his embarrassment with the conventional exclamation: "I'll be damned, he's a man already!" And he continued in the same way even after his body began sending him the first warning signals, because he had always had the iron constitution of the sickly. Tránsito Ariza used to say: "The only disease my son ever had was cholera." She had confused cholera with love, of course, long before her memory failed. But in any event she was mistaken, because her son had suffered from six blennorrhagias, although the doctor had said they were not six but the same one that reappeared after each lost battle. He had also had a swollen lymph gland, four warts, and six cases of impetigo in the groin, but it would not have occurred to him or any man to think of these as diseases; they were only the spoils of war.

When he had just turned forty, he had gone to the doctor because of vague pains in various parts of his body. After many tests, the doctor had said: "It's age." He had returned home without even wondering if any of that had anything to do with him. For his only point of reference in his own past was the ephemeral love affair with Fermina Daza, and only what concerned her had anything to do with reckoning his life. So that on the afternoon when he saw the swallows on the electric wires, he reviewed the past from his earliest memory, he reviewed his chance loves, the countless pitfalls he had been obliged to avoid in order to reach a position of authority, the events without number that had given rise to his bitter determination that Fermina Daza would be his and he would be hers despite everything, in the face of everything, and only then did he realize that his life was passing. He was shaken by a visceral shudder that left his mind blank, and he had to drop the garden tools and lean against the cemetery wall so that the first blow of old age would not knock him down.

"Damn it," he said, appalled, "that all happened thirty years ago!"

And it had. Thirty years that had also gone by for Fermina Daza, of course, but had been for her the most pleasant and exhilarating years of her life. The days of horror in the Palace of Casalduero were relegated to the trash heap of memory. She was living in her new house in La Manga, absolute mistress of her own destiny, with a husband she would have preferred to all the men in the world if she had to choose again, a son who was continuing the family tradition in the Medical School, and a daughter so much like her when she was her age that at times she was disturbed by the impression of feeling herself duplicated. She had returned to Europe three times after the unfortunate trip from which she had intended never to return so that she would not have to live in perpetual turmoil.

God must have finally listened to someone's prayers: after two years in Paris, when Fermina Daza and Juvenal Urbino were just beginning to find what remained of their love in the ruins, a midnight telegram awoke them with the news that Doña Blanca de Urbino was gravely ill, and almost on its heels came another with the news of her death. They returned without delay. Fermina Daza walked off the ship wearing a black tunic whose fullness could not hide her condition. In fact she was pregnant again, and this news gave rise to a popular song, more mischievous than malicious, whose chorus was heard for the rest of the year: *What d'you think she does over there, this beauty from our earth? Whenever she comes back from Paris, she's ready to give birth.* Despite the vulgarity of the words, for many years afterward Dr. Juvenal Urbino would request it at Social Club dances to prove he was a good sport.

The noble palace of the Marquis de Casalduero, whose existence and coat of arms had never been documented, was sold to the municipal treasury for a decent price, and then resold for a fortune to the central government when a Dutch researcher began excavations to prove that the real grave of Christopher Columbus was located there: the fifth one so far. The sisters of Dr. Urbino, without taking vows, went to live in seclusion in the Convent of the Salesians, and Fermina Daza stayed in her father's old house until the villa in La Manga was completed. She walked in with a firm step, she walked in prepared to command, with the English furniture brought back on their honeymoon and the complementary furnishings they sent for after their reconciliation trip, and from the first day she began to fill it with exotic animals that she herself went to buy on the schooners from the Antilles. She walked in with the husband she had won back, the son she had raised with propriety, the daughter who was born four months after their return and whom they baptized Ofelia. Dr. Urbino, for his part, understood that it was impossible to possess his wife as completely as he had on their honeymoon, because the part of love he wanted was what she had given, along with her best hours, to her children, but he learned to live and be happy with what was left over. The harmony they had longed for reached its culmination when they least expected it, at a gala dinner at which a delicious food was served that Fermina Daza could not identify. She began with a good portion, but she liked it so much that she took another of the same size, and she was lamenting the fact that urbane etiquette did not permit her to help herself to a third, when she learned that she had just eaten, with unsuspected pleasure, two heaping plates of pureed eggplant. She accepted defeat with good grace, and from that time on, eggplant in all its forms was served at the villa in La Manga with almost as much frequency as at the Palace of Casalduero, and it was enjoyed so much by everyone that Dr. Juvenal Urbino would lighten the idle hours of his old age by insisting that he wanted to have another daughter so that he could give her the best-loved word in the house as a name: Eggplant Urbino.

Fermina Daza knew then that private life, unlike public life, was fickle and unpredictable. It was not easy for her to establish real differences between children and adults, but in the last analysis she preferred children, because their judgment was more reliable. She had barely turned the corner into maturity, free at last of illusions, when she began to detect the disillusionment of never having been what she had dreamed of being when she was young, in the Park of the Evangels. Instead, she was something she never dared admit even to herself: a deluxe servant. In society she came to be the woman most loved, most catered to, and by the same token most feared, but in nothing was she more demanding or less forgiving than in the management of her house. She always felt as if her life had been lent to her by her husband: she was absolute monarch of a vast empire of happiness, which had been built by him and for him alone. She knew that he loved her above all else, more than anyone else in the world, but only for his own sake: she was in his holy service.

If anything vexed her, it was the perpetual chain of daily meals. For they not only had to be served on time: they had to be perfect, and they had to be just what he wanted to eat, without his having to be asked. If she ever did ask, in one of the innumerable useless ceremonies of their domestic ritual, he would not even look up from the newspaper and would reply: "Anything." In his amiable way he was telling the truth, because one could not imagine a less despotic husband. But when it was time to eat, it could not be anything, but just what he wanted, and with no defects: the meat should not taste of meat, and the fish should not taste of fish, and the pork should not taste of mange, and the chicken should not taste of feathers. Even when it was not the season for asparagus, it had to be found regardless of cost, so that he could take pleasure in the vapors of his own fragrant urine. She did not blame him: she blamed life. But he was an implacable protagonist in that life. At the mere hint of a doubt, he would push aside his plate and say: "This meal has been prepared without love." In that sphere he would achieve moments of fantastic inspiration. Once he tasted some chamomile tea and sent it back, saying only: "This stuff tastes of window." Both she and the servants were surprised because they had never heard of anyone who had drunk boiled window, but when they tried the tea in an effort to understand, they understood: it did taste of window.

He was a perfect husband: he never picked up anything from the floor, or turned out a light, or closed a door. In the morning darkness, when he found a button missing from his clothes, she would hear him say: "A man should have two wives: one to love and one to sew on his buttons." Every day, at his first swallow of coffee and at his first spoonful of soup, he would break into a heartrending howl that no longer frightened anyone, and then unburden himself: "The day I leave this house, you will know it is because I grew tired of always having a burned mouth." He would say that they never prepared lunches as appetizing and unusual as on the days when he could not eat because he had taken a laxative, and he was so convinced that this was treachery on the part of his wife that in the end he refused to take a purgative unless she took one with him.

Tired of his lack of understanding, she asked him for an unusual birthday gift: that for one day he would take care of the domestic chores. He accepted in amusement, and indeed took charge of the house at dawn. He served a splendid breakfast, but he forgot that fried eggs did not agree with her and that she did not drink *café con leche*. Then he ordered a birthday luncheon for eight guests and gave instructions for tidying the house, and he tried so hard to manage better than she did that before noon he had to capitulate without a trace of embarrassment. From the first moment he realized he did not have the slightest idea where anything was, above all in the kitchen, and the servants let him upset everything to find each item, for they were playing the game too. At ten o'clock no decisions had been made regarding lunch because the housecleaning was not finished yet, the bedroom was not straightened, the bathroom was not scrubbed; he forgot to replace the toilet paper, change the sheets, and send the coachmen for the children, and he confused the servants' duties: he told the cook to make the beds and set the chambermaids to cooking. At eleven o'clock, when the guests were about to arrive, the chaos in the house was such that Fermina Daza resumed command, laughing out loud, not with the triumphant attitude she would have liked but shaken instead with compassion for the domestic helplessness of her husband. He was bitter as he offered the argument he always used: "Things did not go as badly for me as they would for you if you tried to cure the sick." But it was a useful lesson, and not for him alone. Over the years they both reached the same wise conclusion by different paths: it was not possible to live together in any other way, or love in any other way, and nothing in this world was more difficult than love.

In the fullness of her new life, Fermina Daza would see Florentino Ariza on various public occasions, with more frequency as he improved his position, but she learned to see him with so much naturalness that more than once, in sheer distraction, she forgot to greet him. She heard about him often, because in the world of business his cautious but inexorable advance in the R.C.C. was a constant topic of conversation. She saw him improve his manners, his timidity was passed off as a certain enigmatic distance, a slight increase in weight suited him, as did the slowness of age, and he had known how to handle his absolute baldness with dignity. The only area in which he persisted in defying time and fashion was in his somber attire, his anachronistic frock coats, his unique hat, the poet's string ties from his mother's notions shop, his sinister umbrella. Fermina Daza grew accustomed to seeing him with other eyes, and in the end she did not connect him to the languid adolescent who would sit and sigh for her under the gusts of yellow leaves in the Park of the Evangels. In any case, she never saw him with indifference, and she was always pleased by the good news she heard about him, because that helped to alleviate her guilt.

However, when she thought he was completely erased from her memory, he reappeared where she least expected him, a phantom of her nostalgia. It was during the first glimmering of old age, when she began to feel that something irreparable had occurred in her life whenever she heard thunder before the rain. It was the incurable wound of solitary, stony, punctual thunder that would sound every afternoon in October at three o'clock in the Sierra Villanueva, a memory that was becoming more vivid as the years went by. While more recent events blurred in just a few days, the memories of her legendary journey through Cousin Hildebranda's province were as sharp as if they had happened yesterday, and they had the perverse clarity of nostalgia. She remembered Manaure, in the mountains, its one straight, green street, its birds of good omen, the haunted house where she would wake to find her nightgown soaked by the endless tears of Petra Morales, who had died of love many years before in the same bed where she lay sleeping. She remembered the taste of the guavas, which had never been the same again, the warning thunder, which had been so intense that its sound was confused with the sound of rain, the topaz afternoons in San Juan del César when she would go walking with her court of excited cousins and clench her teeth so that her heart would not leap out of her mouth as they approached the telegraph office. She had to sell her father's house because she could not bear the pain of her adolescence, the view of the desolate little park from the balcony, the sibylline fragrance of gardenias on hot nights, the frightening face of an old lady on the February afternoon when her fate was decided, and regardless of where she turned her memory of those times, she would find herself face to face with Florentino Ariza. But she always had enough serenity to know that they were not memories of love or repentance, but the image of a sorrow that left a trail of tears on her cheeks. Without realizing it, she was menaced by the same trap of pity that had been the downfall of so many of Florentino Ariza's defenseless victims.

She clung to her husband. And it was just at the time when he needed her most, because he suffered the disadvantage of being ten years ahead of her as he stumbled alone through the mists of old age, with the even greater disadvantage of being a man and weaker than she was. In the end they knew each other so well that by the time they had been married for thirty years they were like a single divided being, and they felt uncomfortable at the frequency with which they guessed each other's thoughts without intending to, or the ridiculous accident of one of them anticipating in public what the other was going to say. Together they had overcome the daily incomprehension, the instantaneous hatred, the reciprocal nastiness and fabulous flashes of glory in the conjugal conspiracy. It was the time when they loved each other best, without hurry or excess, when both were most conscious of and grateful for their incredible victories over adversity. Life would still present them with other mortal trials, of course, but that no longer mattered: they were on the other shore.

ON THE OCCASION of the celebration of the new century, there was an innovative program of public ceremonies, the most memorable of which was the first journey in a balloon, the fruit of the boundless initiative of Dr. Juvenal Urbino. Half the city gathered on the Arsenal Beach to express their wonderment at the ascent of the enormous balloon made of taffeta in the colors of the flag, which carried the first airmail to San Juan de la Ciénaga, some thirty leagues to the northeast as the crow flies. Dr. Juvenal Urbino and his wife, who had experienced the excitement of flight at the World's Fair in Paris, were the first to climb into the wicker basket, followed by the pilot and six distinguished guests. They were carrying a letter from the Governor of the Province to the municipal offices of San Juan de la Ciénaga, in which it was documented for all time that this was the first mail transported through the air. A journalist from the *Commercial Daily* asked Dr. Juvenal Urbino for his final words in the event he perished during the adventure, and he did not even take the time to think about the answer that would earn him so much abuse.

"In my opinion," he said, "the nineteenth century is passing for everyone except us."

Lost in the guileless crowd that sang the national anthem as the balloon gained altitude, Florentino Ariza felt himself in agreement with the person whose comments he heard over the din, to the effect that this was not a suitable exploit for a woman, least of all one as old as Fermina Daza. But it was not so dangerous after all. Or at least not so much dangerous as depressing. The balloon reached its destination without incident after a peaceful trip through an incredible blue sky. They flew well and very low, with a calm, favorable wind, first along the spurs of the snow-covered mountains and then over the vastness of the Great Swamp.

From the sky they could see, just as God saw them, the ruins of the very old and heroic city of Cartagena de Indias, the most beautiful in the world, abandoned by its inhabitants because of the cholera panic after three centuries of resistance to the sieges of the English and the atrocities of the buccaneers. They saw the walls still intact, the brambles in the streets, the fortifications devoured by heartsease, the marble palaces and the golden altars and the Viceroys rotting with plague inside their armor.

They flew over the lake dwellings of the Trojas in Cataca, painted in lunatic colors, with pens holding iguanas raised for food and balsam apples

355

and crepe myrtle hanging in the lacustrine gardens. Excited by everyone's shouting, hundreds of naked children plunged into the water, jumping out of windows, jumping from the roofs of the houses and from the canoes that they handled with astonishing skill, and diving like shad to recover the bundles of clothing, the bottles of cough syrup, the beneficent food that the beautiful lady with the feathered hat threw to them from the basket of the balloon.

They flew over the dark ocean of the banana plantations, whose silence reached them like a lethal vapor, and Fermina Daza remembered herself at the age of three, perhaps four, walking through the shadowy forest holding the hand of her mother, who was almost a girl herself, surrounded by other women dressed in muslin, just like her mother, with white parasols and hats made of gauze. The pilot, who was observing the world through a spyglass, said: "They seem dead." He passed the spyglass to Dr. Juvenal Urbino, who saw the oxcarts in the cultivated fields, the boundary lines of the railroad tracks, the blighted irrigation ditches, and wherever he looked he saw human bodies. Someone said that the cholera was ravaging the villages of the Great Swamp. Dr. Urbino, as he spoke, continued to look through the spyglass.

"Well, it must be a very special form of cholera," he said, "because every single corpse has received the coup de grace through the back of the neck."

A short while later they flew over a foaming sea, and they landed without incident on a broad, hot beach whose surface, cracked with niter, burned like fire. The officials were there with no more protection against the sun than ordinary umbrellas, the elementary schools were there waving little flags in time to the music, and the beauty queens with scorched flowers and crowns made of gold cardboard, and the brass band of the prosperous town of Gayra, which in those days was the best along the Caribbean coast. All that Fermina Daza wanted was to see her birthplace again, to confront it with her earliest memories, but no one was allowed to go there because of the dangers of the plague. Dr. Juvenal Urbino delivered the historic letter, which was then mislaid among other papers and never seen again, and the entire delegation almost suffocated in the tedium of the speeches. The pilot could not make the balloon ascend again, and at last they were led on muleback to the dock at Pueblo Viejo, where the swamp met the sea. Fermina Daza was sure she had passed through there with her mother when she was very young, in a cart drawn by a team of oxen. When she was older, she had repeated the story several times to her father, who died insisting that she could not possibly recall that.

"I remember the trip very well, and what you say is accurate," he told her, "but it happened at least five years before you were born."

Three days later the members of the balloon expedition, devastated by a bad night of storms, returned to their port of origin, where they received a heroes' welcome. Lost in the crowd, of course, was Florentino Ariza, who recognized the traces of terror on Fermina Daza's face. Nevertheless he saw her again that same afternoon in a cycling exhibition that was also sponsored by her husband, and she showed no sign of fatigue. She rode an uncommon velocipede that resembled something from a circus, with a very high front wheel, over which she was seated, and a very small back wheel that gave almost no support. She wore a pair of loose trousers trimmed in red, which scandalized the older ladies and disconcerted the gentlemen, but no one was indifferent to her skill.

That, along with so many other ephemeral images in the course of so many years, would suddenly appear to Florentino Ariza at the whim of fate, and disappear again in the same way, leaving behind a throb of longing in his heart. Taken together, they marked the passage of his life, for he experienced the cruelty of time not so much in his own flesh as in the imperceptible changes he discerned in Fermina Daza each time he saw her.

One night he went to Don Sancho's Inn, an elegant colonial restaurant, and sat in the most remote corner, as was his custom when he ate his frugal meals alone. All at once, in the large mirror on the back wall, he caught a glimpse of Fermina Daza sitting at a table with her husband and two other couples, at an angle that allowed him to see her reflected in all her splendor. She was unguarded, she engaged in conversation with grace and laughter that exploded like fireworks, and her beauty was more radiant under the enormous teardrop chandeliers: once again, Alice had gone through the looking glass.

Holding his breath, Florentino Ariza observed her at his pleasure: he saw her eat, he saw her hardly touch her wine, he saw her joke with the fourth in the line of Don Sanchos; from his solitary table he shared a moment of her life, and for more than an hour he lingered, unseen, in the forbidden precincts of her intimacy. Then he drank four more cups of coffee to pass the time until he saw her leave with the rest of the group. They passed so close to him that he could distinguish her scent among the clouds of other perfumes worn by her companions.

From that night on, and for almost a year afterward, he laid unrelenting siege to the owner of the inn, offering him whatever he wanted, money or favors or whatever he desired most in life, if he would sell him the mirror. It was not easy, because old Don Sancho believed the legend that the beautiful frame, carved by Viennese cabinetmakers, was the twin of another, which had belonged to Marie Antoinette and had disappeared without a trace: a pair of unique jewels. When at last he surrendered, Florentino Ariza hung the mirror in his house, not for the exquisite frame but because of the place inside that for two hours had been occupied by her beloved reflection.

When he saw Fermina Daza she was almost

always on her husband's arm, the two of them in perfect harmony, moving through their own space with the astonishing fluidity of Siamese cats, which was broken only when they stopped to greet him. Dr. Juvenal Urbino, in fact, shook his hand with warm cordiality, and on occasion even permitted himself a pat on the shoulder. She, on the other hand, kept him relegated to an impersonal regime of formalities and never made the slightest gesture that might allow him to suspect that she remembered him from her unmarried days. They lived in two different worlds, but while he made every effort to reduce the distance between them, every step she took was in the opposite direction. It was a long time before he dared to think that her indifference was no more than a shield for her timidity. This occurred to him suddenly, at the christening of the first freshwater vessel built in the local shipyards, which was also the first official occasion at which Florentino Ariza, as First Vice President of the R.C.C., represented Uncle Leo XII. This coincidence imbued the ceremony with special solemnity, and everyone of any significance in the life of the city was present.

Florentino Ariza was looking after his guests in the main salon of the ship, still redolent of fresh paint and tar, when there was a burst of applause on the docks, and the band struck up a triumphal march. He had to repress the trembling that was almost as old as he was when he saw the beautiful woman of his dreams on her husband's arm, splendid in her maturity, striding like a queen from another time past the honor guard in parade uniform, under the shower of paper streamers and flower petals tossed at them from the windows. Both responded to the ovation with a wave of the hand, but she was so dazzling, dressed in imperial gold from her high-heeled slippers and the foxtails at her throat to her bell-shaped hat, that she seemed to be alone in the midst of the crowd.

Florentino Ariza waited for them on the bridge with the provincial officials, surrounded by the crash of the music and the fireworks and the three heavy screams from the ship, which enveloped the dock in steam. Juvenal Urbino greeted the members of the reception line with that naturalness so typical of him, which made everyone think the Doctor bore him a special fondness: first the ship's captain in his dress uniform, then the Archbishop, then the Governor with his wife and the Mayor with his, and then the military commander, who was a newcomer from the Andes. Beyond the officials stood Florentino Ariza, dressed in dark clothing and almost invisible among so many eminent people. After greeting the military commander, Fermina seemed to hesitate before Florentino Ariza's outstretched hand. The military man, prepared to introduce them, asked her if they did not know each other. She did not say yes and she did not say no, but she held out her hand to Florentino Ariza with a salon smile. The same thing had occurred twice in the past, and would occur again, and Florentino Ariza always accepted these occasions with a strength of character worthy of Fermina Daza. But that afternoon he asked himself, with his infinite capacity for illusion, if such pitiless indifference might not be a subterfuge for hiding the torments of love.

The mere idea excited his youthful desires. Once again he haunted Fermina Daza's villa, filled with the same longings he had felt when he was on duty in the little Park of the Evangels, but his calculated intention was not that she see him, but rather that he see her and know that she was still in the world. Now, however, it was difficult for him to escape notice. The District of La Manga was on a semi-deserted island, separated from the historic city by a canal of green water and covered by thickets of icaco plum, which had sheltered Sunday lovers in colonial times. In recent years, the old stone bridge built by the Spaniards had been torn down, and in its stead was one made of brick and lined with streetlamps for the new mule-drawn trolleys. At first the residents of La Manga had to endure a torture that had not been anticipated during construction, which was sleeping so close to the city's first electrical plant whose vibration was a constant earthquake. Not even Dr. Juvenal Urbino, with all his prestige, could persuade them to move it where it would not disturb anyone, until his proven complicity with Divine Providence interceded on his behalf. One night the boiler in the plant blew up in a fearful explosion, flew over the new houses, sailed across half the city, and destroyed the largest gallery in the former convent of St. Julian the Hospitaler. The old ruined building had been abandoned at the beginning of the year, but the boiler caused the deaths of four prisoners who had escaped from the local jail earlier that night and were hiding in the chapel.

The peaceful suburb with its beautiful tradition of love was, however, not the most propitious for unrequited love when it became a luxury neighborhood. The streets were dusty in summer, swamp-like in winter, and desolate all year round, and the scattered houses were hidden behind leafy gardens and had mosaic tile terraces instead of old-fashioned projecting balconies, as if they had been built for the purpose of discouraging furtive lovers. It was just as well that at this time it became fashionable to drive out in the afternoon in hired old Victorias that had been converted to one-horse carriages, and that the excursion ended on a hill where one could appreciate the heartbreaking twilights of October better than from the lighthouse, and observe the watchful sharks lurking at the seminarians' beach, and see the Thursday ocean liner, huge and white, that could almost be touched with one's hands as it passed through the harbor channel. Florentino Ariza would hire a Victoria after a hard day at the office, but instead of folding down the top, as was customary during the hot months, he would stay hidden in the depths of the seat, invisible in the darkness, always alone, and requesting unexpected routes so as not to arouse the evil thoughts of the driver. In reality, the only thing that interested him on the drive was the pink marble Parthenon half hidden among leafy banana and mango trees, a luckless replica of the idyllic mansions on Louisiana cotton plantations. Fermina Daza's children returned home a little before five. Florentino Ariza would see them arrive in the family carriage, and then he would see Dr. Juvenal Urbino leave for his routine house calls, but in almost a year of vigilance he never even caught the glimpse he so desired.

One afternoon when he insisted on his solitary drive despite the first devastating rains of June, the horse slipped and fell in the mud. Florentino Ariza realized with horror that they were just in front of Fermina Daza's villa, and he pleaded with the driver, not thinking that his consternation might betray him.

"Not here, please," he shouted. "Anywhere but here."

Bewildered by his urgency, the driver tried to raise the horse without unharnessing him, and the axle of the carriage broke. Florentino Ariza managed to climb out of the coach in the driving rain and endure his embarrassment until passersby in other carriages offered to take him home. While he was waiting, a servant of the Urbino family had seen him, his clothes soaked through, standing in mud up to his knees, and she brought him an umbrella so that he could take refuge on the terrace. In the wildest of his deliriums Florentino Ariza had never dreamed of such good fortune, but on that afternoon he would have died rather than allow Fermina Daza to see him in that condition.

When they lived in the old city, Juvenal Urbino and his family would walk on Sundays from their house to the Cathedral for eight o'clock Mass, which for them was more a secular ceremony than a religious one. Then, when they moved, they continued to drive there for several years, and at times they visited with friends under the palm trees in the park. But when the temple of the theological seminary was built in La Manga, with a private beach and its own cemetery, they no longer went to the Cathedral except on very solemn occasions. Ignorant of these changes, Florentino Ariza waited Sunday after Sunday on the terrace of the Parish Café, watching the people coming out of all three Masses. Then he realized his mistake and went to the new church, which was fashionable until just a few years ago, and there, at eight o'clock sharp on four Sundays in August, he saw Dr. Juvenal Urbino with his children, but Fermina Daza was not with them. On one of those Sundays he visited the new cemetery adjacent to the church, where the residents of La Manga were building their sumptuous pantheons, and his heart skipped a beat when he discovered the most sumptuous of all in the shade of the great ceiba trees. It was already complete, with Gothic stained-glass windows and marble angels and gravestones with gold lettering for the entire family. Among them, of course, was that of Doña Fermina Daza de Urbino de la Calle, and next to it her husband's, with a common epitaph: *Together still in the peace of the Lord*.

For the rest of the year, Fermina Daza did not attend any civic or social ceremonies, not even the Christmas celebrations, in which she and her husband had always been illustrious protagonists. But her absence was most notable on the opening night of the opera season. During intermission, Florentino Ariza happened on a group that, beyond any doubt, was discussing her without mentioning her name. They said that one midnight the previous June someone had seen her boarding the Cunard ocean liner en route to Panama, and that she wore a dark veil to hide the ravages of the shameful disease that was consuming her. Someone asked what terrible illness would dare to attack a woman with so much power, and the answer he received was saturated with black bile:

"A lady so distinguished could suffer only from consumption."

Florentino Ariza knew that the wealthy of his country did not contract short-term diseases. Either they died without warning, almost always on the eve of a major holiday that could not be celebrated because of the period of mourning, or they faded away in long, abominable illnesses whose most intimate details eventually became public knowledge. Seclusion in Panama was almost an obligatory penance in the life of the rich. They submitted to God's will in the Adventist Hospital, an immense white warehouse lost in the prehistoric downpours of Darién, where the sick lost track of the little life that was left to them, and in whose solitary rooms with their burlap windows no one could tell with certainty if the smell of carbolic acid was the odor of health or of death. Those who recovered came back bearing splendid gifts that they would distribute with a free hand and a kind of agonized longing to be pardoned for their indiscretion in still being alive. Some returned with their abdomens crisscrossed by barbarous stitches that seemed to have been sewn with cobbler's hemp; they would raise their shirts to display them when people came to visit, they compared them with those of others who had suffocated from excesses of joy, and for the rest of their days they would describe and describe again the angelic visions they had seen under the influence of chloroform. On the other hand, no one ever learned about the visions of those who did not return, including the saddest of them all: those who had died as exiles in the tuberculosis pavilion, more from the sadness of the rain than because of the complications of their disease.

If he had been forced to choose, Florentino Ariza did not know which fate he would have wanted for Fermina Daza. More than anything else he wanted the truth, but no matter how unbearable, and regardless of how he searched, he could not find it. It was inconceivable to him that no one could even give him a hint that would confirm the story he had heard. In the world of riverboats, which was his world, no mystery could be maintained, no secret could be kept. And yet no one had heard anything about the woman in the black veil. No one knew anything in a city where everything was known, and where many things were known even before they happened, above all if they concerned the rich. But no one had any explanation for the disappearance of Fermina Daza. Florentino Ariza continued to patrol La Manga, continued to hear Mass without devotion in the basilica of the seminary, continued to attend civic ceremonies that never would have interested him in another state of mind, but the passage of time only increased the credibility of the story he had heard. Everything seemed normal in the Urbino household, except for the mother's absence.

As he carried on his investigation, he learned about other events he had not known of or into which he had made no inquiries, including the death of Lorenzo Daza in the Cantabrian village where he had been born. He remembered seeing him for many years in the rowdy chess wars at the Parish Café, hoarse with so much talking, and growing fatter and rougher as he sank into the quicksand of an unfortunate old age. They had never exchanged another word since their disagreeable breakfast of anise in the previous century, and Florentino Ariza was certain that even after he had obtained for his daughter the successful marriage that had become his only reason for living, Lorenzo Daza remembered him with as much rancor as he felt toward Lorenzo Daza. But he was so determined to find out the unequivocal facts regarding Fermina Daza's health that he returned to the Parish Café to learn them from her father, just at the time of the historic tournament in which Jeremiah de Saint-Amour alone confronted forty-two opponents. This was how he discovered that Lorenzo Daza had died, and he rejoiced with all his heart, although the price of his joy might be having to live without the truth. At last he accepted as true the story of the hospital for the terminally ill, and his only consolation was the old saying: *Sick women live forever*. On the days when he felt disheartened, he resigned himself to the notion that the news of Fermina Daza's death, if it should occur, would find him without his having to look for it.

It never did, for Fermina Daza was alive and well on the ranch, half a league from the village of Flores de María, where her Cousin Hildebranda Sánchez was living, forgotten by the world. She had left with no scandal, by mutual agreement with her husband, both of them as entangled as adolescents in the only serious crisis they had suffered during so many years of stable matrimony. It had taken them by surprise in the repose of their maturity, when they felt themselves safe from misfortune's sneak attacks, their children grown and well-behaved, and the future ready for them to learn how to be old without bitterness. It had been something so unexpected for them both that they wanted to resolve it not with shouts, tears, and intermediaries, as was the custom in the Caribbean, but with the wisdom of the nations of Europe, and there was so much vacillation as to whether their loyalties lay here or over there that they ended up mired in a puerile situation that did not belong anywhere. At last she decided to leave, not even knowing why or to what purpose, out of sheer fury, and he, inhibited by his sense of guilt, had not been able to dissuade her.

Fermina Daza, in fact, had sailed at midnight in the greatest secrecy and with her face covered by a black mantilla, not on a Cunard liner bound for Panama, however, but on the regular boat to San Juan de la Ciénaga, the city where she had been born and had lived until her adolescence, and for which she felt a growing homesickness that became more and more difficult to bear as the years went by. In defiance of her husband's will, and of the customs of the day, her only companion was a fifteen-year-old goddaughter who had been raised as a family servant, but the ship captains and the officials at each port had been notified of her journey. When she made her rash decision, she told her children that she was going to have a change of scene for three months or so with Aunt Hildebranda, but her determination was not to return. Dr. Juvenal Urbino knew the strength of her character very well, and he was so troubled that he accepted her decision with humility as God's punishment for the gravity of his sins. But the lights on the boat had not yet been lost to view when they both repented of their weakness.

Although they maintained a formal correspondence concerning their children and other household matters, almost two years went by before either one could find a way back that was not mined with pride. During the second year, the children went to spend their school vacation in Flores de María, and Fermina Daza did the impossible and appeared content with her new life. That at least was the conclusion drawn by Juvenal Urbino from his son's letters. Moreover, at that time the Bishop of Riohacha went there on a pastoral visit, riding under the pallium on his celebrated white mule with the trappings embroidered in gold. Behind him came pilgrims from remote regions, musicians playing accordions, peddlers selling food and amulets; and for three days the ranch was overflowing with the crippled and the hopeless, who in reality did not come for the learned sermons and the plenary indulgences but for the favors of the mule who, it was said, performed miracles behind his master's back. The Bishop had frequented the home of the Urbino de la Calle family ever since his days as an ordinary priest, and one afternoon he escaped from the public festivities to have lunch at Hildebranda's ranch. After the meal, during which they spoke only of earthly matters, he took Fermina Daza aside and asked to hear her confession. She refused in an amiable but firm manner, with the explicit argument that she had nothing to repent of. Although it was not her purpose, at least not her conscious purpose, she was certain that her answer would reach the appropriate ears.

Dr. Juvenal Urbino used to say, not without a

certain cynicism, that it was not he who was to blame for those two bitter years of his life but his wife's bad habit of smelling the clothes her family took off, and the clothes that she herself took off, so that she could tell by the odor if they needed to be laundered even though they might appear to be clean. She had done this ever since she was a girl, and she never thought it worthy of comment until her husband realized what she was doing on their wedding night. He also knew that she locked herself in the bathroom at least three times a day to smoke, but this did not attract his attention because the women of his class were in the habit of locking themselves away in groups to talk about men and smoke, and even to drink as much as two liters of aguardiente until they had passed out on the floor in a brickmason's drunken stupor. But her habit of sniffing at all the clothing she happened across seemed to him not only inappropriate but unhealthy as well. She took it as a joke, which is what she did with everything she did not care to discuss, and she said that God had not put that diligent oriole's beak on her face just for decoration. One morning, while she was at the market, the servants aroused the entire neighborhood in their search for her three-year-old son, who was not to be found anywhere in the house. She arrived in the middle of the panic, turned around two or three times like a tracking mastiff, and found the boy asleep in an armoire where no one thought he could possibly be hiding. When her astonished husband asked her how she had found him, she replied:

"By the smell of caca."

The truth is that her sense of smell not only served her in regard to washing clothes or finding lost children: it was the sense that oriented her in all areas of life, above all in her social life. Juvenal Urbino had observed this throughout his marriage, in particular at the beginning, when she was the parvenue in a milieu that had been prejudiced against her for three hundred years, and yet she had made her way through coral reefs as sharp as knives, not colliding with anyone, with a power over the world that could only be a supernatural instinct. That frightening faculty, which could just as well have had its origin in a millenarian wisdom as in a heart of stone, met its moment of misfortune one ill-fated Sunday before Mass when, out of simple habit, Fermina Daza sniffed the clothing her husband had worn the evening before and experienced the disturbing sensation that she had been in bed with another man.

First she smelled the jacket and the vest while she took the watch chain out of the buttonhole and removed the pencil holder and the billfold and the loose change from the pockets and placed everything on the dresser, and then she smelled the hemmed shirt as she removed the tiepin and the topaz cuff links and the gold collar button, and then she smelled the trousers as she removed the keyholder with its eleven keys and the penknife with its mother-of-pearl handle, and finally she smelled the underwear and the socks and the linen handkerchief with the embroidered monogram. Beyond any shadow of a doubt there was an odor in each of the articles that had not been there in all their years of life together, an odor impossible to define because it was not the scent of flowers or of artificial essences but of something peculiar to human nature. She said nothing, and she did not notice the odor every day, but she now sniffed at her husband's clothing not to decide if it was ready to launder but with an unbearable anxiety that gnawed at her innermost being.

Fermina Daza did not know where to locate the odor of his clothing in her husband's routine. It could not be placed between his morning class and lunch, for she supposed that no woman in her right mind would make hurried love at that time of day, least of all with a visitor, when the house still had to be cleaned, and the beds made, and the marketing done, and lunch prepared, and perhaps with the added worry that one of the children would be sent home early from school because somebody threw a stone at him and hurt his head and he would find her at eleven o'clock in the morning, naked in the unmade bed and, to make matters worse, with a doctor on top of her. She also knew that Dr. Juvenal Urbino made love only at night, better yet in absolute darkness, and as a last resort before breakfast when the first birds began to chirp. After that time, as he would say, it was more work than the pleasure of daytime love was worth to take off one's clothes and put them back on again. So that the contamination of his clothing could occur only during one of his house calls or during some moment stolen from his nights of chess and films. This last possibility was difficult to prove, because unlike so many of her friends, Fermina Daza was too proud to spy on her husband or to ask someone else to do it for her. His schedule of house calls, which seemed best suited to infidelity, was also the easiest to keep an eye on, because Dr. Juvenal Urbino kept a detailed record of each of his patients, including the payment of his fees, from the first time he visited them until he ushered them out of this world with a final sign of the cross and some words for the salvation of their souls.

In the three weeks that followed, Fermina Daza did not find the odor in his clothing for a few days, she found it again when she least expected it, and then she found it, stronger than ever, for several days in a row, although one of those days was a Sunday when there had been a family gathering and the two of them had not been apart for even a moment. Contrary to her normal custom and even her own desires, she found herself in her husband's office one afternoon as if she were someone else, doing something that she would never do, deciphering with an exquisite Bengalese magnifying glass his intricate notes on the house calls he had made during the last few months. It was the first time she had gone alone into that office, saturated with showers of creosote and crammed with books bound in the hides of unknown animals, blurred school pictures, honorary degrees, astrolabes, and elaborately worked daggers collected over the years: a secret sanctuary that she always considered the only part of her husband's private life to which she had no access because it was not part of love, so that the few times she had been there she had gone with him, and the visits had always been very brief. She did not feel she had the right to go in alone, much less to engage in what seemed to be indecent prying. But there she was. She wanted to find the truth, and she searched for it with an anguish almost as great as her terrible fear of finding it, and she was driven by an irresistible wind even stronger than her innate haughtiness, even stronger than her dignity: an agony that bewitched her.

She was able to draw no conclusions, because her husband's patients, except for mutual friends, were part of his private domain; they were people without identity, known not by their faces but by their pains, not by the color of their eyes or the evasions of their hearts but by the size of their livers, the coating on their tongues, the blood in their urine, the hallucinations of their feverish nights. They were people who believed in her husband, who believed they lived because of him when in reality they lived for him, and who in the end were reduced to a phrase written in his own hand at the bottom of the medical file: *Be calm. God awaits you at the door*. Fermina Daza left his study after two fruitless hours, with the feeling that she had allowed herself to be seduced by indecency.

Urged on by her imagination, she began to discover changes in her husband. She found him evasive, without appetite at the table or in bed, prone to exasperation and ironic answers, and when he was at home he was no longer the tranquil man he had once been but a caged lion. For the first time since their marriage, she began to monitor the times he was late, to keep track of them to the minute, to tell him lies in order to learn the truth, but then she felt wounded to the quick by the contradictions. One night she awoke with a start, terrified by a vision of her husband staring at her in the darkness with eyes that seemed full of hatred. She had suffered a similar fright in her youth, when she had seen Florentino Ariza at the foot of her bed, but that apparition had been full of love, not hate. Besides, this time it was not fantasy: her husband was awake at two in the morning, sitting up in bed to watch her while she slept, but when she asked him why, he denied it. He lay back on the pillow and said:

"You must have been dreaming."

After that night, and after similar episodes that occurred during that time, when Fermina Daza could not tell for certain where reality ended and where illusion began, she had the overwhelming revelation that she was losing her mind. At last she realized that her husband had not taken Communion on the Thursday of Corpus Christ or on any Sunday in recent weeks, and he had not found time for that year's retreats. When she asked him the reason for those unusual changes in his spiritual health, she received an evasive answer. This was the decisive clue, because he had not failed to take Communion on an important feast day since he had made his first Communion, at the age of eight. In this way she realized not only that her husband was in a state of mortal sin but that he had resolved to persist in it, since he did not go to his confessor for help. She had never imagined that she could suffer so much for something that seemed to be the absolute opposite of love, but she was suffering, and she resolved that the only way she could keep from dying was to burn out the nest of vipers that was poisoning her soul. And that is what she did. One afternoon she began to darn socks on the terrace while her husband was reading, as he did every day after his siesta. Suddenly she interrupted her work, pushed her eyeglasses up onto her forehead, and without any trace of harshness, she asked for an explanation:

"Doctor."

He was immersed in *L'Ile des pingouins*, the novel that everyone was reading in those days, and he answered without surfacing: *"Oui."* She insisted:

"Look at me."

He did so, looking without seeing her through the fog of his reading glasses, but he did not have to take them off to feel burned by the raging fire in her eyes.

"What is going on?" he asked.

"You know better than I," she said.

That was all she said. She lowered her glasses and continued darning socks. Dr. Juvenal Urbino knew then that the long hours of anguish were over. The moment had not been as he had foreseen it; rather than a seismic tremor in his heart, it was a calming blow, and a great relief that what was bound to happen sooner or later had happened sooner rather than later: the ghost of Miss Barbara Lynch had entered his house at last.

Dr. Juvenal Urbino had met her four months earlier as she waited her turn in the clinic of Misericordia Hospital, and he knew immediately that something irreparable had just occurred in his destiny. She was a tall, elegant, large-boned mulatta, with skin the color and softness of molasses, and that morning she wore a red dress with white polka dots and a broad-brimmed hat of the same fabric, which shaded her face down to her eyelids. Her sex seemed more pronounced than that of other human beings. Dr. Juvenal Urbino did not attend patients in the clinic, but whenever he passed by and had time to spare, he would go in to remind his more advanced students that there is no medicine better than a good diagnosis. So that he arranged to be present at the examination of the unforeseen mulatta, making certain that his pupils would not notice any gesture of his that did not appear to be casual and barely looking at her, but fixing her name and address with care in his memory. That afternoon, after his last house call, he had his carriage pass by the address that she had given in the consulting room, and in fact there she was, enjoying the coolness on her terrace.

It was a typical Antillean house, painted yellow even to the tin roof, with burlap windows and pots of carnations and ferns hanging in the doorway. It rested on wooden pilings in the salt marshes of Mala Crianza. A troupial sang in the cage that hung from the eaves. Across the street was a primary school, and the children rushing out obliged the coachman to keep a tight hold on the reins so that the horse would not shy. It was a stroke of luck, for Miss Barbara Lynch had time to recognize the Doctor. She waved to him as if they were old friends, she invited him to have coffee while the confusion abated, and he was delighted to accept (although it was not his custom to drink coffee) and to listen to her talk about herself, which was the only thing that had interested him since the morning and the only thing that was going to interest him, without a moment's respite, during the months to follow. Once, soon after he had married, a friend told him, with his wife present, that sooner or later he would have to confront a mad passion that could endanger the stability of his marriage. He, who thought he knew himself, knew the strength of his moral roots, had laughed at the prediction. And now it had come true.

Miss Barbara Lynch, Doctor of Theology, was the only child of the Reverend Jonathan B. Lynch, a lean black Protestant minister who rode on a mule through the poverty-stricken settlements in the salt marshes, preaching the word of one of the many gods that Dr. Juvenal Urbino wrote with a small *g* to distinguish them from his own. She spoke good Spanish, with a certain roughness in the syntax, and her frequent slips heightened her charm. She would be twenty-eight years old in December, not long ago she had divorced another minister, who was a student of her father's and to whom she had been unhappily married for two years, and she had no desire to repeat the offense. She said: "I have no more love than my troupial." But Dr. Urbino was too serious to think that she said it with hidden intentions. On the contrary: he asked himself in bewilderment if so many opportunities coming together might not be one of God's pitfalls, which he would then have to pay for dearly, but he dismissed the thought without delay as a piece of theological nonsense resulting from his state of confusion.

As he was about to leave, he made a casual remark about that morning's medical consultation, knowing that nothing pleases patients more than talking about their ailments, and she was so splendid talking about hers that he promised he would return the next day, at four o'clock sharp, to examine her with greater care. She was dismayed: she knew that a doctor of his qualifications was far above her ability to pay, but he reassured her: "In this profession we try to have the rich pay for the poor." Then he marked in his notebook: *Miss Barbara Lynch, Mala Crianza Salt Marsh, Saturday, 4 p.m.* Months later, Fermina Daza was to read that notation, augmented by details of the diagnosis, treatment, and evolution of the disease. The name attracted her attention, and it suddenly occurred to her that she was one of those dissolute artists from the New Orleans fruit boats, but the address made her think that she must come from Jamaica, a black woman, of course, and she eliminated her without a second thought as not being to her husband's taste.

Dr. Juvenal Urbino came ten minutes early for the Saturday appointment, and Miss Lynch had not finished dressing to receive him. He had not felt so much tension since his days in Paris when he had to present himself for an oral examination. As she lay on her canvas bed, wearing a thin silk slip, Miss Lynch's beauty was endless. Everything about her was large and intense: her siren's thighs, her slow-burning skin, her astonished breasts, her diaphanous gums with their perfect teeth, her whole body radiating a vapor of good health that was the human odor Fermina Daza had discovered in her husband's clothing. She had gone to the clinic because she suffered from something that she, with much charm, called "twisted colons," and Dr. Urbino thought that it was a symptom that should not be ignored. So he palpated her internal organs with more intention than attention, and as he did so he discovered in amazement that this marvelous creature was as beautiful inside as out, and then he gave himself over to the delights of touch, no longer the best-qualified physician along the Caribbean coastline but a poor soul tormented by his tumultuous instincts. Only once before in his austere professional life had something similar happened to him, and that had been the day of his greatest shame, because the indignant patient had moved his hand away, sat up in bed, and said to him: "What you want may happen, but it will not be like this." Miss Lynch, on the other hand, abandoned herself to his hands, and when she was certain that the Doctor was no longer thinking about his science, she said:

"I thought this not permitted by your ethics."

He was as drenched by perspiration as if he had just stepped out of a pool wearing all his clothes, and he dried his hands and face with a towel.

"Our code of ethics supposes," he said, "that we doctors are made of wood."

"The fact I thought so does not mean you cannot do," she said. "Just think what it mean for poor black woman like me to have such a famous man notice her."

"I have not stopped thinking about you for an instant," he said.

It was so tremulous a confession that it might have inspired pity. But she saved him from all harm with a laugh that lit up the bedroom.

"I know since I saw you in hospital, Doctor," she said. "Black I am but not a fool."

It was far from easy. Miss Lynch wanted her honor protected, she wanted security and love, in that order, and she believed that she deserved them. She gave Dr. Urbino the opportunity to seduce her but not to penetrate her inner sanctum, even when she was alone in the house. She would go no further than allowing him to repeat the ceremony of palpation and auscultation with all the ethical violations he could desire, but without taking off her clothes. For his part, he could not let go of the bait once he had bitten, and he continued his almost daily incursions. For reasons of a practical nature, it was close to impossible for him to maintain a continuing relationship with Miss Lynch, but he was too weak to stop, as he would later be too weak to go any further. This was his limit.

The Reverend Lynch did not lead a regular life, for he would ride away on his mule on the spur of the moment, carrying Bibles and evangelical pamphlets on one side and provisions on the other, and he would return when least expected. Another difficulty was the school across the street, for the children would recite their lessons as they looked out the windows, and what they saw with greatest clarity was the house across the way, with its doors and windows open wide from six o'clock in the morning, they saw Miss Lynch hanging the birdcage from the eaves so that the troupial could learn the recited lessons, they saw her wearing a bright-colored turban and going about her household tasks as she recited along with them in her brilliant Caribbean voice, and later they saw her sitting on the porch, reciting the afternoon psalms by herself in English.

They had to choose a time when the children were not there, and there were only two possibilities: the afternoon recess for lunch, between twelve and two, which was also when the Doctor had his lunch, or late in the afternoon, after the children had gone home. This was always the best time, although by then the Doctor had made his rounds and had only a few minutes to spare before it was time for him to eat with his family. The third problem, and the most serious for him, was his own situation. It was not possible for him to go there without his carriage, which was very well known and always had to wait outside her door. He could have made an accomplice of his coachman, as did most of his friends at the Social Club, but that was not in his nature. In fact, when his visits to Miss Lynch became too obvious, the liveried family coachman himself dared to ask if it would not be better for him to come back later so that the carriage would not spend so much time at her door. Dr. Urbino, in a sharp response that was not typical of him, cut him off.

"This is the first time since I know you that I have heard you say something you should not have," he said. "Well, then: I will assume it was never said."

There was no solution. In a city like this, it was impossible to hide an illness when the Doctor's carriage stood at the door. At times the Doctor himself took the initiative and went on foot, if distance permitted, or in a hired carriage, to avoid malicious or premature assumptions. Such deceptions, however, were to little avail. Since the prescriptions ordered in pharmacies revealed the truth,

Dr. Urbino would always prescribe counterfeit medicines along with the correct ones in order to preserve the sacred right of the sick to die in peace along with the secret of their illness. Similarly, he was able in various truthful ways to account for the presence of his carriage outside the house of Miss Lynch, but he could not allow it to stay there too long, least of all for the amount of time he would have desired, which was the rest of his life.

The world became a hell for him. For once the initial madness was sated, they both became aware of the risks involved, and Dr. Juvenal Urbino never had the resolve to face a scandal. In the deliriums of passion he promised everything, but when it was over, everything was left for later. On the other hand, as his desire to be with her grew, so did his fear of losing her, so that their meetings became more and more hurried and problematic. He thought about nothing else. He waited for the afternoons with unbearable longing, he forgot his other commitments, he forgot everything but her, but as his carriage approached the Mala Crianza salt marsh he prayed to God that an unforeseen obstacle would force it to drive past. He went to her in a state of such anguish that at times as he turned the corner he was glad to catch a glimpse of the woolly head of the Reverend Lynch, who read on the terrace while his daughter catechized neighborhood children in the living room with recited passages of scripture. Then he would go home relieved that he was not defying fate again, but later he would feel himself going mad with the desire for it to be five o'clock in the afternoon all day, every day.

So their love became impossible when the carriage at her door became too conspicuous, and after three months it became nothing less than ridiculous. Without time to say anything, Miss Lynch would go to the bedroom as soon as she saw her agitated lover walk in the door. She took the precaution of wearing a full skirt on the days she expected him, a charming skirt from Jamaica with red flowered ruffles, but with no underwear, nothing, in the belief that this convenience was going to help him ward off his fear. But he squandered everything she did to make him happy. Panting and drenched with perspiration, he rushed after her into the bedroom, throwing everything on the floor, his walking stick, his medical bag, his Panama hat, and he made panic-stricken love with his trousers down around his knees, with his jacket buttoned so that it would not get in his way, with his gold watch chain across his vest, with his shoes on, with everything on, and more concerned with leaving as soon as possible than with achieving pleasure. She was left dangling, barely at the entrance of her tunnel of solitude, while he was already buttoning up again, as exhausted as if he had made absolute love on the dividing line between life and death, when in reality he had accomplished no more than the physical act that is only a part of the feat of love. But he had finished in time: the exact time needed to give

387

an injection during a routine visit. Then he returned home ashamed of his weakness, longing for death, cursing himself for the lack of courage that kept him from asking Fermina Daza to pull down his trousers and burn his ass on the brazier.

He did not eat, he said his prayers without conviction, in bed he pretended to continue his siesta reading while his wife walked round and round the house putting the world in order before going to bed. As he nodded over his book, he began to sink down into the inevitable mangrove swamp of Miss Lynch, into her air of recumbent forest glade, his deathbed, and then he could think of nothing except tomorrow's five minutes to five o'clock in the afternoon and her waiting for him in bed with nothing but the mound of her dark bush under her madwoman's skirt from Jamaica: the hellish circle.

In the past few years he had become conscious of the burden of his own body. He recognized the symptoms. He had read about them in textbooks, he had seen them confirmed in real life, in older patients with no history of serious ailments who suddenly began to describe perfect syndromes that seemed to come straight from medical texts and yet turned out to be imaginary. His professor of children's clinical medicine at La Salpêtrière had recommended pediatrics as the most honest specialization, because children become sick only when in fact they are sick, and they cannot communicate with the physician using conventional words but only with concrete symptoms of real diseases. After a certain age, however, adults either had the symptoms without the diseases, or, what was worse, serious diseases with the symptoms of minor ones. He distracted them with palliatives, giving time enough time to teach them not to feel their ailments, so that they could live with them in the rubbish heap of old age. Dr. Juvenal Urbino never thought that a physician his age, who believed he had seen everything, would not be able to overcome the uneasy feeling that he was ill when he was not. Or what was worse, not believe he was, out of pure scientific prejudice, when perhaps he really was. At the age of forty, half in earnest and half in jest, he had said in class: "All I need in life is someone who understands me." But when he found himself lost in the labyrinth of Miss Lynch, he no longer was jesting.

All the real or imaginary symptoms of his older patients made their appearance in his body. He felt the shape of his liver with such clarity that he could tell its size without touching it. He felt the dozing cat's purr of his kidneys, he felt the iridescent brilliance of his vesicles, he felt the humming blood in his arteries. At times he awoke at dawn gasping for air, like a fish out of water. He had fluid in his heart. He felt it lose the beat for a moment, he felt it syncopate like a school marching band, once, twice, and then, because God is good, he felt it recover at last. But instead of having recourse to the same distracting remedies he gave to his patients, he went mad with terror. It was true: all he needed in life, even at the age of fifty-eight, was someone who understood him. So he turned to Fermina Daza, the person who loved him best and whom he loved best in the world, and with whom he had just eased his conscience.

For this occurred after she interrupted his afternoon reading to ask him to look at her, and he had the first indication that his hellish circle had been discovered. But he did not know how, because it would have been impossible for him to conceive of Fermina Daza's learning the truth by smell alone. In any case, for a long time this had not been a good city for keeping secrets. Soon after the first home telephones were installed, several marriages that seemed stable were destroyed by anonymous tale-bearing calls, and a number of frightened families either canceled their service or refused to have a telephone for many years. Dr. Urbino knew that his wife had too much self-respect to allow so much as an attempt at anonymous betrayal by telephone, and he could not imagine anyone daring to try it under his own name. But he feared the old method: a note slipped under the door by an unknown hand could be effective, not only because it guaranteed the double anonymity of sender and receiver, but because its time-honored ancestry permitted one to attribute to it some kind of metaphysical connection to the designs of Divine Providence.

Jealousy was unknown in his house: during more than thirty years of conjugal peace, Dr. Urbino had often boasted in public—and until now it had been true—that he was like those Swedish matches that light only with their own box. But he did not know how a woman with as much pride, dignity, and strength of character as his wife would react in the face of proven infidelity. So that after looking at her as she had asked, nothing occurred to him but to lower his eyes again in order to hide his embarrassment and continue the pretense of being lost among the sweet, meandering rivers of Alca Island until he could think of something else. Fermina Daza, for her part, said nothing more either. When she finished darning the socks, she tossed everything into the sewing basket in no particular order, gave instructions in the kitchen for supper, and went to the bedroom.

Then he reached the admirable decision not to go to Miss Lynch's house at five o'clock in the afternoon. The vows of eternal love, the dream of a discreet house for her alone where he could visit her with no unexpected interruptions, their unhurried happiness for as long as they lived—everything he had promised in the blazing heat of love was canceled forever after. The last thing Miss Lynch received from him was an emerald tiara in a little box wrapped in paper from the pharmacy, so that the coachman himself thought it was an emergency prescription and handed it to her with no comment, no message, nothing in writing. Dr. Urbino never saw her again, not even by accident, and God alone knows how much grief his heroic resolve cost him or how many bitter tears he had to shed behind the locked lavatory door in order to survive this private catastrophe. At five o'clock, instead of going to see her, he made a profound act of contrition before his confessor, and on the following Sunday he took Communion, his heart broken but his soul at peace.

That night, following his renunciation, as he was undressing for bed, he recited for Fermina Daza the bitter litany of his early morning insomnia, his sudden stabbing pains, his desire to weep in the afternoon, the encoded symptoms of secret love, which he recounted as if they were the miseries of old age. He had to tell someone or die, or else tell the truth, and so the relief he obtained was sanctified within the domestic rituals of love. She listened to him with close attention, but without looking at him, without saying anything as she picked up every article of clothing he removed, sniffed it with no gesture or change of expression that might betray her wrath, then crumpled it and tossed it into the wicker basket for dirty clothes. She did not find the odor, but it was all the same: tomorrow was another day. Before he knelt down to pray before the altar in the bedroom, he ended the recital of his misery with a sign as mournful as it was sincere: "I think I am going to die." She did not even blink when she replied.

"That would be best," she said. "Then we could both have some peace."

Years before, during the crisis of a dangerous illness, he had spoken of the possibility of dying, and she had made the same brutal reply. Dr. Urbino attributed it to the natural hardheartedness of women, which allows the earth to continue revolving around the sun, because at that time he did not know that she always erected a barrier of wrath to hide her fear. And in this case it was the most terrible one of all, the fear of losing him.

That night, on the other hand, she wished him dead with all her heart, and this certainty alarmed him. Then he heard her slow sobbing in the darkness as she bit the pillow so he would not hear. He was puzzled, because he knew that she did not cry easily for any affliction of body or soul. She cried only in rage, above all if it had its origins in her terror of culpability, and then the more she cried the more enraged she became, because she could never forgive her weakness in crying. He did not dare to console her, knowing that it would have been like consoling a tiger run through by a spear, and he did not have the courage to tell her that the reason for her weeping had disappeared that afternoon, had been pulled out by the roots, forever, even from his memory.

Fatigue overcame him for a few minutes. When he awoke, she had lit her dim bedside lamp and lay there with her eyes open, but without crying. Something definitive had happened to her while he slept: the sediment that had accumulated at the bottom of her life over the course of so many years had been stirred up by the torment of her jealousy and had floated to the surface, and it had aged her all at once. Shocked by her sudden wrinkles, her faded lips, the ashes in her hair, he risked telling her that she should try to sleep: it was after two o'clock. She spoke, not looking at him but with no trace of rage in her voice, almost with gentleness.

"I have a right to know who she is," she said.

And then he told her everything, feeling as if he were lifting the weight of the world from his shoulders, because he was convinced that she already knew and only needed to confirm the details. But she did not, of course, so that as he spoke she began to cry again, not with her earlier timid sobs but with abundant salty tears that ran down her cheeks and burned her nightdress and inflamed her life, because he had not done what she, with her heart in her mouth, had hoped he would do, which was to be a man: deny everything, and swear on his life it was not true, and grow indignant at the false accusation, and shout curses at this ill-begotten society that did not hesitate to trample on one's honor, and remain imperturbable even when faced with crushing proofs of his disloyalty. Then, when he told her that he had been with his confessor that afternoon, she feared she would go blind with rage. Ever since her days at the Academy she had been convinced that the men and women of the Church lacked any virtue inspired by God. This was a discordant note in the harmony of the house, which they had managed to overlook without mishap. But her husband's allowing his confessor to be privy to an intimacy that was not only his but hers as well was more than she could bear.

"You might as well have told a snake charmer in the market," she said.

394

For her it was the end of everything. She was sure that her honor was the subject of gossip even before her husband had finished his penance, and the feeling of humiliation that this produced in her was much less tolerable than the shame and anger and injustice caused by his infidelity. And worst of all, damn it: with a black woman. He corrected her: "With a mulatta." But by then it was too late for accuracy: she had finished.

"Just as bad," she said, "and only now I understand: it was the smell of a black woman."

This happened on a Monday. On Friday at seven o'clock in the evening, Fermina Daza sailed away on the regular boat to San Juan de la Ciénaga with only one trunk, in the company of her god-daughter, her face covered by a mantilla to avoid questions for herself and her husband. Dr. Juvenal Urbino was not at the dock, by mutual agreement, following an exhausting three-day discussion in which they decided that she should go to Cousin Hildebranda Sánchez's ranch in Flores de María for as long a time as she needed to think before coming to a final decision. Without knowing her reasons, the children understood it as a trip she had often put off and that they themselves had wanted her to make for a long time. Dr. Urbino arranged matters so that no one in his perfidious circle could engage in malicious speculation, and he did it so well that if Florentino Ariza could find no clue to Fermina Daza's disappearance it was because in fact there was none, not because he lacked the means to investigate. Her husband had no doubts that she would come home as soon as she got over her rage. But she left certain that her rage would never end.

However, she was going to learn very soon that her drastic decision was not so much the fruit of resentment as of nostalgia. After their honeymoon she had returned several times to Europe, despite the ten days at sea, and she had always made the trip with more than enough time to enjoy it. She knew the world, she had learned to live and think in new ways, but she had never gone back to San Juan de la Ciénaga after the aborted flight in the balloon. To her mind there was an element of redemption in the return to Cousin Hildebranda's province, no matter how belated. This was not her response to her marital catastrophe: the idea was much older than that. So the mere thought of revisiting her adolescent haunts consoled her in her unhappiness.

When she disembarked with her goddaughter in San Juan de la Ciénaga, she called on the great reserves of her character and recognized the town despite all the evidence to the contrary. The Civil and Military Commander of the city, who had been advised of her arrival, invited her for a drive in the official Victoria while the train was preparing to leave for San Pedro Alejandrino, which she wanted to visit in order to see for herself if what they said was true, that the bed in which The Liberator had died was as small as a child's. Then Fermina Daza saw her town again in the somnolence of two o'clock in the afternoon. She saw the streets that seemed more like beaches with scum-covered pools, and she saw the mansions of the Portuguese, with their coats of arms carved over the entrance and bronze jalousies at the windows, where the same hesitant, sad piano exercises that her recently married mother had taught to the daughters of the wealthy houses were repeated without mercy in the gloom of the salons. She saw the deserted plaza, with no trees growing in the burning lumps of sodium nitrate, the line of carriages with their funereal tops and their horses asleep where they stood, the yellow train to San Pedro Alejandrino, and on the corner next to the largest church she saw the biggest and most beautiful of the houses, with an arcaded passageway of greenish stone, and its great monastery door, and the window of the bedroom where Álvaro would be born many years later when she no longer had the memory to remember it. She thought of Aunt Escolástica, for whom she continued her hopeless search in heaven and on earth, and thinking of her, she found herself thinking of Florentino Ariza with his literary clothes and his book of poems under the almond trees in the little park, as she did on rare occasions when she recalled her unpleasant days at the Academy. She drove around and around, but she could not recognize the old family house, for where she supposed it to be she found only a pigsty, and around the corner was a street lined with brothels where whores from all over the world took their siestas in the doorways in case there was something for them in the mail. It was not the same town.

When they began their drive, Fermina Daza had covered the lower half of her face with her mantilla, not for fear of being recognized in a place where no one could know her but because of the dead bodies she saw everywhere, from the railroad station to the cemetery, bloating in the sun. The Civil and Military Commander of the city told her: "It's cholera." She knew it was, because she had seen the white lumps in the mouths of the sweltering corpses, but she noted that none of them had the coup de grace in the back of the neck as they had at the time of the balloon.

"That is true," said the officer. "Even God improves His methods."

The distance from San Juan de la Ciénaga to the old plantation of San Pedro Alejandrino was only nine leagues, but the yellow train took the entire day to make the trip because the engineer was a friend of the regular passengers, who were always asking him to please stop so they could stretch their legs by strolling across the golf courses of the banana company, and the men bathed naked in the clear cold rivers that rushed down from the mountains, and when they were hungry they got off the train to milk the cows wandering in the pastures. Fermina Daza was terrified when they reached their destination, and she just had time to marvel at the Homeric tamarinds where The Liberator had hung his dying man's hammock and to confirm that the bed where he had died, just as they had said, was small not only for so glorious a man but even for a seven-month-old infant. Another visitor, however, who seemed very well informed, said that the bed was a false relic, for the truth was that the father of his country had been left to die on the floor. Fermina Daza was so depressed by what she had seen and heard since she left her house that for the rest of the trip she took no pleasure in the memory of her earlier trip, as she had longed to do, but instead she avoided passing through the villages of her nostalgia. In this way she could still keep them, and keep herself from disillusionment. She heard the accordions in her detours around disenchantment, she heard the shouts from the cockfighting pits, the bursts of gunfire that could just as well signal war as revelry, and when she had no other recourse and had to pass through a village, she covered her face with her mantilla so that she could remember it as it once had been.

One night, after so much avoidance of the past, she arrived at Cousin Hildebranda's ranch, and when she saw her waiting at the door she almost fainted: it was as if she were seeing herself in the mirror of truth. She was fat and old, burdened with unruly children whose father was not the man she still loved without hope but a soldier living on his pension whom she had married out of spite and who loved her to distraction. But she was still the same person inside her ruined body. Fermina Daza recovered from her shock after just a few days of country living and pleasant memories, but she did not leave the ranch except to go to Mass on Sundays with the grandchildren of her wayward conspirators of long ago, cowboys on magnificent horses and beautiful, well-dressed girls who were just like their mothers at their age and who rode standing in oxcarts and singing in chorus until they reached the mission church at the end of the valley. She only passed through the village of Flores de María, where she had not gone on her earlier trip because she had not thought she would like it, but when she saw it she was fascinated. Her misfortune, or the village's, was that she could never remember it afterward as it was in reality, but only as she had imagined it before she had been there.

Dr. Juvenal Urbino made the decision to come for her after receiving a report from the Bishop of Riohacha, who had concluded that his wife's long stay was caused not by her unwillingness to return but by her inability to find a way around her pride. So he went without notifying her after an exchange of letters with Hildebranda, in which it was made clear that his wife was filled with nostalgia: now she thought only of home. At eleven o'clock in the morning, Fermina Daza was in the kitchen preparing stuffed eggplant when she heard the shouts of the peons, the neighing of the horses, the shooting of guns into the air, then the resolute steps in the courtyard and the man's voice:

"It is better to arrive in time than to be invited."

She thought she would die of joy. Without time to think about it, she washed her hands as well as she could while she murmured: "Thank you, God, thank you, how good you are," thinking that she had not yet bathed because of the damned eggplant that Hildebranda had asked her to prepare without telling her who was coming to lunch, thinking that she looked so old and ugly and that her face was so raw from the sun that he would regret having come when he saw her like this, damn it. But she dried her hands the best she could on her apron, arranged her appearance the best she could, called on all the haughtiness she had been born with to calm her maddened heart, and went to meet the man with her sweet doe's gait, her head high, her eyes shining, her nose ready for battle, and grateful to her fate for the immense relief of going home, but not as pliant as he thought, of course, because she would be happy to leave with him, of course, but she was also determined to make him pay with her silence for the bitter suffering that had ended her life.

Almost two years after the disappearance of Fermina Daza, an impossible coincidence occurred, the sort that Tránsito Ariza would have characterized as one of God's jokes. Florentino Ariza had not been impressed in any special way by the invention of moving pictures, but Leona Cassiani took him, unresisting, to the spectacular opening of *Cabiria*, whose reputation was based on the dialogues written by the poet Gabriele D'Annunzio. The great open-air patio of Don Galileo Daconte, where on some nights one enjoyed the splendor of the stars more than the silent lovemaking on the screen, was filled to overflowing with a select public. Leona Cassiani followed the wandering plot with her heart in her mouth. Florentino Ariza, on the other hand, was nodding his head in sleep because of the overwhelming tedium of the drama. At his back, a woman's voice seemed to read his thoughts:

"My God, this is longer than sorrow!"

That was all she said, inhibited perhaps by the resonance of her voice in the darkness, for the custom of embellishing silent films with piano accompaniment had not yet been established here, and in the darkened enclosure all that one could hear was the projector murmuring like rain. Florentino Ariza did not think of God except in the most extreme circumstances, but now he thanked Him with all his heart. For even twenty fathoms underground he would instantly have recognized the husky voice he had carried in his soul ever since the afternoon when he heard her say in a swirl of yellow leaves in a solitary park: "Now go, and don't come back until I tell you to." He knew that she was sitting in the seat behind his, next to her inevitable husband, and he could detect her warm, even breathing, and he inhaled with love the air purified by the health of her breath. Instead of imagining her under attack by the devouring worms of death, as he had in his despondency of recent months, he recalled her at a radiant and joyful age, her belly rounded under the Minervan tunic with the seed of her first child. In utter detachment from the historical disasters that were crowding the screen, he did not need to turn around to see her in his imagination. He delighted in the scent of almonds that came wafting back to him from his innermost being, and he longed to know how she thought women in films should fall in love so that their loves would cause less pain than they did in life. Just before the film ended, he realized in a flash of exultation that he had never been so close, so long, to the one he loved so much.

When the lights went on, he waited for the others to stand up. Then he stood, unhurried, and turned around in a distracted way as he buttoned his vest that he always opened during a performance, and the four of them found themselves so close to one another that they would have been obliged to exchange greetings even if one of them had not wanted to. First Juvenal Urbino greeted Leona Cassiani, whom he knew well, and then he shook Florentino Ariza's hand with his customary gallantry. Fermina Daza smiled at both of them with courtesy, only courtesy, but in any event with the smile of someone who had seen them often, who knew who they were, and who therefore did not need an introduction. Leona Cassiani responded with her mulatta grace. But Florentino Ariza did not know what to do, because he was flabbergasted at the sight of her.

She was another person. There was no sign in her face of the terrible disease that was in fashion, or of any other illness, and her body had kept the proportion and slenderness of her better days, but it was evident that the last two years had been as hard on her as ten difficult ones. Her short hair was becoming, with a curved wing on each cheek, but it was the color of aluminum, not honey, and behind her grandmother's spectacles her beautiful lanceolate eyes had lost half a lifetime of light. Florentino Ariza saw her move away from her husband's arm in the crowd that was leaving the theater, and he was surprised that she was in a public place wearing a poor woman's mantilla and house slippers. But what moved him most was that her husband had to take her arm to help her at the exit, and even then she miscalculated the height of the step and almost tripped on the stairs at the door.

Florentino Ariza was very sensitive to the faltering steps of age. Even as a young man he would interrupt his reading of poetry in the park to observe elderly couples who helped each other across the street, and they were lessons in life that had aided him in detecting the laws of his own aging. At Dr. Juvenal Urbino's time of life, that night at the film, men blossomed in a kind of autumnal youth, they seemed more dignified with their first gray hairs, they became witty and seductive, above all in the eyes of young women, while their withered wives had to clutch at their arms so as not to trip over their own shadows. A few years later, however, the husbands fell without warning down the precipice of a humiliating aging in body and soul, and then it was their wives who recovered and had to lead them by the arm as if they were blind men on charity, whispering in their ear, in order not to wound their masculine pride, that they should be careful, that there were three steps, not two, that there was a puddle in the middle of the street, that the shape lying across the sidewalk was a dead beggar, and with great difficulty helped them to cross the street as if it were the only ford across the last of life's rivers. Florentino Ariza had seen himself reflected so often in that mirror that he was never as afraid of death as he was of reaching that humiliating age when he would have to be led on a woman's arm. On that day, and only on that day, he knew he would have to renounce his hope of Fermina Daza.

The meeting frightened away sleep. Instead of driving Leona Cassiani in the carriage, he walked with her through the old city, where their footsteps echoed like horses' hooves on the cobblestones. From time to time, fragments of fugitive voices escaped through the open balconies, bedroom confidences, sobs of love magnified by phantasmal acoustics and the hot fragrance of jasmine in the narrow, sleeping streets. Once again Florentino Ariza had to summon all his strength not to reveal to Leona Cassiani his repressed love for Fermina Daza. They walked together with measured steps, loving each other like unhurried old sweethearts, she thinking about the charms of Cabiria and he thinking about his own misfortune. A man was singing on a balcony in the Plaza of the Customhouse, and his song was repeated throughout the area in a chain of echoes: *When I was sailing across the immense waves of the sea.* On Saints of Stone Street, just when he should have said good night at her door, Florentino Ariza asked Leona Cassiani to invite him in for a brandy. It was the second time he had made such a request to her under comparable circumstances. The first time, ten years before, she had said to him: "If you come in at this hour you will have to stay forever." He did not go in. But he would do so now, even if he had to break his word afterward. Nevertheless, Leona Cassiani invited him in and asked for no promises.

That was how he found himself, when he least expected it, in the sanctuary of a love that had been extinguished before it was born. Her parents had died, her only brother had made his fortune in Curaçao, and she was living alone in the old family house. Years before, when he had still not renounced the hope of making her his lover, with the consent of her parents Florentino Ariza would visit her on Sundays, and sometimes until very late at night, and he had contributed so much to the household that he came to consider it his own. But that night after the film he had the feeling that his memory had been erased from the drawing room. The furniture had been moved, there were new prints hanging on the walls, and he thought that so many heartless changes had been made in order to perpetuate the certainty that he had never lived. The cat did not recognize him.

Dismayed by the cruelty of oblivion, he said: "He does not remember me anymore." But she replied over her shoulder, as she was fixing the brandies, that if he was bothered by that he could rest easy, because cats do not remember anyone.

Leaning back as they sat close together on the sofa, they spoke about themselves, about what they had been before they met one afternoon who knows how long ago on the mule-drawn trolley. Their lives were spent in adjacent offices, and until now they had never spoken of anything except their daily work. As they talked, Florentino Ariza put his hand on her thigh, he began to caress her with the gentle touch of an experienced seducer, and she did not stop him, but she did not respond either, not even with a shudder for courtesy's sake. Only when he tried to go further did she grasp his exploratory hand and kiss him on the palm.

"Behave yourself," she said. "I realized a long time ago that you are not the man I am looking for."

While she was still very young, a strong, able man whose face she never saw took her by surprise, threw her down on the jetty, ripped her clothes off, and made instantaneous and frenetic love to her. Lying there on the rocks, her body covered with cuts and bruises, she had wanted that man to stay forever so that she could die of love in his arms. She had not seen his face, she had not heard his voice, but she was sure she would have known him in a crowd of a thousand men because of his shape and size and his way of making love. From that time on, she would say to anyone who would listen to her: "If you ever hear of a big, strong fellow who raped a poor black girl from the street on Drowned Men's Jetty, one October fifteenth at about half-past eleven at night, tell him where he can find me." She said it out of habit, and she had said it to so many people that she no longer had any hope. Florentino Ariza had heard the story as many times as he had heard a boat sailing away in the night. By two o'clock in the morning they had each drunk three brandies and he knew, in truth, that he was not the man she was waiting for, and he was glad to know it.

"Bravo, lionlady," he said when he left. "We have killed the tiger."

It was not the only thing that came to an end that night. The evil lie about the pavilion of consumptives had ruined his sleep, for it had instilled in him the inconceivable idea that Fermina Daza was mortal and as a consequence might die before her husband. But when he saw her stumble at the door of the movie theater, by his own volition he took another step toward the abyss with the sudden realization that he, and not she, might be the one to die first. It was the most fearful kind of presentiment, because it was based on reality. The years of immobilized waiting, of hoping for good luck, were behind him, but on the horizon he could see nothing more than the unfathomable sea of imaginary illnesses, the drop-by-drop urinations of sleepless nights, the daily death at twilight. He thought that all the moments in the day, which had once been his allies and sworn accomplices, were beginning to conspire against him. A few years before he had gone to a dangerous assignation, his heart heavy with terror of what might happen, and he had found the door unlocked and the hinges recently oiled so that he could come in without a sound, but he repented at the last moment for fear of causing a decent married woman irreparable harm by dying in her bed. So that it was reasonable to think that the woman he loved most on earth, the one he had waited for from one century to the next without a sigh of disenchantment, might not have the opportunity to lead him by the arm across a street full of lunar grave mounds and beds of windblown poppies in order to help him reach the other side of death in safety.

The truth is that by the standards of his time, Florentino Ariza had crossed the line into old age. He was fifty-six well-preserved years old, and he thought them well lived because they were years of love. But no man of the time would have braved the ridicule of looking young at his age, even if he did or thought he did, and none would have dared to confess without shame that he still wept in secret over a rebuff received in the previous century. It was a bad time for being young: there was a style of dress for each age, but the style of old age began soon after adolescence, and lasted until the grave. More than age, it was a matter of social dignity. The young men dressed like their grandfathers, they made themselves more respectable with premature spectacles, and a walking stick was looked upon with favor after the age of thirty. For women there were only two ages: the age for marrying, which did not go past twenty-two, and the age for being eternal spinsters: the ones left behind. The others, the married women, the mothers, the widows, the grandmothers, were a race apart who tallied their age not in relation to the number of years they had lived but in relation to the time left to them before they died.

Florentino Ariza, on the other hand, faced the insidious snares of old age with savage temerity, even though he knew that his peculiar fate had been to look like an old man from the time he was a boy. At first it was a matter of necessity. Tránsito Ariza pulled apart and then sewed together again for him the clothes that his father decided to discard, so that he went to primary school wearing frock coats that dragged on the ground when he sat down, and ministerial hats that came down over his ears despite the cotton batting on the inside to make them smaller. Since he had also worn glasses for myopia from the age of five, and had his mother's Indian hair, as bristly and coarse as horsehair, his appearance clarified nothing. It was fortunate that after so much governmental instability because of so many superimposed civil wars, academic standards were less selective than they had been, and there was a jumble of backgrounds and social positions in the public schools. Half-grown children would come to class from the barricades, smelling of gunpowder, wearing the insignias and uniforms of rebel officers captured at gunpoint in inconclusive battles, and carrying their regulation weapons in full view at their waists. They shot each other over disagreements in the playground, they threatened the teachers if they received low grades on examinations, and one of them, a third-year student at La Salle Academy and a retired colonel in the militia, shot and killed Brother Juan Eremita, Prefect of the Community, because he said in catechism class that God was a full-fledged member of the Conservative Party.

On the other hand, the sons of the great ruined families were dressed like old-fashioned princes, and some very poor boys went barefoot. Among so many oddities originating in so many places, Florentino Ariza was certainly among the oddest, but not to the point of attracting undue attention. The harshest thing he heard was when someone shouted to him on the street: "When you're ugly and poor, you can only want more." In any event, the apparel imposed by necessity became, from that time on and for the rest of his life, the kind best suited to his enigmatic nature and solemn character. When he was promoted to his first important position in the R.C.C., he had clothes made to order in the same style as those of his father, whom he recalled as an old man who had died at Christ's venerable age of thirty-three. So that Florentino Ariza always looked much older than he was. As a matter of fact, the loose-tongued Brígida Zuleta, a brief love who dished up unwashed truths, told him on the very first day

411

that she liked him better without his clothes because he looked twenty years younger when he was naked. However, he never knew how to remedy that, first because his personal taste would not allow him to dress in any other way, and second because at the age of twenty no one knew how to dress like a younger man, unless he were to take his short pants and sailor hat out of the closet again. On the other hand, he himself could not escape the notion of old age current in his day, so it was to be expected that when he saw Fermina Daza stumble at the door of the movie theater he would be shaken by a thunderbolt of panic that death, the son of a bitch, would win an irreparable victory in his fierce war of love.

Until that time his greatest battle, fought tooth and nail and lost without glory, was against baldness. From the moment he saw the first hairs tangled in his comb, he knew that he was condemned to a hell whose torments cannot be imagined by those who do not suffer them. He struggled for years. There was not a pomade or lotion he did not try, a belief he did not accept, a sacrifice he did not endure, in order to defend every inch of his head against the ravages of that devastation. He memorized the agricultural information in the *Bristol Almanac* because he had heard that there was a direct relationship between the growth of hair and the harvesting cycles. He left the totally bald barber he had used all his life for a foreign newcomer who cut hair only when the moon was in the first quarter. The new barber had begun to demonstrate that in fact he had a fertile hand, when it was discovered that he was wanted by several Antillean police forces for raping novices, and he was taken away in chains.

By then Florentino Ariza had cut out every advertisement concerning baldness that he found in the newspapers of the Caribbean basin, the ones in which they printed two pictures of the same man, first as bald as a melon and then with more hair than a lion: before and after using the infallible cure. After six years he had tried one hundred seventy-two of them, in addition to complementary treatments that appeared on the labels of the bottles, and all that he achieved was an itching, foul-smelling eczema of the scalp called ringworm borealis by the medicine men of Martinique because it emitted a phosphorescent glow in the dark. As a last resort he had recourse to all the herbs that the Indians hawked in the public market and to all the magical specifics and Oriental potions sold in the Arcade of the Scribes, but by the time he realized that he had been swindled, he already had the tonsure of a saint. In the year 1900, while the Civil War of a Thousand Days bled the country, an Italian who made custom-fitted wigs of human hair came to the city. The wigs cost a fortune, and the manufacturer took no responsibility after three months of use, but there were few solvent bald men who did not succumb to the temptation. Florentino Ariza was one of the first. He tried on a wig that was so similar to his own hair that he was afraid it would stand on end with his changes in mood, but he could not accept the idea of wearing a dead man's hair on his head. His only consolation was that his raging baldness meant that he would not have to watch his hair turn gray. One day, one of the genial drunks on the river docks embraced him with more enthusiasm than usual when he saw him leave the office, and then he removed Florentino Ariza's hat, to the mocking laughter of the stevedores, and gave him a resounding kiss on the head.

"Hairless wonder!" he shouted.

That night, at the age of forty-eight, he had the few downy strands left at his temples and the nape of his neck cut off, and he embraced with all his heart his destiny of total baldness. Every morning before his bath he lathered not only his chin but the areas on his scalp where stubble was beginning to reappear, and with a barber's razor he left everything as smooth as a baby's bottom. Until then he would not remove his hat even in the office, for his baldness produced a sensation of nakedness that seemed indecent to him. But when he accepted his baldness with all his heart, he attributed to it the masculine virtues that he had heard about and scorned as nothing but the fantasies of bald men. Later he took refuge in the new custom of combing long hairs from his part on the right all the way across his head, and this he never abandoned. But even so, he continued to wear his hat, always the same funereal style, even after the *tartarita*, the local name for the straw skimmer, came into fashion.

The loss of his teeth, on the other hand, did not result from a natural calamity but from the shoddy work of an itinerant dentist who decided to eradicate a simple infection by drastic means. His terror of the drill had prevented Florentino Ariza from visiting a dentist, despite his constant toothaches, until the pain became unbearable. His mother was alarmed by a night of inconsolable moaning from the room next to hers, because these moans seemed to be the same as the ones from another time, which had almost disappeared in the mists of her memory, but when she made him open his mouth to see where love was hurting him, she discovered that he had fallen victim to abscesses.

Uncle Leo XII sent him to Dr. Francis Adonay, a black giant in gaiters and jodhpurs who traveled the riverboats with complete dental equipment that he carried in a steward's saddlebag, and who seemed to be more like a traveling salesman of terror in the villages along the river. With just one glance in his mouth, he decided that Florentino Ariza had to have even his healthy teeth and molars extracted in order to protect him once and for all from further misfortunes. In contrast to baldness, this radical treatment caused him no alarm at all, except for his natural fear of a bloodbath without anesthesia. The idea of false teeth did not disturb him either, first because one of his fondest childhood memories was of a carnival magician who removed his upper and lower teeth and left them chattering by themselves on a table, and second because it would end the toothaches that had tormented him, ever since he was a boy, with almost as much cruelty as the pains of love. Unlike baldness, it did not seem to him an underhanded attack by old age, because he was convinced that despite the bitter breath of vulcanized rubber, his appearance would be cleaner with an orthopedic smile. So he submitted without resistance to the red-hot forceps of Dr. Adonay, and he endured his convalescence with the stoicism of a pack mule.

Uncle Leo XII attended to the details of the operation as if it were being performed on his own flesh. His singular interest in false teeth had developed on one of his first trips along the Magdalena River and was the result of his maniacal love for bel canto. One night when the moon was full, at the entrance to the port of Gamarra, he made a wager with a German surveyor that he could awaken the creatures of the jungle by singing a Neapolitan *romanza* from the Captain's balustrade. He almost lost the bet. In the river darkness one could hear the flapping wings of the cranes in the marshes, the thudding tails of the alligators, the terror of the shad as they tried to leap onto dry land, but on the final note, when it was feared that the singer would burst his arteries with the power of his song, his false teeth dropped out of his mouth with his last breath and fell into the water.

The boat had to wait three days at the port of Tenerife while an emergency set was made for him. It was a perfect fit. But on the voyage home, trying to explain to the Captain how he had lost the first pair, Uncle Leo XII filled his lungs with the burning air of the jungle, sang the highest note he could, held it to his last breath as he tried to frighten the alligators that were sunning themselves and watching the passage of the boat with unblinking eyes, and the new set of false teeth sank into the current as well. From then on, he kept spare sets of teeth everywhere, in various places throughout his house, in his desk drawer, and on each of the three company boats. Moreover, when he ate out he would carry an extra pair in a cough drop box that he kept in his pocket, because he had once broken a pair trying to eat pork cracklings at a picnic. Fearing that his nephew might be the victim of similar unpleasant surprises, Uncle Leo XII told Dr. Adonay to make him two sets right from the start: one of cheap materials for daily use at the office, and the other for Sundays and holidays, with a gold chip in the first molar that would impart a touch of realism. At last, on a Palm Sunday ringing with the sound of holiday bells, Florentino Ariza returned to the street with a new identity, his perfect smile giving him the impression that someone else had taken his place in the world.

This was at the time that his mother died and Florentino Ariza was left alone in his house. It was a haven that suited his way of loving, because the location was discreet despite the fact that the numerous windows that gave the street its name made one think of too many eyes behind the curtains. But the house had been built to make Fermina Daza, and no one but Fermina Daza, happy, so that Florentino Ariza preferred to lose a good many opportunities during his most fruitful years rather than soil his house with other loves. To his good fortune, every step he climbed in the R.C.C. brought new privileges, above all secret privileges, and one of the most practical was the possibility of using the offices at night, or on Sundays or holidays, with the complicity of the watchmen. Once, when he was First Vice President, he was making emergency love to one of the Sunday girls, sitting on a desk chair with her astride him, when the door opened without warning. Uncle Leo XII peered in, as if he had walked into the wrong office, and stared at his terrified nephew over his eyeglasses. "I'll be damned!" said his uncle, without the least sign of shock. "You screw just like your dad!" And before he closed the door, he said, with his eyes looking off into the distance:

"And you, Señorita, feel free to carry on. I swear by my honor that I have not seen your face."

The matter was not mentioned again, but the following week it was impossible to work in Florentino Ariza's office. On Monday the electricians burst in to install a rotating fan on the ceiling. The locksmiths arrived unannounced and with as much noise as if they were going to war, installed a lock on the door so that it could be bolted from the inside. The carpenters took measurements without saying why, the upholsterers brought swatches of cretonne to see if they matched the color of the walls, and the next week an enormous double couch covered in a Dionysian flowered print was delivered through the window because it was too big for the doors. They worked at the oddest hours, with an impertinence that did not seem unintentional, and they offered the same response to all his protests: "Orders from the head office." Florentino Ariza never knew if this sort of interference was a kindness on his uncle's part or a very personal way of forcing him to face up to his abusive behavior. The truth never occurred to him, which was that Uncle Leo XII was encouraging his nephew, because he, too, had heard the rumors that his habits were different from those of most men, and this obstacle to naming him as his successor had caused him great distress.

Unlike his brother, Leo XII Loayza had enjoyed a stable marriage of sixty years' duration, and he was always proud of not working on Sundays. He had four sons and a daughter, and he wanted to prepare all of them as heirs to his empire, but by a series of coincidences that were common in the novels of the day, but that no one believed in real life, his four sons died, one after the other, as they rose to positions of authority, and his daughter had no river vocation whatsoever and preferred to die watching the boats on the Hudson from a window fifty meters high. There were even those who accepted as true the tale that

419

Florentino Ariza, with his sinister apperance and his vampire's umbrella, had somehow been the cause of all those coincidences.

When doctor's orders forced his uncle into retirement, Florentino Ariza began, with good grace, to sacrifice some of his Sunday loves. He accompanied his uncle to his country retreat in one of the city's first automobiles, whose crank handle had such a powerful recoil that it had dislocated the shoulder of the first driver. They talked for many hours, the old man in the hammock with his name embroidered in silk thread, removed from everything and with his back to the sea, in the old slave plantation from whose terraces, filled with crepe myrtle, one could see the snow-covered peaks of the sierra in the afternoon. It had always been difficult for Florentino Ariza and his uncle to talk about anything other than river navigation, and it still was on those slow afternoons when death was always an unseen guest. One of Uncle Leo XII's constant preoccupations was that river navigation not pass into the hands of entrepreneurs from the interior with connections to European corporations. "This has always been a business run by people from the coast," he would say. "If the inlanders get hold of it, they will give it back to the Germans." His preoccupation was consistent with a political conviction that he liked to repeat even when it was not to the point.

"I am almost one hundred years old, and I have seen everything change, even the position of the stars in the universe, but I have not seen anything

420

change yet in this country," he would say. "Here they make new constitutions, new laws, new wars every three months, but we are still in colonial times."

To his brother Masons, who attributed all evils to the failure of federalism, he would always reply: "The War of a Thousand Days was lost twenty-three years ago in the war of '76." Florentino Ariza, whose indifference to politics hovered on the limits of the absolute, listened to these increasingly frequent and tiresome speeches as one listens to the sound of the sea. But he was a rigorous debater when it came to company policy. In opposition to his uncle's opinion, he thought that the setbacks in river navigation, always on the edge of disaster, could be remedied only by a voluntary renunciation of the riverboat monopoly that the National Congress had granted to the River Company of the Caribbean for ninety-nine years and a day. His uncle protested: "My namesake Leona with her worthless anarchist theories has put those ideas in your head." But that was only half true. Florentino Ariza based his thinking on the experience of the German commodore Johann B. Elbers, whose noble intelligence had been destroyed by excessive personal ambition. His uncle, however, believed that the failure of Elbers was due not to privileges but to the unrealistic commitments he had contracted for, which had almost been tantamount to his assuming responsibility for the geography of the nation: he had taken charge of maintaining the navigability of the river, the port installations, the access routes on land, the means of transportation. Besides, he would say, the virulent opposition of President Simón Bolívar was no laughing matter.

Most of his business associates viewed those disputes as if they were matrimonial arguments, in which both parties are right. The old man's obstinacy seemed natural to them, not because, as it was too easy to say, old age had made him less visionary than he had always been, but because renouncing the monopoly must have seemed to him like throwing away the victories of a historic battle that he and his brothers had waged unaided, back in heroic times, against powerful adversaries from all over the world. Which is why no one opposed him when he kept so tight a hold on his rights that no one could touch them before their legal expiration. But suddenly, when Florentino Ariza had already surrendered his weapons during those meditative afternoons on the plantation, Uncle Leo XII agreed to renounce the centenarian privilege, on the one honorable condition that it not take place before his death.

It was his final act. He did not speak of business again, he did not even allow anyone to consult with him, he did not lose a single ringlet from his splendid imperial head or an iota of his lucidity, but he did everything possible to keep anyone from seeing him who might pity him. He passed the days in contemplation of the perpetual snows from his terrace, rocking slowly in a Viennese rocker next to a table where the servants always kept a pot of black coffee hot for him, along with a glass of water with boric acid that contained two plates of false teeth, which he no longer used except to receive visitors. He saw very few friends, and he would speak only of a past so remote that it antedated river navigation. But he still had one new topic of conversation left: his desire that Florentino Ariza marry. He expressed his wish to him several times, and always in the same way:

"If I were fifty years younger," he would say, "I would marry my namesake Leona. I cannot imagine a better wife."

Florentino Ariza trembled at the idea of his labor of so many years being frustrated at the last moment by this unforeseen circumstance. He would have preferred to renounce everything, throw it all away, die, rather than fail Fermina Daza. Fortunately, Uncle Leo XII did not insist. When he turned ninety-two, he recognized his nephew as sole heir and retired from the company.

Six months later, by unanimous agreement, Florentino Ariza was named President of the Board of Directors and General Manager of the company. After the champagne toast on the day he took over the post, the old lion in retirement excused himself for speaking without getting up from the rocker, and he improvised a brief speech that seemed more like an elegy. He said that his life had begun and ended with two providential events. The first was that The Liberator had carried him in his arms in the village of Turbaco when he was making his ill-fated journey toward death. The other had been finding, despite all the obstacles that destiny had interposed, a successor worthy of the company. At last, trying to undramatize the drama, he concluded:

"The only frustration I carry away from this life is that of singing at so many funerals except my own."

It goes without saying that to close the ceremony he sang the "addio alla vita" from *Tosca*. He sang it a capella, which was the style he preferred, in a voice that was still steady. Florentino Ariza was moved, but he showed it only in the slight tremor in his voice as he expressed his thanks. In just the same way that he had done and thought everything he had done and thought in life, he had scaled the heights only because of his fierce determination to be alive and in good health at the moment he would fulfill his destiny in the shadow of Fermina Daza.

However, it was not her memory alone that accompanied him to the party Leona Cassiani gave for him that night. The memory of them all was with him: those who slept in the cemeteries, thinking of him through the roses he planted over them, as well as those who still laid their heads on the pillow where their husbands slept, their horns golden in the moonlight. Deprived of one, he wanted to be with them all at the same time, which is what he always wanted whenever he was fearful. For even during his most difficult times and at his worst moments, he had maintained some link, no matter how weak, with his countless lovers of so many years: he always kept track of their lives.

And so that night he remembered Rosalba, the very first one, who had carried off the prize of his virginity and whose memory was still as painful as it had been the first day. He had only to close his eyes to see her in her muslin dress and her hat with the long silk ribbons, rocking her child's cage on the deck of the boat. Several times in the course of the numerous years of his life he had been ready to set out in search of her, without knowing where, or her last name, or if she was the one he was looking for, but certain of finding her somewhere among groves of orchids. Each time, because of a real difficulty at the last minute or because of an ill-timed failure of his own will, his trip was postponed just as they were about to raise the gangplank: always for a reason that had something to do with Fermina Daza.

He remembered the Widow Nazaret, the only one with whom he had profaned his mother's house on the Street of Windows, although it had been Tránsito Ariza and not he who had asked her in. He was more understanding of her than of any of the others, because she was the only one who radiated enough tenderness to compensate for Fermina Daza despite her sluggishness in bed. But she had the inclinations of an alleycat, which were more indomitable than the strength of her tenderness, and this meant that both of them were condemned to infidelity. Still, they continued to be intermittent lovers for almost thirty years, thanks

425

to their musketeers' motto: *Unfaithful but not disloyal*. She was also the only one for whom Florentino Ariza assumed any responsibility: when he heard that she had died and was going to a pauper's grave, he buried her at his own expense and was the only mourner at the funeral.

He remembered other widows he had loved. He remembered Prudencia Pitre, the oldest of those still alive, who was known to everyone as the Widow of Two because she had outlived both her husbands. And the other Prudencia, the Widow Arellano, the amorous one, who would rip the buttons from his clothes so that he would have to stay in her house while she sewed them back on. And Josefa, the Widow Zúñiga, mad with love for him, who was ready to cut off his penis with gardening shears while he slept, so that he would belong to no one else even if he could not belong to her.

He remembered Ángeles Alfaro, the most ephemeral and best loved of them all, who came for six months to teach string instruments at the Music School and who spent moonlit nights with him on the flat roof of her house, as naked as the day she was born, playing the most beautiful suites in all music on a cello whose voice became human between her golden thighs. From the first moonlit night, both of them broke their hearts in the fierce love of inexperience. But Ángeles Alfaro left as she had come, with her tender sex and her sinner's cello, on an ocean liner that flew the flag of oblivion, and all that remained of her on the moonlit roofs was a fluttered farewell with a white hand-kerchief like a solitary sad dove on the horizon, as if she were a verse from the Poetic Festival. With her Florenino Ariza learned what he had already experienced many times without realizing it: that one can be in love with several people at the same time, feel the same sorrow with each, and not betray any of them. Alone in the midst of the crowd on the pier, he said to himself in a flash of anger: "My heart has more rooms than a whorehouse." He wept copious tears at the grief of parting. But as soon as the ship had disappeared over the horizon, the memory of Fermina Daza once again occupied all his space.

He remembered Andrea Varón, outside whose house he had spent the previous week, but the orange light in the bathroom had been a warning that he could not go in: someone had arrived before him. Someone: man or woman, because Andrea Varón did not hesitate over such details when it came to the follies of love. Of all those on the list, she was the only one who earned a living with her body, but she did so at her pleasure and without a business manager. In her day she had enjoyed a legendary career as a clandestine courte-san who deserved her nom de guerre, Our Lady of Everybody. She drove governors and admirals mad, she watched eminent heroes of arms and letters who were not as illustrious as they believed, and even some who were, as they wept on her shoulder. It was true, however, that President Rafael Reyes, after only a hurried half hour between appointments in the city, granted her a lifetime pension for distinguished service to the Ministry of Finance, where she had never worked a day of her life. She distributed her gifts of pleasure as far as her body could reach, and although her indecent conduct was public knowledge, no one could have made a definitive case against her, because her eminent accomplices gave her the same protection they gave themselves, knowing that they had more to lose in a scandal than she did. For her sake Florentino Ariza had violated his sacred principle of never paying, and she had violated hers of never doing it free of charge, even with her husband. They had agreed upon a symbolic fee of one peso, which she did not take and he did not hand to her, but which they put in the piggy bank until enough of them had accumulated to buy something charming from overseas in the Arcade of the Scribes. It was she who attributed a distinctive sensuality to the enemas he used for his crises of constipation, who convinced him to share them with her, and they took them together in the course of their mad afternoons as they tried to create even more love within their love.

He considered it a stroke of good fortune that among so many hazardous encounters, the only woman who had made him taste a drop of bitterness was the sinuous Sara Noriega, who ended her days in the Divine Shepherdess Asylum, reciting senile verses of such outrageous obscenity that they were forced to isolate her so that she would not drive the rest of the madwomen crazy. However, when he took over complete responsibility for the R.C.C., he no longer had much time or desire to attempt to replace Fermina Daza with anyone else: he knew that she was irreplaceable. Little by little he had fallen into the routine of visiting the ones who were already established, sleeping with them for as long as they pleased him, for as long as he could, for as long as they lived. On the Pentecost Sunday when Juvenal Urbino died, he had only one left, only one, who had just turned fourteen and had everything that no one else until then had had to make him mad with love.

Her name was América Vicuña. She had arrived two years before from the fishing village of Puerto Padre, entrusted by her family to Florentino Ariza as her guardian and recognized blood relative. They had sent her with a government scholarship to study secondary education, with her *petate* and her little tin trunk as small as a doll's, and from the moment she walked off the boat, with her high white shoes and her golden braid, he had the awful presentiment that they were going to take many Sunday siestas together. She was still a child in every sense of the word, with braces on her teeth and the scrapes of elementary school on her knees, but he saw right away the kind of woman she was soon going to be, and he cultivated her during a slow year of Saturdays at the circus, Sundays in the park with ice cream, childish late afternoons, and he won her confidence, he won

429

her affection, he led her by the hand, with the gentle astuteness of a kind grandfather, toward his secret slaughterhouse. For her it was immediate: the doors of heaven opened to her. All at once she burst into flower, which left her floating in a limbo of happiness and which motivated her studies, for she was always at the head of her class so that she would not lose the privilege of going out on weekends. For him it was the most sheltered inlet in the cove of his old age. After so many years of calculated loves, the mild pleasure of innocence had the charm of a restorative perversion.

They were in full agreement. She behaved like what she was, a girl ready to learn about life under the guidance of a venerable old man who was not shocked by anything, and he chose to behave like what he had most feared being in his life: a senile lover. He never identified her with the young Fermina Daza despite a resemblance that was more than casual and was not based only on their age, their school uniform, their braid, their untamed walk, and even their haughty and unpredictable character. Moreover, the idea of replacement, which had been so effective an inducement for his mendicancy of love, had been completely erased from his mind. He liked her for what she was, and he came to love her for what she was, in a fever of crepuscular delights. She was the only one with whom he took drastic precautions against accidental pregnancy. After half a dozen encounters, there was no dream for either of them except their Sunday afternoons.

Since he was the only person authorized to take her out of the boarding school, he would call for her in the six-cylinder Hudson that belonged to the R.C.C., and sometimes they would lower the top if the afternoon was not sunny and drive along the beach, he with his somber hat and she, weak with laughter, holding the sailor hat of her school uniform with both hands so that the wind would not blow it off. Someone had told her not to spend more time with her guardian than necessary, not to eat anything he had tasted, and not to put her face too close to his, for old age was contagious. But she did not care. They were both indifferent to what people might think of them because their family kinship was well known, and what is more, the extreme difference in their ages placed them beyond all suspicion.

They had just made love on Pentecost Sunday when the bells began to toll at four o'clock. Florentino Ariza had to overcome the wild beating of his heart. In his youth, the ritual of the tolling bells had been included in the price of the funeral and was denied only to the indigent. But after our last war, just at the turn of the century, the Conservative regime consolidated its colonial customs, and funeral rites became so expensive that only the wealthiest could pay for them. When Archbishop Dante de Luna died, bells all over the province tolled unceasingly for nine days and nine nights, and the public suffering was so great that his successor reserved the tolling of bells for the funeral services of the most illustrious of the dead.

431

Therefore, when Florentino Ariza heard the Cathedral bells at four o'clock in the afternoon on a Pentecost Sunday, he felt as if he had been visited by a ghost from his lost youth. He never imagined they were the bells he had so longed to hear for so many years, ever since the Sunday when he saw Fermina Daza in her sixth month of pregnancy as she was leaving High Mass.

"Damn," he said in the darkness. "It must be a very big fish for them to ring the Cathedral bells."

América Vicuña, completely naked, had just awakened.

"It must be for Pentecost," she said.

Florentino Ariza was in no way expert in matters pertaining to the Church, and he had not gone to Mass again since he had played the violin in the choir with a German who also taught him the science of the telegraph and about whose fate he had never been able to obtain any definite news. But he knew beyond any doubt that the bells were not ringing for Pentecost. There was public mourning in the city, that was certain, and that is what he knew. A delegation of Caribbean refugees had come to his house that morning to inform him that Jeremiah de Saint-Amour had been found dead in his photography studio. Although Florentino Ariza was not an intimate friend of his, he was close to many other refugees who always invited him to their public ceremonies, above all to their funerals. But he was sure that the bells were not tolling for Jeremiah de Saint-Amour, who was a militant unbeliever and a committed anarchist and who had, moreover, died by his own hand.

"No," he said, "tolling like that must be for a governor at least."

América Vicuña, her pale body dappled by the light coming in through the carelessly drawn blinds, was not of an age to think about death. They had made love after lunch and they were lying together at the end of their siesta, both of them naked under the ceiling fan, whose humming could not hide the sound like falling hail that the buzzards made as they walked across the hot tin roof. Florentino Ariza loved her as he had loved so many other casual women in his long life, but he loved her with more anguish than any other, because he was certain he would be dead by the time she finished secondary school.

The room resembled a ship's cabin, its walls made of wooden laths covered by many coats of paint, as were the walls of boats, but at four o'clock in the afternoon, even with the electric fan hanging over the bed, the heat was more intense than in the riverboat cabins because it reflected off the metal roof. It was not so much a formal bedroom as a cabin on dry land, which Florentino Ariza had built behind his office in the R.C.C. with no other purpose or pretext than to have a nice little refuge for his old man's loves. On ordinary days it was difficult to sleep there, with the shouts of the stevedores, and the noise of the cranes from the river harbor, and the enormous bellowing of the ships moored at the dock. For the girl, however, it was a Sunday paradise.

They had planned to be together on Pentecost until she had to return to school, five minutes before the Angelus, but the tolling of the bells reminded Florentino Ariza of his promise to attend the funeral of Jeremiah de Saint-Amour, and he dressed with more haste than usual. First, as always, he plaited her single braid that he himself had loosened before they made love, and he sat her on the table to tie the bow on her school shoes, which was something she never did well. He helped her without malice, and she helped him to help her, as if it were an obligation: after their first encounters they had both lost awareness of their ages, and they treated each other with the familiarity of a husband and wife who had hidden so many things in this life that there was almost nothing left for them to say to each other.

The offices were closed and dark because of the holiday, and at the deserted dock there was only one ship, its boilers damped. The sultry weather presaged the first rains of the year, but the transparent air and the Sunday silence in the harbor seemed to belong to a more benevolent month. The world was harsher here than in the shadowy cabin, and the bells caused greater grief, even if one did not know for whom they tolled. Florentino Ariza and the girl went down to the patio of saltpeter, which the Spaniards had used as a port for blacks and where there were still the remains of weights and other rusted irons from the slave

434

trade. The automobile was waiting for them in the shade of the warehouses, and they did not awaken the driver, asleep with his head on the steering wheel, until they were settled in their seats. The automobile turned around behind the warehouses enclosed by chicken wire, crossed the area of the old market on Las Ánimas Bay, where near-naked adults were playing ball, and drove out of the river harbor in a burning cloud of dust. Florentino Ariza was sure that the funerary honors could not be for Jeremiah de Saint-Amour, but the insistent tolling filled him with doubts. He put his hand on the driver's shoulder and asked him, shouting into his ear, for whom the bells tolled.

"It's for that doctor with the goatee," said the driver. "What's his name?"

Florentino Ariza did not have to wonder who that was. Nevertheless, when the driver told him how he had died, his instantaneous hope vanished because he could not believe what he heard. Nothing resembles a person as much as the way he dies, and no death could resemble the man he was thinking about less than this one. But it was he, although it seemed absurd: the oldest and best-qualified doctor in the city, and one of its illustrious men for many other meritorious reasons, had died of a broken spine, at the age of eighty-one, when he fell from the branch of a mango tree as he tried to catch a parrot.

All that Florentino Ariza had done since Fermina Daza's marriage had been based on his hope for this event. But now that it had come, he did not feel the thrill of triumph he had imagined so often in his sleeplessness. Instead, he was seized by terror: the fantastic realization that it could just as well have been himself for whom the death knell was tolling. Sitting beside him in the automobile that jolted along the cobbled streets, América Vicuña was frightened by his pallor, and she asked him what was the matter. Florentino Ariza grasped her hand with his icy one.

"Oh, my dear," he sighed, "I would need another fifty years to tell you about it."

He forgot Jeremiah de Saint-Amour's funeral. He left the girl at the door of the school with a hurried promise that he would come back for her the following Saturday, and he told the driver to take him to the house of Dr. Juvenal Urbino. He was confronted by an uproar of automobiles and hired carriages in the surrounding streets and a multitude of curious onlookers outside the house. The guests of Dr. Lácides Olivella, who had received the bad news at the height of the celebration, came rushing in. It was not easy to move inside the house because of the crowd, but Florentino Ariza managed to make his way to the master bedroom, peered on tiptoe over the groups of people blocking the door, and saw Juvenal Urbino in the conjugal bed as he had wanted to see him since he had first heard of him—wallowing in the indignity of death. The carpenter had just taken his measurements for the coffin, and at his side, still wearing the dress of a newlywed grandmother that she had put on for the party, Fermina Daza was introspective and dejected.

Florentino Ariza had imagined that moment down to the last detail since the days of his youth when he had devoted himself completely to the cause of his reckless love. For her sake he had won fame and fortune without too much concern for his methods, for her sake he had cared for his health and personal appearance with a rigor that did not seem very manly to other men of his time, and he had waited for this day as no one else could have waited for anything or anyone in this world: without an instant of discouragement. The proof that death had at last interceded on his behalf filled him with the courage he needed to repeat his vow of eternal fidelity and everlasting love to Fermina Daza on her first night of widowhood.

He did not deny the accusations of his conscience that it had been a thoughtless and inappropriate act, one he had rushed into for fear that the opportunity would never be repeated. He would have preferred something less brutal, something in the manner he had so often imagined, but fate had given him no choice. He left the house of mourning, full of sorrow at leaving her in the same state of upheaval in which he found himself, but there was nothing he could have done to prevent it because he felt that this barbarous night had been forever inscribed in both their destinies.

For the next two weeks he did not sleep through a single night. He asked himself in despair where

Fermina Daza could be without him, what she could be thinking, what she would do, in the years of life remaining to her, with the burden of consternation he had left in her hands. He suffered a crisis of constipation that swelled his belly like a drum, and he had to resort to remedies less pleasant than enemas. The complaints of old age, which he endured better than his contemporaries because he had known them since his youth, all attacked at the same time. On Wednesday he appeared at the office after a week at home, and Leona Cassiani was horrified at seeing him so pale and enervated. But he reassured her: it was insomnia again, as always, and once more he bit his tongue to keep the truth from pouring out through the bleeding wounds in his heart. The rain did not allow him a moment of sun to think in. He spent another unreal week unable to concentrate on anything, eating badly and sleeping worse, trying to find the secret signs that would show him the road to salvation. But on Friday he was invaded by an unreasoning calm, which he interpreted as an omen that nothing new was going to happen, that everything he had done in his life had been in vain, that he could not go on: it was the end. On Monday, however, when he returned to his house on the Street of Windows, he discovered a letter floating in a puddle inside the entrance, and on the wet envelope he recognized at once the imperious handwriting that so many changes in life had not changed, and he even thought he could detect the nocturnal perfume of withered gardenias, because after the initial shock, his heart told him everything: it was the letter he had been waiting for, without a moment's respite, for over half a century.

FERMINA DAZA COULD not have imagined that her letter, inspired by blind rage, would have been interpreted by Florentino Ariza as a love letter. She had put into it all the fury of which she was capable, her cruelest words, the most wounding, most unjust vilifications, which still seemed minuscule to her in light of the enormity of the offense. It was the final act in a bitter exorcism through which she was attempting to come to terms with her new situation. She wanted to be herself again, to recover all that she had been obliged to give up in half a century of servitude that had doubtless made her happy but which, once her husband was dead, did not leave her even the vestiges of her identity. She was a ghost in a strange house that overnight had become immense and solitary and through which she wandered without purpose, asking herself in anguish which of them was deader: the man who had died or the woman he had left behind.

She could not avoid a profound feeling of rancor toward her husband for having left her alone in the middle of the ocean. Everything of his made her cry: his pajamas under the pillow, his slippers that had always looked to her like an invalid's, the memory of his image in the back of the mirror as he undressed while she combed her hair before bed, the odor of his skin, which was to linger on hers for a long time after his death. She would stop in the middle of whatever she was doing and slap herself on the forehead because she suddenly remembered something she had forgotten to tell him. At every moment countless ordinary questions would come to mind that he alone could answer for her. Once he had told her something that she could not imagine: that amputees suffer pains, cramps, itches, in the leg that is no longer there. That is how she felt without him, feeling his presence where he no longer was.

When she awoke on her first morning as a widow, she turned over in bed without opening her eyes, searching for a more comfortable position so that she could continue sleeping, and that was the moment when he died for her. For only then did it become clear that he had spent the night away from home for the first time in years. The other place where this struck her was at the table, not because she felt alone, which in fact she was, but because of her strange belief that she was eating with someone who no longer existed. It was not until her daughter Ofelia came from New Orleans with her husband and the three girls that she sat at a table again to eat, but instead of the usual one, she ordered a smaller, improvised table set up in the corridor. Until then she did not take

441

a regular meal. She would walk through the kitchen at any hour, whenever she was hungry, and put her fork in the pots and eat a little of everything without placing anything on a plate, standing in front of the stove, talking to the serving women, who were the only ones with whom she felt comfortable, the ones she got along with best. Still, no matter how hard she tried, she could not elude the presence of her dead husband: wherever she went, wherever she turned, no matter what she was doing, she would come across something of his that would remind her of him. For even though it seemed only decent and right to grieve for him, she also wanted to do everything possible not to wallow in her grief. And so she made the drastic decision to empty the house of everything that would remind her of her dead husband, which was the only way she could think of to go on living without him.

It was a ritual of eradication. Her son agreed to take his library so that she could replace his office with the sewing room she had never had when she was married. And her daughter would take some furniture and countless objects that she thought were just right for the antique auctions in New Orleans. All of this was a relief for Fermina Daza, although she was not at all amused to learn that the things she had bought on her honeymoon were now relics for antiquarians. To the silent stupefaction of the servants, the neighbors, the women friends who came to visit her during that time, she had a bonfire built in a vacant lot behind the

house, and there she burned everything that reminded her of her husband: the most expensive
and elegant clothes seen in the city since the last
century, the finest shoes, the hats that resembled
him more than his portraits, the siesta rocking
chair from which he had arisen for the last time to
die, innumerable objects so tied to her life that by
now they formed part of her identity. She did it
without the shadow of a doubt, in the full certainty that her husband would have approved, and
not only for reasons of hygiene. For he had often
expressed his desire to be cremated and not shut
away in the seamless dark of a cedar box. His
religion would not permit it, of course: he had
dared to broach the subject with the Archbishop,
just in case, and his answer had been a categorical
no. It was pure illusion, because the Church did
not permit the existence of crematoriums in our
cemeteries, not even for the use of religions other
than Catholic, and the advantage of building them
would not have occurred to anyone but Juvenal
Urbino. Fermina Daza did not forget her husband's terror, and even in the confusion of the
first hours she remembered to order the carpenter
to leave a chink where light could come into the
coffin as a consolation to him.

In any event, the holocaust was in vain. In a
very short while Fermina Daza realized that the
memory of her dead husband was as resistant to
the fire as it seemed to be to the passage of time.
Even worse: after the incineration of his clothing,
she continued to miss not only the many things

she had loved in him but also what had most annoyed her: the noises he made on arising. That memory helped her to escape the mangrove swamps of grief. Above all else, she made the firm decision to go on with her life, remembering her husband as if he had not died. She knew that waking each morning would continue to be difficult, but it would become less and less so.

At the end of the third week, in fact, she began to see the first light. But as it grew larger and brighter, she became aware that there was an evil phantom in her life who did not give her a moment's peace. He was not the pitiable phantom who had haunted her in the Park of the Evangels and whom she had evoked with a certain tenderness after she had grown old, but the hateful phantom with his executioner's frock coat and his hat held against his chest, whose thoughtless impertinence had disturbed her so much that she found it impossible not to think about him. Ever since her rejection of him at the age of eighteen, she had been convinced that she had left behind a seed of hatred in him that could only grow larger with time. She had always counted on that hatred, she had felt it in the air when the phantom was near, and the mere sight of him had upset and frightened her so that she never found a natural way to behave with him. On the night when he reiterated his love for her, while the flowers for her dead husband were still perfuming the house, she could not believe that his insolence was not the first step in God knows what sinister plan for revenge.

Her persistent memory of him increased her rage. When she awoke thinking about him on the day after the funeral, she succeeded in removing him from her thoughts by a simple act of will. But the rage always returned, and she realized very soon that the desire to forget him was the strongest inducement for remembering him. Then, overcome by nostalgia, she dared to recall for the first time the illusory days of that unreal love. She tried to remember just how the little park was then, and the shabby almond trees, and the bench where he had loved her, because none of it still existed as it had been then. They had changed everything, they had removed the trees with their carpet of yellow leaves and replaced the statue of the decapitated hero with that of another, who wore his dress uniform but had no name or dates or reasons to justify him, and who stood on an ostentatious pedestal in which they had installed the electrical controls for the district. Her house, sold many years before, had fallen into total ruin at the hands of the Provincial Government. It was not easy for her to imagine Florentino Ariza as he had been then, much less to believe that the taciturn boy, so vulnerable in the rain, was the moth-eaten old wreck who had stood in front of her with no consideration for her situation, or the slightest respect for her grief, and had seared her soul with a flaming insult that still made it difficult for her to breathe.

Cousin Hildebranda Sánchez had come to visit a short while after Fermina Daza returned from the ranch in Flores de María, where she had gone to recuperate from the misfortune of Miss Lynch. Old, fat, and contented, she had arrived in the company of her oldest son who, like his father, had been a colonel in the army but had been repudiated by him because of his contemptible behavior during the massacre of the banana workers in San Juan de la Ciénaga. The two cousins saw each other often and spent endless hours feeling nostalgia for the time when they first met. On her last visit, Hildebranda was more nostalgic than ever, and very affected by the burden of old age. In order to add even greater poignancy to their memories, she had brought her copy of the portrait of them dressed as old-fashioned ladies, taken by the Belgian photographer on the afternoon that a young Juvenal Urbino had delivered the coup de grace to a willful Fermina Daza. Her copy of the photograph had been lost, and Hildebranda's was almost invisible, but they could both recognize themselves through the mists of disenchantment: young and beautiful as they would never be again.

For Hildebranda it was impossible not to speak of Florentino Ariza, because she always identified his fate with her own. She evoked him as she evoked the day she had sent her first telegram, and she could never erase from her heart the memory of the sad little bird condemned to oblivion. For her part, Fermina had often seen him without speaking to him, of course, and she could not imagine that he had been her first love. She always heard news about him, as sooner or later she heard news about anyone of any significance in the city. It was said that he had not married because of his unusual habits, but she paid no attention to this, in part because she never paid attention to rumors, and in part because such things were said in any event about men who were above suspicion. On the other hand, it seemed strange to her that Florentino Ariza would persist in his mystic attire and his rare lotions, and that he would continue to be so enigmatic after making his way in life in so spectacular and honorable a manner. It was impossible for her to believe he was the same person, and she was always surprised when Hildebranda would sigh: "Poor man, how he must have suffered!" For she had seen him without grief for a long time: a shadow that had been obliterated.

Nevertheless, on the night she met him in the movie theater just after her return from Flores de María, something strange occurred in her heart. She was not surprised that he was with a woman, and a black woman at that. What did surprise her was that he was so well preserved, that he behaved with the greatest self-assurance, and it did not occur to her that perhaps it was she, not he, who had changed after the troubling explosion of Miss Lynch in her private life. From then on, and for more than twenty years, she saw him with more compassionate eyes. On the night of the vigil for her husband, it not only seemed reasonable for

447

him to be there, but she even understood it as the natural end of rancor: an act of forgiving and forgetting. That was why she was so taken aback by his dramatic reiteration of a love that for her had never existed, at an age when Florentino Ariza and she could expect nothing more from life.

The mortal rage of the first shock remained intact after the symbolic cremation of her husband, and it grew and spread as she felt herself less capable of controlling it. Even worse: the spaces in her mind where she managed to appease her memories of the dead man were slowly but inexorably being taken over by the field of poppies where she had buried her memories of Florentino Ariza. And so she thought about him without wanting to, and the more she thought about him the angrier she became, and the angrier she became the more she thought about him, until it was something so unbearable that her mind could no longer contain it. Then she sat down at her dead husband's desk and wrote Florentino Ariza a letter consisting of three irrational pages so full of insults and base provocations that it brought her the consolation of consciously committing the vilest act of her long life.

Those weeks had been agonizing for Florentino Ariza as well. The night he reiterated his love to Fermina Daza he had wandered aimlessly through streets that had been devastated by the afternoon flood, asking himself in terror what he was going to do with the skin of the tiger he had just killed after having resisted its attacks for more than half a century. The city was in a state of emergency because of the violent rains. In some houses, half-naked men and women were trying to salvage whatever God willed from the flood, and Florentino Ariza had the impression that everyone's calamity had something to do with his own. But the wind was calm and the stars of the Caribbean were quiet in their places. In the sudden silence of other voices, Florentino Ariza recognized the voice of the man whom Leona Cassiani and he had heard singing many years before, at the same hour and on the same corner: *I came back from the bridge bathed in tears*. A song that in some way, on that night, for him alone, had something to do with death.

He needed Tránsito Ariza then as he never had before, he needed her wise words, her head of a mock queen adorned with paper flowers. He could not avoid it: whenever he found himself on the edge of catastrophe, he needed the help of a woman. So that he passed by the Normal School, seeking out those who were within reach, and he saw a light in the long row of windows in América Vicuña's dormitory. He had to make a great effort not to fall into the grandfather's madness of carrying her off at two o'clock in the morning, warm with sleep in her swaddling clothes and still smelling of the cradle's tantrums.

At the other end of the city was Leona Cassiani, alone and free and doubtless ready to provide him with the compassion he needed at two o'clock in the morning, at three o'clock, at any hour and

449

under any circumstances. It would not be the first time he had knocked at her door in the wasteland of his sleepless nights, but he knew that she was too intelligent, and that they loved each other too much, for him to come crying to her lap and not tell her the reason. After a good deal of thought as he sleepwalked through the deserted city, it occurred to him that he could do no better than Prudencia Pitre, the Widow of Two, who was younger than he. They had first met in the last century, and if they stopped meeting it was because she refused to allow anyone to see her as she was, half blind and verging on decrepitude. As soon as he thought of her, Florentino Ariza returned to the Street of the Windows, put two bottles of port and a jar of pickles in a shopping bag, and went to visit her, not even knowing if she was still in her old house, if she was alone, or if she was alive.

Prudencia Pitre had not forgotten his scratching signal at the door, the one he had used to identify himself when they thought they were still young although they no longer were, and she opened the door without any questions. The street was dark, he was barely visible in his black suit, his stiff hat, and his bat's umbrella hanging over his arm, and her eyes were too weak to see him except in full light, but she recognized him by the gleam of the streetlamp on the metal frame of his eyeglasses. He looked like a murderer with blood still on his hands.

"Sanctuary for a poor orphan," he said.

It was the only thing he could think of to say, just to say something. He was surprised at how much she had aged since the last time he saw her, and he was aware that she saw him the same way. But he consoled himself by thinking that in a moment, when they had both recovered from the initial shock, they would notice fewer and fewer of the blows that life had dealt the other, and they would again seem as young as they had been when they first met.

"You look as if you are going to a funeral," she said.

It was true. She, along with almost the entire city, had been at the window since eleven o'clock, watching the largest and most sumptuous funeral procession that had been seen here since the death of Archbishop De Luna. She had been awakened from her siesta by the thundering artillery that made the earth tremble, by the dissonances of the marching bands, the confusion of funeral hymns over the clamoring bells in all the churches, which had been ringing without pause since the previous day. From her balcony she had seen the cavalry in dress uniform, the religious communities, the schools, the long black limousines of an invisible officialdom, the carriage drawn by horses in feathered headdresses and gold trappings, the flag-draped yellow coffin on the gun carriage of a historic cannon, and at the very end a line of old open Victorias that kept themselves alive in order to carry funeral wreaths. As soon as they had passed by Prudencia Pitre's balcony, a little after

451

midday, the deluge came and the funeral procession dispersed in a wild stampede.

"What an absurd way to die," she said.

"Death has no sense of the ridiculous," he said, and added in sorrow: "above all at our age."

They were seated on the terrace, facing the open sea, looking at the ringed moon that took up half the sky, looking at the colored lights of the boats along the horizon, enjoying the mild, perfumed breeze after the storm. They drank port and ate pickles on slices of country bread that Prudencia Pitre cut from a loaf in the kitchen. They had spent many nights like this after she had been left a widow without children. Florentino Ariza had met her at a time when she would have received any man who wanted to be with her, even if he were hired by the hour, and they had established a relationship that was more serious and longer-lived than would have seemed possible.

Although she never even hinted at it, she would have sold her soul to the devil to marry him. She knew that it would not be easy to submit to his miserliness, or the foolishness of his premature appearance of age, or his maniacal sense of order, or his eagerness to ask for everything and give nothing at all in return, but despite all this, no man was better company because no other man in the world was so in need of love. But no other man was as elusive either, so that their love never went beyond the point it always reached for him: the point where it would not interfere with his determination to remain free for Fermina Daza.

Nevertheless, it lasted many years, even after he had arranged for Prudencia Pitre to marry a salesman who was home for three months and traveled for the next three and with whom she had a daughter and four sons, one of whom, she swore, was Florentino Ariza's.

They talked, not concerned about the hour, because both were accustomed to sharing the sleepless nights of their youth, and they had much less to lose in the sleeplessness of old age. Although he almost never had more than two glasses of wine, Florentino Ariza still had not caught his breath after the third. He was dripping with perspiration, and the Widow of Two told him to take off his jacket, his vest, his trousers, to take off everything if he liked, what the hell: after all, they knew each other better naked than dressed. He said he would if she did the same, but she refused: some time ago she had looked at herself in the wardrobe mirror and suddenly realized that she would no longer have the courage to allow anyone—not him, not anyone—to see her undressed.

Florentino Ariza, in a state of agitation that he could not calm with four glasses of port, talked at length about the same subject: the past, the good memories from the past, for he was desperate to find the hidden road in the past that would bring him relief. For that was what he needed: to let his soul escape through his mouth. When he saw the first light of dawn on the horizon, he attempted an indirect approach. He asked, in a way that seemed casual: "What would you do if someone proposed marriage to you, just as you are, a widow of your age?" She laughed with a wrinkled old woman's laugh, and asked in turn:

"Are you speaking of the Widow Urbino?"

Florentino Ariza always forgot when he should not have that women, and Prudencia Pitre more than any other, always think about the hidden meanings of questions more than about the questions themselves. Filled with sudden terror because of her chilling marksmanship, he slipped through the back door: "I am speaking of you." She laughed again: "Go make fun of your bitch of a mother, may she rest in peace." Then she urged him to say what he meant to say, because she knew that he, or any other man, would not have awakened her at three o'clock in the morning after so many years of not seeing her just to drink port and eat country bread with pickles. She said: "You do that only when you are looking for someone to cry with." Florentino Ariza withdrew in defeat.

"For once you are wrong," he said. "My reasons tonight have more to do with singing."

"Let's sing, then," she said.

And she began to sing, in a very good voice, the song that was popular then: *Ramona, I cannot live without you.* The night was over, for he did not dare to play forbidden games with a woman who have proven too many times that she knew the dark side of the moon. He walked out into a different city, one that was perfumed by the last dahlias of June, and onto a street out of his youth, where the shadowy widows from five o'clock Mass were filing by. But now it was he, not they, who crossed the street, so they would not see the tears he could no longer hold back, not his midnight tears, as he thought, but other tears: the ones he had been swallowing for fifty-one years, nine months and four days.

He had lost all track of time, and did not know where he was when he awoke facing a large, dazzling window. The voice of América Vicuña playing ball in the garden with the servant girls brought him back to reality: he was in his mother's bed. He had kept her bedroom intact, and he would sleep there to feel less alone on the few occasions when he was troubled by his solitude. Across from the bed hung the large mirror from Don Sancho's Inn, and he had only to see it when he awoke to see Fermina Daza reflected in its depths. He knew that it was Saturday, because that was the day the chauffeur picked up América Vicuña at her boarding school and brought her back to his house. He realized that he had slept without knowing it, dreaming that he could not sleep, in a dream that had been disturbed by the wrathful face of Fermina Daza. He bathed, wondering what his next step should be, he dressed very slowly in his best clothing, he dabbed on cologne and waxed the ends of his white mustache, he left the bedroom, and from the second-floor hallway he saw the beautiful child in her uniform catching the ball with the grace that had made him tremble on so many Saturdays but this morning did not disquiet him in the least. He indicated that she should come with him, and before he climbed into the automobile he said, although it was not necessary: "Today we are not going to do our things." He took her to the American Ice Cream Shop, filled at this hour with parents eating ice cream with their children under the long blades of the fans that hung from the smooth ceiling. América Vicuña ordered an enormous glass filled with layers of ice cream, each a different color, her favorite dish and the one that was the most popular because it gave off an aura of magic. Florentino Ariza drank black coffee and looked at the girl without speaking, while she ate the ice cream with a spoon that had a very long handle so that one could reach the bottom of the glass. Still looking at her, he said without warning:

"I am going to marry."

She looked into his eyes with a flash of uncertainty, her spoon suspended in midair, but then she recovered and smiled.

"That's a lie," she said. "Old men don't marry."

That afternoon he left her at her school under a steady downpour just as the Angelus was ringing, after the two of them had watched the puppet show in the park, had lunch at the fried-fish stands on the jetties, seen the caged animals in the circus that had just come to town, bought all kinds of candies at the outdoor stalls to take back to school, and driven around the city several times with the top down, so that she could become accustomed to the idea that he was her guardian and no longer her lover. On Sunday he sent the automobile for her in the event she wanted to take a drive with her friends, but he did not want to see her, because since the previous week he had come to full consciousness of both their ages. That night he decided to write a letter of apology to Fermina Daza, its only purpose to show that he had not given up, but he put it off until the next day. On Monday, after exactly three weeks of agony, he walked into his house, soaked by the rain, and found her letter.

It was eight o'clock at night. The two servant girls were in bed, and they had left on the light in the hallway that lit Florentino Ariza's way to his bedroom. He knew that his Spartan, bland supper was on the table in the dining room, but the slight hunger he felt after so many days of haphazard eating vanished with the emotional upheaval of the letter. His hands were shaking so much that it was difficult for him to turn on the overhead light in the bedroom. He put the rain-soaked letter on the bed, lit the lamp on the night table, and with the feigned tranquillity that was his customary way of calming himself, he took off his wet jacket and hung it on the back of the chair, he took off his vest, folded it with care, and placed it on top of the jacket, he took off his black silk string tie and the celluloid collar that was no longer fashionable in the world, he unbuttoned his shirt down to his waist and loosened his belt so that he could breathe with greater ease, and at last he took off his hat and put it by the window to dry. Then he began to tremble because he did not know where the letter was, and his nervous excitement was so great that he was surprised when he found it, for he did not remember placing it on the bed. Before opening it, he dried the envelope with his handkerchief, taking care not to smear the ink in which his name was written, and as he did so it occurred to him that the secret was no longer shared by two people but by three, at least, for whoever had delivered it must have noticed that only three weeks after the death of her husband, the Widow Urbino was writing to someone who did not belong to her world, and with so much urgency that she did not use the regular mails and so much secretiveness that she had ordered that it not be handed to anyone but slipped under the door instead, as if it were an anonymous letter. He did not have to tear open the envelope, for the water had dissolved the glue, but the letter was dry: three closely written pages with no salutation, and signed with the initials of her married name.

He sat on the bed and read it through once as quickly as he could, more intrigued by the tone than by the content, and before he reached the second page he knew that it was in fact the insulting letter he had expected to receive. He laid it, unfolded, in the light shed by the bedlamp, he took off his shoes and his wet socks, he turned out the overhead light, using the switch next to the door, and at last he put on his chamois mustache cover and lay down without removing his trousers and shirt, his head supported by two large pillows that he used as a backrest for reading. Now he read it again, this time syllable by syllable, scrutinizing each so that none of the letter's secret intentions would be hidden from him, and then he read it four more times, until he was so full of the written words that they began to lose all meaning. At last he placed it, without the envelope, in the drawer of the night table, lay on his back with his hands behind his head, and for four hours he did not blink, he hardly breathed, he was more dead than a dead man, as he stared into the space in the mirror where she had been. Precisely at midnight he went to the kitchen and prepared a thermos of coffee as thick as crude oil, then he took it to his room, put his false teeth into the glass of boric acid solution that he always found ready for him on the night table, and resumed the posture of a recumbent marble statue, with momentary shifts in position when he took a sip of coffee, until the maid came in at six o'clock with a fresh thermos.

Florentino Ariza knew by then what one of his next steps was going to be. In truth, the insults caused him no pain, and he was not concerned with rectifying the unjust accusations that could have been worse, considering Fermina Daza's character and the gravity of the cause. All that interested him was that the letter, in and of itself, gave him the opportunity, and even recognized his right, to respond. Even more: it demanded that he respond. So that life was now at the point where he had wanted it to be. Everything else depended on him, and he was convinced that his private hell of over half a century's duration would still present him with many mortal challenges, which he was prepared to confront with more ardor and more sorrow and more love than he had brought to any of them before now, because these would be the last.

When he went to his office five days after receiving the letter from Fermina Daza, he felt as if he were floating in an abrupt and unusual absence of the noise of the typewriters, whose sound, like rain, had become less noticeable than silence. It was a moment of calm. When the sound began again, Florentino Ariza went to Leona Cassiani's office and watched her as she sat in front of her own personal typewriter, which responded to her fingertips as if it were human. She knew she was being observed, and she looked toward the door with her awesome solar smile, but she did not stop typing until the end of the paragraph.

"Tell me something, lionlady of my soul," asked Florentino Ariza. "How would you feel if you received a love letter written on that thing?"

Her expression—she who was no longer surprised at anything—was one of genuine surprise.

"My God, man!" she exclaimed. "It never occurred to me."

For that very reason she could make no other reply. Florentino Ariza had not thought of it either until that moment, and he decided to risk it with no reservations. He took one of the office typewriters home, his subordinates joking good-naturedly: "You can't teach an old dog new tricks." Leona Cassiani, enthusiastic about anything new, offered to give him typing lessons at home. But he had been opposed to methodical learning ever since Lotario Thugut had wanted to teach him to play the violin by reading notes and warned him that he would need at least a year to begin, five more to qualify for a professional orchestra, and six hours a day for the rest of his life in order to play well. And yet he had convinced his mother to buy him a blind man's violin, and with the five basic rules given him by Lotario Thugut, in less than a year he had dared to play in the choir of the Cathedral and to serenade Fermina Daza from the paupers' cemetery according to the direction of the winds. If that had been the case at the age of twenty, with something as difficult as the violin, he did not see why it could not also be the case at the age of seventy-six, with a one-finger instrument like the typewriter.

He was right. He needed three days to learn the position of the letters on the keyboard, another six to learn to think while he typed, and three more to complete the first letter without errors after tearing up half a ream of paper. He gave it a solemn salutation—*Señora*—and signed it with his initial, as he had done in the perfumed love letters of his youth. He mailed it in an envelope with the mourning vignettes that were de rigueur for a letter to a recent widow, and with no return address on the back.

It was a six-page letter, unlike any he had ever written before. It did not have the tone, or the style, or the rhetorical air of his early years of love, and his argument was so rational and measured that the scent of a gardenia would have been out of place. In a certain sense it was his closest approximation to the business letters he had never been able to write. Years later, a typed personal letter would be considered almost an insult, but at that time the typewriter was still an office animal without its own code of ethics, and its domestication for personal use was not foreseen in the books on etiquette. It seemed more like bold modernity, which was how Fermina Daza must have understood it, for in her second letter to Florentino Ariza, she began by begging his pardon for any difficulties in reading her handwriting, since she did not have at her disposal any means more advanced than her steel pen.

Florentino Ariza did not even refer to the terrible letter that she had sent him, but from the very beginning he attempted a new method of seduction, without any reference to past loves or even to the past itself: a clean slate. Instead, he wrote an extensive meditation on life based on his ideas about, and experience of, relations between men and women, which at one time he had intended to write as a complement to the *Lovers' Companion*. Only now he disguised it in the patriarchal style of an old man's memories so that it would not be too obvious that it was really a document of love. First he wrote many drafts in his old style, which took longer to read with a cool head than to throw into the fire. But he knew that any conventional slip, the slightest nostalgic indiscretion, could revive the unpleasant taste of the past in her heart, and although he foresaw her returning a hundred letters to him before she dared open the first, he preferred that it not happen even once. And so he planned everything down to the last detail, as if it were the final battle: new intrigues, new hopes in a woman who had already lived a full and complete life. It had to be a mad dream, one that would give her the courage she would need to discard the prejudices of a class that had not always been hers but had become hers more than anyone's. It had to teach her to think of love as a state of grace: not the means to anything but the alpha and omega, an end in itself.

He had the good sense not to expect an immediate reply, to be satisfied if the letter was not returned to him. It was not, nor were any of the ones that followed, and as the days passed, his excitement grew, for the more days that passed without his letters being returned, the greater his hope of a reply. In the beginning, the frequency of his letters was conditioned by the dexterity of his fingers: first one a week, then two, and at last one a day. He was happy about the progress made in the mail service since his days as a standard-bearer, for he would not have risked being seen every day in the post office mailing a letter to the same person, or sending it with someone who might talk. On the other hand, it was very easy to send an employee to buy enough stamps for a month, and then slip the letter into one of the three mailboxes located in the old city. He soon made that ritual a part of his routine: he took advantage of his insomnia to write, and the next day, on his way to the office, he would ask the driver to stop for a moment at a corner box, and he would get out to mail the letter. He never allowed the chauffeur to do it for him, as he attempted to do one rainy morning, and at times he took the precaution of carrying several letters rather than just one, so that it would seem more natural. The chauffeur did not know, of course, that the additional letters were blank pages that Florentino Ariza addressed to himself, for he had never carried on a private correspondence with anyone, with the exception of the guardian's report that he sent at the end of each month to the parents of América Vicuña, with his personal impressions of the girl's conduct, her state of mind and health, and the progress she was making in her studies.

After the first month he began to number the letters and to head them with a synopsis of the previous ones, as in the serialized novels in the newspapers, for fear that Fermina Daza would not realize that they had a certain continuity. When they became daily letters, moreover, he replaced the envelopes that had mourning vignettes with long white envelopes, and this gave them the added impersonality of business letters. When he began, he was prepared to subject his patience to a crucial test, at least until he had proof that he was wasting his time with the only new approach he could think of. He waited, in fact, not with the many kinds of suffering that waiting had caused him in his youth, but with the stubbornness of an old man made of stone who had nothing else to think about, nothing else to do in a riverboat company that by this time was sailing without his help before favorable winds, and who was also convinced that he would be alive and in perfect possession of his male faculties the next day, or the day after that, or whenever Fermina Daza at last was convinced that there was no other remedy for her solitary widow's yearnings than to lower the drawbridge for him.

Meanwhile, he continued with his normal life. In anticipation of a favorable reply, he began a second renovation of his house so that it would be worthy of the woman who could have considered herself its lady and mistress from the day of its purchase. He visited Prudencia Pitre again several times, as he had promised, in order to prove to her that he loved her despite the devastation wrought by age, loved her in full sunlight and with the doors open, and not only on his nights of desolation. He continued to pass by Andrea Varón's house until he found the bathroom light turned off, and he tried to lose himself in the wildness of her bed even though it was only so he would not lose the habit of love, in keeping with another of his superstitions, not disproved so far, that the body carries on for as long as you do.

His relations with América Vicuña were the only difficulty. He had repeated the order to his chauffeur to pick her up on Saturdays at ten o'clock in the morning at the school, but he did not know what to do with her during the weekends. For the first time he did not concern himself with her, and she resented the change. He placed her in the care of the servant girls and had them take her to the afternoon film, to the band concerts in the children's park, to the charity bazaars, or he arranged Sunday activities for her and her classmates so that he would not have to take her to the hidden paradise behind his offices, to which she had always wanted to return after the first time he took her there. In the fog of his new illusion, he did not realize that women can become adults in three days, and that three years had gone by since he had met her boat from Puerto Padre. No matter how he tried to soften the blow, it was a brutal change for her, and she could not imagine the reason for it. On the day in the ice cream parlor when he told her he was going to marry, when he revealed the truth to her, she had reeled with panic, but then the possibility seemed so absurd that she forgot about it. In a very short while, however, she realized that he was behaving with inexplicable evasiveness, as if it was true, as if he were not sixty years older than she, but sixty years younger.

One Saturday afternoon, Florentino Ariza found her trying to type in his bedroom, and she was doing rather well, for she was studying typing at school. She had completed more than half a page of automatic writing, but it was not difficult to isolate an occasional phrase that revealed her state of mind. Florentino Ariza leaned over her shoulder to read what she had written. She was disturbed by his man's heat, by his ragged breathing, by the scent on his clothes, which was the same as the scent on his pillow. She was no longer the little girl, the newcomer, whom he had undressed, one article of clothing at a time, with little baby games: first these little shoes for the little baby bear, then this little chemise for the little puppy dog, next these little flowered panties for the little bunny rabbit, and a little kiss on her papa's delicious little dickey-bird. No: now she was a full-fledged woman, who liked to take the initiative. She continued typing with just one finger of her right hand, and with her left she felt for his leg, explored him, found him, felt him come to life, grow, heard him sigh with excitement, and his old man's breathing became uneven and labored. She knew him: from that point on he was going to lose control, his speech would become disjointed, he would be at her mercy, and he would not find his way back until he had reached the end. She led him by the hand to the bed as if he were a blind beggar on the street, and she cut him into pieces with malicious tenderness; she added salt to taste, pepper, a clove of garlic, chopped onion, lemon juice, bay leaf, until he was seasoned and on the platter, and the oven was heated to the right temperature. There was no one in the house. The servant girls had gone out, and the masons and carpenters who were renovating the house did not work on Saturdays: they had the whole world to themselves. But on the edge of the abyss he came out of his ecstasy, moved her hand away, sat up, and said in a tremulous voice:

"Be careful, we have no rubbers."

She lay on her back in bed for a long time, thinking, and when she returned to school an hour early she was beyond all desire to cry, and she had sharpened her sense of smell along with her claws so that she could track down the miserable whore who had ruined her life. Florentino Ariza, on the other hand, made another masculine misjudgment: he believed that she had been convinced of the futility of her desires and had resolved to forget him.

He was back in his element. At the end of six months he had heard nothing at all, and he found himself tossing and turning in bed until dawn, lost in the wasteland of a new kind of insomnia. He thought that Fermina Daza had opened the first letter because of its appearance, had seen the initial she knew from the letters of long ago, and had thrown it out to be burned with the rest of the trash without even taking the trouble to tear it up. Just seeing the envelopes of those that followed would be enough for her to do the same thing without even opening them, and to continue to do so until the end of time, while he came at last to his final written meditation. He did not believe that the woman existed who could resist her curiosity about half a year of almost daily letters when she did not even know the color of ink they were written in, but if such a woman existed, it had to be her.

Florentino Ariza felt that his old age was not a rushing torrent but a bottomless cistern where his memory drained away. His ingenuity was wearing thin. After patrolling the villa in La Manga for several days, he realized that this strategy from his youth would never break down the doors sealed by mourning. One morning, as he was looking for a number in the telephone directory, he happened to come across hers. He called. It rang many times, and at last he recognized her grave, husky voice: "Hello?" He hung up without speaking, but the infinite distance of that unapproachable voice weakened his morale.

It was at this time that Leona Cassiani celebrated her birthday and invited a small group of friends to her house. He was distracted and spilled chicken gravy on himself. She cleaned his lapel with the corner of his napkin dampened in a glass of water, and then she tied it around his neck like a bib to avoid a more serious accident: he looked like an old baby. She noticed that several times during dinner he took off his eyeglasses and dried them with his handkerchief because his eyes were watering. During coffee he fell asleep holding his cup in his hand, and she tried to take it away without waking him, but his embarrassed response was: "I was just resting my eyes." Leona Cassiani went to bed astounded at how his age was beginning to show.

On the first anniversary of the death of Juvenal Urbino, the family sent out invitations to a memorial Mass at the Cathedral. Florentino Ariza had still received no reply, and this was the driving force behind his bold decision to attend the Mass although he had not been invited. It was a social event more ostentatious than emotional. The first few rows of pews were reserved for their lifetime owners, whose names were engraved on copper nameplates on the backs of their seats. Florentino Ariza was among the first to arrive so that he might sit where Fermina Daza could not pass by without seeing him. He thought that the best seats would be in the central nave, behind the reserved pews, but there were so many people he could not find a seat there either, and he had to sit in the nave for poor relations. From there he saw Fermina Daza walk in on her son's arm, dressed in an unadorned long-sleeved black velvet dress buttoned all the way from her neck to the tips of her shoes, like a bishop's cassock, and a narrow scarf of Castilian lace instead of the veiled hat worn by other widows, and even by many other ladies who longed for that condition. Her uncovered face shone like alabaster, her lanceolate eyes had a life of their own under the enormous chandeliers of the central nave, and as she walked she was so erect, so haughty, so self-possessed, that she seemed no older than her son. As he stood, Florentino Ariza leaned the tips of his fingers against the back of the pew until his dizziness passed, for he felt that he and she were not separated by seven paces, but existed in two different times.

Through almost the entire ceremony, Fermina Daza stood in the family pew in front of the main altar, as elegant as when she attended the opera. But when it was over, she broke with convention and did not stay in her seat, according to the custom of the day, to receive the spiritual renewal of condolences, but made her way instead through the crowd to thank each one of the guests: an innovative gesture that was very much in harmony with her style and character. Greeting one guest after another, she at last reached the pews of the poor relations, and then she looked around to make certain she had not missed anyone she knew. At that moment Florentino Ariza felt a supernatural wind lifting him out of himself: she had seen him. Fermina Daza moved away from her companions with the same assurance she brought to everything in society, held out her hand, and with a very sweet smile, said to him:

"Thank you for coming."

For she had not only received his letters, she had read them with great interest and had found in them serious and thoughtful reasons to go on living. She had been at the table, having breakfast with her daughter, when she received the first one. She opened it because of the novelty of its being typewritten, and a sudden blush burned her face when she recognized the initial of the signature. But she immediately regained her self-possession and put the letter in her apron pocket. She said: "It is a condolence letter from the government." Her daughter was surprised: "All of them came already." She was imperturbable: "This is another one." Her intention was to burn the letter later, when she was away from her daughter's questions, but she could not resist the temptation of looking it over first. She expected the reply that her insulting letter deserved, a letter that she began to regret the very moment she sent it, but from the majestic salutation and the subject of the first paragraph, she realized that something had changed in the world. She was so intrigued that she locked herself in her bedroom to read it at her ease before she burned it, and she read it three times without pausing.

It was a meditation on life, love, old age, death: ideas that had often fluttered around her head like nocturnal birds but dissolved into a trickle of feathers when she tried to catch hold of them. There they were, precise, simple, just as she would have liked to say them, and once again she grieved that her husband was not alive to discuss them with her as they used to discuss certain events of the day before going to sleep. In this way an unknown Florentino Ariza was revealed to her, one possessed of a clear-sightedness that in no way corresponded to the feverish love letters of his youth or to the somber conduct of his entire life. They were, rather, the words of a man who, in the opinion of Aunt Escolástica, was inspired by the Holy Spirit, and this thought astounded her now as much as it had the first time. In any case, what most calmed her spirit was the certainty that this letter from a wise old man was not an attempt to repeat the impertinence of the night of the vigil over the body but a very noble way of erasing the past.

The letters that followed brought her complete calm. Still, she burned them after reading them with a growing interest, although burning them left her with a sense of guilt that she could not dissipate. So that when they began to be numbered, she found the moral justification she had been seeking for not destroying them. At any rate, her initial intention was not to keep them for herself but to wait for an opportunity to return them to Florentino Ariza so that something that seemed of such great human value would not be lost. The difficulty was that time passed and the letters continued to arrive, one every three or four days throughout the year, and she did not know how to return them without that appearing to be the rebuff she no longer wanted to give, and without having to explain everything in a letter that her pride would not permit her to write.

That first year had been enough time for her to adjust to her widowhood. The purified memory of her husband, no longer an obstacle in her daily actions, in her private thoughts, in her simplest intentions, became a watchful presence that guided but did not hinder her. On the occasions when she truly needed him she would see him, not as an apparition but as flesh and blood. She was encouraged by the certainty that he was there, still alive but without his masculine whims, his patriarchal demands, his consuming need for her to love him in the same ritual of inopportune kisses and tender words with which he loved her. For now she understood him better than when he was alive, she understood the yearning of his love, the urgent need he felt to find in her the security that seemed to be the mainstay of his public life and that in reality he never possessed. One day, at the height of desperation, she had shouted at him: "You don't understand how unhappy I am." Unperturbed, he took off his eyeglasses with a characteristic gesture, he flooded her with the transparent waters of his childlike eyes, and in a single phrase he burdened her with the weight of his unbearable wisdom: "Always remember that the most important thing in a good marriage is not happiness, but stability." With the first loneliness of her widowhood she had understood that the phrase did not conceal the miserable threat that she had attributed to it at the time, but was the lodestone that had given them both so many happy hours.

On her many journeys through the world, Fermina Daza had bought every object that attracted her attention because of its novelty. She desired these things with a primitive impulse that her husband was happy to rationalize, and they were beautiful, useful objects as long as they remained in their original environment, in the show windows of Rome, Paris, London, or in the New York, vibrating to the Charleston, where skyscrapers were beginning to grow, but they could not withstand the test of Strauss waltzes with pork cracklings or Poetic Festivals when it was ninety degrees in the shade. And so she would return with half a dozen enormous standing trunks made of polished metal, with copper locks and corners like decorated coffins, lady and mistress of the world's latest marvels, which were worth their price not in gold but in the fleeting moment when someone from her local world would see them for the first time. For that is why they had been bought: so that others could see them. She became aware of her frivolous public image long before she began to grow old, and in the house she was often heard to say: "We have to get rid of all these trinkets; there's no room to turn around." Dr. Urbino would laugh at her fruitless efforts, for he knew that the emptied spaces were only going to be filled again. But she persisted, because it was true that there was no room for anything else and nothing anywhere served any purpose, not the shirts hanging on the doorknobs or the overcoats for European winters squeezed into the kitchen cupboards. So that on a morning when she awoke in high spirits she would raze the clothes closets, empty the trunks, tear apart the attics, and wage a war of separation against the piles of clothing that had been seen once too often, the hats she had never worn because there had been no occasion to wear them while they were still in fashion, the shoes copied by European artists from those used by empresses for their coronations, and which were scorned here by highborn ladies because they were identical to the ones that black women bought at the market to wear in the house. For the entire morning the interior terrace would be in a state of crisis, and in the house it would be difficult to breathe because of bitter gusts from the mothballs.

But in a few hours order would be reestablished because she at last took pity on so much silk strewn on the floor, so many leftover brocades and useless pieces of passementerie, so many silver fox tails, all condemned to the fire.

"It is a sin to burn this," she would say, "when so many people do not even have enough to eat."

And so the burning was postponed, it was always postponed, and things were only shifted from their places of privilege to the stables that had been transformed into storage bins for remnants, while the spaces that had been cleared, just as he predicted, began to fill up again, to overflow with things that lived for a moment and then went to die in the closets: until the next time. She would say: "Someone should invent something to do with things you cannot use anymore but that you still cannot throw out." That was true: she was dismayed by the voracity with which objects kept invading living spaces, displacing the humans, forcing them back into the corners, until Fermina Daza pushed the objects out of sight. For she was not as ordered as people thought, but she did have her own desperate method for appearing to be so: she hid the disorder. The day that Juvenal Urbino died, they had to empty out half of his study and pile the things in the bedrooms so there would be space to lay out the body.

Death's passage through the house brought the solution. Once she had burned her husband's clothes, Fermina Daza realized that her hand had not trembled, and on the same impulse she continued to light the fire at regular intervals, throwing everything on it, old and new, not thinking about the envy of the rich or the vengeance of the poor who were dying of hunger. Finally, she had the mango tree cut back at the roots until there was nothing left of that misfortune, and she gave the live parrot to the new Museum of the City. Only then did she draw a free breath in the kind of house she had always dreamed of: large, easy, and all hers.

Her daughter Ofelia spent three months with her and then returned to New Orleans. Her son brought his family to lunch on Sundays and as often as he could during the week. Fermina Daza's closest friends began to visit her once she had overcome the crisis of her mourning, they played cards facing the bare patio, they tried out new recipes, they brought her up to date on the secret life of the insatiable world that continued to exist without her. One of the most faithful was Lucrecia del Real del Obispo, an aristocrat of the old school who had always been a good friend and who drew even closer after the death of Juvenal Urbino. Stiff with arthritis and repenting her wayward life, in those days Lucrecia del Real not only provided her with the best company, she also consulted with her regarding the civic and secular projects that were being arranged in the city, and this made her feel useful for her own sake and not because of the protective shadow of her husband. And yet she was never so closely identified with him as she was then, for she was no longer called by her maiden name, and she became known as the Widow Urbino.

It seemed incredible, but as the first anniversary of her husband's death approached, Fermina Daza felt herself entering a place that was shady, cool, quiet: the grove of the irremediable. She was not yet aware, and would not be for several months, of how much the written meditations of Florentino Ariza had helped her to recover her peace of mind. Applied to her own experiences, they were what allowed her to understand her own life and to await the designs of old age with serenity. Their meeting at the memorial Mass was a providential opportunity for her to let Florentino Ariza know that she, too, thanks to his letters of encouragement, was prepared to erase the past.

Two days later she received a different kind of letter from him: handwritten on linen paper and his complete name inscribed with great clarity on the back of the envelope. It was the same ornate handwriting as in his earlier letters, the same will to lyricism, but applied to a simple paragraph of gratitude for the courtesy of her greeting in the Cathedral. For several days after she read the letter Fermina Daza continued to think about it with troubled memories, but with a conscience so clear that on the following Thursday she suddenly asked Lucrecia del Real del Obispo if she happened to know Florentino Ariza, the owner of the riverboats. Lucrecia replied that she did: "He seems to be a wandering succubus." She repeated the common gossip that he had never had a woman although he was such a good catch, and that he had a secret office where he took the boys he pursued at night along the docks. Fermina Daza had heard that story for as long as she could remember, and she had never believed it or given it any importance. But when she heard it repeated with so much conviction by Lucrecia del Real del Obispo, who had also been rumored at one time to have strange tastes, she could not resist the urge to clarify matters. She said she had known Florentino Ariza since he was a boy. She reminded her that his mother had owned a notions shop on the Street of Windows and also bought old shirts and sheets, which she unraveled and sold as bandages during the civil wars. And she concluded with conviction: "He is an honorable man, and he is the soul of tact." She was so vehement that Lucrecia took back what she had said: "When all is said and done, they also say the same sort of thing about me." Fermina Daza was not curious enough to ask herself why she was making so passionate a defense of a man who had been no more than a shadow in her life. She continued to think about him, above all when the mail arrived without another letter from him. Two weeks of silence had gone by when one of the servant girls woke her during her siesta with a warning whisper:

"Señora," she said, "Don Florentino is here."

He was there. Fermina Daza's first reaction was panic. She thought no, he should come back another day at a more appropriate hour, she was in no condition to receive visitors, there was nothing to talk about. But she recovered instantly and told her to show him into the drawing room and bring him coffee, while she tidied herself before seeing him. Florentino Ariza had waited at the street door, burning under the infernal three o'clock sun, but in full control of the situation. He was prepared not to be received, even with an amiable excuse, and that certainty kept him calm. But the decisiveness of her message shook him to his very marrow, and when he walked into the cool shadows of the drawing room he did not have time to think about the miracle he was experiencing because his intestines suddenly filled in an explosion of painful foam. He sat down, holding his breath, hounded by the damnable memory of the bird droppings on his first love letter, and he remained motionless in the shadowy darkness until the first attack of shivering had passed, resolved to accept any mishap at that moment except this unjust misfortune.

He knew himself well: despite his congenital constipation, his belly had betrayed him in public three or four times in the course of his many years, and those three or four times he had been obliged to give in. Only on those occasions, and on others of equal urgency, did he realize the truth of the words that he liked to repeat in jest: "I do not believe in God, but I am afraid of Him." He did not have time for doubts: he tried to say any prayer he could remember, but he could not think of a single one. When he was a boy, another boy had taught him magic words for hitting a bird with a stone: "Aim, aim, got my aim—if I miss you I'm not to blame." He used it when he went to the country for the first time with a new slingshot, and the bird fell down dead. In a confused way he thought that one thing had something to do with the other, and he repeated the formula now with the fervor of a prayer, but it did not have the desired effect. A twisting in his guts like the coil of a spring lifted him from his seat, the foaming in his belly grew thicker and more painful, it grumbled a lament and left him covered with icy sweat. The maid who brought him the coffee was frightened by his corpse's face. He sighed: "It's the heat." She opened the window, thinking she would make him more comfortable, but the afternoon sun hit him full in the face and she had to close it again. He knew he could not hold out another moment, and then Fermina Daza came in, almost invisible in the darkness, dismayed at seeing him in such a state.

"You can take off your jacket," she said to him.

He suffered less from the deadly griping of his bowels than from the thought that she might hear them bubbling. But he managed to endure just an instant longer to say no, he had only passed by to ask her when he might visit. Still standing, she said to him in confusion: "Well, you are here now." And she invited him to the terrace in the patio, where it was cooler. He refused in a voice that seemed to her like a sigh of sorrow.

"I beg you, let it be tomorrow," he said.

She remembered that tomorrow was Thursday,

the day when Lucrecia del Real del Obispo made her regular visit, but she had the perfect solution: "The day after tomorrow at five o'clock." Florentino Ariza thanked her, bid an urgent farewell with his hat, and left without tasting the coffee. She stood in the middle of the drawing room, puzzled, not understanding what had just happened, until the sound of his automobile's backfiring faded at the end of the street. Then Florentino Ariza shifted into a less painful position in the back seat, closed his eyes, relaxed his muscles, and surrendered to the will of his body. It was like being reborn. The driver, who after so many years in his service was no longer surprised at anything, remained impassive. But when he opened the door for him in front of his house, he said:

"Be careful, Don Floro, that looks like cholera."

But it was only his usual ailment. Florentino Ariza thanked God for that on Friday, at five o'clock sharp, when the maid led him through the darkness of the drawing room to the terrace in the patio, where he saw Fermina Daza sitting beside a small table set for two. She offered him tea, chocolate, or coffee. Florentino Ariza asked for coffee, very hot and very strong, and she told the maid: "The usual for me." The usual was a strong infusion of different kinds of Oriental teas, which raised her spirits after her siesta. By the time she had emptied the teapot and he the coffeepot, they had both attempted and then broken off several topics of conversation, not so much because they were really interested in them but in order to avoid others that neither dared to broach. They were both intimidated, they could not understand what they were doing so far from their youth on a terrace with checkerboard tiles in a house that belonged to no one and that was still redolent of cemetery flowers. It was the first time in half a century that they had been so close and had enough time to look at each other with some serenity, and they had seen each other for what they were: two old people, ambushed by death, who had nothing in common except the memory of an ephemeral past that was no longer theirs but belonged to two young people who had vanished and who could have been their grandchildren. She thought that he would at last be convinced of the unreality of his dream, and that this would redeem his insolence.

In order to avoid uncomfortable silences or undesirable subjects, she asked obvious questions about riverboats. It seemed incredible that he, the owner, had only traveled the river once, many years ago, before he had anything to do with the company. She did not know his reasons, and he would have been willing to sell his soul if he could have told them to her. She did not know the river either. Her husband had an aversion to the air of the Andes that he concealed with a variety of excuses: the dangers to the heart of the altitude, the risks of pneumonia, the duplicity of the people, the injustices of centralism. And so they knew half the world, but they did not know their own country. Nowadays there was a Junkers seaplane that flew from town to town along the basin of the Magdalena like an aluminum grasshopper, with two crew members, six passengers, and many sacks of mail. Florentino Ariza commented: "It is like a flying coffin." She had been on the first balloon flight and had experienced no fear, but she could hardly believe that she was the same person who had dared such an adventure. She said: "Things have changed." Meaning that she was the one who had changed, and not the means of transportation.

At times the sound of airplanes took her by surprise. She had seen them flying very low and performing acrobatic maneuvers on the centenary of the death of The Liberator. One of them, as black as an enormous turkey buzzard, grazed the roofs of the houses in La Manga, left a piece of wing in a nearby tree, and was caught in the electrical wires. But not even that had convinced Fermina Daza of the existence of airplanes. In recent years she had not even had the curiosity to go to Manzanillo Bay, where seaplanes landed on the water after the police launches had warned away the fishermen's canoes and the growing numbers of recreational boats. Because of her age, she had been chosen to greet Charles Lindbergh with a bouquet of roses when he came here on his goodwill flight, and she could not understand how a man who was so tall, so blond, so handsome, could go up in a contraption that looked as if it were made of corrugated tin and that two mechanics had to push by the tail to help lift it off the ground. She just could not get it through her head that airplanes not much larger than that one could carry eight people. On the other hand, she had heard that the riverboats were a delight because they did not roll like ocean liners, although there were other, more serious dangers, such as sandbars and attacks by bandits.

Florentino Ariza explained that those were all legends from another time: these days the riverboats had ballrooms and cabins as spacious and luxurious as hotel rooms, with private baths and electric fans, and there had been no armed attacks since the last civil war. He also explained, with the satisfaction of a personal triumph, that these advances were due more than anything else to the freedom of navigation that he had fought for and which had stimulated competition: instead of a single company, as in the past, there were now three, which were very active and prosperous. Nevertheless, the rapid progress of aviation was a real threat to all of them. She tried to console him: boats would always exist because there were not many people crazy enough to get into a contraption that seemed to go against nature. Then Florentino Ariza spoke of improvements in mail service, transportation as well as delivery, in an effort to have her talk about his letters. But he was not successful.

Soon afterward, however, the occasion arose on its own. They had moved far afield of the subject when a maid interrupted them to hand Fermina

Daza a letter that had just arrived by special urban mail, a recent creation that used the same method of distribution as telegrams. As always, she could not find her reading glasses. Florentino Ariza remained calm.

"That will not be necessary," he said. "The letter is mine."

And so it was. He had written it the day before, in a terrible state of depression because he could not overcome the embarrassment of his first frustrated visit. In it he begged her pardon for the impertinence of attempting to visit her without first obtaining her permission, and he promised never to return. He had mailed it without thinking, and when he did have second thoughts it was too late to retrieve it. But he did not believe so many explanations were necessary, and he simply asked Fermina Daza please not to read the letter.

"Of course," she said. "After all, letters belong to the person who writes them. Don't you agree?"

He made a bold move.

"I do," he said. "That is why they are the first things returned when an affair is ended."

She ignored his hidden intentions and returned the letter to him, saying: "It is a shame that I cannot read it, because the others have helped me a great deal." He took a deep breath, astounded that she had said so much more than he had hoped for in so spontaneous a manner, and he said: "You cannot imagine how happy I am to know that." But she changed the subject, and he could not manage to bring it up again for the rest of the afternoon.

He left well after six o'clock, as they were beginning to turn on the lights in the house. He felt more secure but did not have many illusions, because he could not forget Fermina Daza's fickle character and unpredictable reactions at the age of twenty, and he had no reason to think that she had changed. Therefore he risked asking, with sincere humility, if he might return another day, and once again her reply took him by surprise.

"Come back whenever you like," she said. "I am almost always alone."

Four days later, on Tuesday, he returned unannounced, and she did not wait for the tea to be served to tell him how much his letters had helped her. He said that they were not letters in the strict sense of the word, but pages from a book that he would like to write. She, too, had understood them in that way. In fact, she had intended to return them, if he would not take that as an insult, so that they could be put to better use. She continued speaking of how they had helped her during this difficult time, with so much enthusiasm, so much gratitude, perhaps with so much affection, that Florentino Ariza risked something more than a bold move: it was a somersault.

"We called each other *tú* before," he said.

It was a forbidden word: "before." She felt the chimerical angel of the past flying overhead, and she tried to elude it. But he went even further: "Before, I mean, in our letters." She was annoyed, and she had to make a serious effort to conceal it. But he knew, and he realized that he had to move with more tact, although the blunder showed him that her temper was still as short as it had been in her youth although she had learned to soften it.

"I mean," he said, "that these letters are something very different."

"Everything in the world has changed," she said.

"I have not," he said. "Have you?"

She sat with her second cup of tea halfway to her mouth and rebuked him with eyes that had survived so many inclemencies.

"By now it does not matter," she said. "I have just turned seventy-two."

Florentino Ariza felt the blow in the very center of his heart. He would have liked to find a reply as rapid and well aimed as an arrow, but the burden of his age defeated him: he had never been so exhausted by so brief a conversation, he felt pain in his heart, and each beat echoed with a metallic resonance in his arteries. He felt old, forlorn, useless, and his desire to cry was so urgent that he could not speak. They finished their second cup in a silence furrowed by presentiments, and when she spoke again it was to ask a maid to bring her the folder of letters. He was on the verge of asking her to keep them for herself, since he had made carbon copies, but he thought this precaution would seem ignoble. There was nothing else to say. Before he left he suggested coming back on the following Tuesday at the same time. She asked herself whether she should be so acquiescent.

"I don't see what sense so many visits would make," she said.

"I hadn't thought they made any sense," he said.

And so he returned on Tuesday at five o'clock, and then every Tuesday after that, and he ignored the convention of notifying her, because by the end of the second month the weekly visits had been incorporated into both their routines. Florentino Ariza brought English biscuits for tea, candied chestnuts, Greek olives, little salon delicacies that he would find on the ocean liners. One Tuesday he brought her a copy of the picture of her and Hildebranda taken by the Belgian photographer more than half a century before, which he had bought for fifteen centavos at a postcard sale in the Arcade of the Scribes. Fermina Daza could not understand how it had come to be there, and he could only understand it as a miracle of love. One morning, as he was cutting roses in his garden, Florentino Ariza could not resist the temptation of taking one to her on his next visit. It was a difficult problem in the language of flowers because she was a recent widow. A red rose, symbol of flaming passion, might offend her mourning. Yellow roses, which in another language were the flowers of good fortune, were an expression of jealousy in the common vocabulary. He had heard of the black roses of Turkey, which were perhaps the most appropriate, but he had not been able to obtain any for acclimitization in his patio. After much thought he risked a white rose, which he liked less than the others because it was insipid and mute: it did not say anything. At the last minute, in case Fermina Daza was suspicious enough to attribute some meaning to it, he removed the thorns.

It was well received as a gift with no hidden intentions, and the Tuesday ritual was enriched, so that when he would arrive with the white rose, the vase filled with water was ready in the center of the tea table. One Tuesday, as he placed the rose in the vase, he said in an apparently casual manner:

"In our day it was camellias, not roses."

"That is true," she said, "but the intention was different, and you know it."

That is how it always was: he would attempt to move forward, and she would block the way. But on this occasion, despite her ready answer, Florentino Ariza realized that he had hit the mark, because she had to turn her face so that he would not see her blush. A burning, childish blush, with a life of its own and an insolence that turned her vexation on herself. Florentino Ariza was very careful to move to other, less offensive topics, but his courtesy was so obvious that she knew she had been found out, and that increased her anger. It was an evil Tuesday. She was on the point of asking him not to return, but the idea of a lovers' quarrel seemed so ridiculous at their age and in their circumstances that it provoked a fit of laughter. The following Tuesday, when Florentino Ariza was placing the rose in the vase, she examined her conscience and discovered to her joy that not a vestige of resentment was left over from the previous week.

His visits soon began to acquire an awkward familial amplitude, for Dr. Urbino Daza and his wife would sometimes appear as if by accident, and they would stay to play cards. Florentino Ariza did not know how to play, but Fermina taught him in just one visit and they both sent a written challenge to the Urbino Dazas for the following Tuesday. The games were so pleasant for everyone that they soon became as official as his visits, and patterns were established for each person's contribution. Dr. Urbino and his wife, who was an excellent confectioner, brought exquisite pastries, a different one each time. Florentino Ariza continued to bring delicacies from the European ships, and Fermina Daza found a way to contribute a new surprise each time. They played on the third Tuesday of every month, and although they did not wager with money, the loser was obliged to contribute something special to the next game.

There was no difference between Dr. Urbino Daza and his public image: his talents were limited, his manner awkward, and he suffered from sudden twitching, caused by either happiness or annoyance, and from inopportune blushing, which made one fear for his mental fortitude. But it was evident on first meeting him that he was, beyond

491

the shadow of a doubt, what Florentino Ariza most feared people would call him: a good man. His wife, on the other hand, was vivacious and had a plebeian spark of sharp wit that gave a more human note to her elegance. One could not wish for a better couple to play cards with, and Florentino Ariza's insatiable need for love overflowed with the illusion of feeling that he was part of a family.

One night, as they were leaving the house together, Dr. Urbino Daza asked him to have lunch with him: "Tomorrow, at twelve-thirty, at the Social Club." It was an exquisite dish served with a poisonous wine: the Social Club reserved the right to refuse admission for any number of reasons, and one of the most important was illegitimate birth. Uncle Leo XII had experienced great annoyance in this regard, and Florentino Ariza himself had suffered the humiliation of being asked to leave when he was already sitting at the table as the guest of one of the founding members, for whom Florentino Ariza had performed complex favors in the area of river commerce, and who had no other choice but to take him elsewhere to eat.

"Those of us who make the rules have the greatest obligation to abide by them," he had said to him.

Nevertheless Floretino Ariza took the risk with Dr. Urbino Daza, and he was welcomed with special deference, although he was not asked to sign the gold book for notable guests. The lunch was brief, there were just the two of them, and its tone was subdued. The fears regarding the meeting that had troubled Florentino Ariza since the previous afternoon vanished with the port he had as an aperitif. Dr. Urbino Daza wanted to talk to him about his mother. Because of everything that he said, Florentino Ariza realized that she had spoken to her son about him. And something still more surprising: she had lied on his behalf. She told him that they had been childhood friends, playmates from the time of her arrival from San Juan de la Ciénaga, and that he had introduced her to reading, for which she was forever grateful. She also told him that after school she had often spent long hours in the notions shop with Tránsito Ariza, performing prodigious feats of embroidery, for she had been a notable teacher, and that if she had not continued seeing Florentino Ariza with the same frequency, it had not been through choice but because of how their lives had diverged.

Before he came to the heart of his intentions, Dr. Urbino Daza made several digressions on the subject of aging. He thought that the world would make more rapid progress without the burden of old people. He said: "Humanity, like armies in the field, advances at the speed of the slowest." He foresaw a more humanitarian and by the same token a more civilized future in which men and women would be isolated in marginal cities when they could no longer take care of themselves so that they might be spared the humiliation, suffering, and frightful loneliness of old age. From the medical point of view, according to him, the proper age limit would be seventy. But until they reached that degree of charity, the only solution was nursing homes, where the old could console each other and share their likes and dislikes, their habits and sorrows, safe from their natural disagreements with the younger generation. He said: "Old people, with other old people, are not so old." Well, then: Dr. Urbino Daza wanted to thank Florentino Ariza for the good companionship he gave his mother in the solitude of her widowhood, he begged him to continue doing so for the good of them both and the convenience of all, and to have patience with her senile whims. Florentino Ariza was relieved with the outcome of their interview. "Don't worry," he said. "I am now four years older than she is, and have been since long, long before you were born." Then he succumbed to the temptation of giving vent to his feelings with an ironic barb.

"In the society of the future," he concluded, "you would have to visit the cemetery now to bring her and me a bouquet of arum lilies for lunch."

Until that moment Dr. Urbino Daza had not noticed the inappropriateness of his prognostications, and he became enmeshed in a long series of explanations that only made matters worse. But Florentino Ariza helped him to extricate himself. He was radiant, for he knew that sooner or later he was going to have another meeting like this one with Dr. Urbino Daza in order to satisfy an unavoidable social convention: the formal request for his mother's hand in marriage. The lunch had been very encouraging, not only in and of itself but because it showed him how simple and well received that inexorable request was going to be. If he could have counted on Fermina Daza's consent, no occasion would have been more propitious. Moreover, after their conversation at this historic lunch, the formality of a request was almost *de trop*.

Even in his youth Florentino Ariza climbed up and down stairs with special care, for he had always believed that old age began with one's first minor fall and that death came with the second. The staircase in his offices seemed the most dangerous of all to him because it was so steep and narrow, and long before he had to make a special effort not to drag his feet, he would climb it with his eyes fixed on each step and both hands clutching the banister. It had often been suggested that he replace it with one that was less dangerous, but he always put off the decision until next month because he thought it was a concession to old age. As the years passed, it took him longer and longer to walk up the stairs, not because it was harder for him, as he himself hurried to explain, but because he used greater and greater care in the climb. Nevertheless, on the afternoon when he returned from lunch with Dr. Urbino Daza, after the aperitif of port and half a glass of red wine with the meal, and above all after their triumphal conversation, he tried to reach the third stair with so youthful a dance step that he twisted his left ankle, fell backward, and only by a miracle did not kill himself. As he was falling he had enough lucidity to think that he was not going to die of this accident because the logic of life would not allow two men, who had loved the same woman so much for so many years, to die in the same way within a year of each other. He was right. He was put into a plaster cast from his foot to his calf and forced to remain immobile in bed, but he was livelier than he had been before his fall. When the doctor ordered sixty days of convalescence, he could not believe his misfortune.

"Don't do this to me, Doctor," he begged. "Two months for me are like ten years for you."

He tried to get up several times, holding his leg that was like a statue's, with both hands, and reality always defeated him. But when at last he walked again, his ankle still painful and his back raw, he had more than enough reasons to believe that destiny had rewarded his perseverance with a providential fall.

The first Monday was his worst day. The pain had eased and the medical prognosis was very encouraging, but he refused to accept the fatality of not seeing Fermina Daza the following afternoon for the first time in four months. Nevertheless, after a resigned siesta, he submitted to reality and wrote her a note excusing himself. He wrote it by hand on perfumed paper and in luminous ink so that it could be read in the dark, and with no sense of shame he dramatized the gravity of his accident in an effort to arouse her compassion. She answered him two days later, very sympathetic, very kind, without one word extra, just as in the great days of their love. He seized the opportunity as it flew by and wrote to her again. When she answered a second time, he decided to go much further than in their coded Tuesday conversations, and he had a telephone installed next to his bed on the pretext of keeping an eye on the company's daily affairs. He asked the operator to connect him with the three-digit number that he had known by heart since the first time he dialed it. The quiet voice strained by the mystery of distance, the beloved voice answered, recognized the other voice, and said goodbye after three conventional phrases of greeting. Florentino Ariza was devastated by her indifference: they were back at the beginning.

Two days later, however, he received a letter from Fermina Daza in which she begged him not to call again. Her reasons were valid. There were so few telephones in the city that all communication took place through an operator who knew all the subscribers, their lives, their miracles, and it did not matter if they were not at home: she would find them wherever they might be. In return for such efficiency she kept herself informed of their conversations, she uncovered the secrets, the best-kept dramas of their private lives, and it was not unusual for her to interrupt a conversation in order to express her point of view or to calm tempers. Then, too, that year marked the founding of *Justice*, an evening newspaper whose sole purpose was to attack the families with long last names, inherited and unencumbered names, which was the publisher's revenge because his sons had not been admitted to the Social Club. Despite her unimpeachable life, Fermina Daza was more careful now than ever of everything she said or did, even with her closest friends. So that she maintained her connection to Florentino Ariza by means of the anachronistic thread of letters. The correspondence back and forth became so frequent and intense that he forgot about his leg and the chastisement of the bed, he forgot about everything, and he dedicated himself totally to writing on the kind of portable table used in hospitals to serve meals to patients.

They called each other *tú* again, again they exchanged commentaries on their lives as they had done once before in their letters, and again Florentino Ariza tried to move too quickly: he wrote her name with the point of a pin on the petals of a camellia and sent it to her in a letter. Two days later it was returned with no message. Fermina Daza could not help it: all that seemed like children's games to her, most of all when Florentino Ariza insisted on evoking the afternoons of melancholy verses in the Park of the Evangels, the letters hidden along her route to school, the embroidery lessons under the almond trees. With sorrowing heart she reprimanded him in what appeared to be a casual question in the midst of other trivial remarks: "Why do you insist on talking about what does not exist?" Later she reproached him for his fruitless insistence on not permitting himself to grow old in a natural way. This was, according to her, the reason for his haste and constant blundering as he evoked the past. She could not understand how a man capable of the thoughts that had given her the strength to endure her widowhood could become entangled in so childish a manner when he attempted to apply them to his own life. Their roles were reversed. Now it was she who tried to give him new courage to face the future, with a phrase that he, in his reckless haste, could not decipher: *Let time pass and we will see what it brings*. For he was never as good a student as she was. His forced immobility, the growing lucidity of his conviction that time was fleeting, his mad desire to see her, everything proved to him that his fear of falling had been more accurate and more tragic than he had foreseen. For the first time, he began to think in a reasoned way about the reality of death.

Leona Cassiani helped him to bathe and to change his pajamas every other day, she gave him his enemas, she held the portable urinal for him, she applied arnica compresses to the bedsores on his back, she gave him the massages recommended by the doctor so that his immobility would not cause other, more severe ailments. On Saturdays and Sundays she was relieved by América Vicuña, who was to receive her teaching degree in December of that year. He had promised to send her to Alabama for further study, at the expense of the river company, in part to quiet his conscience and above all in order not to face either the reproaches that she did not know how to make to him or the explanations that he owed to her. He never imagined how much she suffered during her sleepless nights at school, during the weekends without him, during her life without him, because he never imagined how much she loved him. He had been informed in an official letter from the school that she had fallen from her perpetual first place in the class to last, and that she had almost failed her final examinations. But he ignored his duty as guardian: he said nothing to América Vicuña's parents, restrained by a sense of guilt that he tried to elude, and he did not discuss it with her because of a well-founded fear that she would try to implicate him in her failure. And so he left things as they were. Without realizing it, he was beginning to defer his problems in the hope that death would resolve him.

The two women who took care of him, and Florentino Ariza himself, were surprised at how much he had changed. Less than ten years before, he had assaulted one of the maids behind the main staircase in the house, dressed and standing as she was, and in less time than a Filipino rooster he had left her in a family way. He had to give her a furnished house in exchange for her swearing that the author of her dishonor was a part-time, Sunday sweetheart who had never even kissed her, and her father and uncles, who were proficient sugarcane cutters, forced them to marry. It did not seem possible that this could be the same man, this man handled front and back by two women who just a few months earlier had made him tremble with love and who now soaped him above his waist and below, dried him with towels of Egyptian cotton, and massaged his entire body, while he did not emit a single sigh of passion. Each of them had a different explanation for his lack of desire. Leona Cassiani thought it was the prelude to death. América Vicuña attributed it to a hidden cause whose intricacies she could not decipher. He alone knew the truth, and it had its own name. In any case, it was unfair: they suffered more in serving him than he did in being so well served.

Fermina Daza needed no more than three Tuesdays to realize how much she missed Florentino Ariza's visits. She enjoyed the friends who were frequent visitors, and she enjoyed them even more as time distanced her from her husband's habits. Lucrecia del Real del Obispo had gone to Panama to have her ear examined because of a pain that nothing could ease, and after a month she came back feeling much better, but hearing less than she had before and using an ear trumpet. Fermina Daza was the friend who was most tolerant of her confusions of questions and answers, and this was so encouraging to Lucrecia that hardly a day went by that she did not stop in at any hour. But for Fermina Daza no one could take the place of her calming afternoons with Florentino Ariza.

The memory of the past did not redeem the future, as he insisted on believing. On the contrary, it strengthened the conviction that Fermina

Daza had always had, that the feverish excitement of twenty had been something very noble, very beautiful, but it had not been love. Despite her rough honesty she did not intend to disclose that to him, either by mail or in person, nor did she have it in her heart to tell him how false the sentimentalities of his letters sounded after the miraculous consolation of his written meditations, how his lyrical lies cheapened him, how detrimental his maniacal insistence on recapturing the past was to his cause. No: not one line of his letters of long ago, not a single moment of her own despised youth, had made her feel that Tuesday afternoons without him could be as tedious, as lonely, and as repetitious as they really were.

In one of her attacks of simplification, she had relegated to the stables the radioconsole that her husband had given her as an anniversary gift, and which both of them had intended to present to the Museum as the first in the city. In the gloom of her mourning she had resolved not to use it again, for a widow bearing her family names could not listen to any kind of music without offending the memory of the dead, even if she did so in private. But after her third solitary Tuesday she had it brought back to the drawing room, not to enjoy the sentimental song on the Riobamba station, as she had done before, but to fill her idle hours with the soap operas from Santiago de Cuba. It was a good idea, for after the birth of her daughter she had begun to lose the habit of reading that her husband had inculcated with so much diligence ever since their honeymoon, and with the progressive fatigue of her eyes she had stopped altogether, so that months would go by without her knowing where she had left her reading glasses.

She took such a liking to the soap operas from Santiago de Cuba that she waited with impatience for each day's new episode. From time to time she listened to the news to find out what was going on in the world, and on the few occasions when she was alone in the house she would turn the volume very low and listen to distant, clear merengues from Santo Domingo and plenas from Puerto Rico. One night, on an unknown station that suddenly came in as strong and clear as it if were next door, she heard heartbreaking news: an elderly couple, who for forty years had been repeating their honeymoon every year in the same spot, had been murdered, bludgeoned to death with oars by the skipper of the boat they were riding in, who then robbed them of all the money they were carrying: fourteen dollars. The effect on her was even more devastating when Lucrecia del Real told her the complete story, which had been published in a local newspaper. The police had discovered that the elderly couple beaten to death were clandestine lovers who had taken their vacations together for forty years, but who each had a stable and happy marriage as well as very large families. Fermina Daza, who never cried over the soap operas on the radio, had to hold back the knot of tears that choked her. In his next letter, without any comment, Florentino Ariza sent her the news item that he had cut out of the paper.

These were not the last tears that Fermina Daza was going to hold back. Florentino Ariza had not yet finished his sixty days of seclusion when *Justice* published a front-page story, complete with photographs of the two protagonists, about the alleged secret love affair between Dr. Juvenal Urbino and Lucrecia del Real del Obispo. There was speculation on the details of their relationship, the frequency of their meetings and how they were arranged, and the complicity of her husband, who was given to excesses of sodomy with the blacks on his sugar plantation. The story, published in enormous block letters in an ink the color of blood, fell like a thundering cataclysm on the enfeebled local aristocracy. Not a line of it was true: Juvenal Urbino and Lucrecia del Real had been close friends in the days when they were both single, and they had continued their friendship after their marriages, but they had never been lovers. In any case, it did not seem that the purpose of the story was to sully the name of Dr. Juvenal Urbino, whose memory enjoyed universal respect, but to injure the husband of Lucrecia del Real, who had been elected President of the Social Club the week before. The scandalous story was suppressed in a few hours. But Lucrecia del Real did not visit Fermina Daza again, and Fermina Daza interpreted this as a confession of guilt.

It was soon obvious, however, that Fermina Daza was not immune to the hazards of her class.

Justice attacked her one weak flank: her father's business. When he was forced into exile, she knew of only one instance of his shady dealings, which had been told to her by Gala Placidia. Later, when Dr. Urbino confirmed the story after his interview with the Governor, she was convinced that her father had been the victim of slander. The facts were that two government agents had come to the house on the Park of the Evangels with a warrant, searched it from top to bottom without finding what they were looking for, and at last ordered the wardrobe with the mirrored doors in Fermina Daza's old bedroom to be opened. Gala Placidia, who was alone in the house and lacked the means to stop anyone from doing anything, refused to open it, with the excuse that she did not have the keys. Then one of the agents broke the mirror on the door with the butt of his revolver and found the space between the glass and the wood stuffed with counterfeit hundred-dollar bills. This was the last in a chain of clues that led to Lorenzo Daza as the final link in a vast international operation. It was a masterful fraud, for the bills had the water-marks of the original paper: one-dollar bills had been erased by a chemical process that seemed to be magic, and reprinted as hundred-dollar notes. Lorenzo Daza claimed that the wardrobe had been purchased long after his daughter's wedding, and that it must have come into the house with the bills already in it, but the police proved that it had been there since the days when Fermina Daza had been in school. He was the only one who could have hidden the counterfeit fortune behind the mirrors. This was all Dr. Urbino told his wife when he promised the Governor that he would send his father-in-law back to his own country in order to cover up the scandal. But the newspaper told much more.

It said that during one of the many civil wars of the last century, Lorenzo Daza had been the intermediary between the government of the Liberal President Aquileo Parra and one Joseph T. K. Korzeniowski, a native of Poland and a member of the crew of the merchant ship *Saint Antoine*, sailing under the French flag, who had spent several months here trying to conclude a complicated arms deal. Korzeniowski, who later became famous as Joseph Conrad, made contact somehow with Lorenzo Daza, who bought the shipment of arms from him on behalf of the government, with his credentials and his receipts in order and the purchase price in gold. According to the story in the newspaper, Lorenzo Daza claimed that the arms had been stolen in an improbable raid, and then he sold them again, for twice their value, to the Conservatives who were at war with the government.

Justice also said that at the time that General Rafael Reyes founded the navy, Lorenzo Daza bought a shipment of surplus boots at a very low price from the English army, and with that one deal he doubled his fortune in six months. According to the newspaper, when the shipment reached this port, Lorenzo Daza refused to accept

506

it because it contained only boots for the right foot, but he was the sole bidder when Customs auctioned it according to the law, and he bought it for the token sum of one hundred pesos. At the same time, under similar circumstances, an accomplice purchased the shipment of boots for the left foot that had reached Riohacha. Once they were in pairs, Lorenzo Daza took advantage of his relationship by marriage to the Urbino de la Calle family and sold the boots to the new navy at a profit of two thousand percent.

The story in *Justice* concluded by saying that Lorenzo Daza did not leave San Juan de la Ciénaga at the end of the last century in search of better opportunities for his daughter's future, as he liked to say, but because he had been found out in his prosperous business of adulterating imported tobacco with shredded paper, which he did with so much skill that not even the most sophisticated smokers noticed the deception. They also uncovered his links to a clandestine international enterprise whose most profitable business at the end of the last century had been the illegal smuggling of Chinese from Panama. On the other hand, his suspect mule trading, which had done so much harm to his reputation, seemed to be the only honest business he had ever engaged in.

When Florentino Ariza left his bed, with his back on fire and carrying a walking stick for the first time instead of his umbrella, his first excursion was to Fermina Daza's house. She was like a stranger, ravaged by age, whose resentment had destroyed her desire to live. Dr. Urbino Daza, in the two visits he had made to Florentino Ariza during his exile, had spoken to him of how disturbed his mother was by the two stories in *Justice*. The first provoked her to such irrational anger at her husband's infidelity and her friend's disloyalty that she renounced the custom of visiting the family mausoleum one Sunday each month, for it infuriated her that he, inside his coffin, could not hear the insults she wanted to shout at him: she had a quarrel with a dead man. She let Lucrecia del Real know, through anyone who would repeat it to her, that she should take comfort in having had at least one real man in the crowd of people who had passed through her bed. As for the story about Lorenzo Daza, there was no way to know which affected her more, the story itself or her belated discovery of her father's true character. But one or the other, or both, had annihilated her. Her hair, the color of stainless steel, had ennobled her face, but now it looked like ragged yellow strands of corn silk, and her beautiful panther eyes did not recover their old sparkle even in the brilliant heat of her anger. Her decision not to go on living was evident in every gesture. She had long ago given up smoking, whether locked in the bathroom or anywhere else, but she took it up again, for the first time in public, and with an uncontrolled voracity, at first with cigarettes she rolled herself, as she had always liked to do, and then with ordinary ones sold in stores because she no longer had time or patience to do it herself. Anyone else would have asked himself what the future could hold for a lame old man whose back burned with a burro's saddle sores and a woman who longed for no other happiness but death. But not Florentino Ariza. He found a glimmer of hope in the ruins of disaster, for it seemed to him that Fermina Daza's misfortune glorified her, that her anger beautified her, and that her rancor with the world had given her back the untamed character she had displayed at the age of twenty.

She had new reasons for being grateful to Florentino Ariza, because in response to the infamous stories, he had written *Justice* an exemplary letter concerning the ethical responsibilities of the press and respect for other people's honor. They did not publish it, but the author sent a copy to the *Commercial Daily*, the oldest and most serious newspaper along the Caribbean coast, which featured the letter on the front page. Signed with the pseudonym "Jupiter," it was so reasoned, incisive, and well written that it was attributed to some of the most notable writers in the province. It was a lone voice in the middle of the ocean, but it was heard at great depth and great distance. Fermina Daza knew who the author was without having to be told, because she recognized some of the ideas and even a sentence taken directly from Florenino Ariza's moral reflections. And so she received him with renewed affection in the disarray of her solitude. It was at this time that América Vicuña found herself alone one Saturday afternoon in the bedroom on the Street of Windows, and without looking for them, by sheer accident, she found the typed copies of the meditations of Florentino Ariza and the handwritten letters of Fermina Daza, in a wardrobe without a key.

Dr. Urbino Daza was happy about the resumption of the visits that gave so much encouragement to his mother. But Ofelia, his sister, came from New Orleans on the first fruit boat as soon as she heard that Fermina Daza had a strange friendship with a man whose moral qualifications were not the best. Her alarm grew to critical proportions during the first week, when she became aware of the familiarity and self-possession with which Florentino Ariza came into the house, and the whispers and fleeting lovers' quarrels that filled their visits until all hours of the night. What for Dr. Urbino Daza was a healthy affection between two lonely old people was for her a vice-ridden form of secret concubinage. Ofelia Urbino had always been like that, resembling Doña Blanca, her paternal grandmother, more than if she had been her daughter. Like her she was distinguished, like her she was arrogant, and like her she lived at the mercy of her prejudices. Even at the age of five she had been incapable of imagining an innocent friendship between a man and a woman, least of all when they were eighty years old. In a bitter argument with her brother, she said that all Florentino Ariza needed to do to complete his consolation of their mother was to climb into her widow's bed. Dr. Urbino Daza did not have the courage to face her, he had never had the courage to face her, but his wife intervened with a serene justification of love at any age. Ofelia lost her temper.

"Love is ridiculous at our age," she shouted, "but at theirs it is revolting."

She insisted with so much vehemence on her determination to drive Florentino Ariza out of the house that it reached Fermina Daza's ears. She called her to her bedroom, as she always did when she wanted to talk without being heard by the servants, and she asked her to repeat her accusations. Ofelia did not soften them: she was certain that Florentino Ariza, whose reputation as a pervert was known to everyone, was carrying on an equivocal relationship that did more harm to the family's good name than the villainies of Lorenzo Daza or the ingenuous adventures of Juvenal Urbino. Fermina Daza listened to her without saying a word, without even blinking, but when she finished, Fermina Daza was another person: she had come back to life.

"The only thing that hurts me is that I do not have the strength to give you the beating you deserve for being insolent and evil-minded," she said. "But you will leave this house right now, and I swear to you on my mother's grave that you will not set foot in it again as long as I live."

There was no power that could dissuade her. Ofelia went to live in her brother's house, and from there she sent all kinds of petitions with distinguished emissaries. But it was in vain. Neither the mediation of her son nor the intervention of her friends could break Fermina Daza's resolve. At last, in the colorful language of her better days, she allowed herself to confide in her daughter-in-law, with whom she had always maintained a certain plebeian camaraderie. "A century ago, life screwed that poor man and me because we were too young, and now they want to do the same thing because we are too old." She lit a cigarette with the end of the one she was smoking, and then she gave vent to all the poison that was gnawing at her insides.

"They can all go to hell," she said. "If we widows have any advantage, it is that there is no one left to give us orders."

There was nothing to be done. When at last she was convinced that she had no more options, Ofelia returned to New Orleans. After much pleading, her mother would only agree to say goodbye to her, but she would not allow her in the house: she had sworn on her mother's grave, and for her, during those dark days, that was the only thing left that was still pure.

On one of his early visits, when he was talking about his ships, Florentino Ariza had given Fermina Daza a formal invitation to take a pleasure cruise along the river. With one more day of traveling by train she could visit the national capital, which they, like most Caribbeans of their generation, still called by the name it bore until the last century: Santa Fe. But she maintained the prejudices of her husband, and she did not want to visit a cold, dismal city where the women did not leave their houses except to attend five o'clock Mass and where, she had been told, they could not enter ice cream parlors or public offices, and where the funerals disrupted traffic at all hours of the day or night, and where it had been drizzling since the year one: worse than in Paris. On the other hand, she felt a very strong attraction to the river, she wanted to see the alligators sunning themselves on the sandy banks, she wanted to be awakened in the middle of the night by the woman's cry of the manatees, but the idea of so arduous a journey at her age, and a lone widow besides, seemed unrealistic to her.

Florentino Ariza repeated the invitation later on, when she had decided to go on living without her husband, and then it had seemed more plausible. But after her quarrel with her daughter, embittered by the insults to her father, by her rancor toward her dead husband, by her anger at the hypocritical duplicities of Lucrecia del Real, whom she had considered her best friend for so many years, she felt herself superfluous in her own house. One afternoon, while she was drinking her infusion of worldwide leaves, she looked toward the morass of the patio where the tree of her misfortune would never bloom again.

"What I would like is to walk out of this house, and keep going, going, going, and never come back," she said.

"Take a boat," said Florentino Ariza.

Fermina Daza looked at him thoughtfully.

"Well, I might just do that," she said.

A moment before she said it, the thought had not even occurred to her, but all she had to do was admit the possibility for it to be considered a reality. Her son and daughter-in-law were delighted when they heard the news. Florentino Ariza hastened to point out that on his vessels Fermina Daza would be a guest of honor, she would have a cabin to herself which would be just like home, she would enjoy perfect service, and the Captain himself would attend to her safety and well-being. He brought route maps to encourage her, picture postcards of furious sunsets, poems to the primitive paradise of the Magdalena written by illustrious travelers and by those who had become travelers by virtue of the poems. She would glance at them when she was in the mood.

"You do not have to cajole me as if I were a baby," she told him. "If I go, it will be because I have decided to and not because the landscape is interesting."

When her son suggested that his wife accompany her, she cut him off abruptly: "I am too big to have anyone take care of me." She herself arranged the details of the trip. She felt immense relief at the thought of spending eight days traveling upriver and five on the return, with no more than the bare necessities: half a dozen cotton dresses, her toiletries, a pair of shoes for embarking and disembarking, her house slippers for the journey, and nothing else: her lifetime dream.

In January 1824, Commodore Johann Bernard Elbers, the father of river navigation, had registered the first steamboat to sail the Magdalena River, a primitive old forty-horsepower wreck named *Fidelity*. More than a century later, one seventh of July at six o'clock in the evening, Dr. Urbino Daza and his wife accompanied Fermina Daza as she boarded the boat that was to carry her on her first river voyage. It was the first vessel built in the local shipyards and had been christened *New Fidelity* in memory of its glorious ancestor. Fermina Daza could never believe that so significant a name for them both was indeed a historical coincidence and not another conceit born of Florentino Ariza's chronic romanticism.

In any case, unlike the other riverboats, ancient and modern, *New Fidelity* boasted a suite next to the Captain's quarters that was spacious and comfortable: a sitting room with bamboo furniture covered in festive colors, a double bedroom decorated in Chinese motifs, a bathroom with tub and shower, a large, enclosed observation deck with hanging ferns and an unobstructed view toward the front and both sides of the boat, and a silent cooling system that kept out external noises and maintained a climate of perpetual spring. These deluxe accommodations, known as the Presidential Suite because three Presidents of the Republic had already made the trip in them, had no commercial purpose but were reserved for high-ranking officials and very special guests. Florentino Ariza had ordered the suite built for that public purpose as soon as he was named President of the R.C.C., but his private conviction was that sooner or later

515

it was going to be the joyous refuge of his wedding trip with Fermina Daza.

When in fact the day arrived, she took possession of the Presidential Suite as its lady and mistress. The ship's Captain honored Dr. Urbino Daza and his wife, and Florentino Ariza, with champagne and smoked salmon. His name was Diego Samaritano, he wore a white linen uniform that was absolutely correct, from the tips of his boots to his cap with the R.C.C. insignia embroidered in gold thread, and he possessed, in common with other river captains, the stoutness of a ceiba tree, a peremptory voice, and the manners of a Florentine cardinal.

At seven o'clock the first departure warning was sounded, and Fermina Daza felt it resonate with a sharp pain in her left ear. The night before, her dreams had been furrowed with evil omens that she did not dare to decipher. Very early in the morning she had ordered the car to take her to the nearby seminary burial ground, which in those days was called La Manga Cemetery, and as she stood in front of his crypt, she made peace with her dead husband in a monologue in which she freely recounted all the just recriminations she had choked back. Then she told him the details of the trip and said goodbye for now. She refused to tell anyone anything except that she was going away, which is what she had done whenever she had gone to Europe, in order to avoid exhausting farewells. Despite all her travels, she felt as if this were her first trip, and as the day approached her agitation increased. Once she was on board she felt abandoned and sad, and she wanted to be alone to cry.

When the final warning sounded, Dr. Urbino Daza and his wife bade her an undramatic goodbye, and Florentino Ariza accompanied them to the gangplank. Dr. Urbino Daza tried to stand aside so that Florentino Ariza could follow his wife, and only then did he realize that Florentino Ariza was also taking the trip. Dr. Urbino Daza could not hide his confusion.

"But we did not discuss this," he said.

Florentino Ariza showed him the key to his cabin with too evident an intention: an ordinary cabin on the common deck. But to Dr. Urbino Daza this did not seem sufficient proof of innocence. He glanced at his wife in consternation, with the eyes of a drowning man looking for support, but her eyes were ice. She said in a very low, harsh voice: "You too?" Yes: he too, like his sister Ofelia, thought there was an age at which love began to be indecent. But he was able to recover in time, and he said goodbye to Florentino Ariza with a handshake that was more resigned than grateful.

From the railing of the salon, Florentino Ariza watched them disembark. Just as he had hoped and wished, Dr. Urbino Daza and his wife turned to look at him before climbing into their automobile, and he waved his hand in farewell. They both responded in kind. He remained at the railing until the automobile disappeared in the dust of

517

the freight yard, and then he went to his cabin to change into clothing more suitable for his first dinner on board in the Captain's private dining room.

It was a splendid evening, which Captain Diego Samaritano seasoned with succulent tales of his forty years on the river, but Fermina Daza had to make an enormous effort to appear amused. Despite the fact that the final warning had been sounded at eight o'clock, when visitors had been obliged to leave and the gangplank had been raised, the boat did not set sail until the Captain had finished eating and gone up to the bridge to direct the operation. Fermina Daza and Florentino Ariza stayed at the railing, surrounded by noisy passengers who made bets on how well they could identify the lights in the city, until the boat sailed out of the bay, moved along invisible channels and through swamps spattered with the undulating lights of the fishermen, and at last took a deep breath in the open air of the Great Magdalena River. Then the band burst into a popular tune, there was a joyous stampede of passengers, and in a mad rush, the dancing began.

Fermina Daza preferred to take refuge in her cabin. She had not said a word for the entire evening, and Florentino Ariza allowed her to remain lost in her thoughts. He interrupted her only to say good night outside her cabin, but she was not tired, just a little chilly, and she suggested that they sit for a while on her private deck to watch the river. Florentino Ariza wheeled two wicker easy chairs to the railing, turned off the lights, placed a woolen shawl around her shoulders, and sat down beside her. With surprising skill, she rolled a cigarette from the little box of tobacco that he had brought her. She smoked it slowly, with the lit end inside her mouth, not speaking, and then she rolled another two and smoked them one right after the other. Sip by sip, Florentino Ariza drank two thermoses of mountain coffee.

The lights of the city had disappeared over the horizon. Seen from the darkened deck in the light of a full moon, the smooth, silent river and the pastureland on either bank became a phosphorescent plain. From time to time one could see a straw hut next to the great bonfires signaling that wood for the ships' boilers was on sale. Florentino Ariza still had dim memories of the journey of his youth, and in dazzling flashes of lightning the sight of the river called them back to life as if they had happened yesterday. He recounted some of them to Fermina Daza in the belief that this might animate her, but she sat smoking in another world. Florentino Ariza renounced his memories and left her alone with hers, and in the meantime he rolled cigarettes and passed them to her already lit, until the box was empty. The music stopped after midnight, the voices of the passengers dispersed and broke into sleepy whispers, and two hearts, alone in the shadows on the deck, were beating in time to the breathing of the ship.

After a long while, Florentino Ariza looked at Fermina Daza by the light of the river. She seemed ghostly, her sculptured profile softened by a tenuous blue light, and he realized that she was crying in silence. But instead of consoling her or waiting until all her tears had been shed, which is what she wanted, he allowed panic to overcome him.

"Do you want to be alone?" he asked.

"If I did, I would not have told you to come in," she said.

Then he reached out with two icy fingers in the darkness, felt for the other hand in the darkness, and found it waiting for him. Both were lucid enough to realize, at the same fleeting instant, that the hands made of old bones were not the hands they had imagined before touching. In the next moment, however, they were. She began to speak of her dead husband in the present tense, as if he were alive, and Florentino Ariza knew then that for her, too, the time had come to ask herself with dignity, with majesty, with an irrepressible desire to live, what she should do with the love that had been left behind without a master.

Fermina Daza stopped smoking in order not to let go of the hand that was still in hers. She was lost in her longing to understand. She could not conceive of a husband better than hers had been, and yet when she recalled their life she found more difficulties than pleasures, too many mutual misunderstandings, useless arguments, unresolved angers. Suddenly she sighed: "It is incredible how one can be happy for so many years in the midst of so many squabbles, so many problems, damn it, and not really know if it was love or not." By

the time she finished unburdening herself, someone had turned off the moon. The boat moved
ahead at its steady pace, one foot in front of the
other: an immense, watchful animal. Fermina Daza
had returned from her longing.

"Go now," she said.

Florentino Ariza pressed her hand, bent toward
her, and tried to kiss her on the cheek. But she
refused, in her hoarse, soft voice.

"Not now," she said to him. "I smell like an
old woman."

She heard him leave in the darkness, she heard
his steps on the stairs, she heard him cease to exist
until the next day. Fermina Daza lit another cigarette, and as she smoked she saw Dr. Juvenal
Urbino in his immaculate linen suit, with his professional rigor, his dazzling charm, his official love,
and he tipped his white hat in a gesture of farewell
from another boat out of the past. "We men are
the miserable slaves of prejudice," he had once
said to her. "But when a woman decides to sleep
with a man, there is no wall she will not scale, no
fortress she will not destroy, no moral consideration she will not ignore at its very root: there is
no God worth worrying about." Fermina Daza sat
motionless until dawn, thinking about Florentino
Ariza, not as the desolate sentinel in the little Park
of the Evangels, whose memory did not awaken
even a spark of nostalgia in her, but as he was
now, old and lame, but real: the man who had
always been within reach and whom she could
never acknowledge. As the breathing boat carried

her toward the splendor of the day's first roses, all that she asked of God was that Florentino Ariza would know how to begin again the next day.

He did. Fermina Daza instructed the steward to let her sleep as long as she wanted, and when she awoke there was a vase on the night table with a fresh white rose, drops of dew still on it, as well as a letter from Florentino Ariza with as many pages as he had written since his farewell to her. It was a calm letter that did not attempt to do more than express the state of mind that had held him captive since the previous night: it was as lyrical as the others, as rhetorical as all of them, but it had a foundation in reality. Fermina Daza read it with some embarrassment because of the shameless racing of her heart. It concluded with the request that she advise the steward when she was ready, for the Captain was waiting on the bridge to show them the operation of the ship.

She was ready at eleven o'clock, bathed and smelling of flower-scented soap, wearing a very simple widow's dress of gray etamine, and completely recovered from the night's turmoil. She ordered a sober breakfast from the steward, who was dressed in impeccable white, and in the Captain's personal service, but she did not send a message for anyone to come for her. She went up alone, dazzled by the cloudless sky, and she found Florentino Ariza talking to the Captain on the bridge. He looked different to her, not only because she saw him now with other eyes, but because in reality he had changed. Instead of the funereal clothing he had worn all his life, he was dressed in comfortable white shoes, slacks, and a linen shirt with an open collar, short sleeves, and his monogram embroidered on the breast pocket. He also had on a white Scottish cap and removable dark lenses over his perpetual eyeglasses for myopia. It was evident that everything was being used for the first time and had been bought just for the trip, with the exception of the well-worn belt of dark brown leather, which Fermina Daza noticed at first glance as if it were a fly in the soup. Seeing him like this, dressed just for her in so patent a manner, she could not hold back the fiery blush that rose to her face. She was embarrassed when she greeted him, and he was more embarrassed by her embarrassment. The knowledge that they were behaving as if they were sweethearts was even more embarrassing, and the knowledge that they were both embarrassed embarrassed them so much that Captain Samaritano noticed it with a tremor of compassion. He extricated them from their difficulty by spending the next two hours explaining the controls and the general operation of the ship. They were sailing very slowly up a river without banks that meandered between arid sandbars stretching to the horizon. But unlike the troubled waters at the mouth of the river, these were slow and clear and gleamed like metal under the merciless sun. Fermina Daza had the impression that it was a delta filled with islands of sand.

"It is all the river we have left," said the Captain.

Florentino Ariza, in fact, was surprised by the changes, and would be even more surprised the following day, when navigation became more difficult and he realized that the Magdalena, father of waters, one of the great rivers of the world, was only an illusion of memory. Captain Samaritano explained to them how fifty years of uncontrolled deforestation had destroyed the river: the boilers of the riverboats had consumed the thick forest of colossal trees that had oppressed Florentino Ariza on his first voyage. Fermina Daza would not see the animals of her dreams: the hunters for skins from the tanneries in New Orleans had exterminated the alligators that, with yawning mouths, had played dead for hours on end in the gullies along the shore as they lay in wait for butterflies, the parrots with their shrieking and the monkeys with their lunatic screams had died out as the foliage was destroyed, the manatees with their great breasts that had nursed their young and wept on the banks in a forlorn woman's voice were an extinct species, annihilated by the armored bullets of hunters for sport.

Captain Samaritano had an almost maternal affection for the manatees, because they seemed to him like ladies damned by some extravagant love, and he believed the truth of the legend that they were the only females in the animal kingdom that had no mates. He had always opposed shooting at them from the ship, which was the custom despite

524

the laws prohibiting it. Once, a hunter from North Carolina, his papers in order, had disobeyed him, and with a well-aimed bullet from his Springfield rifle had shattered the head of a manatee mother whose baby became frantic with grief as it wailed over the fallen body. The Captain had the orphan brought on board so that he could care for it, and left the hunter behind on the deserted bank, next to the corpse of the murdered mother. He spent six months in prison as the result of diplomatic protests and almost lost his navigator's license, but he came out prepared to do it again, as often as the need arose. Still, that had been a historic episode: the orphaned manatee, which grew up and lived for many years in the rare-animal zoo in San Nicolás de las Barrancas, was the last of its kind seen along the river.

"Each time I pass that bank," he said, "I pray to God that the gringo will board my ship so that I can leave him behind all over again."

Fermina Daza, who had felt no fondness for the Captain, was so moved by the tenderhearted giant that from that morning on he occupied a privileged place in her heart. She was not wrong: the trip was just beginning, and she would have many occasions to realize that she had not been mistaken.

Fermina Daza and Florentino Ariza remained on the bridge until it was time for lunch. It was served a short while after they passed the town of Calamar on the opposite shore, which just a few years before had celebrated a perpetual fiesta and now was a ruined port with deserted streets. The only creature they saw from the boat was a woman dressed in white, signaling to them with a handkerchief. Fermina Daza could not understand why she was not picked up when she seemed so distressed, but the Captain explained that she was the ghost of a drowned woman whose deceptive signals were intended to lure ships off course into the dangerous whirlpools along the other bank. They passed so close that Fermina Daza saw her in sharp detail in the sunlight, and she had no doubt that she did not exist, but her face seemed familiar.

It was a long, hot day. Fermina Daza returned to her cabin after lunch for her inevitable siesta, but she did not sleep well because of a pain in her ear, which became worse when the boat exchanged mandatory greetings with another R.C.C. vessel as they passed each other a few leagues above Barranca Vieja. Florentino Ariza fell into instantaneous sleep in the main salon, where most of the passengers without cabins were sleeping as if it were midnight, and close to the spot where he had seen her disembark, he dreamed of Rosalba. She was traveling alone, wearing her Mompox costume from the last century, and it was she and not the child who slept in the wicker cage that hung from the ceiling. It was a dream at once so enigmatic and so amusing that he enjoyed it for the rest of the afternoon as he played dominoes with the Captain and two of the passengers who were friends of his.

It grew cooler as the sun went down, and the ship came back to life. The passengers seemed to emerge from a trance; they had just bathed and changed into fresh clothing, and they sat in the wicker armchairs in the salon, waiting for supper, which was announced at exactly five o'clock by a waiter who walked the deck from one end to the other and rang a sacristan's bell, to mocking applause. While they were eating, the band began to play fandangos, and the dancing continued until midnight.

Fermina Daza did not care to eat because of the pain in her ear, and she watched as the first load of wood for the boilers was taken on from a bare gully where there was nothing but stacked logs and a very old man who supervised the operation. There did not seem to be another person for many leagues around. For Fermina Daza it was a long, tedious stop that would have been unthinkable on the ocean liners to Europe, and the heat was so intense that she could feel it even on her cooled observation deck. But when the boat weighed anchor again there was a cool breeze scented with the heart of the forest, and the music became more lively. In the town of Sitio Nuevo there was only one light in only one window in only one house, and the port office did not signal either cargo or passengers, so the boat passed by without a greeting.

Fermina Daza had spent the entire afternoon wondering what stratagems Florentino Ariza would use to see her without knocking at her cabin door, and by eight o'clock she could no longer bear the longing to be with him. She went out into the passageway, hoping to meet him in what would seem a casual encounter, and she did not have to go very far: Florentino Ariza was sitting on a bench in the passageway, as silent and forlorn as he had been in the Park of the Evangels, and for over two hours he had been asking himself how he was going to see her. They both made the same gesture of surprise that they both knew was feigned, and together they strolled the first-class deck, crowded with young people, most of them boisterous students who, with some eagerness, were exhausting themselves in the final fling of their vacation. In the lounge, Florentino Ariza and Fermina Daza sat at the bar as if they were students themselves and drank bottled soft drinks, and suddenly she saw herself in a frightening situation. She said: "How awful!" Florentino Ariza asked her what she was thinking that caused her so much distress.

"The poor old couple," she said. "The ones who were beaten to death in the boat."

They both decided to turn in when the music stopped, after a long, untroubled conversation on the dark observation deck. There was no moon, the sky was cloudy, and on the horizon flashes of lightning, with no claps of thunder, illuminated them for an instant. Florentino Ariza rolled cigarettes for her, but she did not smoke more than a few, for she was tormented by pain that would ease for a few moments and flare up again when the boat bellowed as it passed another ship or a sleeping village, or when it slowed to sound the depth of the river. He told her with what longing he had watched her at the Poetic Festival, on the balloon flight, on the acrobat's velocipede, with what longing he had waited all year for public festivals just so he could see her. She had often seen him as well, and she had never imagined that he was there only to see her. However, it was less than a year since she had read his letters and wondered how it was possible that he had never competed in the Poetic Festival: there was no doubt he would have won. Florentino Ariza lied to her: he wrote only for her, verses for her, and only he read them. Then it was she who reached for his hand in the darkness, and she did not find it waiting for her as she had waited for his the night before. Instead, she took him by surprise, and Florentino Ariza's heart froze.

"How strange women are," he said.

She burst into laughter, a deep laugh like a young dove's, and she thought again about the old couple in the boat. It was incised: the image would always pursue her. But that night she could bear it because she felt untroubled and calm, as she had few times in her life: free of all blame. She would have remained there until dawn, silent, with his hand perspiring ice into hers, but she could not endure the torment in her ear. So that when the music was over, and then the bustle of the ordinary passengers hanging their hammocks in the salon had ended, she realized that her pain was stronger than her desire to be with him. She knew that telling him about it would alleviate her suffering, but she did not because she did not want to worry him. For now it seemed to her that she knew him as well as if she had lived with him all her life, and she thought him capable of ordering the boat back to port if that would relieve her pain.

Florentino Ariza had foreseen how things would be that night, and he withdrew. At the door of her cabin he tried to kiss her good night, but she offered him her left cheek. He insisted, with labored breath, and she offered him her other cheek, with a coquettishness that he had not known when she was a schoolgirl. Then he insisted again, and she offered him her lips, she offered her lips with a profound trembling that she tried to suppress with the laugh she had forgotten after her wedding night.

"My God," she said, "ships make me so crazy."

Florentino Ariza shuddered: as she herself had said, she had the sour smell of old age. Still, as he walked to his cabin, making his way through the labyrinth of sleeping hammocks, he consoled himself with the thought that he must give off the same odor, except his was four years older, and she must have detected it on him, with the same emotion. It was the smell of human fermentation, which he had perceived in his oldest lovers and they had detected in him. The Widow Nazaret, who kept nothing to herself, had told him in a cruder way: "Now we stink like a henhouse."

They tolerated each other because they were an even match: my odor against yours. On the other hand, he had often taken care of América Vicuña, whose diaper smell awakened maternal instincts in him, but he was disturbed at the idea that she had disliked his odor: the smell of a dirty old man. But all that belonged to the past. The important thing was that not since the afternoon when Aunt Escolástica left her missal on the counter in the telegraph office had Florentino Ariza felt the happiness he felt that night: so intense it frightened him.

At five o'clock he was beginning to doze off, when the ship's purser woke him in the port of Zambrano to hand him an urgent telegram. It was signed by Leona Cassiani and dated the previous day, and all its horror was contained in a single line: *América Vicuña dead yesterday reasons unknown*. At eleven o'clock in the morning he learned the details from Leona Cassiani in a telegraphic conference during which he himself operated the transmitting equipment for the first time since his years as a telegraph operator. América Vicuña, in the grip of mortal depression because she had failed her final examinations, had drunk a flask of laudanum stolen from the school infirmary. Florentino Ariza knew in the depths of his soul that the story was incomplete. But no: América Vicuña had left no explanatory note that would have allowed anyone to be blamed for her decision. The family, informed by Leona Cassiani, was arriving now from Puerto Padre, and the funeral would take place that afternoon at five o'clock. Florentino Ariza took a breath. The only thing he could do to stay alive was not to allow himself the anguish of that memory. He erased it from his mind, although from time to time in the years that were left to him he would feel it revive, with no warning and for no reason, like the sudden pang of an old scar.

The days that followed were hot and interminable. The river became muddy and narrow, and instead of the tangle of colossal trees that had astonished Florentino Ariza on his first voyage, there were calcinated flatlands stripped of entire forests that had been devoured by the boilers of the riverboats, and the debris of god-forsaken villages whose streets remained flooded even in the cruelest droughts. At night they were awakened not by the siren songs of manatees on the sandy banks but by the nauseating stench of corpses floating down to the sea. For there were no more wars or epidemics, but the swollen bodies still floated by. The Captain, for once, was solemn: "We have orders to tell the passengers that they are accidental drowning victims." Instead of the screeching of the parrots and the riotous noise of invisible monkeys, which at one time had intensified the stifling midday heat, all that was left was the vast silence of the ravaged land.

There were so few places for taking on wood, and they were so far apart from each other, that by the fourth day of the trip the *New Fidelity* had run out of fuel. She was stranded for almost a week while her crew searched bogs of ashes for the last scattered trees. There was no one else: the woodcutters had abandoned their trails, fleeing the ferocity of the lords of the earth, fleeing the invisible cholera, fleeing the larval wars that governments were bent on hiding with distracted decrees. In the meantime, the passengers in their boredom held swimming contests, organized hunting expeditions, and returned with live iguanas that they split open from top to bottom and sewed up again with baling needles after removing the clusters of soft, translucent eggs that they strung over the railings to dry. The poverty-stricken prostitutes from nearby villages followed in the path of the expeditions, improvised tents in the gullies along the shore, brought music and liquor with them, and caroused across the river from the stranded vessel.

Long before he became President of the R.C.C., Florentino Ariza had received alarming reports on the state of the river, but he barely read them. He would calm his associates: "Don't worry, by the time the wood is gone there will be boats fueled by oil." With his mind clouded by his passion for Fermina Daza, he never took the trouble to think about it, and by the time he realized the truth, there was nothing anyone could do except bring in a new river. Even in the days when the waters were at their best, the boats had to anchor at night, and then even the simple fact of being alive became unendurable. Most of the passengers, above all the Europeans, abandoned the pestilential stench of their cabins and spent the night walking the decks, brushing away all sorts of predatory creatures with the same towel they used to dry their incessant perspiration, and at dawn they were exhausted and swollen with bites. An English traveler at the beginning of the nineteenth century, referring to the journey by canoe and mule that could last as long as fifty days, had written: "This is one of the most miserable and uncomfortable pilgrimages that a human being can make." This had no longer been true during the first eighty years of steam navigation, and then it became true again forever when the alligators ate the last butterfly and the maternal manatees were gone, the parrots, the monkeys, the villages were gone: everything was gone.

"There's no problem," the Captain laughed. "In a few years, we'll ride the dry riverbed in luxury automobiles."

For the first three days Fermina Daza and Florentino Ariza were protected by the soft springtime of the enclosed observation deck, but when the wood was rationed and the cooling system began to fail, the Presidential Suite became a steam bath. She survived the nights because of the river breeze that came in through the open windows, and she frightened off the mosquitoes with a towel because the insecticide bomb was useless when the boat was anchored. Her earache had become unbearable, and one morning when she awoke it stopped suddenly and completely, like the sound of a smashed cicada. But she did not realize that she had lost the hearing in her left ear until that night, when Florentino Ariza spoke to her on that side and she had to turn her head to hear what he was saying. She did not tell anyone, for she was resigned to the fact that it was one of the many irremediable defects of old age.

In spite of everything, the delay had been a providential accident for them. Florentino Ariza had once read: "Love becomes greater and nobler in calamity." The humidity in the Presidential Suite submerged them in an unreal lethargy in which it was easier to love without questions. They spent unimaginable hours holding hands in the armchairs by the railing, they exchanged unhurried kisses, they enjoyed the rapture of caresses without the pitfalls of impatience. On the third stupefying night she waited for him with a bottle of anisette, which she used to drink in secret with Cousin Hildebranda's band and later, after she was married and had children, behind closed doors with the friends from her borrowed world. She needed to be somewhat intoxicated in order not to think about her fate with too much lucidity, but Florentino Ariza thought it was to give herself courage for the final step. Encouraged by that illusion, he dared to explore her withered neck with his fingertips, her bosom armored in metal stays, her hips with their decaying bones, her thighs with their aging veins. She accepted with pleasure, her eyes closed, but she did not tremble, and she smoked and drank at regular intervals. At

535

last, when his caresses slid over her belly, she had enough anisette in her heart.

"If we're going to do it, let's do it," she said, "but let's do it like grownups."

She took him to the bedroom and, with the lights on, began to undress without false modesty. Florentino Ariza was on the bed, lying on his back and trying to regain control, once again not knowing what to do with the skin of the tiger he had slain. She said: "Don't look." He asked why without taking his eyes off the ceiling.

"Because you won't like it," she said.

Then he looked at her and saw her naked to her waist, just as he had imagined her. Her shoulders were wrinkled, her breasts sagged, her ribs were covered by a flabby skin as pale and cold as a frog's. She covered her chest with the blouse she had just taken off, and she turned out the light. Then he sat up and began to undress in the darkness, throwing everything at her that he took off, while she tossed it back, dying of laughter.

They lay on their backs for a long time, he more and more perturbed as his intoxication left him, and she peaceful, almost without will, but praying to God that she would not laugh like a fool, as she always did when she overindulged in anisette. They talked to pass the time. They spoke of themselves, of their divergent lives, of the incredible coincidence of their lying naked in a dark cabin on a stranded boat when reason told them they had time only for death. She had never heard of his having a woman, not even one, in that city where everything was known even before it happened. She spoke in a casual manner, and he replied without hesitation in a steady voice:

"I've remained a virgin for you."

She would not have believed it in any event, even if it had been true, because his love letters were composed of similar phrases whose meaning mattered less than their brilliance. But she liked the spirited way in which he said it. Florentino Ariza, for his part, suddenly asked himself what he would never have dared to ask himself before: what kind of secret life had she led outside of her marriage? Nothing would have surprised him, because he knew that women are just like men in their secret adventures: the same stratagems, the same sudden inspirations, the same betrayals without remorse. But he was wise not to ask the question. Once, when her relations with the Church were already strained, her confessor had asked her out of the blue if she had ever been unfaithful to her husband, and she had stood up without responding, without concluding, without saying goodbye, and had never gone to confession again, with that confessor or with any other. But Florentino Ariza's prudence had an unexpected reward: she stretched out her hand in the darkness, caressed his belly, his flanks, his almost hairless pubis. She said: "You have skin like a baby's." Then she took the final step: she searched for him where he was not, she searched again without hope, and she found him, unarmed.

"It's dead," he said.

It had happened to him sometimes, and he had learned to live with the phantom: each time he had to learn again, as if it were the first time. He took her hand and laid it on his chest: Fermina Daza felt the old, untiring heart almost bursting through his skin, beating with the strength, the rapidity, the irregularity of an adolescent's. He said: "Too much love is as bad for this as no love at all." But he said it without conviction: he was ashamed, furious with himself, longing for some reason to blame her for his failure. She knew it, and began to provoke his defenseless body with mock caresses, like a kitten delighting in cruelty, until he could no longer endure the martyrdom and he returned to his cabin. She thought about him until dawn, convinced at last of her love, and as the anisette left her in slow waves, she was invaded by the anguished fear that he was angry and would never return.

But he returned the same day, refreshed and renewed, at the unusual hour of eleven o'clock, and he undressed in front of her with a certain ostentation. She was pleased to see him in the light just as she had imagined him in the darkness: an ageless man, with dark skin that was as shiny and tight as an opened umbrella, with no hair except for a few limp strands under his arms and at his groin. His guard was up, and she realized that he did not expose his weapon by accident, but displayed it as if it were a war trophy in order to give himself courage. He did not even give her time to take off the nightgown that she had put on when the dawn breeze began to blow, and his beginner's haste made her shiver with compassion. But that did not disturb her, because in such cases it was not easy to distinguish between compassion and love. When it was over, however, she felt empty.

It was the first time she had made love in over twenty years, and she had been held back by her curiosity concerning how it would feel at her age after so long a respite. But he had not given her time to find out if her body loved him too. It had been hurried and sad, and she thought: Now we've screwed up everything. But she was wrong: despite the disappointment that each of them felt, despite his regret for his clumsiness and her remorse for the madness of the anisette, they were not apart for a moment in the days that followed. Captain Samaritano, who uncovered by instinct any secret that anyone wanted to keep on his ship, sent them a white rose every morning, had them serenaded with old waltzes from their day, had meals prepared for them with aphrodisiac ingredients as a joke. They did not try to make love again until much later, when the inspiration came to them without their looking for it. They were satisfied with the simple joy of being together.

They would not have thought of leaving the cabin if the Captain had not written them a note informing them that after lunch they would reach golden La Dorada, the last port on the eleven-day journey. From the cabin Fermina Daza and Florentino Ariza saw the promontory of houses lit by a pale sun, and they thought they understood the reason for its name, but it seemed less evident to them when they felt the heat that steamed like a caldron and saw the tar bubbling in the streets. Moreover, the boat did not dock there but on the opposite bank, where the terminal for the Santa Fe Railroad was located.

They left their refuge as soon as the passengers disembarked. Fermina Daza breathed the good air of impunity in the empty salon, and from the gunwale they both watched a noisy crowd of people gathering their luggage in the cars of a train that looked like a toy. One would have thought they had come from Europe, above all the women, in their Nordic coats and hats from the last century that made no sense in the sweltering, dusty heat. Some wore beautiful potato blossoms in their hair, but they had begun to wither in the heat. They had just come from the Andean plateau after a train trip through a dreamlike savannah, and they had not had time to change their clothes for the Caribbean.

In the middle of the bustling market, a very old man with an inconsolable expression on his face was pulling chicks out of the pockets of his beggar's coat. He had appeared without warning, making his way through the crowd in a tattered overcoat that had belonged to someone much taller and heavier than he. He took off his hat, placed it brim up on the dock in case anyone wanted to throw him a coin, and began to empty his pockets of handfuls of pale baby chicks that seemed to proliferate in his fingers. In only a moment the dock appeared to be carpeted with cheeping chicks running everywhere among hurried travelers who trampled them without realizing it. Fascinated by the marvelous spectacle that seemed to be performed in her honor, for she was the only person watching it, Fermina Daza did not notice when the passengers for the return trip began to come on board. The party was over: among them she saw many faces she knew, some of them friends who until a short while ago had attended her in her grief, and she rushed to take refuge in her cabin. Florentino Ariza found her there, distraught: she would rather die than be seen on a pleasure trip, by people she knew, so soon after the death of her husband. Her preoccupation affected Florentino Ariza so much that he promised to think of some way to protect her other than keeping her in the cabin.

The idea came to him all at once as they were having supper in the private dining room. The Captain was troubled by a problem he had wanted to discuss for a long time with Florentino Ariza, who always evaded him with his usual answer: "Leona Cassiani can handle those problems better than I can." This time, however, he listened to him. The fact was that the boats carried cargo upriver, but came back empty, while the opposite occurred with passengers. "And the advantage of cargo is that it pays more and eats nothing," he said. Fermina Daza, bored with the men's enervated discussion concerning the possibility of establishing differential fares, ate without will. But Florentino Ariza pursued the discussion to its end, and only then did he ask the question that the Captain thought was the prelude to a solution:

"And speaking hypothetically," he said, "would it be possible to make a trip without stopping, without cargo or passengers, without coming into any port, without anything?"

The Captain said that it was possible, but only hypothetically. The R.C.C. had business commitments that Florentino Ariza was more familiar with than he was, it had contracts for cargo, passengers, mail, and a great deal more, and most of them were unbreakable. The only thing that would allow them to bypass all that was a case of cholera on board. The ship would be quarantined, it would hoist the yellow flag and sail in a state of emergency. Captain Samaritano had needed to do just that on several occasions because of the many cases of cholera along the river, although later the health authorities had obliged the doctors to sign death certificates that called the cases common dysentery. Besides, many times in the history of the river the yellow plague flag had been flown in order to evade taxes, or to avoid picking up an undesirable passenger, or to elude inopportune inspections. Florentino Ariza reached for Fermina Daza's hand under the table.

"Well, then," he said, "let's do that."

The Captain was taken by surprise, but then, with the instinct of an old fox, he saw everything clearly.

"I command on this ship, but you command us," he said. "So if you are serious, give me the order in writing and we will leave right now."

Florentino Ariza was serious, of course, and he signed the order. After all, everyone knew that the time of cholera had not ended despite all the joyful statistics from the health officials. As for the ship, there was no problem. The little cargo they had taken on was transferred, they told the passengers there had been a mechanical failure, and early that morning they sent them on their way on a ship that belonged to another company. If such things were done for so many immoral, even contemptible reasons, Florentino Ariza could not see why it would not be legitimate to do them for love. All that the Captain asked was that they stop in Puerto Nare to pick up someone who would accompany him on the voyage: he, too, had his secret heart.

So the *New Fidelity* weighed anchor at dawn the next day, without cargo or passengers, and with the yellow cholera flag waving jubilantly from the mainmast. At dusk in Puerto Nare they picked up a woman who was even taller and stouter than the Captain, an uncommon beauty who needed only a beard to be hired by a circus. Her name was Zenaida Neves, but the Captain called her "my wild woman": an old friend whom he would pick up in one port and leave in another, and who came on board followed by the winds of joy. In that sad place of death, where Florentino Ariza relived his memories of Rosalba when he saw the train from Envigado struggling to climb the old mule trail, there was an Amazonian downpour that would continue with very few pauses for the rest of the trip. But no one cared: the floating fiesta had its own roof. That night, as a personal contribution to the revelry, Fermina Daza went down to the galley amid the ovations of the crew and prepared a dish for everyone that she created and that Florentino Ariza christened Eggplant al Amor.

During the day they played cards, ate until they were bursting, took gritty siestas that left them exhausted, and as soon as the sun was down the orchestra began to play, and they had anisette with salmon until they could eat and drink no more. It was a rapid journey: the boat was light and the currents favorable and even improved by the floods that rushed down from the headwaters, where it rained as much that week as it had during the entire voyage. Some villages fired charitable cannons for them to frighten away the cholera, and they expressed their gratitude with a mournful bellow. The ships they passed on the way, regardless of the company they belonged to, signaled their condolences. In the town of Magangué, where Mercedes was born, they took on enough wood for the rest of the trip.

Fermina Daza was horrified when she heard the boat's horn with her good ear, but by the second day of anisette she could hear better with both of them. She discovered that roses were more fragrant than before, that the birds sang at dawn much better than before, and that God had created a manatee and placed it on the bank at

544

Tamalameque just so it could awaken her. The Captain heard it, had the boat change course, and at last they saw the enormous matron nursing the baby that she held in her arms. Neither Florentino nor Fermina was aware of how well they understood each other: she helped him to take his enemas, she got up before he did to brush the false teeth he kept in a glass while he slept, and she solved the problem of her misplaced spectacles, for she could use his for reading and mending. When she awoke one morning, she saw him sewing a button on his shirt in the darkness, and she hurried to do it for him before he could say the ritual phrase about needing two wives. On the other hand, the only thing she needed from him was that he cup a pain in her back.

Florentino Ariza, for his part, began to revive old memories with a violin borrowed from the orchestra, and in half a day he could play the waltz of "The Crowned Goddess" for her, and he played it for hours until they forced him to stop. One night, for the first time in her life, Fermina Daza suddenly awoke choking on tears of sorrow, not of rage, at the memory of the old couple in the boat beaten to death by the boatman. On the other hand, the incessant rain did not affect her, and she thought too late that perhaps Paris was not as gloomy as it had seemed, that Santa Fe did not have so many funerals passing along the streets. The dream of other voyages with Florentino Ariza appeared on the horizon: mad voyages, free of trunks, free of social commitments: voyages of love.

The night before their arrival they had a grand party with paper garlands and colored lights. The weather cleared at nightfall. Holding each other very close, the Captain and Zenaida danced the first boleros that were just beginning to break hearts in those days. Florentino Ariza dared to suggest to Fermina Daza that they dance their private waltz, but she refused. Nevertheless she kept time with her head and her heels all night, and there was even a moment when she danced sitting down without realizing it, while the Captain merged with his young wild woman in the shadows of the bolero. She drank so much anisette that she had to be helped up the stairs, and she suffered an attack of laughing until she cried, which alarmed everyone. However, when at last she recovered her self-possession in the perfumed oasis of her cabin, they made the tranquil, wholesome love of experienced grandparents, which she would keep as her best memory of that lunatic voyage. Contrary to what the Captain and Zenaida supposed, they no longer felt like newlyweds, and even less like belated lovers. It was as if they had leapt over the arduous calvary of conjugal life and gone straight to the heart of love. They were together in silence like an old married couple wary of life, beyond the pitfalls of passion, beyond the brutal mockery of hope and the phantoms of disillusion: beyond love. For they had lived together long enough to know that love was always love, anytime and anyplace, but it was more solid the closer it came to death.

They awoke at six o'clock. She had a headache scented with anisette, and her heart was stunned by the impression that Dr. Juvenal Urbino had come back, plumper and younger than when he had fallen from the tree, and that he was sitting in his rocking chair, waiting for her at the door of their house. She was, however, lucid enough to realize that this was the result not of the anisette but of her imminent return.

"It is going to be like dying," she said.

Florentino Ariza was startled, because her words read a thought that had given him no peace since the beginning of the voyage home. Neither one could imagine being in any other home but the cabin, or eating in any other way but on the ship, or living any other life, for that would be alien to them forever. It was, indeed, like dying. He could not go back to sleep. He lay on his back in bed, his hands crossed behind his head. At a certain moment, the pangs of grief for América Vicuña made him twist with pain, and he could not hold off the truth any longer: he locked himself in the bathroom and cried, slowly, until his last tear was shed. Only then did he have the courage to admit to himself how much he had loved her.

When they went up, already dressed for going ashore, the ship had left behind the narrow channels and marshes of the old Spanish passage and was navigating around the wrecks of boats and the platforms of oil wells in the bay. A radiant Thursday was breaking over the golden domes of the city of the Viceroys, but Fermina Daza, standing at the railing, could not bear the pestilential stink of its glories, the arrogance of its bulwarks profaned by iguanas: the horror of real life. They did not say anything, but neither one felt capable of capitulating so easily.

They found the Captain in the dining room, in a disheveled condition that did not accord with his habitual neatness: he was unshaven, his eyes were bloodshot from lack of sleep, his clothing was still sweaty from the previous night, his speech was interrupted by belches of anisette. Zenaida was asleep. They were beginning to eat their breakfast in silence, when a motor launch from the Health Department ordered them to stop the ship.

The Captain, standing on the bridge, shouted his answers to the questions put to him by the armed patrol. They wanted to know what kind of pestilence they carried on board, how many passengers there were, how many of them were sick, what possibility there was for new infections. The Captain replied that they had only three passengers on board and all of them had cholera, but they were being kept in strict seclusion. Those who were to come on board in La Dorada, and the twenty-seven men of the crew, had not had any contact with them. But the commander of the patrol was not satisfied, and he ordered them to leave the bay and wait in Las Mercedes Marsh until two o'clock in the afternoon, while the forms were prepared for placing the ship in quarantine.

The Captain let loose with a wagon driver's fart, and with a wave of his hand he ordered the pilot to turn around and go back to the marshes.

Fermina Daza and Florentino Ariza had heard everything from their table, but that did not seem to matter to the Captain. He continued to eat in silence, and his bad humor was evident in the manner in which he breached the rules of etiquette that sustained the legendary reputation of the riverboat captains. He broke apart his four fried eggs with the tip of his knife, and he ate them with slices of green plantain, which he placed whole in his mouth and chewed with savage delight. Fermina Daza and Florentino Ariza looked at him without speaking, as if waiting on a school bench to hear their final grades. They had not exchanged a word during his conversation with the health patrol, nor did they have the slightest idea of what would become of their lives, but they both knew that the Captain was thinking for them: they could see it in the throbbing of his temples.

While he finished off his portion of eggs, the tray of fried plantains, and the pot of *café con leche*, the ship left the bay with its boilers quiet, made its way along the channels through blankets of taruya, the river lotus with purple blossoms and large heart-shaped leaves, and returned to the marshes. The water was iridescent with the universe of fishes floating on their sides, killed by the dynamite of stealthy fishermen, and all the birds of the earth and the water circled above them with metallic cries. The wind from the Caribbean blew in the windows along with the racket made by the birds, and Fermina Daza felt in her blood the wild beating of her free will. To her right, the muddy, frugal estuary of the Great Magdalena River spread out to the other side of the world.

When there was nothing left to eat on the plates, the Captain wiped his lips with a corner of the tablecloth and broke into indecent slang that ended once and for all the reputation for fine speech enjoyed by the riverboat captains. For he was not speaking to them or to anyone else, but was trying instead to come to terms with his own rage. His conclusion, after a string of barbaric curses, was that he could find no way out of the mess he had gotten into with the cholera flag.

Florentino Ariza listened to him without blinking. Then he looked through the windows at the complete circle of the quadrant on the mariner's compass, the clear horizon, the December sky without a single cloud, the waters that could be navigated forever, and he said:

"Let us keep going, going, going, back to La Dorada."

Fermina Daza shuddered because she recognized his former voice, illuminated by the grace of the Holy Spirit, and she looked at the Captain: he was their destiny. But the Captain did not see her because he was stupefied by Florentino Ariza's tremendous powers of inspiration.

"Do you mean what you say?" he asked.

"From the moment I was born," said Florenino Ariza, "I have never said anything I did not mean."

The Captain looked at Fermina Daza and saw on her eyelashes the first glimmer of wintry frost. Then he looked at Florentino Ariza, his invincible power, his intrepid love, and he was overwhelmed by the belated suspicion that it is life, more than death, that has no limits.

"And how long do you think we can keep up this goddamn coming and going?" he asked.

Florentino Ariza had kept his answer ready for fifty-three years, seven months, and eleven days and nights.

"Forever," he said.

The publishers hope that this
Large Print Book has brought
you pleasurable reading.
Each title is designed to make
the text as easy to see as possible.
G.K. Hall Large Print Books
are available from your library and
your local bookstore. Or, you can
receive information by mail on
upcoming and current Large Print Books
and order directly from the publishers.
Just send your name and address to:

G.K. Hall & Co.
70 Lincoln Street
Boston, Mass. 02111

or call, toll-free:

1-800-343-2806

A note on the text
Large print edition designed by
Bernadette Montalvo.
Composed in 16 pt Plantin
on a Xyvision 300/Linotron 202N

of G.K. Hall & Co.